A MARKET KILLING

A MARKET KILLING

a novel
by Frank Pierson

iUniverse, Inc.
New York Lincoln Shanghai

A MARKET KILLING

iUniverse books may be ordered through booksellers or by contacting:

iUniverse
2021 Pine Lake Road, Suite 100
Lincoln, NE 68512
www.iuniverse.com
1-800-Authors (1-800-288-4677)

ISBN-13: 978-0-595-37210-2 (pbk)
ISBN-13: 978-0-595-81609-5 (ebk)
ISBN-10: 0-595-37210-4 (pbk)
ISBN-10: 0-595-81609-6 (ebk)

Printed in the United States of America

CHAPTER 1

▼

SUNDAY, OCTOBER 8

John Blanchard rose slightly from a squat, shifted his weight from one foot to the other, and then settled back into the shadows between a Dumpster that reeked of rotting fish and a large, low-hanging spruce tree. The only illumination came from the dim light bulb in a rusting fixture over the door of the bar across the parking lot. Under the light, a sign proclaimed the name of the place to be "Marty's." The condition of the sign, barely legible now, added that the bar had seen better days.

Blanchard instinctively crouched lower as the lights of a sedan passed to his left and headed down Garner Avenue toward the center of town.

He wasn't worried about being seen from a passing car. He had been trained in camouflage by the best in the world, the U.S. Navy Seals. His blackened face, the black hat covering his sandy blond hair, and his dark blue sweat suit made him nearly invisible to anyone who wasn't looking for him. His only concern was being seen once the mission required his leaving cover. He counted on there being little traffic this late on a Sunday night.

His watch said 11:51 PM. He had been waiting for nearly an hour for his target to emerge from the bar. As the minutes ticked by, he mentally checked off the gear in his backpack and rehearsed his plan. He would have preferred to be in a less public place, but he needed to have everyone in town think there had been an accident, that the target had been driving drunk.

Blanchard tensed as the door to the bar swung open.

"So long," Kevin Armstrong yelled over his shoulder as he wobbled out the front door. A chorus of good-byes and hoots sang out from inside. Despite the late hour, there were a number of people in the bar, their cars still in the parking lot. Marty's was one of the few businesses in town that could boast a steady clientele, and Kevin Armstrong was one of its most dependable clients.

Someone inside yelled, "Close the fucking door." Kevin flipped the man the finger and let the door slam closed. He pulled a pack of Marlboros out of a pocket in his worn denim jacket and extracted a cigarette. He struck the lighter unsteadily, lit the cigarette, and took a long drag. As he started across the parking lot, he slowly let the smoke drift out of his nose.

"Oooof," Kevin said through gritted teeth, as a cold burst of wind slapped him in the face. Holding the cigarette unsteadily in his teeth, he fumbled with the zipper of his jacket. After four attempts to close the jacket, which was two sizes too small, he gave up and held the coat closed as best he could with his hand.

Blanchard watched intently, comparing the man walking toward him to the photo he had memorized. The photo had arrived by e-mail from his anonymous employer a week earlier. It must have been taken some time ago, he concluded. The short, styled hair was now stringy and nearly shoulder-length, much thinner and grayer. The face was more haggard and fleshy, and the body had become paunchy and soft. Despite the changes, there was no doubt this was the man in the photo. The intel had been correct.

Kevin took a few unsteady steps forward. He stopped, wavering, to scan the parking lot for his truck. His dented, rusting ten-year-old Ford Ranger blended in well with the other trucks parked outside Marty's.

"There it is," he announced when he spotted his truck. He shuffled forward, kicking up a small cloud of dirt with each step. Blanchard slipped his arms through the straps of his backpack and smoothly stood.

Flicking the stub of his cigarette into the night, Kevin stopped three feet from the truck, swaying back and forth as he reached into his pants pocket, fumbling for his keys. They were stuck. He gave a final tug and they flew into the air, landing in the gravel near the back of his truck. "Shit," he muttered as he walked back to retrieve them.

As Kevin struggled to stand back up, Blanchard came up behind him and clamped a hand holding an ether-soaked cloth over his mouth and nose. Kevin dropped his keys and reached up to pull the hand away, but could only put up a brief, ineffectual struggle before going limp.

Blanchard caught the unconscious man under the arms as he collapsed and unceremoniously heaved him into the back of the pickup truck. He tossed a tarp over the body in case someone cared enough to look in the bed of the truck. Moments later, the Ford Ranger, with Blanchard behind the wheel, pulled out of the parking lot. At the stoplight, it turned right onto Tuckers Road, heading east toward the river.

Fifteen minutes later, the pickup truck pulled to the side of the road at the base of a small hill leading up to an old, rusted, little-used bridge that crossed the Pawnee River. The nearest farmhouse, visible only as a darkened box surrounded by snow-covered moonlit fields, was more than a mile away. No lights shone through any of the windows. Most people out here, except those that hung out at Marty's, went to bed early, especially on a Sunday night.

Blanchard got out of the truck and strode across the road to a Chevy Suburban, careful to leave as few footprints as possible. The SUV, partially hidden by a small stand of linden trees, started easily and idled almost silently. He pulled the Suburban up behind the pickup truck, leaving it on the pavement to minimize any tire tracks.

Staggering under the weight, Blanchard carried Kevin piggyback style to the rear of the Suburban and dumped the body inside the car. Blanchard opened the rear passenger door, leaned inside, grabbed the unconscious man, and pulled him into the car far enough that the tailgate could be closed.

He carried a large blue and white Coleman cooler back to the waiting pickup truck, put on a pair of heavy gloves, pulled out two large blocks of ice, and tossed them onto the passenger seat. He drove the truck slowly forward, stopped and put the truck in neutral fifteen feet from the bridge, where the embankment was steepest. The truck pointed toward the river. Blanchard jammed one of the blocks of ice under the driver's seat and positioned the second block so it pushed down on the accelerator. The engine roared.

Blanchard jumped out of the truck and checked the alignment of the wheels one last time, then reached in and yanked the gearshift into drive. The truck jerked forward and accelerated down the hill, leaping the bank and landing in the river several feet from the shore. It floated upright for a few seconds before slowly tilting on its side as the force of the current swept it downriver.

Without so much as a glance back at the half-submerged pickup truck, Blanchard carried the empty cooler back to the Suburban and tossed it in the back. He checked Kevin's breathing. Satisfied that everything was as it should be, he pulled out and crossed the bridge, heading toward the interstate. After setting the cruise control at the speed limit on the highway, Blanchard pulled out a cell phone and hit the one preprogrammed number. The call was answered by the click and beep of an answering machine with no recorded greeting.

"I got the package," Blanchard said. "I'll drop it at the motel within forty-eight hours and you can come and get it as we discussed." He hit the disconnect button and tossed the phone on the passenger seat. After dropping off the package, he would discard the phone, forgoing the one-hundred-dollar deposit.

The important thing now was to complete the mission. He did not want to get caught speeding. Even though he might be able to convince police that the man in the back was simply sleeping one off, which wasn't too far from the truth, he'd rather not take the chance. He picked up the thermos of coffee from the passenger seat, poured a cup, and took a swig. It was still lukewarm, which wasn't bad given how long it had been sitting in the cold. After another self-congratulatory sip, he reached down and clicked on the radio.

CHAPTER 2

▼

MONDAY, OCTOBER 9

Ted Saunders sat in his lower Manhattan office, overlooking the Hudson River. He reached out a long, thick finger to punch the disconnect button on the speakerphone, ending the conference call with the Deputy Chief Litigation Counsel of the SEC and the Deputy Assistant Attorney General from the Department of Justice.

Although Saunders was no longer the darling of Wall Street, he still looked and dressed as Wall Street expected of its stars. He stood five foot, eleven inches tall and weighed 170 pounds, a trim build that he maintained by making daily trips to the gym. He kept his auburn hair stylishly short, doing nothing to fight the touch of gray at the temples, and his blue-gray eyes could silence even the hardiest analyst. Even his age, fifty-two, seemed to be perfect. Only trouble was, his life was all an illusion, just like his company, which had at one point been one of the biggest corporations in America.

"It doesn't look good, does it?" Saunders said. He sat back in his chair, crossed his legs, and waited for a response from the man sitting on the other side of the desk.

The man he addressed, his lawyer and longtime confidant Whittaker Harden, didn't answer immediately. He never answered right away, which was the principal reason he had made it to the top of Garrison, Harden and Tilden, one of the most influential law firms in Washington. His firm handled the personal legal work of many of the biggest players on Wall Street and many of the most successful politicians in Washington. In addition to the old-money clients the firm had always represented, it had a new breed of clients, the nouveau riche created by the dot-com boom, which included the ex-CEO of GenergTex now aiming this desperate question at Harden.

Unlike Saunders, Whit Harden was of modest height and weight. Indeed, nearly everything about him was modest. He eschewed two-thousand-dollar suits in favor of lower-priced apparel on sale at Brooks Brothers. He ordered his shirts and ties through the Lands' End or L.L. Bean catalog. Although not physically intimidating, he knew that he intimidated people with his intellect. He had been valedictorian of every one of his graduating classes, from high school to his undergraduate class at Harvard to Harvard Law School, and he had been editor of the Law Review. After receiving his JD, he had interned under the Chief Justice of the Supreme Court. Even in those circles, his intellect was intimidating.

Harden reached out for the fine bone china coffee cup on the desk and took a sip. "I agree. The news is not good. The real question now is not if but when the government will file charges. You heard them. They're talking about insider trading, securities fraud, conspiracy to defraud, stock manipulation."

"They don't have a case."

"Don't have a case! Weren't you listening? They've got one hell of a case and it just got a whole lot better with George's testimony." The lawyer was referring to George MacIntosh, the former chief financial officer of GenergTex. Both Saunders and George MacIntosh had been fired by the board of directors a month ago, shortly before the SEC forced the company to file revised financial statements. Those statements showed a net worth of only about a fifth of what had previously been reported. The stock had dropped like a rock since then, and the company was nearing bankruptcy. After that point, immense pressure had been put on George to cooperate with the government's investigation. It had only been a matter of time before they offered a deal that was too good for him to pass up.

"How was I to know that the little twerp would keep those e-mails and then testify about them?" Saunders fumed. "I told that asshole to delete them."

"Well, that ship's sailed," the lawyer said in a calm voice. "The worst thing is it makes you look like a liar. You've probably added perjury to all of the other charges. You told me you weren't involved in the day-to-day finances of the company, that George handled that."

"But…" Saunders stopped, sat back suddenly, and remained quiet.

"Ted, if you're not going to be truthful with your own lawyer…"

"I was…I am. Damn it! I wasn't involved like he said. Those e-mails were taken out of context." Saunders swung his arm across his desk as if he were trying to sweep his problems away, but his hand merely caught the corner of the sole picture on his desk and sent it flying.

Harden reacted quickly and snatched it in midair. He handed it back without looking at it.

Saunders studied the photo for a moment before putting it back in its place. An old, grainy image of a woman standing next to a little boy smiled up at him from the frame. It had been taken on the boy's first day home from the orphanage. Saunders sat back in his chair, eyes downcast.

"Sorry. Where were we?" He finally said in a softer tone.

"George's e-mails," Harden said. "They seem pretty self-explanatory."

"Well they aren't!" His usual combative tone returned almost instantly. "Do you think they'll get Canfield to testify? Isn't there some sort of client-attorney privilege or something that we could use to keep him quiet?"

"I've gone over that before," the lawyer said in an exasperated voice. "No. He wasn't your attorney. He worked for the company."

Saunders considered that for a moment. Victor Canfield, the ex-general counsel of GenergTex, had been with the company almost from the beginning. Given his role, he would likely be indicted too. Faced with the threat of a long jail term, Victor was sure to cooperate with the Feds.

"Let's look at this objectively," Harden said, raising his hand to quell the anticipated rebuttal. "There were a number of questionable accounting practices going on here, not to mention all those bogus deals." He took another sip of coffee. "In the end, the huge numbers are the decider. Three and a half, four billion? How do you expect anyone to believe that you didn't know about it? You were the CEO for god's sake."

"I know, Whit, but it was all George's doing. He ran the finances and set up those companies. I believed him when he told me those deals were legit. Hell, even the auditors agreed with him."

"That doesn't matter now. George admitted he lied to them."

"Shit! He lied to me too!" Saunders slammed his hand down on the desk.

"He says you knew all about it. He says you ordered it."

"Fuck him! He never told me a thing until it was all over and the Feds were about to walk in the door."

The lawyer sat quietly, shaking his head. "Ted, think about how this looks. You were never a hands-off manager. It seems awfully convenient to claim to be one now."

"I don't give a damn how it looks! You've got to get me out of this."

"Ted, you know I'll do all I can, but my professional opinion is that you're pretty far up the proverbial creek."

"Then you'd better get me a big fucking paddle, or I'll find someone who can."

"It's fine with me either way, Ted," Harden said. "Just tell me where to send my final bill."

Saunders sat forward, elbows on the desk, and rubbed his temples until they turned red. He had resisted making a deal because he couldn't give it all up. He couldn't go back to being poor and alone. He reached out and picked up the picture. The images of his childhood swirled in his mind—the small, white clapboard house, his dad going to work every day delivering the mail and his mom scrimping to make ends meet. He studied the look on the boy's face. He could see the sadness and the fear in his eyes. He remembered those feelings, the same feelings that had driven him his whole life. Should he give up? Should he simply give in and cut a deal with the Feds? What would Whit think? Did it really matter anymore? Not really, he decided.

"Okay, Whit, what do you propose we do?"

"I think you should try to cut a deal."

"Okay. But let's wait until they file the formal charges. Another few days won't matter."

Whit Harden didn't usually give away his feelings, but his face showed genuine surprise. They had discussed making a deal for months and his client had always flatly rejected the idea. "Ted, you'd be better off going to them first…"

"No, wait," Saunders said softly. "I'll let you know when the papers arrive." He stood up, indicating that the meeting was over.

Harden stopped at the door. "Regardless of what you do about the charges, I think it's a really bad idea to go to Dallas tomorrow." He took another step and turned. "No, let me rephrase that. It's probably one of the worst ideas you've ever had. As your lawyer *and* your friend, I'm going to tell you again: you shouldn't go to the meeting."

"But I'm still a stockholder."

"I know. But there are a lot of people down there who want your head on a silver platter."

"Hey, what ever happened to innocent until proven guilty?"

"If that ever applies, it's only in the courtroom, not out on the street. And…not in Texas, for God's sake!" Harden stared at his client for a moment. "What about the letters? There's a good chance that one of those lunatics will be there and want to make good on the threats."

"Don't worry. I know what I'm doing." Saunders brought both hands up to his chest, fingers pointing inward. "Trust me."

They shook hands and Saunders watched his lawyer get on the elevator. He shrugged, turned, and strode back to his desk.

A short time later, the intercom buzzed and the voice of Betty Goodman, his secretary, announced that his next appointment was here. Saunders checked his watch and was surprised to find that it was almost one o'clock. The conference call and talk with Whit had lasted a lot longer than he had realized.

Two seconds later, Charlie Wong burst into the office, marched across the room, and sat down in the chair that Whit Harden had just vacated, not waiting for a greeting or wanting to shake hands. He was dressed, as always, in an expensive suit he had bought back in Hong Kong, where it had, no doubt, been expertly altered to fit his size 46-short body. The shirt and tie were likely purchased on Saville Row in London.

Betty Goodman stepped into the open doorway and raised her arms and shrugged to indicate that she was sorry. Saunders nodded to indicate that it was fine. What could she have done? Betty's face relaxed. She left the room and closed the door behind her.

Charlie yelled at Saunders as soon as the door snapped closed. "You bastard!"

"Good to see you too, Charlie. I take it something's wrong?" ignoring Charlie's lack of manners, Saunders hit the intercom button and asked for coffee.

"I don't want coffee and you bet there's something wrong. I just got the latest financials on Pan-Oil." Charlie and Saunders had been partners in many overseas investments, the latest being Pan-Oil Limited, an oil exploration and drilling company they had formed in the Cayman Islands. Charlie headed a large trading company in Bermuda. The company, East Wind Trading, traced its roots back more than two hundred years. Charlie's father, Chen, had moved the company out of Hong Kong just before the British handed the colony back to China in 1997. It was rumored that the Wongs had loose ties to various criminal groups in both Asia and the United States, but Saunders didn't care. If he let such rumors limit his choices of business partners, he'd never have gotten to where he was today.

"Calm down, Charlie."

"Why should I? You gave yourself a thirty-five-million-dollar dividend out of the company. It was supposed to be five million."

"Come on, Charlie. Thirty-five million was always the number if the spot price dropped below thirty-seven bucks a barrel. That happened last Thursday and I took the money out. End of story."

"Bullshit."

"Well, that's the number in the documents." Saunders kept his voice calm.

The door to the office opened and Betty stood in the doorframe. At Saunders's wave, she walked across the room carrying a small, sterling silver tray with two mugs emblazoned with the GenergTex logo and filled with black coffee, a small pitcher of milk, a bowl with packets of sugar and sweeteners, and a plate stacked high with Oreo cookies, her boss's favorite. She placed the tray on the desk between the two men, turned without saying a word, and left the office.

Despite what he had said earlier about not wanting coffee, Charlie reached forward and grabbed a cup, poured in a small amount of milk, and took a sip before he said, "I don't care what the docs say, that's not how I thought the deal was supposed to work."

"Then I suggest next time you get the documents and your understanding of the deal to agree," Saunders replied calmly, picking up a cup and adding a dash of milk and a teaspoon of sugar. He took a sip without stirring the mixture, then grabbed three cookies and munched the first one whole.

"Fuck you!"

"If you're going to be like this, maybe I should have a little chat with Chen. Maybe he and I could sort this all out."

Charlie's face reddened at the mention of his father. "Keep him out of this. This is between you and me."

"Okay, but let's keep it civil, shall we?" Saunders liked to keep meetings as civil as possible, but only as long as it helped him. Otherwise, he would act just like his visitor was now. Was Charlie acting, he wondered. He tried to read the man's face, but it revealed very little, for all the anger on the surface.

"Fine, just put the money back into the company and everything will go back to the way it should be."

"C'mon Charlie, that's not going to happen. You knew the deal and your lawyers knew it. It's a bit late to whine about it now." He had no intention of ever putting the cash back in. For one thing, it was already spent.

Struggling to keep calm, Charlie said in a controlled voice, "We never agreed you could declare yourself an extraordinary dividend and take that much cash out of the company."

"Of course we did. That's why I got voting control at the outset. I don't know what you're so pissed off about. You'll still do all right in the deal." Of course, that was going to take seven or eight years.

"I wasn't planning on doing just *all right*."

"I don't know what to say, Charlie. We've been involved in a lot of deals before and…"

"Well…That won't happen again."

"I had hoped that we'd stay partners. There're plenty of other deals out there."

"You think I'd be your partner again after this?"

"I'm sorry you feel that way," he lied. He would be happy if he never had to work with Charlie again. Charlie's dad, Chen, was a different story. He had been a decent enough partner—smart, and with plenty of cash, most of it illegal, to invest. Unfortunately, Charlie had inherited none of his father's brains or temperament, a fact that Saunders had taken advantage of in the Pan-Oil deal.

"You're not going to get away with this. I'll see you in court."

"You've got to be kidding," Saunders laughed heartily. "In the Caymans? Go ahead. Their courts take a very literal reading of contracts."

"I'll move it to the States."

"On what grounds? Everything's in the Caymans. There's no way the U.S. has any jurisdiction."

"You bastard," Charlie repeated. "You tricked me."

"Oh, come on. You're too good a businessman for that." Saunders paused for a second or two. "Why not join me out at the ranch. I'm going out there in a couple of days. We can work this out."

"There's nothing to work out! I do not know how, but I will make you pay for this," Charlie announced, rising out of his chair and heading toward the door.

"Yeah, I've heard that before," he said to Charlie's back.

Saunders sat for several minutes thinking about the exchange that had just occurred. It wasn't often that the Wongs came out on the wrong end of a deal. Chen Wong, who really ran the company in spite of Charlie's title, wasn't going to be happy. Bad things, he knew, usually happened to people who made Old Man Wong unhappy. But, if all went according to plan, he wouldn't have to worry about Charlie or his father ever again.

*   *   *   *

"Sheriff's office," Jake Carter bellowed into the phone after stabbing the speakerphone button with one of his pudgy fingers.

"Sheriff Carter?"

"Speaking."

"Sheriff. This is Ken Little, state police."

"Yes." Jake sat up straight in his chair and snatched up the handset.

"We've got a single-vehicle accident out here on Highway 10b. Registration comes back as Kevin Armstrong." The last was said in a tone indicating to Jake that the trooper already had experience with Kevin Armstrong.

"Yep. What happened? Is Kevin okay?"

"We don't know. All we found was his pickup in the river, wedged against a tree downstream from the bridge. A farmer out looking for a runaway cow called it in this morning."

Shit, the sheriff said to himself, what had Kevin done now? "Was anyone hurt?"

"As I said, I can't say. No one was in the truck when we found it. The water runs pretty fast down there, even at this time of the year. We're afraid he's been swept downstream."

"Could be he got out before it went in."

"Could be, but we checked near the bridge and along the riverbanks. We didn't see any footprints or anything that indicated someone got out. That's why I'm calling. Could you send someone out to his place to see if he made it home somehow? Maybe someone picked him up and gave him a lift home. We checked the hospital. The only person admitted since last night was a pregnant woman whose water broke this morning."

"I'll send someone over to check it out." He'd also send someone around town to see if anyone had seen Kevin. "Thanks for the call."

Twenty minutes later, Patrolman Dave Henderson drove down the dirt road that led to the tumbled-down, rusting trailer where Kevin Armstrong had lived for the last seven years. The road was bumpy and rutted and the patrol car creaked and groaned as it lurched back and forth. Dave cringed at each bounce.

He knocked on the door, waited a minute, and knocked again. No one came to the door. Knowing that most folks around town didn't lock their doors, Dave turned the doorknob. It turned and the door opened with a gentle push. He entered the trailer cautiously, not wanting to startle Kevin in case he was inside. He could be real ornery when he was hung over.

The patrolman stepped over piles of dirty clothes and empty beer bottles as he made his way through the small living room and the adjoining kitchen to the bedroom door at the rear of the trailer. The bed was empty, and it looked as if it hadn't been made in a week or more. It was impossible to tell whether anyone had slept in it the night before or not. He turned and looked around the kitchen again. The coffeepot on the counter was cold and dishes were piled in the sink. A silvery-gray cat with white paws curled around his leg, meowing for food. Dave reached down and scratched its head and ears while looking around the cramped kitchen area for cat food. There was a little bit of food left in a bowl on the counter, but it was hard and crusted over. Obviously, no one had fed the cat that morning. He found a bag of Friskies dry cat food and poured some into the bowl and walked out.

"No one's here, sheriff," Dave reported over the radio. "It doesn't look like anyone came home last night either."

"Damn! Okay, get your sorry ass on back here," Jake said. That wasn't good news. "I got Annemarie over at Marty's now. It doesn't look like anyone has seen Kevin today. Steve Henley remembers him leaving Marty's last night around midnight, drunk as a skunk."

"No surprise there," the patrolman sniggered.

"Nope," the sheriff grunted in agreement. Kevin had been a problem ever since he had moved here with his folks. Kevin's father, Dick Armstrong, had grown up in town and had gone off to the University of Indiana, vowing never to come back. Dick then surprised everyone by showing up ten years later with a wife and an eight-year-old son. Unfortunately, Doris Armstrong had died a couple of years later and Dick had never remarried. Everyone now agreed on how tough his mother's death must have been on the boy, but back then, no one recognized just how hard. Dick couldn't afford to send him to college, but that had been a moot point because no college would have been willing to take someone with his grades and penchant for trouble. So, after high school, Kevin ended up working at Nicky's Auto Repair, and worked there still.

"Sheriff, if he left Marty's at midnight, what was he doing way out on 10b that time of night? There ain't nothing out that way."

"Who knows?" No one ever knew what Kevin was going to do next. Maybe he drove into the river on purpose. The sheriff considered that idea for a minute, but decided that Kevin didn't have it in him to commit suicide.

Patrolwoman Annemarie D'Angelo pulled up in front of the low red brick building that housed the police department while the town hall was being renovated. She marched straight into the sheriff's office just as the sheriff replaced the phone in its cradle. "No one's seen him anywhere, Jake," she announced, placing her hands on her hips.

Jake winced. Annemarie never addressed him as sheriff and he had only himself to blame for that. He had invited her to call him by his first name shortly after she had joined the force, hoping that such familiarity would lead to something, but it hadn't. She had told him she didn't believe in dating her boss. He later found out the real reason: she couldn't get interested in anyone who didn't take care of his body as well as she did. That would have been hard for almost anybody given that Annemarie looked like one of the spokeswomen for a fitness center. Jake, on the other hand, looked like every film's version of a small-town sheriff. He was short, overweight, and balding. Any hair he had was kept clipped military length. He wore wire-rim sunglasses most of the time and carried a 357 Magnum revolver, although he stopped short of having a pearl handle on it. By the time he realized she had no interest in him, it was too late to change the first-name arrangement and he was deathly afraid of a sexual harassment lawsuit.

"Okay, I'll alert the state cops. They'll have to drag the river for him. They'll be royally pissed off if Kevin shows up after sleeping one off somewhere." He relayed the information to the state police and hung up.

"I doubt they'll find the body any time soon," he said to Annemarie, who stood throughout the call. "The Pawnee only runs a few miles before emptying into the Arkansas River. The body could be twenty or thirty miles downstream by now."

"Should we notify his next of kin?" Annemarie asked. She was too young to know Kevin well.

"No point. His dad died last year from cancer. His mom died years ago in a car crash."

"Any brothers or sisters?"

"Nope No aunts or uncles either, at least not alive. Dick's brother died in 'Nam. Kevin's mother didn't have any siblings that I know of."

*   *   *   *

John Blanchard yawned again. He rolled down the window to let in the cold night air, blinked a couple of times, and rubbed his eyes. He checked his watch: 12:45 PM. He had been driving for thirteen hours. He pulled off the exit of Interstate 27 just outside of Amarillo, in middle of the Texas panhandle. He had hoped to drive farther, but he just couldn't keep his eyes open any longer.

He checked into an isolated, decrepit motel a mile off the highway, and parked the Suburban at the far end of the parking lot. There was only one other car in the lot, which was one of the reasons he had chosen the motel.

The room was pretty much what one would expect from a roadside motel in the middle of nowhere. All it offered was a single queen-sized bed, a couple of night tables, and a television on a flimsy metal stand against the wall across from the end of the bed. It wasn't much, but it would do.

Kevin was still unconscious in the back of the Suburban. Blanchard had debated whether to carry him into the motel room, but decided it was highly likely that someone would see him carrying the body into or out of the room and begin asking a lot of questions he didn't want to answer. It would be better to leave the body in the car. It was a risk, but one he had to take.

Blanchard opened a small plastic box and pulled out a small hypodermic, stuck the needle through the rubber seal of a bottle, and siphoned out three ccs of the serum. He stuck the needle into Kevin's arm and depressed the plunger. He returned the bottle to its case, tossed the used needle into a paper trash bag, and waited a minute to make sure that there was no adverse reaction. Seeing none, he covered Kevin with a blanket, closed the tailgate, and locked the car. He looked through the dark tinted windows and could barely make out the body in the back, and he was looking for it. Satisfied that it was unlikely that anyone would discover his cargo, he walked back into his room, set the alarm for three hours later, lay down on the bed, and was asleep in minutes.

Chapter 3

▼

Tuesday, October 10

Ted Saunders marched out of the Dallas Hyatt and climbed into the backseat of the limousine sent by KDAL-TV to chauffeur him across town to the station's main studio. He was scheduled to appear on that's morning's "AM Dallas" show in an hour. He moved quickly, not wanting to face any angry crowds that early in the morning. There would be a time and place for that later. In fact, he was looking forward to it.

Despite driving through the city at rush hour, Saunders was sitting in his chair on the set, with his makeup on, forty-seven minutes after he had left the hotel. The station had wanted him there earlier, but he had no desire to wait around before the show started. The station manager had been relieved to see his guest walk through the door and rushed him straight to makeup and onto the set in record time.

Carrie Cornfeld, who sat in the opposite chair, adjusted her microphone for the third time in five minutes. The interview would begin in three minutes. She fumbled with a number of note cards, dropping several to the floor. "Oh, my God," she blurted out and stooped down to pick them up.

As she bent down, her white blouse parted, giving Saunders a clear view of her ample cleavage. He stared involuntarily for a few seconds; the deep tan skin of her breasts was highlighted against her white, lacy bra. Sitting up, she noticed his gaze and blushed.

Carrie sat back and occupied herself with adjusting her blouse and jacket. Without thinking, she pushed back a stray lock of blond hair that had fallen over her face. She looked up, cleared her throat, and said, "Any last questions, Mr. Saunders?"

"No. But, please, call me Ted."

"Thank you, but I think I'll stick with Mr. Saunders." She reddened again.

Saunders continued to look at her, taking in her features. Under any other circumstances, he could imagine taking her to bed. She was young, extremely beautiful, even by television standards, and ambitious. That used to be a perfect combination for getting a woman into bed. Not any more, he sighed.

"And now," the anchorman announced, "as we promised at the top of the show, we have a special guest in our studio with our own Carrie Cornfeld." He turned to look at them.

"Thank you, Bob," Carrie said, looking straight ahead at the camera positioned directly behind her guest. "First of all, let me welcome you back to Dallas, Mr. Saunders. I believe that this is your first trip back since you lost your position as CEO of GenergTex."

"That's right, Carrie. Thank you for having me here today."

"What brings you back to Dallas?"

Saunders grinned. It was a typical opening question for an interview like this. Hopefully, she'd stay on form, and he'd be able to lead her where he wanted the interview to go. "I needed a break, so I'm going out to my ranch for a week of R and R. I thought I'd stop here on my way and attend the GenergTex annual meeting."

"But you're no longer CEO? Why are you attending the meeting?"

"I may not be part of management anymore, but I'm still a big shareholder and I plan to attend the meeting as a shareholder."

"But...um, what kind of welcome do you expect?"

"Mixed, I guess. I think some will welcome me, some will not. But that's irrelevant. I need to protect the value of my stock just like any other investor."

"But you're not really like any other investor, are you?"

"I am now."

"How do you think those people will react when you show up at the meeting? Um...There're many people just here in Dallas who think you destroyed their lives."

"I am terribly sorry about what happened. I know some think we cooked the books and overstated profits for personal gain. That's not true. We did what we thought the shareholders wanted and that was to push the stock price up. I never expected it to all fall apart."

"But it did fall apart and…"

"Yes, it did. But…" He raised his hand with his index finger up, "under slightly different conditions, everything would have worked out fine and all of those who vilify me now would be sitting here kissing my ass instead." The station, running the interview on a five-second delay, was able to block the word *ass*.

The interviewer's face showed a momentary loss of composure, which she struggled to regain. After a couple of seconds, she said, "What about the charge that you engaged in insider trading?"

"Yeah, well, it might appear that way, but someone had to sell their shares so that the people who wanted to buy GenergTex's stock could buy it. It isn't as if I've sold all of my stock. In fact, given how much I owned and how much I held onto, I've actually suffered the biggest loss of anybody. Put on top of that the fact that I've lost my job, and have a ton of legal fees to look forward to. I don't see anyone feeling sorry for me."

"What a crock!" Bill Dayton, a cameraman, said, just loud enough to be heard on the set.

Saunders stood up and turned around. "Do you have something to say to me?" he said to the cameraman.

The cameraman peeked out from behind the camera, but didn't say another word.

"I said, do you have something you want to say?"

"Um…er…no."

"Mr. Saunders," Carrie said loud enough to catch her guest's attention. "Could you tell our audience how you spend your days now that you're, um, *retired?*"

"Huh?" Saunders said, turning back to her.

"I think our audience would like to know what you're doing these days to keep busy."

"Besides defending myself from the media, you mean?" He sat down.

The station manager, who had been watching the segment from just off the set, frantically waved his outstretched hand under his chin.

"Um…well, I think that's all the time we've got. Mr. Saunders, thank you for coming in to speak with us. Good luck today and we hope you can join us again soon. Back to you, Bob and Robin."

The red lights blinked off on all the cameras pointed at the interview set. Saunders stood up, tore off his microphone, and threw it on the floor. He turned to face the cameraman who had spoken during the interview.

"I'm sorry about that, Mr. Saunders," the station manager said as he stepped forward, getting between the two men. A stagehand grabbed Dayton by the shirt to hold him back. "Please forgive Bill. His wife used to work at GenergTex and they lost most of their savings when the stock dropped."

Saunders glowered at the cameraman without moving. Unexpectedly, his face softened. "That's okay. I understand."

"Can we take you back to the hotel?"

"No. One of my ranch hands drove down to get me. He should be outside waiting for me."

*   *   *   *

Saunders drove up to the entrance to the Hyatt, where he had stayed the night before and where GenergTex was holding its annual meeting. Hundreds of angry workers surrounded his Hummer, shouting obscenities and holding signs denouncing the man who once ran their company. A small contingent of police struggled to keep the crowd away from the car.

Since he had left the hotel that morning, camera crews from a couple of the local television stations, probably alerted to his attending the GenergTex annual meeting by his interview, had set up to capture the scene. They panned the crowd and focused from time to time on a few of the more vocal protestors.

Saunders stepped out of his Hummer into a cordon of police, who pushed ahead of him to make a path into the hotel. Back in the car, Pete Tucker, the foreman on Saunders's ranch, heaved his two hundred twenty pounds across the console into the driver's seat. The angry crowds outside convinced him not to try to walk around the car. He put the car in gear and inched away from the front of the hotel. The crowd thinned dramatically by the time he reached the corner. He drove around to the hotel parking lot to wait for his boss's call to bring the Hummer back.

The ex-CEO of GenergTex walked into the cavernous grand ballroom. Row after row of seats, filled with GenergTex shareholders and employees, covered most of the floor space. At the front of the room, a long table sat on a raised platform. Seated at the table was the new management of GenergTex. He scanned the faces. Most were unknown to him. The new CEO was speaking, but paused momentarily when he noticed his predecessor in the back of the room.

The pause, though short, caught everyone's attention, and all heads turned in unison toward the back of the room. Saunders was used to seeing faces containing a mix of awe and gratitude, but now all he saw was anger. No, it was closer to hate, he decided. He smiled, but the faces didn't smile back.

An instant later, many people screamed out obscenities and demanded that he leave. A few people near the back of the room stepped into the aisle and started toward him. Saunders took a step back. Two hotel security guards stepped forward hesitantly. The angry shareholders stopped when confronted by the uniformed men and merely glared past them at the man who had betrayed their trust.

"I don't think you're welcome here, Mr. Saunders," the CEO said over the loudspeakers. "Perhaps you should leave." There were cries of agreement from all around the room.

Saunders stood quietly for a moment. He could sense that the anger in the room was rising with each passing second. He waited until he felt the rage of the audience was about to get out of control and yelled out, "I'll leave, but under protest." He turned and walked out of the room. Boos and hisses followed him out. A few water bottles thumped against the doors as they closed behind him.

Twenty minutes after he walked out of the ballroom, Saunders merged his Hummer into the westbound traffic on Interstate 30 for the six-hour drive to his ranch outside of Sandy Creek, Texas. Saunders settled into his seat, adjusted his seatbelt, and turned on the radio. Pete Tucker flipped a page of the book he was reading and held his tongue at his boss's choice of music.

Just to the west of Fort Worth, the phone in his shirt pocket rang. Saunders fished it out, flipped it open, and held it to his ear. "Saunders, here."

"Well done, Ted," Harden said, dripping sarcasm, without a trace of amusement.

"Hey Whit. What are you talking about?"

"I saw your interview and the subsequent uproar you caused at the annual meeting. CNN carried it."

"Really? Hmm." He hadn't thought that it would go national so quickly. That was good.

"Are you happy now? What the hell did you think you'd accomplish today? If your goal was to get everyone in the country pissed off at you, you succeeded."

"Settle down, Whit. It's no big deal."

"No? You basically admitted that you'd committed both fraud and insider trading."

"Whoa. That's not what I said."

"That's what everyone thinks you said."

"That's their problem."

"No, that's your problem. The DOJ is going to have a field day. You may have blown your chance at a deal."

"Hey, if they can't take a joke…"

"This is no joke!" The lawyer fumed. "Actually," he continued in a calmer voice, "I think the DOJ may be the least of your problems. I warned you about the kooks who might want to mete out some Old West—style justice. The television station has been inundated with hate calls since the show. I'd get out of Dodge if I were you."

"I'll be okay. I'm on my way out to my ranch right now. I'll stay there until things cool down. I can help Pete fix the fence near the Ganter place." He glanced over at his foreman, who nodded in response. "Their herd keeps ending up on my property. It'll give me an excuse to do some real riding."

"You might have to stay out there for a long time given the hornet's nest you've stirred up."

"Whit, I know what I'm doing. Trust me."

"I guess I have no choice," Harden sighed.

"We'll talk when I get back." Saunders snapped the phone closed and put it back into his pocket.

Five hours later, the Hummer turned onto the long gravel driveway to the ranch. The sun had just dropped below the horizon and the road became difficult to see in the twilight, even with the light from the Hummer's halogen headlamps.

They reached the main compound, which encompassed a U-shaped courtyard. The main house formed the bottom of the U, a bunkhouse formed one arm, and the main horse barn and garage formed the other arm. The driveway came right up to the front of the main house, forming a circle.

The main house, which had been built only twenty years ago, looked as if it had been there since the late nineteenth century. The rough hewn logs were weathered, and the white paint around the windows and doors was faded and peeling in places. The peak of the roof ran the length of the house, with a large gable extending from the middle over the main entrance hall. Two large dormers on either side of the gable allowed for guest bedrooms on the third floor.

Saunders threw his bags on the hall floor, knowing they would be taken to his room and unpacked and any dirty laundry washed. He tossed his keys into a Hopi basket sitting on a mission-style side table. He wandered into the family room, which was a bit of a misnomer given that he didn't have any family. The room, the biggest in the house, had walls of unpainted pine paneling. The décor and the furniture was Southwestern rather than Texan, with plums and teals everywhere. In the corner of the room was a monstrous fieldstone fireplace underneath a stuffed antelope head staring out into the room. He grabbed a beer out of the mini-bar, unscrewed the top, and took a swig before he plopped down on the overstuffed sofa and tuned the television to CNN, hoping that they were still carrying his story. He only had to wait five minutes before an excerpt from the interview and footage from outside the Hyatt, both obviously chosen to make him look bad, came on. The whole sequence lasted barely two minutes, but that was enough. He had seen everything he needed. He smiled and clicked off the TV.

CHAPTER 4

▼

WEDNESDAY, OCTOBER 11

On the sixth floor of the New York Times Building, Hank Jenkins pushed a pile of paper aside with his foot, put his size-10 Nikes on his desk, and propped his keyboard on his lap. He hurriedly typed in the last few lines of his latest article on Ted Saunders.

Hank grabbed the oversized Boston Red Sox mug from the file cabinet behind him and gulped some tepid coffee. He corrected a misspelled word, put his hands behind his head, and reread the article from the beginning.

The article focused on Saunders's personal finances rather than the fate of GenergTex, detailing how Saunders had gone from being one of the richest men in America to being nearly eligible for food stamps. It wasn't just his GenergTex stock that was nearly worthless; most of his personal investments had gone bad as well.

He clicked the save icon and e-mailed the article to Adam McMahon, his editor and boss. He checked the time on his Tag Heuer Dive Master watch, which his ex-girlfriend had given him four years ago when she tried to get him to go scuba diving with her. He had quickly found out that he was claustrophobic under the water and he spent the rest of the vacation on the beach, while she went diving every day. She had left him three weeks later for one of the guys she had gone diving with. Despite all that, the parting had been friendly. He now looked on the watch as a reminder to not be pushed into something that he knew wasn't right.

He was ten minutes early. He smiled. "Let's do it," he said and marched down to his editor's office.

"What do you think?" Hank asked as he stood leaning against the doorjamb of the office.

"It's good. It's different from the rest of the stuff you wrote on Saunders." Adam said. Hank liked Adam. He was a reporter's editor, who had earned his chops reporting for a number of papers around the country before coming to the *Times* nearly fifteen years ago. That meant that he understood the reporter temperament and tolerated, somewhat, a missed deadline every once in a while.

"Yeah. I thought it was time to try the up-close-and-personal approach."

"I didn't know you had it in you." Adam looked up and grinned. He then scanned the last couple of paragraphs again. "You come on a bit strong here at the end." He pivoted the screen so Hank could see it and pointed at a passage about Saunders's mental state. The article had questioned whether Saunders was going through a nervous breakdown and pointed to a number of times when Saunders had become enraged and physically assaulted people. That included Hank himself, who had tried to ask his subject a few questions outside a tony restaurant in the East Village.

"I guess I did. You want me to change it?"

The editor sat quietly for a few seconds. "No."

"Are there any other changes?"

"It just needs some clean-up and copy can take care of that."

Hank looked at his watch and smiled.

"Yeah, I know," his editor said, "it's on time for a change. What do you want, a medal? Now get out of here."

A short walk brought Hank to Kelly's, an Irish pub on West 43rd Street. The heavy wooden door closed behind him with a soft thud. He waited a few seconds to let his eyes adjust to the low light, made dimmer by the gray October evening outside. Opposite the door, a long bar ran almost the full length of the room; a large mirror on the wall behind it gave the feeling of being in a much larger space. Most of the rest of the walls were paneled in dark mahogany, its color deepened by layers of cigarette and cigar smoke that had accumulated over the years since the bar had opened shortly after the end of Prohibition.

Hank nodded to a few of the other regulars, shook hands with others as he made his way through the crowd. He glanced over at Patrick behind the bar, pointed over to the corner, held up his index finger, and got a nod and a smile in return. Patrick started to draw a glass of Guinness.

A couple of men dressed in expensive suits parted and Hank saw Maureen O'Connell's cinnamon hair across the room. The hair and fair complexion gave away her Irish ancestry long before anyone knew her last name or heard the delicate lilt of her accent. Maureen was shy and quiet. He recognized that her shyness really disguised a quick wit and an ability to make connections between seemingly unrelated items. Hank knew that a large part of that was because she listened much more than she spoke, a rare talent among the reporters he knew.

He pushed through the gap and made his way toward her.

The rest of the Crew, as they called themselves, had already gathered, taking their usual table in the corner for their Tuesday evening drink and gab session.

"Ahhhh." Matt MacGregor let the single syllable drag out for a couple of seconds. "Hank! Glad you could join us." Matt was wearing his standard bow tie and suspenders that, along with the early onset of gray hair, made him look a lot older than he was, when, in fact, Hank and Matt were about the same age.

"Why?" Hank looked around at the group, hoping to catch a clue as to what was coming next. He was getting used to being on the wrong end of Matt's diatribes. Matt had always envisioned himself as the next Edward R. Murrow, reporting from some far-off war-torn area. Unfortunately for Matt, and everyone else at the *Times* who crossed him, his parrot-like nose, weak chin, and crackly voice kept him off television and radio, so he ended up as a newspaper reporter. Given his decidedly modest ability, it was doubtful that even if he had been an Adonis he would have achieved a Murrowesque stature. This probably accounted for much of the disdain he felt for his colleagues.

"So could you settle an argument about who will go to prison?"

"What are we talking about?"

"Money laundering and American National Federal Bank. You know, the story that finally knocked your GenergTex crap off the front page of the business section." Matt didn't need to mention that it was his story.

"No one's going to jail," Carol Somers said, shaking her head, some of her curly dark brown hair falling loose about her face. "They didn't do the actual laundering. They just *forgot* to report the suspicious activity to the Feds." She flashed a challenging smile at Matt.

"But they let it happen! They still broke the law," Matt retorted, picking up the gauntlet.

"All that'll happen is the bank pays a fine. No one's going to do jail time for that," Carol said in a way to silence Matt. Several heads around the table nodded in knowing agreement.

"She's right," Hank agreed. "No one's going to jail for that."

"Yeah. It's not like they hurt anyone," Henry Cadwaller said with some difficulty. Henry stood a mere five foot six, but weighed nearly three hundred pounds. No one around the table understood how he had reached his fortieth birthday, which they had celebrated a month ago at that very table, without having a major heart attack.

"What do you mean? The stock crashed eighteen percent yesterday after word got out," Matt said, barely repressing a smirk.

"I know, but it's not like," Henry wheezed defensively, "they murdered anyone."

"Tell that to the poor sucker whose retirement just took it in the shorts."

"I guess you're right," Henry retreated. He pulled out a handkerchief and wiped his forehead.

"What about Saunders?" Ravi Bhattacharya asked Hank, "Do you think he'll go to jail?"

"Yes," Hank replied, with a conviction that surprised him, knowing that few white-collar criminals ever actually went to jail. "But, that's different. He was the CEO."

"If anyone deserves it, he does," Carol said.

"So what are you going to do next, now that you've pulled down one of our new-age industrial titans?" Matt asked. "You can't milk that story forever."

"I don't plan to," Hank replied. Not wanting to be pulled into that discussion again, he turned to Ravi. "Saw your cloning article in *Science* today. It was great."

"Thanks."

"Do you really think they'll go as far as cloning people?"

"It's probably close to being technically possible, but should we? That's the real issue. Where do we draw the line?"

"Hey, maybe the Red Sox could make a half dozen clones of Ted Williams," Walt Jansen, one of the *Times* reporters who covered sports, said. "Then maybe they could finally beat the Yankees." Everyone laughed, except Hank and Ravi.

Hank looked at Ravi, who had tried to smile at the joke. He knew that Ravi took the topic seriously and was proud of his work. "Seriously, do you think we should really make duplicates of people?"

"Well, not you, of course," Matt said. "Julia Roberts, that's another story."

"Very funny," Hank said.

"Hey, Hank," Beverly Outerbridge yelled as she pushed her way toward the group. She reached the table panting, her forehead damp with sweat, despite the chill in the air outside.

"What's the matter, Beverly?" Everyone called her Beverly, except Adam McMahon, who called her Bev.

"Just heard it on CNN," She said, in an English accent left over from growing up in Bermuda. "Ted Saunders is dead?"

"What? When?"

"They're reporting it now. At his ranch out in Texas someplace."

"Hey, Patrick," Hank yelled. "Flip on the TV to CNN."

*   *   *   *

The fire chief, or, more correctly, the head of the local volunteer fire department, stood nervously in the glare of the lights, holding his hand in front of his eyes. He could see the cameras and their crews and could just make out the mob of people behind them. It seemed to him that there were almost as many people here as in all of Sandy Creek, the town nearest the Saunders ranch. His department had been the first to respond to the fire that had engulfed the west end of the main house sometime the night before. Two other towns had sent equipment and men to help. All around them was confusion. The firemen had gotten the fire under control after six long hours, and were now just putting out the last smoldering embers. The police were anxious to get in, secure the scene, and begin combing through the remains of the building for evidence of foul play.

The ranch hands milled around the camera crews, not knowing what to do next. They were exhausted from not getting any sleep the night before. Most had spent the night helping the firemen put out the blaze. Others had searched the ranch for Saunders's prized racehorse, Solo, who had somehow gotten out of the barn during the fire. They were all in shock, at the fire and at the thought that their boss was dead.

"We're here this afternoon with fire chief Calvin Irving," the newswoman said, trying not to squint at the camera despite the bright lights. She turned to the man standing next to her and held up a microphone with the station's call letters, KLUE, affixed to it. "Cal, what can you tell us about the fire?"

"Well, we got a call around 2:00 AM last night from one of Mr. Saunders's ranch hands. They had all gone into town for a drink and saw the fire when that got back. They tried to put it out themselves, but they couldn't."

"What did you see when you got here?"

"The whole west end of the house was pretty well involved by then." He turned and swept his arm toward the smoldering pile of timber, which was all that was left of the west wing and central part of the house. "We were unable to keep the fire from totally destroying that end of the house." He turned and pointed at the part of the main house that was still standing. "Fortunately, it didn't spread to the other buildings."

"We heard you found a body. Is that true?"

"Yes. We found the remains on what was left of a sofa in the family room. We can't be sure of the identity yet, but given Mr. Saunders was here alone last night, it would most likely be him."

"How did the fire start?"

"Right now, we're treating it as suspicious."

"Could he have fallen asleep and dropped a cigarette on the sofa?

"As far as I know, Mr. Saunders didn't smoke."

"Is there anything more you can tell us?"

"Not at this time." That was not true, Cal Irving thought, there was a lot more he could tell them. He had seen enough fires in his twenty-five-year firefighting career to spot arson. He could tell that the fire had burned much too hot to have been started by a cigarette or anything else that would normally, accidentally start a house fire. Some kind of accelerant had to have been used. With any luck, they'd find traces of it in the remains of the sofa. The most common accelerant was gasoline and there was a good chance that that's what had been used here. He had seen a gas can out by the garage and it was unlikely that the ranch hands would have left it outside like that. He'd have to ask Pete and the boys about it. If it had been used by the arsonist, maybe they'd get lucky and get some prints or DNA off of it.

They had also found a broken window in the back bedroom and the glass was still on the floor of the room, which meant it had been broken recently. There were also a bunch of footprints outside. The way he saw it, someone broke in, probably surprised Saunders, subdued him in some way, maybe with a blow to the head, and threw him down on the sofa. Maybe there had been a fight. He didn't know yet. That would be for the medical examiner to figure out.

CHAPTER 5

▼

FRIDAY, OCTOBER 13

Dr. Daniel Pendergast glumly stared down at his newest customer. The medical examiner had been looking forward to a leisurely Friday off, until he had received a call from his good friend Tom, the Justice of the Peace of Sandy Creek, Texas. Tom, charged by state law to conduct enquiries into suspicious deaths, had quickly realized that autopsy for the most recent case should be shifted to a bigger city. Sandy Creek, a town with an official population of close to fifteen hundred, thanks to a generous count during the last census, simply didn't have the facilities or the expertise to conduct a proper autopsy. San Antonio, with its relatively new forensics center at the University of Texas, took in cases from all around west central Texas. So the body from the ranch had been taken directly to Dr. Pendergast's morgue in San Antonio.

The body, or what was left of it, rested on the stainless steel autopsy table. A small, hard rubber body block underneath the torso threw the head back to allow the medical examiner better access to the head and neck area. The chest cavity was already open, revealing thoroughly cooked internal organs.

The medical examiner had not found any visible holes in the body and had, therefore, tentatively ruled out death by gunshot or stabbing, but given the degree of burn damage, he'd have to wait for the X-rays before definitively ruling them out as the cause of death.

"Here're the pictures," Dwayne Grogan said, strolling into the autopsy room. He carried a large envelope containing the X-rays of the head and chest of the victim. "Sorry I'm late. I just got a chance to develop them."

Dr. Pendergast snapped the X-rays into the illuminator and flicked on the light, illuminating them from behind. He checked them for a moment or two, looking for anything that might help him determine the actual cause of death. No bullets. No bullet holes. No cracks in the cranium indicating a blow to the head hard enough to kill. There was a ragged hole above the right ear, but that was typical of bodies burned so extremely, the damage caused by steam pressure escaping from the head. The water in the skull heated up and escaped as steam from one of the natural cracks in the cranium. He turned to the chest X-ray and shook his head.

"I don't understand this. This must be some mistake."

"I know."

"The heart valves are still clearly visible. But you have this wrong. No one's heart is on the right side of the chest. You must've put the wrong tags on the pictures."

"I must have, but I've never done that before. Should I take another set?"

"It's too late. I've already removed the organ block."

"Well, that should confirm it."

"No, the organs are damaged. Besides, they've all been detached." He pointed over at the other table where the severely burned internal organs of the victim lay in various stages of dissection. "I wasn't looking for anything like this. I couldn't really tell which side the heart was on before I separated the organs."

Dwayne cringed. "Shit! Sorry."

The doctor ran his hand back and forth through his dark, brown hair as he contemplated the images in front of him. He took off he glasses, held them up to the light, and wiped away a tiny smudge. He had been a medical examiner for nearly twenty years and had never seen a heart on the right side before. It was possible, he knew, but it was extremely rare. The question was, did it matter? "Okay, don't worry about it. I don't have time to go back and reconstruct the internal organs from that mess. I'll make a note of this in the report, but it's no big deal."

A wave of relief swept across Dwayne's face as he scurried from the room.

A second later, Manny Rodriquez poked his head through the door, glanced over at the table, and fought to hold down what remained of his lunch.

"It's time, Doc." Manny said, quickly pulling his head back, not waiting for an answer. The door swung closed automatically.

"Okay. I'm coming." Dr. Pendergast knew this would happen. Answering questions from the media in a high-profile case like this one was just part of the job. Here in San Antonio, with a population of close to one and a half million people, he had seen his share of high-profile cases, but never got used to the lights and the stupid questions asked by most reporters.

He left the room, not bothering to take off his lab coat and boots, locked the door, and trudged down the hall to the front door. Expecting an October afternoon twilight, he was surprised by the bright lights that assaulted him as soon as he stepped through the doors.

"Have you positively identified the deceased as Ted Saunders?" a reporter from one of the local television stations yelled as soon as the doctor appeared.

"Not yet," the doctor said. "We can't make a positive identification at this time, but given the information we have, we have made a tentative ID of Ted Saunders."

"What information is that?" A reporter from the back of the pack called out.

"Mr. Saunders was known to have two webbed toes. Fortunately, the victim was wearing heavy cowboy boots and so the damage to the feet was minimal. Given the presence of webbed toes on the right foot, and the fact that he was the only person known to be in the house, we strongly believe the victim to be Mr. Saunders."

"Why can't you make a positive identification?"

"The fire caused severe damage to the body, including the face, upper body, arms, and hands. The damage was severe enough to make visual identification impossible."

"What about fingerprints?"

The doctor groaned inside. What a stupid question! "The hands were just too severely burned to get any fingerprints."

"If there aren't any fingerprints, how are you going to make the identification?"

Groan. "There are a number of other ways to positively identify a body. We've already requested his dental records. Unfortunately, it will take a couple of days to have them sent to us. If that doesn't work, we'll try DNA profiling, but that will take a couple of weeks, assuming that we get a satisfactory reference sample from his house or a close relative. Despite the damage to the skin, the muscles and the internal organs are still intact. They will give us plenty of usable DNA material to do the analysis."

The doctor held up his hands to stop the barrage of questions, knowing this was a waste of time at this point. "Ladies and gentlemen, that's all for now. We'll share with you everything we can as soon as we know something. I've got to get back to work."

CHAPTER 6

▼

SUNDAY, OCTOBER 15

Candy Harden reached across the breakfast table and pulled down the Washington *Post* that her husband was reading. "What are we going to do now?" she asked. Her face was etched with worry.

Whit Harden looked at his wife and saw, for the first time, that she was beginning to look old. Well, not old exactly, being twenty years his junior, but no longer the trophy wife he had married after his first wife, Doreen, had left him.

"Well, as executor, I'll still get plenty of billable hours. The litigation against the estate will be long and I'm sure Karl will want me to stay involved even though I won't be with the firm anymore," he assured her.

"But, that's still a lot less than you would have gotten if Ted were still alive. Plus it'll end in what, two, three years."

"I know. Maybe I could go back and delay my retirement."

"Could you?" She said, as much a request as a question.

"No, not really. The firm has already announced my retirement and named the new managing partner."

"But Ted was your meal ticket. He promised you a big retainer each year to pay you back for all the losses you suffered."

"Yeah, but that wasn't going to happen anyway. He didn't have the money anymore. I told you already."

"But how are we going to live on what we've got left after those GenergTex losses and what your bitch of a first wife took from you."

He cringed. Why hadn't he followed the advice he had given countless clients over the years and socked away some of his assets overseas? It would have been so easy. That way Doreen wouldn't have gotten so much in the divorce. She had never really been concerned about their finances while they were married. All she had cared about was having enough to throw parties, belong to the right clubs, and take vacations to the "in" place each year. He certainly had the overseas contacts to help him. But, he never thought he'd need to do that. He had truly loved Doreen and was totally shocked when she told him she wanted a divorce, claiming abandonment because of his long hours at the office.

Of course, he wasn't sure that any of that would have mattered. Candy would certainly have given Doreen a run for her, no, he corrected himself, *his* money. The more he saved from Doreen, the more Candy would be spending now.

"I told you," Candy said, not stopping once she started spouting her familiar list of grievances. "You shouldn't have invested so much in Ted's company."

Whit bit his tongue, knowing that there wasn't anything he could say or do to defend himself. He had made that mistake before. He had once pointed out how she had pushed him to invest after she had read about all the money being made in the stock market. Candy had liked it just fine while the stock was going up. Hindsight could cut like a sharp knife, especially in the possession of an angry wife.

True, he had gotten carried away and had put way too much of their portfolio in GenergTex, but he wondered what his wife would do if she knew GenergTex wasn't the only tech stock in their portfolio. Unfortunately, most of them had followed GenergTex into the toilet. When he and his partners had been given the chance to invest in the initial public stock offerings they worked on, they all jumped at the chance. It had all seemed so easy during the roaring nineties, but none of them had cashed out before the crash. All their gains and then some had been lost.

"So, what are we going to do?" Candy gave him a look that told him that she was as angry as she was worried. The only thing Whit didn't know was whether she was angrier with Ted or with him.

CHAPTER 7

▼

MONDAY, NOVEMBER 13

.

The Sandy Creek police issued an update in the death of Ted Saunders, announcing they were on the lookout for a David Oppenheimer, a former employee of GenergTex, who the police had reason to believe had been sending death threats to the former CEO for the last two months. He was also caught on video by one of the network cameras outside the Hyatt when Saunders tried to enter the annual shareholders' meeting. The police believed Oppenheimer had followed the victim out to his ranch and waited until the ranch hands had left, and then had broken in and, either premeditatedly or in the heat of an argument, killed Ted Saunders.

They also concluded that the fire had indeed been arson. There had been traces of gasoline in the remains of the sofa. The gas can the fire chief had seen belonged at the ranch, but no one could explain why it had been left out. The police assumed that the arsonist had gotten it out of the garage and left it out after setting the fire. Unfortunately, there were no prints or DNA on the can.

The autopsy had confirmed that the body was that of Ted Saunders. Preliminary DNA testing, using a previous DNA profile, had provided the only means to positively identify the victim. The fire had damaged too much skin for any fingerprints or facial identification. Dental records had not yet been found, but with the DNA test results, they were not needed.

The autopsy also confirmed that Saunders had been alive when the fire started. Soot particles in the lungs and carbon monoxide levels in the blood were both consistent with someone who was alive when the fire started. There was also evidence of emphysema.

There were traces of amitriptyline in the victim's bloodstream. Saunders's physician confirmed that he had been taking the prescription antidepressant for several months. The level of amitriptyline indicated that it was likely that Saunders had been unconscious when the fire started.

*   *   *   *

Whittaker Harden got off the Amtrak train from Washington and took a cab from Penn Station to the Global Financial Center in lower Manhattan along the Hudson River.

"Good morning, Mr. Harden," Betty Goodman said as the man strode up to her desk.

"Good morning, Betty. How are you doing?"

"I'm doing okay. Each day is a little easier…Not sure what I'm going to do without him."

"Don't worry. I told you, there'll always be a job at of Garrison, Harden and Tilden for you. We have an office here in the city. It's growing pretty quickly and we always need good executive assistants."

"I appreciate that, but I'm thinking about moving back home to Texas to spend more time with my grandkids. I haven't seen them much since moving up here with Mr. Saunders. Gosh, that was almost ten years ago."

"It's been that long? It's amazing how time flies."

"Yes. I was with him for nearly twenty years."

"He was lucky to have you," Harden said, in a tone that let her know that he meant it. Betty smiled weakly at the compliment. "I've got to look through a few things. If I need you, I'll let you know."

"Sure. I'll be right here. I'm still working on that household inventory you asked for. When do you need it?"

"Next week or the week after. Um, Betty, I'd prefer not to be disturbed. Thanks." He closed the door behind him, crossed the room, and sat down behind the desk. He pulled out a set of keys, searched for the right one, and unlocked the desk's drawer, knowing that inside were his late client's most personal files. Pulling each one out, he quickly flipped through them. He replaced all but four in the drawer, pushed the drawer closed and re-locked it.

He spun around in the chair and pulled out the first of the drawers in a file cabinet built into the bookcase in the wall behind the desk. Repeating the process on each drawer in turn, he quickly leafed through every file to ensure that he hadn't overlooked anything. When all the files had been reviewed, he stood up and stuffed the four files he had taken from the desk into his briefcase.

He marched out of the office and said a sympathetic good-bye to Betty. Getting into a cab a few minutes later, he felt a small pang of guilt for taking the files, but they would be worthless to him if they were found in Saunders's office.

CHAPTER 8

▼

TUESDAY, NOVEMBER 14

As on most mornings, Hank Jenkins's e-mail inbox was full of articles from various online news services, sent because they contained one or more keywords. Prior to Ted Saunders's death, the inbox would be full of stories about Generg-Tex. Now, there was only the occasional one about the company or its late former CEO. Near the end of that day's offerings, he noticed one from a Fort Wayne, Indiana, daily, the *News-Sentinel*. Over the last year, he had watched Saunders's hometown paper swing from a mix of support and pride in the local boy making it big to a sense of betrayal.

The article used Saunders's death to demonstrate the scientific advances in identifying crime victims. Hank skimmed the article and was about to close it when he read something that stopped him:

> Edna Grouse, Saunders's nurse when he was a child, has questioned the accuracy of the autopsy. She stated that "the webbed toes were on the left foot, not the right." A check with the medical examiner in Texas confirmed the toes were on the right. The DNA test, which proved the identity of the victim, makes it clear that a forty-five-year-old memory is not reliable.
> One thing is becoming clear. As new tools are developed to aid forensic science, the role of the eyewitness will decline over time. This is a good thing, as evidenced by the number of death sentences that have been overturned because science has proved the original conviction was wrong. Science can't turn back the hands of time, but it can set innocent people free.

Hank closed the article, opened his word processor, and reread the article he was wrestling with. He spent another twenty minutes revising it. Finally satisfied, he sent it off to his editor.

With his article finished, his thoughts returned to the Fort Wayne article. He clicked on the icon and opened it again, considered it for a while, and then clicked on the Yahoo! white pages to get the number for the *News-Sentinel*.

In minutes he was connected to the reporter whose byline graced the article.

"I'm Hank Jenkins from the *New York Times*. I read your article today. Great article!" It wasn't, but he knew you got more information with a little lie than with the cold truth sometimes.

"Thanks?"

"I really liked the nurse's story. Would you mind if I asked a couple of questions?"

"Sure, what do you want to know?" The voice was a bit tentative.

"Can you give me information on Mrs. Grouse? Did you contact her to check out if she was for real? How was her memory otherwise?"

"Yeah, I talked to her. She seemed okay. She lives in a local old folks' home. She's nearly seventy-five," the Indiana reporter, Chuck O'Brien, began to open up a bit.

"How sure was she of the toes?"

"Absolutely. She nearly convinced me. But the DNA test said otherwise, didn't it?"

"Yes, but maybe there was a mistake at the lab."

"I checked. The medical examiner said that they were able to get a good sample from the body. At first, the police weren't sure that they'd be able to get a DNA match," O'Brien replied. "They tried to get reference samples from the ranch and his apartments, but whoever cleaned those places kept them nearly spotless. Besides, given the number of people who went in and out of the ranch, it would have been difficult to be sure that any sample was his. But..." O'Brien paused for effect. "They got lucky. Saunders had been accused in a paternity suit a few years ago and had given a DNA sample to prove he wasn't the father."

"When was that?" Hank asked, suddenly unable to recall the specifics.

"Oh, it was about four years ago. He had been seeing the woman on the side for a couple of months and then dumped her. Nine months later, she had a son and she tried to get child support money from him. That suit led to his divorce."

"Now I remember. The DNA proved it wasn't his."

"That's right."

"But, this time there was a match?"

"Yes. The DNA profile put the probability at one in a zillion that the body wasn't his. Between that and the fact that he was known to be in the house, there wasn't much doubt that it was Saunders. The toes thing was just a plus, even with Edna Grouse's memory to the contrary. I mean, how many people have webbed toes anyway?"

"Mind if I call the nurse?"

Chuck O'Brien gave him her name, number, and address. "Thanks," Hank said. He hung up the phone and dialed the nursing home where Saunders's childhood nurse now lived.

He identified himself and asked for Edna Grouse. The person on the phone transferred him to the nursing home administrator.

"I'm sorry," the administrator said, "but Edna passed away two nights ago."

"Oh." Hank sat there nonplussed, not sure what to say. "I'm sorry." After another short pause, "Was it expected? I mean, had she been ill?"

"No. The doctors think she had a heart attack."

"Did she have a history of heart trouble?"

"Not at all. That's why we're all in shock about it."

"I'm sorry to have bothered you. Did she have any next of kin?"

"Not living. She's going to be buried next to her late husband and son out at Greenlawn Memorial on Covington Road."

"Will there be an autopsy?"

"I don't know. She was under a doctor's care and seventy-five. That'll be up to the medical examiner, not us."

"That sounds right." He made a note to check on whether an autopsy would be performed or not.

"Um, Mr. Jenkins? You're a reporter, right?"

"Yes. Why?"

"Were you calling about that article?"

"Yes. Why?"

"She wasn't crazy, you know, and her memory was as sharp as a tack."

"That's good to know, but…"

"If she said that the toes were wrong, they were wrong."

"I'm sure that's true, but the DNA test is pretty accurate."

"Well, I don't know about that. I do, um, did know Edna and she knew what she was talking about."

"I'm sure she did. It's a shame she isn't here to defend herself." Hank regretted saying it as soon as it came out.

"Yes. It is." Hank could tell the woman was on the verge of tears.

"I'm sorry. That was an awful thing to say. Thank you for your help." He hung up the phone, felt a lump in his throat. After a few minutes, he picked up the phone and dialed a local number.

At 5:35 PM, Hank walked into Bobbie Roth's office in Bellevue Hospital on First Avenue at 30th Street, where New York City's Chief Medical Examiner's office was located. Dr. Roberta Roth, Bobbie to most people, had worked as a medical examiner for the city for nearly twelve years. She looked up from making some last-minute additions to an autopsy report. She smiled, her pink thin lips parted ever so slightly. She gently bit her lower lip. Her green eyes twinkled as he crossed the office.

As she stood to greet him, her white lab coat opened, revealing a hint of her statuesque figure underneath. Her long, silky raven hair was swept back away from her face. Hank smiled. He knew it was a chauvinistic thing to think, but he couldn't understand why such an attractive woman would dedicate her life to dissecting dead bodies. Come to think of it, he wasn't sure why anyone would want to do that.

"So, Hank, what's the story and how can I help?" She pointed to the chair by her desk and they both sat down.

"I've got some questions about how they use DNA to identify a dead body."

"Any body in particular?"

"Ted Saunders. They used DNA testing to identify his body after the fire."

She nodded. She had read about it in the papers. "Sure, what do you need?"

"I don't know, really. How accurate is a DNA test?"

"It depends. It's all about probability. With the techniques available today, the odds that we're wrong can get pretty small."

"Let's suppose there's a really good match. Could there be a mistake?"

"Mistakes are always a risk. Contamination of a sample happens. Since the amount of DNA used in the test is so small, even a little bit of foreign material could cause misleading results, but that usually leads to a finding of exclusion, meaning no match, rather than inclusion. Given what I know of the case, I doubt that happened."

"How about faking it?"

"What do you mean?" Bobbie asked with a confused look on her face.

"I don't know. Could someone switch a sample intentionally? Maybe rig the report?"

"I doubt it. Medical examiners take this stuff too seriously to let anyone switch a sample. Rig a report? No, I don't think so."

"What about a bribe?"

"That's been known to happen, but it's not likely. There're usually too many people involved for that to happen. It would be too risky in a high-profile case like this one. Too many people look at it. Besides, there's always a chance of a retest, which would catch any falsification."

"What about switching the reference sample?"

"Could happen, I suppose, but I doubt it. The police would keep track of it."

"What if it were an old sample?"

"What do you mean by old?"

"Saunders gave one in a paternity suit a while ago. Years ago."

"Well, to switch that profile so it matches the new sample, someone would have to go in and alter the old profile. That would be nearly impossible since it's part of the court records and probably in a DNA database or two somewhere."

"So you're sure that there couldn't be a mistake?"

"No mistake," Bobbie Roth concluded. "Unless…"

"Unless?" Hank sat forward in his chair.

"Unless," Bobbie had a twinkle in her eye, "the body was a clone?"

"Veeeery funny!" He slumped back into the chair. "Okay. Thanks for the help," he said disappointedly, and stood up to leave.

"You're welcome. What's this all about, Hank?"

"I saw an article in Saunders's hometown paper," he added in response to her quizzical look. "Saunders's childhood nurse questioned the identification of the body, something about the webbed toes being on the wrong foot. I thought there might be a story there, but I guess she was mistaken."

"Sorry, but I don't see how the test could be wrong. I'll check some more if you want."

"Naaah, don't bother. Thanks again."

"Sure. Any time." She watched him leave, than sat at her desk playing with her pen for a minute before returning her attention to the unfinished autopsy report in front of her.

Hank spent the entire forty-five minutes it took him to walk back across town to his office thinking about the idea of a clone. Maybe the cloning process would create the discrepancy with the toes.

He got off the elevator one floor below his office and marched down the hall to Ravi Bhattacharya's cubicle. Ravi looked up from a medical textbook. Other medical books were strewn across his desk.

"Ravi," Hank said, "Just how close are scientists to making human clones?"

"Technically, they're close, but no one's tried anything even close yet."

"What about that sheep in Europe?"

"Dolly? Yeah, that was some years ago, but not much has happened since then. I heard that someone is offering to clone pets, but that's still a long way from humans."

"Doesn't seem like a long way away if someone offered enough cash."

"I suppose. In secret, you mean? Like the government?"

"Yeah, something like that."

"It could be, but for what? Remember, the clone doesn't come out as an adult. It grows just like a normal human being would."

"So to have an adult clone today…"

"It would have to have been born twenty-plus years ago."

"And the technology wasn't available then." Hank said, crestfallen.

"Right!" Ravi eyed Hank for a moment. "What's this all about?"

"Nothing, just a wild idea, but it's not possible. Thanks, Ravi."

Returning to his cubicle, Hank plopped down into his chair. He had hoped that Edna Grouse had been onto something. It would have made a great story.

After a few minutes, he looked at his watch and decided to call it a day. He grabbed his coat and headed straight to Kelly's, which was nearly full by the time he got there. The Crew was already gathered. As he approached the table, Matt MacGregor was pontificating about how the collapse of the second-largest bank in Japan was going to accelerate the worldwide recession and cause the already weak U.S. economy to sink even further.

Hank sat down next to Carol Somers. The waitress brought him a beer. Matt stopped talking just long enough for the waitress to put the beer on the table. "All in all, I think that the economy over the next year's going to be a bust."

"I disagree. I think that the market's going to rebound," Carol tossed out.

"What makes you think that?" Matt said. An annoyed look crossed his face.

"Unemployment's down, wholesale prices are moving up, inventories are low, and new housing starts are picking up. The collapse of the Tokio Sumitomo Bank has been expected for weeks, if not months. If anything, getting rid of the uncertainty will give investors a shot in the arm. So, I'd say the economy's primed for a rebound." Carol looked over at Hank and gave him a mischievous wink.

Hank smiled in return.

"That's a load of crap," Matt retorted after he thought about it for a moment or two. "The market's still nervous about the telecoms and energy companies. Isn't that right, Hank?"

"How would I know?"

"Well, you should be an expert on energy companies by now, given all the time you spent following GenergTex."

"So? That doesn't make me a market guru. I've still got most of my money in CDs."

"You don't invest in the market either?" Henry L. Cadwaller asked, a thin smile creasing his face.

"Are you kidding? Last time I put money into a stock, the company immediately filed for chapter eleven."

"Sounds like you have a lot in common with Ted Saunders," Matt snorted.

"How so?"

"You both seem to have a brown thumb when it comes to growing your portfolios." He snorted. "I just figured out my next investing strategy. I'll simply short whatever you pick. I'd short Saunders's picks too, but he's dead." He laughed even harder.

"That's a morbid thing to say," Ravi Bhattacharya commented, shaking his head in disbelief.

"I agree." Hank paused, then turned to Matt and said, "I'm not that bad."

"But Saunders was," Matt replied. "He seemed to have had a knack for losing money."

"That was only recently. He'd done pretty well before then," Hank exclaimed, not sure why he was defending Saunders's market savvy.

"Yeah, but that must have been luck," Henry said. Wheeze. "How else would you explain his more recent investments? I mean, think about that cockamamie dot-com that sold Oreos and stuff overseas."

"Yeah, what'd he lose on that one? Ten or twenty million?" Matt said.

"Or, how about buying that so-called cattle ranch in Bolivia," Walt Jansen added.

"Argentina," Hank corrected.

"Whatever." Walt shrugged. "You'd think that he'd make sure he could raise cattle on it before he bought it. Maybe it was just too small for him to pay attention. He *only* lost five million on that one."

"I thought the investment in the high-yield certificates from that Antigua bank was the best. Talk about a sucker. What was that? Ten million?"

"Let's change the subject, okay?" Hank suggested strongly.

"Sure. Sure," Matt laughed. "At least he got a nice tax write-off." Clearly, he didn't really want to change the subject.

"He could never use them," Carol jumped in. "He had enough losses on his GenergTex stock to last the rest of his life. Oops." She turned crimson, but then joined in the general laughter all around the table.

An hour later, Hank got up to leave. Maureen O'Connell got up too and walked him to the door. "You know, Hank, I was thinking." Hank knew enough to listen whenever she said that. "They might be on to something. If I didn't know better, and I don't, I'd think he tried to lose that money."

"Why would he?"

"I don't know, but you know him better than anyone else," she smiled warmly. "If you can't you figure it out, nobody can."

"Thanks, Maureen. If you're right, I'll owe you one."

"You still owe me from the last time."

"I know. I'd take you away for a weekend of unrepentant sex, but your husband would kill me."

"Yeah, Donny's like that. I can't understand why." She laughed and left him standing at the door of the bar, deep in thought.

CHAPTER 9

▼

WEDNESDAY, NOVEMBER 15

Arriving at his office building, Hank jumped between the closing doors of the elevator, nearly colliding with Henry Cadwaller and Carol Somers. Carol stepped back quickly to avoid him and dropped the pile of papers she was holding, splaying the sheets all over the floor of the elevator. Hank knelt down and was picking up the last page just as the elevator doors opened to their floor. The three of them stepped out together.

"Too bad you left so early," Carol said, taking the pile of papers back, frowning at the mess in her hands.

"Sorry," Hank said. "It had been a long day."

"We talked about Saunders again," Henry said.

"Really?" Hank could only imagine the conversation after he left.

"Matt thought it was such a waste."

"Yeah, I guess it was," Hank said without much emotion.

"No, it's not what you think," Carol said. "He was referring to all the money Saunders lost. It got us all fantasizing about we'd do with that much money."

"I said I'd be happy with just ten percent," Henry joked, before waddling off to his desk.

"What would you do with that kind of money?" Carol asked, mischievously.

"I've never thought about it."

"Everyone's thought about it. You should try it. It's fun to fantasize, and not just about money." Carol smiled, turned, and walked seductively toward her office.

Hank watched her until she reached the end of the hall and turned. Carol glanced back at him, grinned again, and offered a petite wave. He shook his head. Carol was a beautiful woman. For some reason, perhaps because he had played hard to get, Carol constantly flirted with him. He sometimes fantasized about hopping into bed with her, burying his face between her more than ample breasts, but he always held back. Carol had a history of leading men on and then dumping them. He had decided long ago that he didn't need that kind of rejection.

Hank sat down with his mug of coffee and tried to focus on the story that Adam McMahon had given him a couple of days before. He called up Google and typed in his first search criteria for research for the story. He soon realized he wasn't getting anywhere. He was still thinking about that morning's elevator conversation and Maureen's comments from the night before.

"Hey, what's a five-letter word for blockhead?" Larry Jacobson yelled out suddenly over the wall of his cubicle to no one in particular. Someone offered, "Larry." A chorus of chuckles could be heard in all directions. "Ha-ha. I'm serious."

"So am I," the same voice yelled back. Larry ignored the voice this time.

"Hey, Hank, you know a five-letter word for blockhead?"

"Moron," Hank replied.

"Oh, right." There was more laughter from the surrounding cubicles. Hank could hear the pencil moving across the paper. Larry was one of the world's worst crossword puzzle solvers, but loved to do the *Times* puzzle every morning. He couldn't get more than a half-dozen words on his own, but could usually finish it with the help of the entire office.

"How about a nine-letter name of a Mel Brooks movie, starting with the word *the*?"

"*The Producers*," the same voice as before yelled out.

"*The Producers*? What's that?"

"Yeah, that was a great one," another voice yelled.

"Yeah, the best. You know. Zero Mostel. Gene Wilder. Two Broadway producers who keep producing bomb after bomb until they decide to make a bomb. So they sell shares of a thousand percent in the musical figuring no one will come looking for the money when it bombs. Unfortunately, their play is a big hit and they end up in prison. What was the play called?"

"*Springtime for Hitler*," the voice sang.

"Sounds stupid," Larry concluded.

"You just don't have a sense of humor," a new voice offered.

Hank listened to the back-and-forth without joining in. Once it was quiet again, he started to visit some of the sites that Google had found for him, but his mind kept drifting back to *The Producers*, creating an idea that was fuzzy, just beyond his grasp. What was it? Producing plays that bomb. No, that wasn't it. They wanted it to bomb. Why? Of course, now he knew why Saunders would want to purposefully make bad investments. The question was, could it be done?

He yanked open his file drawer, rummaged through some files, pulled one out, and placed it on his desk, the research for his article now forgotten.

Hank picked up the phone.

"This is Fran Gorski," a woman's voice answered. "Can I help you?" Hank had briefly interviewed Fran a couple of months ago. She worked for one of the major investment brokerage houses in the city and was the personal banker for Saunders, although for only the last year. It had been a big coup for her firm and for her personally when they got the account. They were less than happy now that they had to deal with the fallout from the crash of GenergTex and the death of the account holder.

"This is Hank Jenkins. I'm not sure if you remember me."

"Sure. You're with the *New York Times*, right?"

"Right. Do you mind if I ask you a few more questions."

"I don't think that would be a good idea. Our lawyers don't want me talking to anyone these days." That was understandable, Hank thought. There were already a number of lawsuits by GenergTex employees and investors, and even though Fran's firm wasn't yet a target, one could never be too careful.

"What if it's all off the record? I'm just collecting background stuff for a human-interest piece I'm writing. No attribution."

"Well, okay, but only off the record."

"It's a deal. Have you ever found out why Mr. Saunders switched his account to your firm?" This had been an open issue during their last interview.

"No."

"Do you why you got the account?" He made sure that his tone did not sound condescending. Fran was a junior account manager with only a few years of experience and the Street had been surprised that she had gotten the account in the first place.

"No. All I know is that he asked for me. He said he had heard good things about me."

"Did he say from whom"?

"No, but I didn't ask."

"My recollection is that he used your firm as a broker or agent, but didn't really use you, your firm, I mean, for advice on his finances or investments. Was that right?"

"Yes. I'm still not sure why he was paying for a full-service broker when he didn't use the services."

"That still seems kind of odd to me too. Was it? I mean, do you have many other clients like that?"

"Me? No. Our firm, probably."

"Did you ever try to give him any advice?"

"Sure, many times. But it was usually too late and we were trying to get him to sell things he had just bought. Many of them seemed way too risky or just plain stupid, although I never told him they were stupid."

"And what did he say when you told him that?"

"He said he wanted some high-risk, high-return investments in his portfolio. While we agreed with that basic strategy, I told him that some of his investments bordered on the speculative, involving more risk than anything I'd ever recommend. Especially in light of his, how shall I say it, altered circumstances?"

"Which ones in particular did you discuss with him?"

"Um. I'm not sure I should answer that."

"Listen, I'm not going to hold you to any of this."

"Um, okay. Let me see. Where do I start? We told him that the dot-com bubble had already popped, but he invested in that Internet venture."

Hank quickly scanned his list. He found the one he was looking for, USGoodies.com, which shipped American foods and other stuff around the world to ex-pats living in far-flung parts of the world who wanted a piece of home. He put a check next to that one. "What else?"

"That silver mine in Peru. We actually heard about that one before he invested. We warned him about where silver prices were headed. Even at the then-current price, the mine was losing money. With a little checking, we found out that the mine had been losing money for years. Ted said he was convinced silver was going to jump and wanted to be contrarian. Right after he bought, silver prices collapsed fifteen percent and poof, there went that investment."

Hank found that one on the list. The company was called Argent Trading Limited. Hank smiled. Whoever named the company must have thought he was being clever since Argent meant "silver," but probably didn't realize the Spanish word for silver was "plata." Or, maybe "Plata Trading" didn't sound right.

Fran was warming to the topic.

"We also warned him about the timberland he bought in Canada, but he wouldn't listen. He said that he was sure that Congress would increase quotas on imported lumber, but I'm sure you know what happened."

Hank nodded as he looked for that investment. Saunders had purchased nearly two hundred thousand acres of timberland in Canada, one of the largest single contiguous tracts of private forest to come on the market in many years, for forty million dollars. It had valued at fifteen million dollars less than what he paid for it only six months later. The drop in the demand for lumber coupled with reduced quotas had devastated the value of the land.

"There were others," Fran said, "but I've probably said too much already."

"That's okay. I get the picture. Were any of these deals suspicious to you?"

"What do you mean?"

"Did any of them seem fraudulent?"

"That certainly crossed our minds, but he didn't want to hear about it. He said he made the investments and he was a big boy and would take his lumps."

"Was there anything else odd about them?"

"Not that I can recall."

"Did it ever seem like he was trying to make bad investments?"

"Why would he do that?" She sounded genuinely confused.

"Well," Hank said, not wanting to answer that. "I've taken up enough of your time. Thanks."

With the phone nestled back in its cradle, Hank looked at his notes. Fran Gorski hadn't confirmed his theory, but hadn't discredited it either. At least now Hank knew for sure that the investments had been Saunders's decisions rather than someone else's.

After staring at the list for a couple of minutes, Hank noticed that almost all of the big-money losers had been made in the last six to twelve months before Saunders had died, and all had been made entirely with cash. Almost all of his earlier investments had been made using loans from banks, usually collateralized by the stock of GenergTex. Hank knew the banks had been falling all over themselves to lend to Saunders back then, when his GenergTex stock was worth something, and that would have stopped as soon as the GenergTex stock price fell. But, it appeared that Saunders had started making cash investments before the banks had totally cut off his lines of credit. If Hank's theory about wanting to lose the money was correct, it would make sense to use cash. The last thing Saunders would want was a bunch of bankers poking around into these deals and, besides, they had a nasty habit of wanting their money back.

For his idea to work, Saunders had to have had a way to get the money he lost back. Maybe he got a kickback or something. Hank knew that if he were going to figure this out, he would need some help. He pulled a small slip of paper with a single handwritten phone number on it below the words *call me* out of his wallet. He picked up the phone and dialed.

"Alyson Murphy," the voice on the other end announced.

The sound of her voice brought to his mind the image of her wiry, athletic, and deeply tanned body walking toward him, her naturally wavy, dark, shoulder-length brown hair blowing in the wind. Her sensuous red lips breaking into a broad smile as she approached, lighting up her soft yet seductive deep hazel eyes. He sighed quietly to himself.

"Hello," she said when he didn't answer.

"Oh. Hi. Alyson, it's Hank."

"Hi Hank." She sounded surprised, which was to be expected. They had last met six months ago at their fifteenth college reunion. Hank had promised to call her, but never had, not knowing exactly how to renew their college friendship. Plus, what was the point? She had been there with her boyfriend. After fifteen years, she certainly wasn't looking to renew their college romance. "What's up?"

"I need some help. I wasn't sure who else to turn to." That wasn't exactly true. Hank had other contacts he could call, but had decided to use this as an excuse to call her. "I know that you're into financial investigations of some sort." He hadn't quite figured out exactly what a forensic accountant did, but he knew that her company, Financial Investigations, Inc., specialized in that. "I think you said that you track down money? Is that right?"

"Yes," she replied, "but usually we just help companies, or the Feds or regulators, do that. Why?"

"I'm, um, not exactly sure." Now that he had her on the phone, he wasn't really so sure about what he had in mind. "How hard would it be to stash a lot of money where no one could find it?"

"Is this for you personally?" she asked in a part-playful, part-serious tone.

"I wish. It's for a story. I just wanted to know if it's possible. You know, put it in some numbered account somewhere?"

"The short answer is, it depends. If you're talking about taking some of your paycheck and parking it somewhere, no. But if you're talking about laundering illegal money, then yes."

"Why's that?"

"If you move a lot of money legitimately, you'll almost always leave an electronic or paper trail. If you're moving illegal money, under the radar so to speak, you might get away with it. But that's only going to work if no one knows you've got the cash in the first place."

"Exactly!"

"Exactly what?"

"What if no one knew you had it?"

"Well, it would be a lot harder to find, obviously. But, if you've stolen or embezzled it, there's a good chance someone's going to figure it out, at least eventually. Then, they'll just track you down, wait for you to make a mistake. Everyone makes a mistake sometime."

"What if the money was lost?"

"What do you mean?"

"I don't know. Maybe. What if you purposefully made bad investments so that it looked like the money disappeared by being…um, lost legitimately."

"Why would anyone do that?"

"So nobody would come looking for it, like you said." Hank was clearly fishing now. He hadn't figured things out this far yet.

"I see," she paused to think about it. "Sure, that might work. But, you'd want to get the cash at the end somehow or there wouldn't be much point, would there?"

"Could you give it to someone else for a while and then get it back later?"

"I guess, but you're assuming the person would give it back. What if he doesn't? It's not like you could go to the cops and yell *thief*."

"I guess that's right," Hank said, sitting back in his chair, twirling his pen, seeing his idea slipping away from him.

"No, the better way would be to give the money to yourself," she said after a few moments.

"How could you do that?"

"You could set up a company that no one knows you own. Then that company buys an asset. Then, in a separate transaction, you buy the asset from a company that you already secretly own."

"Can you do that?" Hank asked, sitting up straight again.

"Sure. In any number of countries it would be easy to set up a company where no one would know who actually owned it."

"How?"

"There're lots of ways. The easiest would be for the company to be set up with bearer shares instead of registered shares. Here in the U.S., companies have to keep track of who owns their stock. In some countries, not many, it's still possible for companies to issue stock without having to register who owns it. The ownership can change hands by simply handing over the stock certificates. Once it's set up, the shares are passed to the real owner. Or, you could own the company through an alias. There're other ways as well."

"So, no one would find the money because no one would be looking for it?"

"That's right. Though, if someone really wanted to find it, the money could be traced. Why are you asking? Is this hypothetical or actual?"

"It's only hypothetical at this point."

"Are you sure?"

"Yes. So far." There was a pause. "Alyson, I was wondering…"

"About?"

"Would you like to have dinner over the next few days? Or, maybe sometime this weekend? You know, to talk about this more."

"I'm kind of busy right now and I've got plans for the weekend."

"Oh, okay, um…What about this Monday?"

She was quiet for a moment. "Sure," she said, hesitantly. He suggested an early dinner at a cozy restaurant on Broadway. She agreed.

Hank hung up the phone. So it might be possible to stash the cash somewhere so no one would look for it. Maybe Saunders had meant to disappear or simply hide the cash so he wouldn't have to give it all back. But now that he was dead, the cash was sitting out there somewhere waiting for someone to find it. Maybe there could be some restitution after all. Now all he had to do was convince Adam McMahon to let him try to find it. He got up and marched down to the corner office.

"You want to do what?" the editor demanded of his reporter, after hearing the outline of Hank's idea.

"I want to track down Saunders's lost money?"

"I don't get it. If he lost it, what's the point of trying to get it back?"

"I told you. I think he purposefully made bad investments to hide some of his money so he could keep it after he got out of jail."

"That's crazy." Adam McMahon shook his head.

"No, it's not." Hank outlined what Alyson Murphy had told him and showed the editor the list of bad investments. "Saunders may be a crook, but I don't think he's an idiot. This list proves it."

"That list doesn't prove squat!" Adam spat out. He held up his index finger to stop Hank from saying another word. Hank knew better than to interrupt his boss. Adam sat silently for a few seconds, his head gently bobbing from side to side and his eyebrows dancing up and down. It was obvious that the editor was trying to evaluate the possibilities of the idea and that some part of his story was resonating.

"Okay, I'm intrigued. But, how do we prove this and, more importantly, get the money back?"

"I don't know, yet. I thought I'd get some help from Alyson, er, Ms. Murphy. We might want to hire her as a consultant."

"How much is this going to cost?"

"I don't know. I didn't ask her." He bit his lip, wishing he had.

Hank was about to say something, but his boss asked him first, "Who's going to pay for this? Can we get reimbursed if we find the money?"

"I would think so. I'll find out."

"You'd better. If we're going to lay out some serious money on this, I'd like to get our expenses covered."

Hank got up quickly without saying another word and retreated from the room before his boss had a chance to change his mind.

CHAPTER 10

▼

MONDAY, NOVEMBER 20

Alyson Murphy had trouble keeping her thoughts focused on the report she held in her hands. It was the final draft on the collapse of Arncor Bank, an Internet bank that had grown fairly quickly during the boom years of the late 1990s, but had, just as quickly, fallen into bankruptcy. In this case, they had found that the collapse was due less to mismanagement and fraud than to running afoul of the simple business concept that revenues had to exceed expenses over the long run. The report had been prepared at the request of investors. She usually enjoyed reading final reports before they were sent to clients, but not this time.

Her thoughts kept drifting back to Hank Jenkins and the last time they met at their fifteenth college reunion. She had almost passed on it, dreading the idea of showing up alone. So, even though she had broken up with Zeke, she had asked him to take her. Ironically, she had ended up alone anyway. Shortly after they arrived, Zeke met up with some louts from her class and they went off drinking somewhere, abruptly reminding her of why they had split up. In the end, however, it had turned out all right. She had met Hank a little while later and they had sat by the pool and reminisced for most of the night. She could sense some of the old feelings for Hank resurfacing and she thought he felt the same way too.

Unfortunately, Zeke had come back just past midnight to, as he put it, "reclaim" her, and the two of them had gone back to their room, where Zeke promptly passed out without even taking his clothes off. She had slept fitfully in the other bed. At two in the morning, she had snuck down to Hank's room and slid a piece of paper under the door with the words *call me* and her phone number on it. Either he hadn't seen it or he hadn't wanted to call her.

Until now, that is. Why had he really called her? Was it all business?

She had wanted him to call months ago, but he hadn't. Maybe it was better that he hadn't called until now. She hadn't needed that distraction in her life. Work was crazy and she was seeing someone new, someone who was getting fairly serious judging by the amount of time that he wanted to spend with her. He was even talking about taking a trip to Bali and Tahiti this coming spring, living decadently for two weeks in five-star resorts, the kind with private whirlpools and beaches where you could make love under the stars if you wanted to.

It sounded exciting, but she wasn't going to hold her breath just yet. She had already experienced Gavin unexpectedly canceling at the last minute. The first time had been her birthday. She had felt incredibly foolish sitting by herself at the restaurant. The maitre d' asked her if she wanted to take the birthday cake home, but she told him to give it to staff or just throw it out. She hadn't cared at that point. Gavin had worked hard for the next month to make up for it. The latest example was their upcoming ski trip. Gavin had canceled it because he would be away on business. At least she hadn't made it to the airport before he canceled.

But, if things were so serious with Gavin Matthews, why did her heart race at the thought of having dinner with Hank? Sure, they had been extremely close friends in college, even lovers for a while, but that was over long ago. She had wanted it to go further back then, but Hank hadn't been ready for a commitment. Then, at the reunion, she had given him an opening you could drive a truck through and he hadn't taken it.

So, she had to assume that his call was strictly business. That would be fine with her. She was sure she could keep it that way.

The phone rang. Alyson nearly fell over backwards in her chair in reaction to the sound. It took her a few seconds to regain her balance and reach for the phone.

"Alyson," the receptionist said. "Hank Jenkins is here." Alyson put the phone down and rose to her feet, a little unsteady. She straightened out her dress and marched to the reception area with a lightness in her step that hadn't been there in a long time.

"I thought we were meeting at the restaurant," Alyson said as she walked up to him.

"Sorry, I was in the neighborhood and thought I'd stop by. I know that I'm a bit early. I hope you don't mind."

"Not at all." Alyson would have liked a little time to get ready. "Should we talk a bit before we go?"

"That'd be great."

"Now, what's this all about?" Alyson demanded after they took their seats in her office.

"It's just like I told you on the phone. I think that someone was trying to hide a lot of money by losing it in what looked like bad investments."

"Who? Anyone I would know?" She leaned forward and put her arms on her desk.

"Ted Saunders."

"But he's dead!"

"I know, but I think that's what he was trying to do before he died."

"So you really think he was trying to hide the money by making bad investments?"

"Yes, I do. It seems like the kind of thing he'd do. He had been too good an investor over the years to make that many stupid investments."

"Anyone could lose his touch."

"No, this is more than that. He went out of his way to find bad investments."

"You've given this some thought, I see."

"Yes. Let me show you what I've got." They spent the next thirty minutes going through Hank's file.

"If you're going to find these assets, you'll need a lot more than this."

"I figured you'd say that. What would I need to get?"

"Well," Alyson paused. "Tax returns, account statements, travel records, information on the buyers, exact asset descriptions," she counted them off on her fingers one by one.

Hank sat there for a moment. "Okay, when can you start?"

"Me?"

"Well, not just you. I've already started. When can you start giving me a hand?" He saw her hesitation. "If it's the money, the *New York Times* would be willing to hire you to help me."

"Um, it's not that. I'm not sure I have the time."

"Oh come on. I need you." He said. He cocked his head to one side, his eyes pleading.

"I'll have to check with my boss."

"Good, we can discuss that later, maybe over dinner."

"Sure. That would be great," she said, with false enthusiasm.

"So how would we get that stuff?"

"A lot of it's available online if you know where to look. But, and it's a big but, you have to be willing to bend some laws to get a lot of it. Most of this is supposed to be confidential."

"What do you do on your other jobs?"

"Most of the time we get the client's permission or the Feds ask us to help. Either way, we try to cover our backsides before taking a job." She leaned back. "A financial autopsy, as it were, is slightly less problematic."

"Maybe we can cover your backside." He bent his head a little to look behind her. "I wouldn't want it to get into any trouble," he said playfully.

"Very funny," she said, trying to repress a smile. "How do you propose we do that?" she quipped, in an equally playful voice.

He sat up and said, "I've got an idea. Let's give Whittaker Harden a call."

"Who?" The playfulness instantly evaporated.

"Saunders's lawyer, now his executor. Maybe he'll give us the info you need or permission to look for it."

"Why would he? He doesn't know us from Adam," Alyson said, looking at him skeptically.

"What's he got to lose? We're offering to help him recover money for his client's estate." He picked up the phone and dialed information for Washington DC. "Okay, we've got the number, let's give him a call." He started to dial, but Alyson shook her head and he set the phone back down. "What's wrong?"

"Let's talk about this first." That was the same old Hank she knew from college. Jump in head-first, deal with the consequences later.

After five minutes, they agreed Alyson should call because it was highly unlikely that Saunders's executor was going to hand over a lot of confidential files to a reporter. Besides, Alyson was, at least, someone who could actually find the money.

"Whittaker Harden speaking," the man on the phone announced.

Alyson looked over at Hank and nodded. "Um," she hesitated for a second, still unsure of herself. "Mr. Harden, this is Alyson Murphy. I work for a company called Financial Investigations, Inc."

"Yes. How can I help you?"

"I understand that you were Mr. Saunders's attorney and are now his executor." She started to relax as she spoke.

"That's correct. What's this about?"

"I'd like to talk to you about some money that I believe is missing from your client's estate."

"There isn't any missing money. At least not that I'm aware of." His tone became more lawyer-like.

"Well, it's not missing in the conventional sense of the word."

"I don't know what you're talking about. I'm sorry, but I have a meeting I have to go to."

"Please don't hang up. Let me explain." The next six seconds of silence seemed more like six minutes.

"Go ahead, but you've only got two minutes."

"Thank you," Alyson said. She proceeded to quickly recap their theory about Saunders's investments. "Our firm would like to assist you in getting that money back."

"That's one of the most preposterous things I've ever heard. I've known Ted for years. He'd never even contemplate anything like that. Do you have any proof of this?"

"Er…um, no. Not yet. We hoped that you'd give permission us to look for it."

"I don't have time for any more of this! If you're right, and you get proof, please give me a call. Until then…good-bye." The phone went dead.

"Damn." She shrugged her shoulders and set the phone down.

"I thought it was worth a try," Hank said.

"Yeah, well…"

"Well, we're no worse off than we were. We figured all he could do was say no, and that's what he did." Hank looked at his watch. "We probably should be going." He stood up and grabbed his coat from the back of the empty chair where he had thrown it when he first sat down. "Though, I really thought he might go for it."

"Thinking more about it, why would he? Some wacko woman calling him out of the blue."

"You're probably right," he conceded. She gave him a look. "Not that I'm saying you're a wacko or anything. Are you hungry?" he asked, quickly.

"Famished." She was, having missed lunch for a meeting. The elevator came and they squeezed in. She was pressed up close to Hank. She could smell him and feel his warmth. Unable to stop them, memories of the two of them together flooded over her. She looked down and tried to move away, but the car was too crowded. She closed her eyes and tried to think of other things, but the closeness made it impossible. The doors opened and she stepped briskly away.

A short while later, they were seated in a small booth near the rear of the restaurant. A small candle burned in the middle of the table. They talked about the

Saunders case through most of dinner. It was clear to Alyson that Hank had become a bit fixated on it.

"So what do you think?" Hank asked Alyson, just as the waitress cleared away their entrées.

"I don't know yet. Saunders could certainly have been on both sides of some of his deals, but that doesn't mean he meant to lose money on them."

"Why else would he do that?"

"Who knows," she shrugged. "Maybe he had some ulterior motive for buying them. Maybe he knew something we haven't figured out yet."

"Could be, but I doubt it," Hank said in a determined voice.

She looked at Hank and tried to read his thoughts. He seemed so certain about Saunders's motives. He clearly knew the man a lot better than she did, but was he too close to be objective? He wanted this so badly. Should she work with him or not? She wanted to. But why? Was it because he was right or for some other reason? She struggled to push the thought out of her mind.

"Are you okay?" Hank asked.

"Yes. Um, I was just thinking this through. You know, for your plan to work, Saunders has to get the cash back after making each investment."

"Yeah. So?"

"Well, for that to happen, he has to be paying for something that is already worthless, but looks like it has value. It can't actually lose its value after he buys it; otherwise, he's actually out the money."

"I guess that's right," Hank said, his face dropping as the realization of that statement hit him.

"My question is how would he do that?"

"I don't know. Maybe they never existed in the first place or he played accounting games to make them seem valuable. He certainly had the experience for doing that."

"No, that wouldn't work. It had to look like he lost money on real assets. He couldn't take the chance someone would see through the assets and see that they were fictitious."

"I buy that, but that doesn't help us, does it?"

"Maybe. If they were real, even if grossly overstated in value, we should be able to trace their ownership."

"Can we do that without Harden's approval?"

"Somewhat. We'd be able to look into a few of them, but probably not many."

"Good. When can we start?" he asked eagerly.

"I don't know, but I think I've had enough of this. Can we talk about something else for a while?"

"Sure. Would you like to dance?" She thought for a moment and nodded. He led her out onto the dance floor. They held each other close as the song played.

She was transported back to college. They had been so good for each other. Why hadn't they stayed together back then? She knew the reason. He had wanted to conquer the world, become a world-famous reporter. She had felt obliged, being an only child, to follow her admiral father's footsteps by joining the Navy. Neither one wanted to give up their dreams. Had things changed? For her, the answer was yes. She had given up on the Navy a long time ago, but Hank seemed to be as deep into being a reporter as he had ever been. She pushed back slightly so she could look at him.

Hank looked down and seemed to be studying her face too. What was he seeing, she wondered? Was he seeing someone to help him get a story or more than that? Would it really matter to her if he wanted more?

The song ended and they stood holding each other for a few moments, waiting for the next song to begin. The next song was one that neither recognized. They parted, each looking at the other and then around them. Hank nodded toward the table and Alyson led the way back.

"Anything else," the waiter's words broke the silence. Neither one wanted dessert, so they walked outside, hailed a cab, and were soon headed uptown. Before long, they were standing in front of Alyson's apartment.

"Can I come up?" Hank asked, tentatively.

"Okay, but not for long. I've got a long day ahead of me tomorrow."

"Maybe I should go then."

"No. That's okay. Come on up."

Alyson walked into the kitchen, leaving Hank in the living room, which was large by New York standards. Hank sat on the big, overstuffed sofa between windows that overlooked 71st Street. Even at this hour, plenty of traffic could be heard. Two standing lamps, one at each end of the sofa, illuminated the entire room, giving it a soft glow. Next to them were two low chairs covered in a deep rose-colored fabric that looked like crushed velvet. The color matched the floral print on the sofa. On the walls hung a number of paintings, macramé, and other artwork from around the world. Hank picked up one of the bishops from a hand-carved teak chess set that sat atop a claw-footed Queen Anne coffee table. He was still examining it when Alyson came back into the living room, carrying a glass of white wine in each hand.

She handed a glass to him. "Here's to a successful story." She said, clicking their glasses.

"Here's to you," he replied. She blushed and took a sip of wine.

"It looks like you've been all around the world," he said, gesturing around the room at the wall hangings.

"Yes, but mostly as a kid. I didn't get to *see the world* in the Navy. Being in Naval Intelligence, I was pretty much stuck in Norfolk. I did get a six-month tour at Pearl, but they worked us so hard I didn't get to see much of the islands. You know, the funny thing was that despite all that stuff I used to babble on about in college, after two tours I realized that I didn't really like being in the Navy. I couldn't really deal with the chain of command thing. I think I got too much of that as a kid."

"That's too bad. Was your dad disappointed?"

"Not really. I think he was happy I gave it a shot."

"Well, I'm glad you got that out of your system."

"You are, why?"

They both jumped when the phone rang. Alyson reached out and grabbed it on the second ring. "Hello."

"Oh, hi Gavin." She spun around on the sofa to face away from Hank and lowered her voice.

"Yeah, I just walked in the door and didn't have a chance to play my messages. No, I'm fine. Really." She listened to his questioning tone. "No. Not tonight. I'm really tired. I'll see you tomorrow. Eight o'clock is fine."

She listened for a few more seconds and hung up the phone. Turning back toward Hank, she apologized for the interruption.

"That's okay. Let's call it a night." He put his untouched glass of wine on the table and stood up. "You're tired and you've got a busy day tomorrow."

She looked up at him hesitatingly. After a few moments, she stood up and walked him to the door. "Give me a call and we can figure out what to do next."

"I will. Don't forget to talk to your boss and let us know how much it would cost to hire you."

"I'll talk to him tomorrow."

He leaned down and gave her a quick peck on the cheek. "It was great to see you again. It really was. I'm sorry I never called you before now."

"Thanks for dinner." She waved as he walked down the corridor, then closed the door and slumped against it. What am I getting myself into?

CHAPTER 11

▼

TUESDAY, NOVEMBER 21

She dropped her coat across a chair, put her coffee on the desk, and gently dropped the oversized bag she used as a briefcase on the floor.

The phone rang.

"Ms. Murphy, this is Whittaker Harden. I gave our brief conversation yesterday some more thought. I'd like to discuss the possibility of hiring your firm to help track down the missing money you were talking about, not that I think there's really any missing."

"That's great. I…"

"I'd rather not do this over the phone. Could we meet in your office? I could be in New York any time over the next couple of days."

"Tomorrow's pretty clear."

"Let's make it ten o'clock then."

"Ten it is."

"Um, we'll have to keep this quite confidential. I want as few people as possible to know you're even working on this."

"Of course." They said their good-byes and she replaced the receiver and settled down into the chair behind her desk.

After sitting still for nearly a minute, Alyson reached out and punched the button for her assistant.

"Dylan! Call Carly and tell her that I've got to cancel our 10:00 AM meeting tomorrow. Something just came up."

"Do you want to reschedule it?" Dylan asked.

"Yes. Check my calendar and set something up."

"Right."

"Then check with Mark and see if I can get ten minutes or so with him to discuss a new client."

"I'm not sure he's in yet, but I'll see what I can do." The line went dead.

"Holy cow," she said out loud without realizing it. She leaned back in her chair, absentmindedly picked up her coffee, and took a gulp. She bolted upright, trying to spit the scolding hot coffee back through the tiny hole in the plastic top, dribbling some of it onto her pants. "Damn!" She grabbed a napkin out of her desk drawer and patted herself dry. At least it matched the color of her pants, she thought. She pulled the top off of the cup, blew on the steaming liquid, and carefully took a sip.

Hank had been right. Harden hadn't been able to resist looking into this.

Excitedly, she picked up the phone, but set it down halfway through the number. Wait a minute. Could she call Hank? She had just promised to keep the investigation confidential. What did that mean for Hank? This was his story. She didn't have the right to agree to exclude him, but the last thing that Harden would want would be to have a reporter involved.

At two in the afternoon, Alyson stood in the door of Mark Jackson's office. "Is now a good time?" she asked tentatively. Even though this was the scheduled time for their meeting, Mark notoriously ran late for all meetings.

"Sure," her boss said, waving her in and pointing to the seat in front of his desk. Once she was seated, he continued, "Let me just finish this." He turned to his computer screen and began typing furiously. "There!" he announced triumphantly, hitting the send button. He looked up at Alyson. "I hear we might have another client."

"Yes. Maybe. I think we do, but it's a little difficult."

"Well, why don't you give me the big picture."

She described the theory that Hank and she had developed the prior evening, the call to the lawyer, and his call back that morning. "So, he's interested, but I haven't met with him yet. I wanted to get your advice on a couple of things and get some extra help on the Menlo assignment in case this becomes real." She had been working nearly full-time on Menlo Systems and didn't want it to suffer if she worked on recovering Saunders's assets. "I'm not sure, but if Hank and I are right, it could be one hundred million dollars plus. If we recover the assets, we'd get our standard fee, I assume."

"Who's the client? Harden or the *Times*?"

"That's the thing I need advice on."

"Well, I don't think it can be both and I doubt that Harden will give us permission or his cooperation if he thinks he'll see it all on the front page of the *Times*."

"I know that. But I don't know enough yet. That's why I need to meet with him and…to be free to accept the assignment if the terms and conditions are right."

"Okay. If you think it's real," Mark said. Alyson nodded. "Then, we'll figure out what to do with Menlo."

"Thanks." She stood up.

"Let me know what happens with Harden and what you decide to do with the reporter."

Alyson retreated to her office and dialed Gavin's number. His machine answered and she left a message canceling their plans, vague as they were, for that evening. She would need the time to prepare for the meeting with Harden.

Mark stuck his head in the door and waited for her to hang up. "Got a sec?"

"Sure."

He continued to stand in the doorway. "I was thinking about Harden after you left. He said he wanted you to find the assets after you called him out of the blue." She nodded. "And, we've never worked with him before, at least not directly."

Alyson nodded again, a bit unsure of where Mark was going with this.

"And you think it's possible Saunders could have been murdered by someone who knew about the scheme." She nodded again, more slowly this time. "Well, did you consider that the person most likely to know about the scheme was Saunders's own lawyer before you called him?"

Alyson's eyes grew wide. "No," she stammered, shaking her head.

"I didn't think so. You've got to be real careful tomorrow. First thing you've got to do is figure out if he was involved or not."

"I will," she said softly.

He stood and watched her for a few moments. "You okay?"

She thought about it for a moment. "Yes."

"I don't mean to scare you, but I need you to go into this with your eyes open. I doubt that anything will happen tomorrow, but if you get any sense that he was involved, bail out of the assignment and we'll alert the authorities. Do you want me there?"

She shook her head. "No, I can handle it."

Mark lingered for a moment, then left.

Her hand shook as she held the coffee in front of her lips. "Holy shit," she said. They hadn't considered that. How did she miss that? She had been too busy enjoying the evening and hadn't looked at this assignment objectively. Well, she'd make sure she didn't make the same mistake again. She would keep her relationship with Hank totally business.

CHAPTER 12

▼

WEDNESDAY, NOVEMBER

22

At precisely ten o'clock., Whit Harden walked up to the stainless steel and tinted glass reception desk of Financial Investigations, Inc., gave his name, and asked for Alyson Murphy. The receptionist asked him to have a seat. Harden walked over to the black leather sofa and set his briefcase on the seat. He picked up the latest edition of *Fortune* and flipped through it while he waited.

Two minutes later, Whit Harden and Alyson were seated in a conference room directly behind the reception desk.

"I have to have your assurance of complete confidentiality in this matter," the lawyer said as he pushed a document across the table.

"Of course." Alyson picked up the confidentiality agreement and started to read it. It was identical to the draft the lawyer had faxed last night and she had given to her own lawyer to review first thing this morning.

She had spent the morning with their legal counsel reviewing their options, which they decided were limited. The best they could do, depending on what Harden demanded, was to treat Hank as one of their consultants. That would, they hoped, allow Alyson to share information, but it meant that Hank would not be able to use any of the information that Harden gave them to write a story. He could, however, use whatever information he might dig up on his own.

"We can wait if you want to have one of your lawyers look that over, but I think it's fairly standard."

"No, just give me a minute or two to read it." She finished the four pages quickly. It read just like most of the other confidentiality agreements she had read over the years. Satisfied they could work under the terms and conditions of the agreement, she signed two copies and slid one back across the table.

"Just so you understand," Harden said as he scooped up his copy. "This is on a need-to-know basis. Is that understood?"

"Um," she hesitated, thinking about whether that would work. That wasn't exactly how the document she had just signed laid it out. "I guess that's acceptable. I'll have to tell my boss." She didn't want to admit that she had already told him. "And, I'll need a couple of people on our staff to help me. I can vouch for them all."

"That's fine. But no one but you and your boss is to know why you're looking into these assets."

"That won't work," she said, knowing that she was taking a chance that he might get up and leave. "Knowing why you're looking for something is often crucial to finding it."

Whit Harden sat there for a few moments, his headed bobbing up and down a couple of times. "Okay. I understand that. The same is true in any due diligence, I guess. But, I want you to keep who knows to a minimum."

"I will." She let out an inaudible sigh of relief.

"Now that we've gotten that out of the way, let's begin." With that, he reached down into his briefcase and pulled out a file filed with paper and ceremoniously dropped it on the table. "As you may be aware, my client was accused of a number of illegal actions prior to his death, including insider trading and a number of counts of self-dealing that allegedly defrauded his company, GenergTex, out of nearly six hundred million dollars. This will not involve any of that. Agreed?"

"Yes."

"If I'm telling you things you already know, please stop me and I'll skip ahead."

"No, it's best to start at the beginning, even if it means going over things I already know. I've learned the hard way that skipping over stuff you thought you already knew is the surest way to miss something important." The lawyer nodded knowingly. Alyson got the feeling that starting from the beginning and building a case was the way this man liked to proceed.

"Good. As I was saying," he began to outline the history, as he knew it, without admitting that his client was actually guilty of the things he was accused of.

"With respect to Mr. Saunders's personal fortune, most of that is gone, due to the fact that his remaining stock in GenergTex is basically worthless. Of his various non-GenergTex holdings, there are investments in land, a couple of small businesses, and the ranch, of course, although I'm not sure who would want to buy it after what happened there. Many of his recent investments have turned out to be worth a lot less than he paid for them. Others are still worth a lot, but unfortunately, the debt outstanding on them will take most, if not all, of any remaining value. There might be some value here or there, assuming we don't have to hold a fire sale. All in all, the estate is only a fraction of what it used to be." He paused to let Alyson ask questions. She looked up from her pad, but said nothing.

"As you mentioned on the phone," he continued, "as executor, I have a fiduciary responsibility to Mr. Saunders's heirs-at-law to locate and maximize the value of any assets in the estate. That might be a moot point, with all the lawsuits I'm expecting. If nothing else, the legal fees will eat up a chunk of any remaining value. That being said, I feel that I have to try to recover as much as possible. After you called, I did a quick calculation. If you're right about this, hundreds of millions could be missing. Although I really don't believe your story, it's too much for me to ignore."

"I see."

"Just to let you know, after your call, I checked around. We hear good things about your firm."

"Thank you." For some reason she couldn't pin down, she couldn't tell if the lawyer was sincere or if that was just to make her drop her guard.

"We only want to deal with someone we can trust, particularly someone who would keep this all confidential." He pushed the stack of papers across the table toward Alyson. "Here's some of the documentation I've collected so far. As you can see, I wasn't involved in most of his investments. I'm sure that question had crossed your mind."

"Yes, it did," Alyson figured it didn't do any good to lie about that and was glad to hear that news. She felt that he was being truthful, but wondered if she could really be sure.

"There's also a copy of his holdings as of last June. That's the latest I have, unfortunately. Part of the problem is we don't really know all he's invested in. We did do some checking on the investments, but didn't get very far. There's stuff in here from our prior work. I also included some of the basic documents, but if you need anything more, you'll have to let me know so I can have them sent over. For completeness, there's a copy of the coroner's report, which, as I am sure you know, positively identified the body as my client."

"I heard that. Can we get access to his office? Including his laptop or PC?"

"Of course, with supervision."

"That's okay. Can we start first thing Monday?" She figured no one would want to come in over the Thanksgiving weekend.

The lawyer thought about it for a second and said, "That's fine. I will arrange that with his secretary and I'll get someone to come over from our New York office."

Alyson nodded. She would have preferred not having anyone there from Harden's firm, but that was to be expected.

"I hope you have more luck than we did. As far as the PC is concerned, we looked around, but didn't find much, although I suspect that anything of interest is in the password-protected files on his hard drive. Unfortunately, we don't have the passwords."

"We might be able to fix that," she said. "Did he have any online accounts? If so, we'll have to get access to them. We might be able to track the sites he visited. He may have done a lot of this online. Most of the banks that help wealthy people hide their cash have online banking. It'll be hard to get them to give us any information, but not impossible. It would help if you appointed us as your agent."

"I'll try to get that for you." He paused for a couple of seconds. Alyson waited. "There's one last thing. I assume that you'll want to get paid for your work."

"That's customary when we're hired to find money."

"The standard finder's fee, and expenses?"

"Yes to both."

"Okay, but everything, including your expenses, will have to be contingent. There's no money left in the estate to pay anything. Unless it's paid out of the assets you recover."

"Agreed." She was glad she had anticipated that.

Harden stood up and thanked her. Once outside 145 Broadway, he got into a waiting car to take him to the airport for the flight back to Washington DC.

Forty-one floors above Broadway, Alyson looked out the window, contemplating the task before her. There was a good chance that the investments were really just bad deals. Even if they weren't, there was a better than a fifty-fifty chance that they wouldn't be able to find the money. Unfortunately, there were still a lot of countries around the world that catered to the wealthy who wanted to hide money.

The fact that Saunders was dead should make the job easier. At least they wouldn't have a moving target as they usually did. She hoped that Saunders was not the kind of person who gave account numbers and access codes to someone else. Otherwise, they were in a race against time and they would be starting a lap behind the other runners.

CHAPTER 13

▼

MONDAY, NOVEMBER 27

The door swung open and Alyson Murphy and Joyce Howard entered Ted Saunders's office, followed by Fred Hamilton and Jerry Stockton. Alyson, Joyce, and Fred all worked for Financial Investigations, Inc. Jerry worked for Whittaker Harden.

Joyce Howard wore a blue suit and a white blouse, whose fit indicated that both were tailored rather than off the rack. She wore her nearly jet black hair up in a bun. On her nose perched a pair of small, round wire-rimmed glasses, giving her a serious and somewhat older look. Except for a difference in the cost of clothes, she looked like the academic she had once aspired to be. She was, in reality, the company's resident expert on passwords and how to guess them. In her PhD research in behavioral psychology at Columbia University, she had studied how people used mnemonic devices to remember things. Columbia hadn't been her first choice for her PhD, but it had the advantage of being close to home. She had grown up in Harlem wanting to get as far away as possible. But, her mother developed breast cancer during her senior year at Cornell and wasn't given long to live. Joyce saw going to Columbia and taking of her sick mother as a way to repay some of the debt that she knew she could never truly repay. The only thing she regretted was that her mother hadn't lived to see her get her doctorate.

Fred was, in many ways, Joyce's exact opposite. He stood almost a head taller, with a linebacker's body weighing nearly twice what Joyce did. Although in his late twenties, his frizzy red hair, fair skin, and overly generous supply of freckles made him look like he was still sixteen, causing a roar of laughter among his friends each time he was asked for proof of age when out drinking.

They were opposites in more than appearance. While Joyce had breezed through her studies and saw studying as an end in itself, Fred had struggled to get good grades and saw them as only a means to get a good job, which had meant, at that time, a job on Wall Street. Unfortunately, his timing had been bad and he had graduated along with a near-record number of MBAs just when Wall Street was going through one of its periodic retrenchings. Even a Wharton MBA in finance didn't land him a job at an investment bank, so he settled for Financial Investigations.

Jerry Stockton was an associate with Garrison, Harden and Tilden. He looked every inch the newly minted lawyer, sporting a finely tailored suit, white shirt, and blue-and-red striped power tie. He wore his hair short and blow dried, and was always clean-shaven, although it wasn't obvious that he even needed to shave. Harden had laid out his mission clearly: he was there to keep an eye on Alyson and her team and to report back if they found anything.

Joyce Howard sat down at the desk and the young lawyer pulled over a chair to watch what she was doing, positioning himself so he could also watch Alyson and Fred as they looked through the contents of the file drawers. Joyce set her laptop next to the desktop computer and pulled out a cable, attaching it to the USB port on the back of each. She then powered up both machines.

"What are you doing?" The lawyer asked.

"I'm going to make a digital copy of Mr. Saunders's hard drive onto the hard drive in here," Joyce said, lightly tapping her laptop. "We copy each and every bit on his drive onto a clean second hard drive in here so we have an exact replica. That way, we can try to recover lost or deleted files."

"Why copy it?"

"So we can look at it without worrying about damaging the original. If we ever damaged the original, there'd be no way to fix it, but if we damage a copy, we can make another copy. The real reason is legal. The lawyers would be upset if we were playing around with the original. Someone could claim we destroyed or altered the evidence. This way, it's not an issue."

"Oh. I'm not sure that Mr. Harden has authorized you to take a copy of the hard drive."

"I've cleared it with him," Alyson, overhearing the conversation, jumped in, "but you can call him if you'd like."

The young lawyer looked at her for a moment, stood up and walked over to a corner of the office, pulled out his cell phone, and hit the speed-dial button for his office. He asked a couple of questions in a hushed voice, but most of the time he stood there listening to the other person on the line.

"He says it's okay," the lawyer said sheepishly a minute later as he walked back to the desk.

Joyce hit the execute button on the copy program and pulled out her notes.

"Now what are you doing?" Jerry asked.

Joyce struggled to keep her annoyance under control. "I'm copying the entire hard drive onto my laptop. After that's done, I'll back it up onto CDs in case I screw up and damage or delete the copy on the hard drive. That way, you and I won't have to come back here and do this again." Joyce inserted a CD into the disc drive. Before she was through, she had inserted an entire box of blank discs.

"I'm starting up Passbreaker," Joyce announced to the lawyer before he could ask. "It's our proprietary program to guess passwords."

"Oh, will it take long?"

"Depends on how good the passwords are," Joyce replied. "I don't expect to start it guessing passwords until later. I've got a lot of prep work to do first."

Joyce clicked on the directory icon and brought up a list of all the files she had copied onto her computer's hard drive. Clicking on a sort button, the program eliminated from the list all files that were not password-protected, cutting the list down to a little over one hundred files, which included spreadsheets, letters, and a large accounting file in a format used by a popular personal accounting package.

"Now, what are you doing?"

"Entering personal data about Mr. Saunders into Passbreaker," Joyce said with a growing note of irritation. "His birthday, names of his parents and pets, stuff like that. The program assumes that most people would use this information to create passwords. Your boss gave us a lot of this stuff, but we also got some of it off the Net."

"Based on my work at Columbia and from others' research, we know that people are afraid of forgetting their passwords. So, they typically create passwords out of birth dates, middle names, wife's maiden name, and so on. Passbreaker uses sophisticated artificial intelligence algorithms to guess the mnemonic devices that most people use. It can create hundreds or thousands of them in seconds. Fortunately for us, even when someone tries to use another type of password, the first time she can't get into her computer because she's forgotten it, she usually goes back to using a birthday or her kids' names, or something easier to remember."

She looked over at the lawyer and smiled. "Follow me so far?" He nodded unconvincingly. "Of course, the number of possible combinations is nearly limitless. Our research greatly decreases the combinations to a manageable number by prioritizing the various combinations based on people's habits and general approaches to creating passwords. Passbreaker encrypts each of the generated passwords and then compares them to the encrypted passwords stored by the computer. Since most people use the same password over and over again, once a password is identified, it's tried on all of the remaining files before the program tries another one. Typically, a single password opens many if not all of the files we're working on."

"That's fascinating," Jerry said in a tone that revealed his true feeling, looking around the room. "Let me go check on what Alyson and, um, Fred are doing." He stood up and walked over to the conference table and sat down.

A big grin filled Joyce's face as she watched him sit down. Almost silently, she said, "Let's see if you ask *what are you doing now* again." She began typing again.

Sitting on the table were a number of stacks of files that Fred and Alyson had taken out of Saunders's desk and file cabinets. On the floor were two stacks of files, which they had already read through. One stack had red tabs sticking out of them and the other did not.

"Have you found anything?" Jerry asked.

"We're not sure," Alyson said. We're just marking things that might be of interest. We won't know until we get a chance to study them in detail."

"When are you going to do that?"

"Back at the office," Fred answered.

A look of panic crossed the lawyer's face.

"Don't worry," Fred said. "We only take copies. When we find something we want copied, we attach a small post-it note to it indicating how many pages are to be copied. See?" He pointed to a red plastic tab sticking out of the file in front of him. "That way, we can leave the pages in the file exactly where we found them. We don't want to remove them because we don't to change their order or take the chance that they end up back in the wrong place or, worse, in the trash."

During the course of the day, the stack of files with stickers became two, then three. From time to time, Fred would return the files without stickers to the cabinet drawers and return with a new armful.

"One thing I can say," Fred announced while making his fifth trip to the file cabinets, "Saunders certainly was a pack rat. He kept old bank statements, canceled checks, phone records, credit card statements, tax returns, investment account statements, and shit like that going back years."

"That's good, right?" Jerry asked.

"It's great, except I know what I'm going to be doing for the next few days."

Two hours later, Alyson put the last of the unmarked files away. "I think we're done in here for now," Alyson announced to the room.

Fred stood up and stretched.

"We'll need the things we marked copied," she said to the young lawyer, pointing to the piles.

"I know," he sighed.

"Alyson looked over at Joyce. "How's it going?"

Joyce unplugged the cables and put everything back into her briefcase. "I'm ready too," she announced.

Alyson, Fred, and Joyce gathered up their things and left the office, leaving Jerry Stockton standing at the table with his hands on his hips.

Just outside the office, Alyson stopped. "Wait a sec, guys." She turned around. "Betty, could I ask you a few questions?"

"Yes. Of course."

"Did Mr. Saunders know you kept a list of files?" Alyson was holding the typed list of files that Betty had handed to them on their way in that morning.

"Yes, but he never really looked at it. It was more for me, a way for me to organize things."

"Did you create all the files or did he create some himself?"

"Oh. He created some from time to time."

"Were those files on your list?"

"If I knew about them, I'd put them on it. Otherwise...I'm sure he knew that I put them on my list."

"So, all of these files," Alyson asked, pointing to the pages that Betty had given her when they arrived, "should be in the drawers somewhere."

"Yes. Is there a problem?"

"Well, some files seem to be missing."

"Well, Mr. Saunders took files all the time and didn't always put them back right away." Betty didn't look worried at the news. "I've found some in his apartment or stuck in his briefcase. Sometimes I'd get a call from Pete out at the ranch saying that Mr. Saunders had left a file or two out there, asking if he should FedEx them back here. I guess if they were out at the ranch, they're probably lost for good in the fire. Was there anything important in them?"

"I don't know. I was hoping you'd be able to tell us what was in them. These four files are missing." Alyson had put a check mark next to each file as they went through the file drawers. Four files did not have check marks next to them.

"Those are all files he created," Betty said.

"Do you know what was in them?"

"No. I glanced through them once when I added them to the list. They were loan documents of some sort; I categorize everything. I don't know what they were about. Mr. Saunders didn't tell me."

"You didn't help type those documents?"

"No. Not those."

"Who would have typed them then?"

"I don't know. Some law firm, I guess."

"Could someone other than Mr. Saunders have taken those files?"

"No. No one's been in there since Mr. Saunders died."

Once outside, Alyson grabbed a cab uptown, while Fred and Joyce walked back to the office. Just as the cab passed under the United Nations building, heading north on the FDR Drive, Alyson's phone rang. She fished it out of her bag.

"Miss Murphy?" Betty Goodman said, meekly.

"Yes. Betty?"

"Yes. I think I gave you some wrong information earlier."

"What about?"

"When I told you no one had been in Mr. Saunders's office, I was wrong. I forgot that Mr. Harden has been in there."

"Did he mention anything about taking any files?"

"No, but I doubt that he would do anything like that. I don't know if he even has a key to the desk, but he was in the office alone."

"Did he tell you what he was doing there?"

"No. I assumed that he was working on Mr. Saunders's estate."

"I'm sure you're right, but thank you for telling me."

"I'm not getting Mr. Harden in trouble, am I?"

"Of course not. It'll be okay. Thanks for all your help."

The cab pulled up in front of her apartment forty minutes later. She threw her bag on the sofa, ignored the blinking light on her answering machine, walked into the kitchen, poured a glass of white wine out of the same bottle she had opened a few nights earlier, and walked over to the windows overlooking the street.

Her thoughts returned to the idea that Harden might have taken files out of Saunders office without telling anyone. She had spent the entire cab ride home trying to understand what he was doing. Mark's comments kept intruding into her thoughts. Should she bail out or not? Was it too late?

CHAPTER 14

▼

TUESDAY, NOVEMBER 28

Joyce and Fred sat processing Alyson's description of the call from Betty Good-man.

"Can you believe that?" Fred blurted out. "The old coot stole those files."

"We don't know that," Alyson said. "Saunders could have taken them with him to his ranch."

"I doubt it."

"Even if he took them, Harden's entitled. He *is* the executor," Alyson said.

"I know, but taking the files without telling his secretary. I bet one of those loans was to him. If he takes the file, the paperwork's gone and he never has to pay it back."

"But how does he know that no one else knows about it or that there aren't copies someplace."

"He's Saunders's lawyer. I bet he drew up the document and knew there was only the one copy."

"By why take all four files?" Alyson said.

"Maybe he had more than one loan or, maybe…um…he was in a rush and had to make sure that he took the one he needed," Fred said.

"Why not just take your papers and leave the rest?" Joyce asked. "That would certainly draw less attention."

"He probably didn't know that Betty kept a list." Fred said.

"But, why take the chance?" Alyson asked.

"For enough money," Fred declared, "I'd take that chance."

"Why would he borrow money from Saunders?" Joyce asked. "He's a highly successful lawyer at one of the most prestigious firms in the country."

"Who knows," Fred said, cautiously. "He's divorced, isn't he? Maybe he needs the money to pay alimony to his first wife. Or, maybe he plays the ponies."

Joyce rolled her eyes.

"Just maybe, Fred," Alyson said, "he took the files because he's the executor of the estate."

"But, why didn't he tell anyone he took them?"

"Maybe he didn't think he needed to. It was probably arrogance more than anything nefarious."

Fred sat silently pouting, unconvinced.

"There could be any number of other good reasons he took them," Alyson said, breaking the uncomfortable silence. She checked her watch. "There's one easy way to find out. I'll give him a call later and ask him. He is our client."

An hour later, three large boxes were delivered by a private messenger service. Alyson punched in a number on her phone and, seconds later, Fred stood in her office. "A present for you," she said, pointing at the stack of boxes.

"Thanks. Did you call Harden yet?"

"No. I've been on the phone since we talked. I'll call right now. Have a seat." She hit the speakerphone.

"Mr. Harden. This is Alyson Murphy. I'd like to talk about the files you removed from Mr. Saunders's office last week."

"What files?"

"The ones with the loan documents out of Mr. Saunders's desk. I believe that you might have borrowed them and we'd like to review them."

"I don't know what you're talking about."

"Well, there are four files missing from his office. Betty Goodman kept a record of all Mr. Saunders's files and she says that they were all there when Mr. Saunders left for Texas." Alyson shrugged when Fred gave her a quizzical look. "You were the only one who's been in the office since then."

There was a long silence on the phone. "Yes, Ms. Murphy, I took the files. But, your information isn't exactly correct. They weren't loan documents. My client entered into a number of, how shall I say it, questionable transactions. Ted and I had been discussing how to collect on them. Not so easy as you can imagine. Especially now."

"Would you mind if we reviewed those documents? They may have something to do with our investigation."

"I doubt that, but let me think about it. They aren't something I want to become public."

"I can assure you that won't happen."

"I'll consider it," he said with a tone of authority intended to cut off the conversation.

"Thank you. I hope you let us see them."

"I understand you took a number of files yourself yesterday."

"Copies only," she quickly pointed out.

"Touché," he said. "What exactly are you looking for?"

"Anything that doesn't belong. A phone call that identifies an unknown girlfriend or a credit card purchase of an airline ticket, a meal, or a tank of gas that tells us Saunders went on a secret trip. Everybody makes mistakes."

"Okay. Let me know when…if you find something." Alyson heard a click at the other end.

"We were right," Fred Hamilton exclaimed as soon as she hung up the phone. "We caught him red-handed."

"With what? It sounded as if he might have a valid reason to take those files."

"Then why did he deny knowing about them and then take so long to make up a reason to take them?"

"You heard him. He didn't want them to become public."

"That's bullshit and you know it!"

"Enough!" She slapped the table to get his attention.

"How do we know he'll give us back the complete files even if he returns them at all?"

"He seemed to be surprised that we knew about the files. I don't think he'll make the same mistake and return a partial file."

"I wonder what the deals were."

"Hopefully, we'll find out."

"Well, think about it. Harden knew about the deals and maybe saw them as a way to make some easy dough without anyone ever knowing about it. If they were shady deals, they might never come to anyone's attention. All he'd need would be to get Saunders out of the way."

"What are you saying? That Harden killed Saunders to get the files?"

"Not the files, but what they represent."

"That's ridiculous. Harden's no murderer."

"Money problems make lots of people do things you'd never expect."

Alyson looked at Fred and saw how serious he was. "We're not investigating Harden's finances. So let's keep our focus, huh. I'm sure that we'll get the files back in a couple of days," Alyson said, but wasn't as confident as she tried to sound.

Dylan stuck his head in the door. "There's a Jerry Stockton here to see you."

"Bring him in," Alyson replied. Then she said softly to Fred, "You've got work to do. Let me talk to Jerry one-on-one."

Fred stood up, grabbed the top box, and left the office seconds before Jerry Stockton appeared at the door.

"Come in, Mr. Stockton."

"I bet you didn't expect to see me so soon." She hadn't and didn't see his arrival as a good sign. The last thing she needed was a babysitter.

"Mr. Harden asked me to stop by and see if you needed anything."

"Please, have a seat."

The lawyer sat down and placed his briefcase on the table, flipped it open and pulled out a pad, leaving the top up.

"I have a file for you," he said, rummaging through the papers in his briefcase with one hand, as he nervously grabbed a rectangular box about the size of a jumbo pack of gum with the other. With his thumb, he flicked a small switch at the end. A small, faint green light told him the unit was on. He pulled a plastic tab off a small adhesive strip on the back. "Ah, here it is," he announced, handing her the file. As she scanned the paperwork inside, he reached under the table and pressed the box against the underside of the table next to the pedestal leg in the center. He next pulled the short antenna out to its full six-inch length

"What's this?" Alyson asked.

"It's an updated list of assets."

"I think we have this all ready."

"Oh really?"

"I think so, but we'll check it against the old list. Is there anything else?"

"No, not really. I just wanted to make sure you got the files."

"Yes, thank you."

"How's Ms. Hamilton doing on the passwords?"

"She'll probably get all the data in the program later today. Then it can get started."

"Good. Good."

Alyson thought he looked uncomfortable, but couldn't figure out why.

"Do you need anything more?" he asked.

"Not at the moment," Alyson said. She stared at the lawyer, trying to think where this conversation was leading.

The lawyer's phone rang. He flipped it open. "Yes." He listened for a few moments. "Good." He flipped it close. "I guess I've taken up enough of your time." He stood up, shook her hand, and walked out of her office.

Alyson sat there and stared after him

*　　　*　　　*　　　*

Dan Morris sat at the table in the otherwise empty office one block from Alyson's office. Although he probably only needed it for a week or two, he had had to rent it for an entire month. Fortunately, his employer was willing to foot the bill. It had been surprisingly easy to find an empty office.

He placed the bulky black leather briefcase he had carried with him on the table in front of him. Within minutes, he had finished setting up the recording device, including a high-gain antenna that would minimize any radio interference, although he didn't think he'd need it. The transmitter was only two hundred yards away and it had a range close to five hundred yards, and there was a clear line of sight from where he sat to the other building. The recorder was noise-activated so it would only begin recording when someone spoke near the transmitter, which greatly increased the stated recording time of the machine. This meant he'd probably only have to check back at the end of each week.

He connected the recorder to the laptop sitting next to it, which would allow it to automatically upload the recording each night and save the conversations to his laptop's hard drive. On the floor was an uninterruptible power supply, which would kick in if there was loss of power. Though he considered that unlikely, it was better to be safe than sorry. He wouldn't want to miss any important conversations just because there had been a power outage or spike and he hadn't sprung for the UPS.

He sat back in the chair and marveled at the state of equipment he had to work with today. He had been in the business for long enough to remember using cumbersome tape drives that had to be changed every few hours and transmitters that were three to four times as big and only half as powerful. Now, he could set this up and not return for days, giving him the freedom to follow his subject whenever she left her office.

The best part was that he could pass the digital recording directly through a transcriber program and read the notes at night. If there were any conversations that didn't make sense, he could hit the play button and listen to the original recording. The whole thing took minutes rather than hours or days as in the past.

He could then give his client a printed copy, leaving out anything he found personally interesting.

He put the earphone in, adjusted the volume on the receiver, and listened to the quality of the reception. He fiddled with a couple of dials on the receiver and sat back to listen for a few seconds.

A man's voice said, "Not, not really. I just wanted to make sure you got the files."

"Yes, thank you," a woman's voice said.

"How's Ms. Hamilton doing on the passwords?"

"She hasn't started our program yet. She'll probably get all the data in later today."

"Good. Good." There was a pause. "Do you need anything more?"

"Not at the moment."

He had heard enough. The transmitter was picking up the voices just fine. He pulled out his cell phone, dialed a preprogrammed number, and waited for an answer.

"Yes," a man answered.

"Perfect reception," was all he said.

"Good." The phone went dead.

✳   ✳   ✳   ✳

"Damn!" Whit Harden swore softly as he hung up the phone. He hadn't known that anyone else knew about the loan files. They were in Ted's locked personal file drawer. He thought that Ted kept everyone out of those drawers, but that was clearly not the case. Why had Ted let his secretary know about the files? They could have been the answer to his problems. All those undisclosed "loans" that Ted had made to congressmen, senators, and regulators over the years.

He had been shocked when Ted had told him about them a few months ago and how he was going to call them in to force his "friends" to help him. Ted hadn't seemed concerned that he was talking about blackmailing government officials.

Harden picked up the files. Why had he really taken them? Was it to protect Ted? He had toyed with the idea of burning the files to protect Ted's reputation, but his dead client didn't have a reason to worry about protecting his reputation anymore. Plus, what was to protect after the last few news cycles? So, instead of burning the files, Harden had thought about using them, but not how Ted had planned to—pressuring the Department of Justice to go easy on him—but to get them to repay the money. Of course, he was also going to offer an inducement by discounting the amount. He certainly didn't need to be greedy. Just fifty percent of the total would be enough to recoup his GenergTex losses.

"Damn!" He would have to return the files and let the chips fall where they would. He would have to come up with another idea for keeping his wife in the style to which she had become accustomed.

CHAPTER 15

▼

WEDNESDAY, NOVEMBER 29

Alyson fought her way down the stairs to the Lexington Avenue subway's 68th Street station. She usually left for work much earlier, when the trains were less hectic, but today she had slept late. She had had a hard time falling asleep. The late-night traffic outside her apartment, which she usually found comforting, kept invading her dreams and waking her. She had finally fallen into a deep sleep sometime around 4:00 AM.

The platform was much more crowded than she was used to. She frowned as she made her way slowly to the front of the platform to wait for the number-6 local to take her to the station at 59th Street, where she would change to the downtown express.

Two trains came and went before she could get to the platform edge. The third train roared into the station and the doors opened in front of her. She stepped aside to let two teenage girls get off, freeing up just enough room for her and ten people to jam themselves into the car. It took four attempts to get the doors closed because of the people who were trying to push their way onto the train. The car was so crowded that there wasn't even enough room for her to hold up a newspaper, her usual morning-commute routine. As the train lurched out of the station, she looked around the car. Turning her head to her left, she noticed a man watching her. His cold, small, close-set eyes stared fixedly at her for a moment then turned away. She shivered despite the warmth of the car. She was used to the occasional ogling from men, but this look was different, more intense and more...malevolent.

Just before the train entered the next station, she stole a glance at the man again, but his back was now toward her. A minute later, the doors opened at 59th Street and she got off the train and crossed the platform to wait for the downtown express. The doors of the local train closed and left the station.

Alyson scanned the platform, but she didn't see the man anywhere. He must have stayed on the train, she concluded. Perhaps she was just imagining things. She sighed, pulled the newspaper out of her bag, and began to read the front page.

*   *   *   *

Dan Morris stayed on the local train for the two stops to Grand Central, hoping it would get there before the express. When it arrived, he jumped out and walked across the platform and forward a car length assuming the woman would have walked straight across the platform.

Alyson's train arrived just seconds later and Morris got on, muscled his way into the middle of the car and stretched up to grab the pole that ran along the ceiling. As the car drove on toward Wall Street, he read from a little spiral memo pad.

The woman he had been hired to follow usually left the house around 7:30 AM, though today she left nearer to 8:30 AM. He made a mental note to find out if there was a reason for her being late. All of the people in the other apartments were typically gone by nine. There was no doorman to deal with. There was a custodian who wandered about, but he was only there from time to time and was old and not much of a threat. The mail came around eleven in the morning. A few people had cleaning women come in, but that didn't seem to be every day.

He looked out the window as the train pulled into the Fulton Street station, making a point of not looking back toward the car from which his target would emerge. He stepped away from the train and positioned himself near the wall, keeping his face averted, but checking out the people as they passed by. He caught sight of her about fifteen feet ahead and slipped into the crowd leaving the station.

Alyson pushed through the turnstiles, climbed the first set of stairs to the left and then out to the street, turned south on Broadway, and headed toward her office building.

Morris had taken the stairs to the right and came out across the street from where Alyson had emerged just a few seconds before. He pressed himself against the stonework at the side of the exit, staying in the shadow until he was sure she had started walking away and was unlikely to see him. A number of commuters gave him dirty looks for blocking the exit, but he ignored them.

As soon as Alyson turned the corner onto Broadway, he stepped out from the shadow and followed her again. She passed through the revolving doors of her building a few minutes later. He walked past the entrance without so much as a sideways glance and crossed the street at the next corner. He walked back a half block and entered the building directly across from 145 Broadway. He joined the back of the line at the coffee shop in the lobby, all the while not taking his eyes off the front door of her building. When it was his turn to order, he stepped out of line and left the building, convinced she was staying put. He walked south on Broadway to the subway entrance at Wall Street and was soon on a train heading back uptown.

Forty minutes later, he stood in front of a five-story townhouse. He held a copy of the real estate section of the Sunday *New York Times* and consulted it a number of times while he looked around. The building was a nondescript townhouse, common to the area. There were bars on the basement and first floor windows, but otherwise, there was no obvious security in place. Satisfied that no one was paying him any attention, he climbed the dozen steps leading up to the front door and stepped into the small vestibule. He scanned the row of mailboxes, looking for the one marked *Murphy*. It was 4A. He reached into his coat pocket and pulled out a set of picks and tension wrenches, inspected the lock, and selected the appropriate pair. He inserted the two pieces of metal into the lock, applied slight pressure with the wrench, and then moved the pick along each pin. Five seconds later, the lock yielded and he stepped through the door into the lobby. He climbed the stairs, bypassing the elevator in which he would have no control over stops and who got off and on. Too many people might see him or, worse, remember him. Few people, if any, he knew, would use the stairs when there was an elevator in the building.

The door to the fourth floor hall opened with a light tug. He waited in the stairwell for a few seconds, peeking through the narrow opening and listening. Hearing and seeing no one, he opened the door and checked the other direction. The hall was empty. He stepped out into the hall and moved quickly and silently until he was standing in front of 4A. He quickly picked this lock and slipped into the apartment, shutting the door behind him.

He made a swift tour of the living room, the kitchen, and finally the bedroom. He stood in front of the dresser for a couple of moments, looking at the pictures spread out on top, ignoring the jewelry box. He picked up one of a young girl standing in front of a woman in a floral dress and a man wearing a naval uniform, studied it for a moment, and then put if back on the dresser, careful to return it to precisely where it had been when he entered the room. He pulled open the top drawer in the dresser, rummaged around and pulled out a pair of underpants and a bra, considered them for a few moments, and put them back.

Morris walked into the bathroom and opened the medicine cabinet and made a mental note of the contents, then closed the mirror and walked back into the bedroom.

He stared at the bed, a Queen Anne style four-poster with a high headboard. He smiled at the thought of the woman lying on it naked, beckoning him to come to her. He shook his head to erase the thought, strode over, and pulled the bed away from the wall. He took off his coat, unslung a small knapsack that had been hidden under it and put it on the floor. Reaching inside, he pulled out a small box identical to the one now attached to Alyson's desk in her office and flipped the switch. The small, pale green light indicated the transmitter was working. Morris plugged in the three-foot-long cord that would serve as the antenna, pulled a plastic sheath off the adhesive pad on the back, and reached in behind the bed to stick the transmitter to the back of the headboard. He stretched the cord across the back of the headboard and taped it in place. Finally, he placed the miniature microphone near the top of the headboard and connected it to the transmitter. After checking that everything was working, he pushed the bed back into place.

He unscrewed the back of the phone and inserted a small transmitter that would feed its signal to the box behind the bed, put the phone back together, and walked back into the living room.

The man knelt down on the sofa and lifted the painting off the wall. He placed a similar transmitter and microphone behind the picture and hung the painting back on the wall, making sure that it hung straight. He unscrewed the phone there and inserted another transmitter.

After one last look around, he marched to the door and cracked it open to make sure no one was in the hallway. Satisfied that no one was there, he walked to the stairs and quietly descended to the lobby. Two minutes after leaving her apartment, Morris walked east on 73rd Street, congratulating himself on a job well done. He crossed over Second Avenue, stopped behind a dark blue VW Jetta, opened the trunk, and pulled out a briefcase. He opened the driver's door, slipped in behind the wheel, and put the briefcase on the passenger seat. He pulled a power cord out and plugged it into the cigarette lighter, turned on the receiver, and yanked up the telescoping antenna. The signal indicator told him everything was working.

✳   ✳   ✳   ✳

"Maria Garcia, please." Alyson leaned back in her chair.

"Yes? Can I help you?" the woman replied, with only a faint trace of an accent.

"My name's Alyson Murphy. I'm with Financial Investigations, Inc. I've been hired by Mr. Harden to look into some of Mr. Saunders's investments."

"Yes."

"Did you get the letter from Mr. Harden authorizing you to talk to me? I sent a fax over an hour ago."

"Yes. I just got it. I have not had a chance to read it thoroughly."

"It's fairly standard," Alyson said to reassure her. "I'd just like to reconfirm some of the information Mr. Harden gave me."

"Ah, all right."

"First of all, I just need to make sure that I've got your business information right. You're an associate partner with Banks, Brown and Martinez." Banks, Brown and Martinez was a well-established law firm, located in Miami, that specialized in property law and divorce. Its real expertise was international law, especially in the Caribbean and throughout Central America, where it was well-known for helping spouses, mostly husbands, Alyson frowned at the thought, to hide assets from their soon-to-be-exes. Reputedly, it also used that expertise to help drug dealers and others to hide or launder illegal money. Despite this reputation, or because of it, many reputable firms and affluent individuals used the firm when making investments in the Caribbean and Central America.

"You're originally from Nicaragua, right?"

"Guatemala," the lawyer corrected. The law firm was also well-known for hiring young lawyers who had been born in Central America and the Caribbean, had law degrees from universities in the United States, and were the sons or daughters of highly placed government officials or powerful local families. The firm would often award scholarships to students whose parents worked for the government, but couldn't afford to send their children off to prestigious colleges in the States. Many of the firm's alumni went back home and took significant positions within their governments or business communities, thereby cementing the firm's connections in the region.

"Right. Sorry. Was that where Mr. Martinez is from?"

"No, he's from Costa Rica."

"How long have you been at Banks, Brown?

"Seven years."

"You did a lot of the legal work for Mr. Saunders, correct?"

"Yes."

"I see your firm helped him buy a ranch in Argentina. Did you work on that?"

"Yes."

"And the silver mine in Peru?" She paused, but the lawyer didn't answer. "Yes?"

"Yes," the lawyer hissed.

"You also worked on the Aruba hotel. I assume you specialize in international property law?"

"Yes," the lawyer hissed again.

"That's a lot of work for your firm and for you personally. I assume you'll get a big bonus this year?"

"That's really none of your business."

"Was anyone else at your firm involved in Mr. Saunders's deals?"

"Mr. Martinez. He's the senior partner."

"I assume that you still used a local firm for the title searches and the other local legal stuff?"

"Yes."

"Who were they?"

"Different firms."

"Can I get their names?"

"I'll have to check my files."

Alyson ignored the obvious delaying tactic. "That would be helpful. Were you involved in setting up Cordoba Trading, Limited?"

"Why are you asking about Cordoba?" The woman's voice gained an edge.

"It was the owner of the company that sold the cattle ranch in Argentina to Mr. Saunders."

"I was not involved in setting up that particular company."

Alyson had been engaged in enough of these conversations to know that she had just gotten a very specific answer to a specific question, but not the whole story. There was a good chance that someone else in the firm had set up Cordoba Trading, but she decided she wouldn't gain much by pushing the point at this stage.

"Did Mr. Saunders or anyone from your firm visit the ranch to do due diligence on the property before the closing?"

"We had a local firm do that."

"What was the name of the firm and could I get a copy of the report?"

"No. That's confidential."

"Excuse me. I'm authorized by Mr. Saunders's executor to get this information."

"That may be, but we're under a separate confidentiality agreement with the appraisal company."

"What?"

"The company that did the appraisal wanted to keep its identity and its report confidential."

"Did Mr. Saunders know the name of the firm?"

"I assume he did."

"Did the same company prepare the report on the silver mine or the hotel?"

"I don't think I should answer that."

"Is there anyone else at your firm I could talk to get answers or to tell me the name of the appraisal company?"

Silence.

"Just one last question. The total money that your firm helped Mr. Saunders invest was nearly one hundred million dollars. Is that correct? How much was your fee?"

"The answers to your *two* questions," Maria Garcia said angrily, "are yes and none of your business."

After thanking her, Alyson hung up the phone and turned to Fred, who was listening to her side of the conversation, "She's obviously hiding something," Alyson said.

"Could Harden get the information from her?"

"We could ask him, but I've got a feeling that won't help."

"We could try to get it without his help. I'm sure if they're like any typical law firm, their system security isn't all that tight. Most of what we want is probably on some hard drive somewhere."

"No," Alyson said, knowing where Fred's train of thought was taking him. "We haven't been authorized for that. I'd be fired if I did that without authorization. Maybe even go to jail."

"Could I get your office then?" He flashed a broad, toothy grin.

"Funny. It could be worse, if they really do work for the Calí cartel…" They both shuddered at the thought.

*   *   *   *

"Ms. Murphy, this is Betty Goodman."

"Yes, Betty, what can I do for you?"

"I was going through Mr. Saunders's stuff and I found a computer disc. It fell out of a bag of trash I was taking out to the garbage chute. It should've been thrown out a while ago except Mr. Saunders's housekeeper has been laid up for the last couple of weeks with a broken ankle and hasn't been in his apartment since he died. I was going to get someone else to come in, but then…I guess I just didn't get around to it."

"That's understandable," Alyson said sympathetically.

"I was wondering if you wanted to see it."

"You bet. Did you tell Mr. Harden about it?"

"He's away for a couple of days on business. I left him a message, but I thought that since he let you have all that other stuff from the office that I should just send it to you."

"Okay. We'll make a copy when we get it and send you back the original."

"It's already on its way."

"Thanks, Betty." What was on the CD, she wondered?

The CD arrived by FedEx messenger later that afternoon. Alyson immediately gave it to Joyce Howard and asked her to make a copy and then send the original back to Betty Goodman, which she did after adding the CD's files to the list that Passbreaker was working on.

"Thanks for the CD," Joyce said when she bumped into Alyson in the hallway later that afternoon. "It looks like an archive version of Saunders's hard drive. It has most of the same files, although there are some new ones too. Most of the same ones were password-protected. There's also an archive version of the accounting file, but it appears to be a lot larger than the current version. The date on it is only a week before Saunders died. I'll let you know if I find anything."

*   *   *   *

Fred and Alyson sat next to each other at the table in the conference room just down the hall from Alyson's office, where they had put the boxes of files from Saunders's office. They were reviewing one of Saunders's phone bills, which listed two calls he made in Panama. Both were to the same number and both were short, less than a minute each. There were many calls to and from Costa Rica, but not on the day of the calls in Panama, or the next day.

Fred Hamilton looked up from the pile of credit card and phone records and asked, "Those calls mean he was in Panama that day unless he gave his cell phone to someone else, but why would he?"

Alyson shrugged and lifted her hands. "I don't know. Betty Goodman says he would never let anyone else use it, especially when he was out of the country. He was a fanatic about keeping in touch."

"But if he was in Panama, why didn't he cancel his hotel room in Costa Rica?"

"Well, let me guess," Alyson replied. "Either he didn't want the hassle of checking in and out and didn't care about the cost or he didn't want anyone to know he was leaving Costa Rica. My bet is on the latter."

"Why Panama?"

"Panama? It's easy to set up a shell company there." A shell company was one without any real purpose except to own an asset. "Plus, Panama's secrecy laws are really strict. Good place to hide money. To top it off, it uses the U.S. dollar in addition to the local currency so it wouldn't be necessary to convert his cash into some messy currency like pesos or colones. A number of rich deadbeat husbands that we've been asked to track down have used Panama as a hiding place for their money. We're pretty familiar with it."

"That makes sense."

"We need to figure out how he got there and back. You can't just drive from Costa Rica to Panama in that amount of time. It's too far and the roads aren't good enough."

"What about the Pan-American Highway? Doesn't it run all the way through Central America?"

"Have you ever been on the Pan-American Highway?"

Fred shook his head.

"Calling it a highway is being extremely generous. It's a two-lane road in most places and the back roads out in Oklahoma or Idaho are in better shape."

"So, how'd he get there?"

"The only real option is to fly. Check out the local airlines or the charters. There's got to be a record somewhere."

"What about his corporate jet?"

"I don't think so, but check on it. Remember, he's trying to hide his money. If he didn't check out of the hotel, I doubt he'd get on his own jet and fly there."

"He could've paid off his pilot," Fred said.

"Hmm. Maybe. Let's check on that too. Let's see if we can get the log from the airport. He'd probably fly out of the main airport outside San José. I don't think there's any other place for him to fly out of, but see if there're any other airports nearby that could handle his plane. It's a...um..."

"It's a Gulfstream IV."

"That's right. I bet that needs a pretty decent runway. I doubt they'd risk landing it on some grassy field someplace."

"I doubt it too. So, where does that leave us?"

"My bet is he hopped on a local airline."

"Wouldn't that leave a trail, too?" Fred asked.

"Not if he didn't use his real name."

"Wouldn't he need a passport?"

"Technically yes, but he might have been able to pay off an airline check-in clerk or customs agent."

"If he's not using his own name, how are we going to find him?"

"Let's check for anyone on flights in both directions. He'd probably buy a round-trip ticket, so the same passenger would be on both legs."

"That means getting the passenger lists for all those flights."

"Right."

"That'll take me a while," Fred groaned.

"Then you might as well get started."

"Thanks a lot!"

"Oh, by the way, don't forget to find out who Saunders called in Panama." The phone bill listed the call as being to a private number.

"That will definitely take some time."

✳   ✳   ✳   ✳

"Diga! Habla Miguel Alvarez."

"Miguel. It's Alyson, Alyson Murphy."

"Alyson. ¿Cómo estás?"

"Muy bien. ¿Y usted?"

"Muy bien, also. It's good to hear from you." Miguel switched to English as he did whenever they spoke. His accent was nearly nonexistent, owing to an American mother and a thorough education in the States. Miguel Alvarez worked for the Ministerio de Comercio y Industrias, part of the Comisión Nacional de Valores, the Panamanian Securities Commission that regulated the incorporation of international companies in Panama.

"Miguel, I need your help." Alyson wanted to keep it short and very business-like.

"Sí. How can I help?"

"I'm trying to track down the *real* ownership of some companies set up in Panama."

"Alyson, you know that is against the law down here. I could get into a lot of trouble." Panama had recently passed one of the strictest privacy laws in the world, making it attractive as an international financial center. That law made it a criminal offense, punishable by fines and jail time, to release any information about the owners or directors of any company incorporated in the country. The law was designed to attract customers to Panama, especially those preferring that no one knew who they were or that they were doing business there.

"Was this money stolen or from drugs?" In order to comply with international efforts to cut down on money laundering, principally drug money, Panama's law allowed the information to be released to law enforcement organizations, but only if the funds were known to be from illegal sources.

"I don't know. That would depend on the definition of stolen."

"What do you mean?"

"Well, the money came from stock sales that violated all kinds of laws here. The person may have also embezzled from his company."

"I do not think that we would consider that stolen. It may be drug money. Yes?"

"No. It's not drug money. But in any case, Miguel, the person we're talking about is already dead, so he won't mind."

"What about his wife or children?"

"He doesn't have any. I'm helping his executor track down assets for his estate."

"Hmm."

"Come on, Miguel. It's not like you're going to violate his privacy."

"I do not know. You *sure* it's not drug money? Because, if it were, I'd feel a lot better."

"Oh," Alyson's eyes lit up. "It *could* be drug money."

"Then I might be able to help you."

"That would be great. I'm sure I could make it worth your while, like the last time."

"¡Ay! I almost got caught." His voice trembled.

Alyson remembered how narrowly Miguel had escaped. Thank goodness she had been able to convince the local authorities that she had gotten the information out of the bank's trash. To do that, she actually paid a couple of men to rummage through the bank's trash, where they recovered sensitive information about a number of local politicians. That quickly ended the investigation into Miguel's role.

"But that's because the guy was sure it had to be someone at your Ministry. There's no one here to point the finger this time."

He was silent for a moment. "Okay, but on one condition."

"Yes," she said, cautiously.

"Dinner. Next time I am in New York."

"I'd love to." Alyson had hoped that Miguel had gotten over her, but it didn't seem that way. The last time she had been in Panama, she had flirted a little with him, thinking that would help her get what she needed. It turned out to have been much more than flirtation for Miguel. He had sent her flowers for weeks afterward, then had shown up at her door a few months later when a business trip had brought him to New York. They had had dinner that night, but she had resisted anything more.

"Who is this person?"

"Ted Saunders. The late CEO of GenergTex. I assume you heard about his murder."

"We *do* get CNN down here."

Alyson gently banged a palm against her temple a couple of times for the comment. "We think he set up a bunch of companies in Panama to own some worthless assets that he then sold back to himself."

"Perdón. I did not understand that. Maybe my English is rusty, no?" He said in an affected accent.

"No, your English is better than mine. It's confusing, but we think he tried to hide some of his money by buying assets from companies he secretly owned. He somehow inflated the price before he bought them openly so it would look like he had lost the money when the investments went bad. If we're right, the cash is still stashed somewhere."

"Interesting," Miguel said. "It is amazing, no, how clever rich people can be at hiding their money. I guess that I would do the same thing in their shoes."

"No, you wouldn't."

"Gracias. What do you need?"

"I think that the quickest way would be to get a list of any company that was connected to ones Saunders was involved in as either a buyer or seller."

"How long are we talking about?"

"In terms of his involvement?"

"Sí."

"I would say the last twelve months or so," she said after giving it some thought. "We think that's when he started making bogus investments. Should I e-mail you the list of companies that we know about?"

"Yes. That would be best." He gave her his e-mail address, which she noted was at a private e-mail provider.

"How long will this take?"

"I do not know. It will take some time. It is not always possible to do a search by person across all our databases. Although we have started to put our records online, there are many files that are still only on paper due to a shortage of money. We are, after all, a poor country."

The same was true in the United States, Alyson thought. "Gracias, Miguel."

"De nada." As she hung up the phone there was a knock at her office door. Looking up, she saw Joyce Howard leaning against the side of the door.

"Any luck?" Alyson asked as Joyce walked in and plopped down in a chair.

"Yes and no," she replied, dropping a folder down on the desk.

"Okay. Let's hear it."

"Well, we got into all of the files off his hard drive. That's the good news."

"And the bad news?"

"We didn't find much to help you."

"Let's see what you've got," Alyson said, reaching for the folder.

"Most of the files were spreadsheets detailing his deals. Not surprisingly, given the results, there was little analysis on most of them. See here," she said, pointing to some numbers on a printout. "You've got most of this in hardcopy anyway."

"What else?"

"It seems that Saunders used a personal accounting package to handle his financial info. We printed out a list of accounts and the last twelve months of activity. There's also some correspondence with a couple of law firms in Panama and here in New York. Except for the accounting file and a few others, I'm not sure why he bothered to password-protect them."

"What do you mean?"

"Well, the password, and there was only one, was so easy that we broke it in about two hours of trying. We probably could have broken it without Pass-breaker, but it would've taken longer."

"Well, maybe he didn't worry about stuff like that."

"Could be," she said, sounding unconvinced.

"But you don't think so?"

"No. We also tried to recover any deleted files and e-mails. There weren't any. Either he didn't delete stuff or he used a scrubber program to clean up his drives. My guess is he scrubbed the drive clean. If I'm right, I'd be real surprised he was so cavalier with his password. It was almost as if he knew someone would be looking around and wanted to make it easy, but not too easy, to read these files."

"Why would he do that?"

"Maybe he knew someone would be poking around."

"He was under indictment, which means he may have gotten rid of documents so he wouldn't have to produce them."

"Which is illegal, but that might explain it," Joyce mused, still not sure. "Something about this fact pattern just doesn't feel right."

"I agree."

"We tried the same password on the files on the CD you gave me. No luck. He used a different password."

"And all the files off his office PC used the same password?"

"Yes."

"Maybe he changed them all once a month or something."

"I doubt it," Joyce said, shaking her head slightly. "That wouldn't fit the pattern either. I mean, why would he bother to change it if he used such easy passwords? You only change it from time to time if you're serious about security. It doesn't seem he was overly concerned about that."

"Maybe the program required him to change it periodically."

"Nope. We checked that."

Alyson looked down at the thin file in front of her.

"I wish I had more to give you," Joyce said.

"That's okay. Thanks. Mark will be happy to hear you're off this and can get back to the First Hiberian Bank security audit."

"Yeah, we're setting up for a run at it over the weekend, figuring most of their IT staff will be out."

"You're not going to be the most popular person over there if you force their IT people to come in on a Saturday or Sunday."

"I know, but it's what we agreed to with their security manager."

"Good luck. And Passbreaker's still working on the CD, right?"

"Yeah. I'll let you know when it's finished." Joyce got up and went back to her office down the hall.

Alyson looked over the printouts. Joyce was right, she concluded. A quick scan told her they wouldn't really add much to what they had learned from the paper files and the unprotected files. At least Joyce hadn't wasted too much time getting past the passwords. She picked up the printout from the accounting package and scanned the list of contacts. No names jumped out at her. Three or four of them were listed more than once. She'd ask Fred to check on them.

*   *   *   *

Dan Morris walked up the western side of Third Avenue, watching Alyson on the other side of the street. She suddenly turned east on 70th Street. He frantically tried to cross the street, but was stymied by the heavy southbound traffic. He hurried across the street as soon as the lights changed, dodging a taxi turning onto Third. He picked up the pace, sweating slightly despite the cold. Halfway to Second Avenue, he stopped and looked around.

Alyson Murphy had turned onto 70th Street, having remembered that her dry cleaning would be ready and the shop would close in a few minutes. She climbed down the stairs and stepped into the shop. The windows were nearly covered over with Christmas decorations, even though it was unlikely that the Chois celebrated that holiday in their own home. There were multicolored lights, wreaths, Santas, and a Rudolph with a glowing red nose. She took the plastic bag containing her clothes off the rack next to the cash register and turned to leave. Through a small gap in the decorations, she saw a man up on the sidewalk stop, look around for a moment, and then move off quickly down the street toward Second Avenue. In that brief moment, even thought the darkness hid much of his face, she sensed that he was the man from the subway.

"You okay, Miss Murphy?" Myung Choi asked.

"Excuse me? Uh. Yes. I'm fine. Sorry." Alyson opened the door slowly, climbed up a step, and craned her neck to look through the wrought iron railing. She looked in both directions and saw no one. The man had disappeared. She jumped up the last couple of steps, turned left, walked briskly back to Third Avenue and then north the three blocks to 73rd Street. Minutes later, she bolted the lock on the front door of her apartment, hung up the dry cleaning in the small closet near the front door, walked over to the sofa, and sat down, her legs weak and her hands shaking slightly.

She jumped out of her seat when the phone rang. She reached out and stabbed for the phone, knocking it to the floor. She leaned down and picked it up.

"Hi, honey," Gavin Matthews cooed.

"Oh, Gavin, thank goodness!"

"What's wrong?"

"I think someone's following me."

"What? Who?"

"I don't know. I saw this man in the subway and…" She fought back her tears, "again tonight."

"Are you sure?"

"No. I think it was the same man, but…"

Gavin gave her all the reasons why she was probably imagining things and Alyson began to calm down. "I wish I could be there. I was actually calling to tell you that I'm going to be stuck out in Los Angeles a lot longer than I thought. My deal is heating up and I've got to stay out here until it closes."

"How…how long is that going to be?"

"I don't know. A couple of weeks, maybe more."

Alyson bit her lower lip to stop it from trembling.

They chatted for a few more minutes. "Goodnight," Gavin said. "I love you."

Alyson hesitated for a moment. Did he? Did she love him? She didn't now. "Me too," she finally said and then hung up.

She climbed into bed a little while later, but sleep eluded her for a long time.

CHAPTER 16

▼

THURSDAY, NOVEMBER 30

The alarm woke Alyson from a deep sleep. A long hot shower helped revive her some and a couple of cups of coffee helped some more, but it seemed nothing would clear her head completely.

As she walked toward the subway, her eyes darted unconsciously to her left and right. She couldn't shake the feeling that someone was following her. She had never been stalked before and she didn't like the feeling.

Dan Morris stopped at a sidewalk cart across the street from Alyson's office and bought a cup of coffee. He walked into a small park, where he sat on a bench next to a bronze statue of a woman feeding the pigeons. On the bench next to her were two brass statutes of pigeons. He sipped the coffee and read a copy of the *New York Post* and waited for Alyson to walk by. Halfway through the crossword puzzle, he caught her out of the corner of his eye just before she entered her office building. He scribbled in the remaining answers, got up, tossed the paper into the trash can, and strolled the two blocks to his newly rented office.

Alyson walked into her office, threw her coat and briefcase on the table, and marched down the hall and into the kitchen for a cup of coffee. As she walked around the floor, her muscles started to relax and she stopped looking over her shoulder.

Sitting at her desk, she fumbled with a pen for a minute before reaching out for the phone.

"Twenty-fourth precinct," a woman's voice said.

"Clyde Johnson, please." Music began to play.

"Detective Johnson," a male voice announced, a few seconds later.

"Clyde, this is Alyson."

"Hey, Alyson, long time no hear. What's going on?" Clyde and Alyson had met four years earlier while investigating the apparent suicide of an investment banker who had been under suspicion of embezzling millions of dollars from clients. With Alyson's help, Clyde had proved that a securities broker, who had been a college frat mate of the banker, had murdered the banker. The broker was now serving a life sentence somewhere.

"I need your help," she said, her voice breaking.

"Sure. You name it."

"I think I'm being stalked."

"What makes you think that?"

Alyson told him about seeing the man on the subway and then again outside the dry cleaner near her apartment. "I'm not positive they're the same person, but my gut tells me they are. I didn't see him this morning."

"I'm not saying that I don't believe you, but that's not much to go on. It could be just nerves. Is there anything at work that might be making you edgy?"

"No. Just the usual stuff. It's never affected me this way before. I can't explain this…overwhelming sense of being watched. It's not just two times, it's constant lately."

"Maybe there was just something about the timing of seeing these guys that triggered it. You know," his voice became lighter, "someone staring at you in the subway doesn't sound all that suspicious to me."

"Thanks," she blushed, thankful he couldn't see her. "I know it sounds ridiculous, but the feeling was so strong."

"It's not ridiculous. There're always a couple of cases a year where I wished the victim had acted on her feelings, not that I'm saying this is necessarily one of them."

"Clyde, what should I do?"

"Listen, the best thing you can do is to be aware of your surroundings. Make sure that you stay with crowds and don't work any later than you have to. If you go out at night, make sure someone takes you home." Alyson smiled at the thought of Hank taking her home. "If you see him again, give me a call. My direct dial is 7304. It might be a good idea to program that into your cell."

"Okay."

"And one more thing…"

"What?"

"You might want to get something to defend yourself with."

"Like what? Mace?" Alyson asked.

"No, mace is illegal. A combo of pepper spray and tear gas works almost as well, though."

"Do you really think I need that?" Fear crept back into her voice at the thought of needing to spray someone.

"No. I'm sure this is nothing, but it can't hurt to be careful. And…"

"Yes?"

"Just be careful. If you see this scumbag again, I'll get more manpower on it, but until then that's probably the best I can do."

"I know. Thanks. Just calling you makes me feel better."

✳   ✳   ✳   ✳

The phone on her desk rang. "Oh, Hank. Where are you?" Alyson asked when she recognized the number on her caller ID.

"I'm in a cab heading in from JFK. I just got back from Ireland. I had to cover the signing of the new Ireland-U.S. tax treaty, boring stuff. How are you?"

"Fine. I'll understand if you say no, but are you up for dinner tonight?"

"Sure. What about Gavin?"

"He's out in LA. I'd just like some company tonight." Her voice was pleading.

"Sure. I could be there by 8:00 PM. Is that ok?"

"Perfect. See you at my place at eight. Thanks."

Hank arrived back at his apartment at a little past seven, ran up the stairs into the foyer, and grabbed his mail. A minute later, he threw his luggage and mail on the bed, pulled off his clothes and jumped into the shower. Twenty minutes later, he hailed a cab to go across town. At 7:58 PM, he rang the buzzer next to Alyson's name. There was no response for a dozen seconds. "Hank, is that you?"

"It's me."

"I'll be right down." Two minutes later, Alyson opened the front door, gave him a quick but unexpected hug. "I'm glad you're back. Let's grab a bite around the corner."

"So what's wrong? I could tell something was bothering you on the phone. Did Gavin and you break up?"

Alyson stopped and looked at him, surprised. "What makes you think that?"

"Well," he said, a bit defensively, "you seemed upset and Gavin was out in LA. I guess I just put two and two together."

"And got three!"

"I'm sorry. What's wrong?"

"No. I'm sorry. I shouldn't have reacted like that. Let's talk about it at the restaurant."

The walked in silence over to Third Avenue and got a table at *Roma En Trezo*, one of Alyson's favorite restaurants in all of New York, partly because of its great Italian food and partly because it was frequented only by locals.

They were still early and the restaurant wasn't crowded, which it was most of the time since there were just ten tables. Each one was covered in a red and white checkered tablecloth, with a wax-drenched empty Chianti wine bottle in the middle. A lit white candle was stuck into the opening of each bottle. They, together with a couple of small lights in the ceiling, provided most of the light. The walls were painted with scenes from all over Italy.

She took a sip of wine and said, "Thanks for coming over. You must be tired after your long trip"

He nodded as if to say no problem. "What's wrong?"

Alyson was quiet for a moment. "I think I'm being followed."

"What! What makes you think that?"

"Um, I saw a guy on the subway looking at me and I saw him again the other night. I least I think it was him."

"You sure it's the same guy?"

"No, but at least I think it is. I'm not sure."

"Maybe you should call the police?"

"I did. I've got a friend over at the twenty-fourth precinct."

They talked about Saunders through most of dinner, but then switched to discussing a few college friends. They finished their meal and said no to coffee and dessert.

They strolled back to Alyson's apartment.

"Do you want to come up for a while?" she asked.

They were soon up in her apartment. She brought him a beer and she sat down in the chair next to the end of the sofa where he had taken a seat. She curled her legs under her.

"I forgot to mention," Hank said after the conversation turned back to Saunders, "that my great-grandfather worked on the Canal under George Goethals. He was an army engineer and was there when the USS *Cristobal* became the first ship to pass through the Canal. We had some old photos of him. That seemed the coolest thing in the world when I was a kid."

"Have you ever been there?"

"No. I've always wanted to go, but my folks could never afford it. It looks like I'll finally get to see it. You're not still thinking about coming with me?"

"I don't know. The more I think about it, the more convinced I am I should go."

"I'm not sure my boss will go for it." Hank said. "If not, I'll buy a supersaver fare and take some time off."

They talked about his Ireland trip for a while. The more they talked, the less likely it seemed to her that she was really being stalked. There was a good chance she had been letting her imagination run loose given the current case and the talk about murder.

"I think it's time to call it a night. Thanks for being there when I needed someone."

"Any time. I mean it."

After he left, she double-checked the locks before heading to bed.

*   *   *   *

The phone next to the bed rang. Candy Harden rolled away from her husband. She was used to late-night calls and would let her husband answer it. Whit Harden picked up the phone.

"Mr. Harden, this is Morris."

"What is it?" The lawyer asked, irritated. He looked at the clock on the bedside table. It read 12:17 AM. "Do you know what time it is?"

"Um, no." There was a pause. "Sorry."

"Well, now that I'm awake, what do you want?" Harden said sternly.

"I think she's seen me, but she's not sure. I'll lay low and be extra careful. I know you don't want her to know that I'm tailing her."

"Yes. I don't want her to see you again," his voice became harsher.

"There's one more thing. It sounds like they're planning to go down to Panama."

"They?"

"Her and that reporter."

"Why are they going there?"

"I'm not sure yet."

"Well, find out," the lawyer said, annoyed. "Once you do, call me."

"Oh, by the way, it seems his great-grandfather worked on the Canal."

"How is that relevant?"

"It's not. It's just interesting. It's a small world, huh?"

"Yes, it is a small world." What a weirdo, Harden thought. "Keep me informed, just not after midnight." He hung up the phone.

*   *   *   *

Dan Morris put the receiver down and shook his head. What an asshole! Harden was home sleeping in a nice warm bed with soft silk sheets. His stomach was full of a gourmet meal and some expensive French wine. He probably went to sleep after screwing his trophy wife, unless he got laid before he went home. Probably both. He certainly wasn't sitting in a car at midnight listening to other people's conversations and trying to digest a Big Mac and some fries, washed down with Diet Coke.

Morris turned the key. The engine coughed, but didn't turn over. "Shit!"

He tried again, pumping the gas pedal gently; trying to make sure he didn't flood it. He tried a third time and the engine roared into life.

Someday he wouldn't be sitting in a beat-up Volkswagen. He hit his blinker, looked over his shoulder, and pulled out into traffic for the forty-minute drive back to Brooklyn.

CHAPTER 17

▼

FRIDAY, DECEMBER 1

Alyson rolled her head around trying to get the kinks out of her neck. She sat still with her eyes closed for a few minutes waiting for the Advil to take effect. Giving up, she sat up and clicked on the file for the Estarix project, selecting the final draft of the report she had typed over the weekend. She corrected part of the introduction, found two errors in the analysis section, and sent off an e-mail to Fred and Max Regan asking them to track down the right numbers. She clicked to close the file and clicked yes to save the changes.

Rubbing her eyes again, she looked down at her watch. It was after 6:30 PM already. She looked at the tall pile of paper in her inbox and sagged down farther into her chair. Breathing out, she rocked forward again, pulled a folder off the top of the pile, and started to read. She found it difficult to keep her eyes focused on the words. She had been working all-out for the last two weeks, and it had only gotten worse now that she was working on the Saunders case. Mark had given her some extra help, but he wouldn't let her totally drop her other projects and let her focus only on one contingency case. She was glad to have Fred and Max, but they simply weren't enough. They were too inexperienced to pass a lot of the work off to. Joyce helped, but she was now off on her own projects.

Alyson hesitated to go in and ask Mark to let her go to Panama, sure that he'd hit the roof unless she could show some real progress, which wasn't going to happen without going to Panama. She was caught in a catch-22. Maybe Hank had the right idea. Take some vacation time and put in an expense report after the fact.

She shook her head and tried to refocus on the file in front of her, but her thoughts kept returning to Saunders. She had tried to follow Saunders's online trail. She had reviewed the list of cookies and temp files left on Saunders's laptop to reconstruct where he had surfed, and Harden had given her access to Saunders's e-mail. Unfortunately, other than his personal tastes in pornography, she hadn't learned much in the last few days beyond what they knew earlier. Some of the e-mails pointed to accounts overseas and documented the investments he had made, but nothing in the online record indicated any kind of scheme to purposefully lose money. Instead, the record was nearly perfect in support of Saunders simply being the victim of bad decision making. Maybe this whole thing was just a big mistake—the assets, the offshore companies, the man in the subway. No. Her gut told her she was on to something.

Giving up, she closed the file and put it back on the stack. After opening her Internet connection again, she launched Google and typed in "self-defense products." A second later, the screen filled with a list of Web sites. She clicked on the first site and was amazed at what you could order online. Scrolling down to sprays, she reviewed three other sites and returned to the second one because they guaranteed next-day delivery. She selected the Triple Action Personal Pro that contained OC pepper and CN tear gas and could spray up to ten feet, went to the online checkout, and typed in her address and credit card information. Her finger hovered over the mouse for a couple of seconds before clicking on the submit icon. She smiled as the confirmation of the sale appeared on her screen. She turned her monitor off, stood up, grabbed her coat, and headed for the door.

The phone rang. She hesitated, considered letting the call go into voice mail, but then put down her coat and picked up the phone.

"Hey, Alyson. It's Hank."

"Hi." Her face brightened.

"Are you up for some dinner? I heard you had a bad day."

"When?"

"How about in one minute."

"What? Where are you?"

"I'm in the lobby downstairs. I had an assignment downtown that finished a few minutes ago and I thought I'd surprise you."

"I'll be right down." She glided down the hall and into the ladies room on the way to the elevator to fix her makeup and check her hair. It wasn't the best, but it would do, she concluded. She rode the elevator to the lobby.

"How'd you know I was having a bad day?" She asked as they walked outside.

"I called earlier and Dylan told me."

"It was a long day. I spent it most of it either in meetings or getting ready for them. I'm beat."

"You sure you want to go out? We can skip it."

"No. It'll do me good."

The rain pounded against the windshield of the taxi. The passenger-side wiper screeched as it arced across the window, barely removing any of the water, making it almost impossible to see. Each time, Alyson and Hank cringed, neither knowing how the cab driver could put up with the noise. They chatted about the lousy weather and Hank's latest assignment on the way to the restaurant.

"Here we are," he announced as the cab pulled up to the curb in front of Café Doux, a casual French bistro on Bleecker Street. "It's not too late to change your mind." She shook her head and they ran into the restaurant in a futile effort to stay dry.

The maitre d' showed them to their table after only a short wait. Café Doux was typical of the restaurants in Greenwich Village, with large glass windows across the front, providing a view of people walking by, though they were fewer and farther between due to the downpour. A variety of plants hung from the rafters and numerous objets d'art hung on the walls. Unlike most restaurants, however, the Café Doux was quiet and would allow them to unwind and talk. Drinks and dinner were soon ordered.

"I talked to my boss today about Panama."

"What did he say?"

"He doesn't think the story has legs. He thought there'd be a connection between the missing assets and the murder, but not now."

"Why not?"

"He thinks that employee they arrested killed Saunders."

"I know you don't believe that."

"Not at all. Even without what we're talking about, I just couldn't believe that any employee would really have what it takes to kill someone. It wasn't like it just happened in the heat of a fight or argument. Most murders involving normal people are crimes of passion."

"True, but there was a lot of passion in the GenergTex employees that day. Saunders saw to that."

"It still doesn't fit. For him to be the murderer, he would have had to drive all the way out to the ranch, hope no one would be around, and then kill him in cold blood. Then," Hank took a sip of water, "douse the place with gasoline and set it on fire."

"Maybe he just snapped."

"Twelve hours later? If he snapped, he would have taken his shot at the hotel."

"Did you say all this to your boss?"

"Yes, but he's not listening. I think he just doesn't want me to waste any more time on it."

"So, what are you going to do?"

"I told him I was taking some of the vacation I've accrued over the last couple of years. I haven't really taken any time off in I can't remember how long. I thought I'd go south and try to get some sun."

"Is there anywhere in particular you want to go?" she asked with a slight grin.

"Well, my great-grandfather worked on the Canal and I've always wanted to see it." He grinned. "But first, I think I need to take a trip out west."

"Where out west?"

"I'd like to visit Texas. Maybe see the Alamo."

"I haven't talked to my boss yet."

"That's okay. We've got time, I think."

"I hope so." Alyson thought for a moment. "We both agree Saunders was killed for the money. Right?"

Hank nodded.

"Then we should be focusing all of our attention on who could have known about it."

"It's a short list, isn't it?" Hanks asked.

"So far it is. We know that Maria Garcia and her firm knew about it. Maybe Harden, but I don't think so. Fred thinks he's suspect numero uno."

"I'd have to put him high on my list too." Hank drew a line with his hand about eye-high. "He had the knowledge and opportunity, and then there're the missing files."

"I know, but I got the sense he was surprised about this when we told him."

"But he's a lawyer. Good lawyers are like good poker players: they never let you know what they're thinking."

"Okay, so I put Harden on the list." She wrote the name on a piece of paper she pulled from her purse, looked up, and saw Hank's expression. "Okay, at the top of the list."

"Who else?" he asked.

"Charlie Wong's got to be on the list. He and Saunders were in a lot of deals together."

"Is he one of the Hong Kong Wongs?"

Alyson laughed. "I can't believe you said that."

Hank smiled. He hadn't meant to say that, but he was glad it made her laugh. "Well, is he?"

"I think so, but I'm not sure yet."

"If he is, he probably had the means to find out about the deals. Given the family's reputation, I doubt he'd have any compunction about eliminating Saunders."

Alyson shuddered.

"I'm sorry," Hank said. "How about that guy in Aruba you mentioned earlier?"

"Harold, um, Harold Van Dych. Maybe, but he wasn't really involved. His family owned the land before Saunders bought it, but that was it. He's got a lot of family money."

"Sure, but fortunes change," Hank said. "Who would know about it in Panama?"

Alyson thought about it for a moment and said, "I'm not sure, but if Saunders did this right, not many."

"Well, we'll have to include anyone involved with setting up the companies, like law firms or maybe even someone in the government down there."

She scribbled some notes.

"What about his ex-wife? What was her name? Anne, wasn't it?" Alyson asked

"Yes, but they've been divorced for a number of years."

"Maybe she hired a private investigator to follow him around to protect her alimony? I could imagine she'd be pretty pissed off if she found out about his plan."

"Do you really think she'd be capable of murder?"

"I don't know, but let's put her down just in case."

She wrote down the wife's name, put down the pen, and said, "Say we're right about one of these being the killer." She tapped the paper with her finger. "How'd they do it then? We've got the same logistical problem with any of these that you had with the employee as the killer."

"Maybe not. Saunders could've invited his killer out to the ranch. That would explain why he sent all the ranch hands into town. It could have been someone he didn't want anyone to know was there."

"That could be. But, it still seems unlikely one of them would be any more likely to go out there, kill him, and then set him on fire."

"Maybe he didn't go there intending to kill him. Maybe there was a fight or an accident. Maybe the opportunity just presented itself."

"Are you saying then the money wasn't involved?"

"I don't know," he said, perplexed. "Maybe the killer had help and it was just revenge."

"Now it's a conspiracy!"

"It could be if we're right about the kind of money involved."

"Great. Maybe they're all in it together. Just like that Agatha Christie story, *The Orient Express*, where everyone took part in the murder," Alyson said in a lighthearted voice and then sat there thinking about that for a moment. "But that wouldn't be enough. They'd still have to figure out how to get to the money. The banks would need account numbers and access codes. They wouldn't have them."

"Maybe whoever killed him tortured him to get that information. That's as good a reason to burn the body as any."

"If we're right about this," she said quietly, picking up the pen and tapping the paper, "we'll have to track down where all these people were that night. I can start as soon as I get into the office on Monday."

"Okay. I'll check in from Texas. I've got a flight early on Monday morning."

They finished their entrées and ordered coffee and Café Doux's famous mousse au chocolat and gateaux. After dinner they walked over to Sheridan Square and caught a cab uptown that turned east across 14th Street and then went north on Second Avenue. Thirty-five minutes later, they were pulling up in front of Alyson's apartment. Despite being obviously tired, she asked him to come up for a nightcap and they were soon in her apartment, sipping white wine on the sofa.

Between the meal and the wine, it wasn't long before Alyson began to get sleepy.

"I'd better go," Hank said.

"Please stay. Just a little longer," she said sleepily. "Just a little longer."

Her eyelids soon fluttered and then closed. She slumped toward him, putting her head on his shoulder. He could tell from her breathing that she was nearly asleep.

Hank caressed her hair with his hand, looked down at her, and smiled contently.

Once Alyson was asleep, he slid out from under her and lowered her onto the sofa. He went into the bedroom and grabbed a blanket and a pillow from the closet. Returning to the living room, he tucked her in, gently putting the pillow under her head. Hank stood over her for a minute, studying her face and listening to her steady breathing. She murmured something that he couldn't understand. He waited a few more moments to be sure she was asleep before leaving the apartment, locking the door behind him.

On the way home, he thought back on the conversation. What if they were right? Alyson had asked that, but he hadn't answered her. If they were right, they were both in grave danger.

CHAPTER 18

▼

MONDAY, DECEMBER 4

Alyson awoke on the sofa with a start. She looked around and blinked, unsure of where she was. She rotated her head back and forth to get the kinks out. She got up and looked around the apartment. It was empty.

She made it to work a few minutes after 8:00 AM. The pile of files in her inbox was still there. She sighed. "Damn."

She spent her 11:00 AM meeting with Mark Jackson refraining from telling him about her plans. She hoped Hank would find something she could use to persuade her boss to let her go to Panama.

Dylan handed her a telephone message. Hank had called five minutes earlier. She dialed his cell number.

"Where are you?"

"We just landed in San Antonio. I'm walking to get my rental car." He was panting. "With any luck, I'll be in Sandy Creek by midafternoon."

"Why didn't you fly closer?"

"I'd rather drive."

Hank was still afraid of small planes. She remembered that from college. He had been twelve when he had lost his older brother in a commuter plane crash and he had never gotten over it.

"I'm planning to check in with the local police and then go see the ranch."

"Shouldn't you be going to El Paso where they're holding the murder suspect?"

"No. I figure if he's not guilty, he's not going to know anything. If he is guilty, he's really not all that useful in our search for the money."

"But if he's guilty then maybe our whole premise about the assets is wrong."

"No. I'm sure about the assets. Did you hear from your friend?"

"I just got off the phone with her." Alyson had called Kathy Donovan, an old friend from McCaskey High School in Lancaster, Pennsylvania. Alyson had been a bridesmaid in Kathy's wedding and had helped her through the subsequent painful divorce. Kathy had worked for the U.S. Immigration and Naturalization Service for several years and had given Alyson help from time to time, knowing that Alyson would never misuse the information and that she was helping solve her cases. "I called her first thing this morning and gave her our list and she just called back. It looks like we struck out on most of the names."

"Let's see," she said as she scanned the list on the page lying on the desk in front of her. "Van Dyck wasn't in the States. Charlie Wong was here, but he went back to Bermuda the next day."

"He could have flown back in time to catch that flight."

"We'll have to check that." She looked at the list. "César Hernandez was here and stayed until the twenty-third."

"Who's he again?"

"He's with the Panamanian law firm that helped Maria Garcia's firm on the Argentina cattle ranch deal."

"Right. So he's still on the list."

"What about the rest of the Panamanians on the list?"

"Kathy said it would take some time to match up the entries and the names I gave her."

"But how many Panamanians come into the States during any two week period?" Hank said with a hint of exasperation.

"Enough, I guess, to make the matching difficult." She leaned back in her chair.

"Our list of possibles is shrinking."

"I think it's time to call Mr. Wong again and see if he can tell us where he was the night of the murder."

"You're starting to sound like an investigative reporter."

"Thanks a lot," she said with mock irritation. "Call me later."

She hung up the phone and dialed the number in Bermuda Hank had given to her.

"Charlie Wong speaking."

"Mr. Wong, this is Alyson Murphy. I'm working with Hank Jenkins. I believe you spoke to him last week."

"I remember."

"Well, I was wondering…were you in the States the day Mr. Saunders died?"

"Yes. I was in Atlanta on business."

"Did the two of you meet?"

"Not that it's any of your business, but no, we did not meet on the day he died. I met him in his New York office a few days before. That was the last time I saw him."

"Did you know that Mr. Saunders was going to be at the ranch the night he died?"

"I am not sure I like where you are going with this."

"It's just a simple question."

"No question asked by a reporter is ever simple."

"Did you know he was at the ranch?" Alyson asked again, not bothering to correct his assumption about her occupation.

"Yes," Charlie said. "He asked me to come out there and spend a day going through our *last* deal." Alyson wondered what he meant by that as Charlie continued, "We had a disagreement about it. He thought we could work it out."

"Did you go out there?"

"No. I was in Atlanta that night. I was in meetings until three. I had dinner alone. I stayed at the Peachtree Manor Hotel, room 431, and flew out of Hartsfield the next day back to Bermuda. You can check it out if you want."

"That won't be necessary." She looked down at the notes she had taken during the call with Kathy earlier and made a check mark. "Did you know anyone who would want to kill him?"

"Besides all the investors and employees of GenergTex, you mean?"

"Yes, I guess so."

"No. I did not know him well enough to know who hated him that much."

"You think the killer hated him?"

"Why else would he be killed?" the man asked.

"Money?"

"Yes, that has motivated many a killer," he said in a matter-of-fact way that gave her chills.

"You were his partner on a lot of deals."

"Partner, yes; friend, no. I did not know most of the people he knew. We traveled in very different circles."

"I see. Back to the ranch, if you don't mind. Did you ever visit it?"

"The ranch? No. Any more questions?" He was clearly tiring of answering her questions.

"Not at the moment. Thank you for your time." She hung up the phone and replayed the conversation in her head. The information about Atlanta had come out pretty pat, almost as if he were waiting for it. The hotel would probably check out since it was unlikely he'd make something up that was so easy to check. She'd have to ask Fred to check out Charlie Wong's credit card records to see if he had charged a dinner anywhere in Atlanta.

She looked down at her list again, looking for names that hadn't been checked off. The only one they had come up with at the restaurant that wasn't accounted for was César Hernandez. So she looked up Maria Garcia's number and gave her a call. She wasn't in, but her secretary gave her the number of their office in Panama. After a couple of tries, she connected with César Hernandez.

"Yes, Señorita Murphy, I was in the States the night that Señor Saunders died, but I was at a basketball game at your Madison Square Garden. The New York Knicks played the Los Angeles Lakers. I am a Lakers fan, but the Knicks won."

"I don't know exactly how to ask this, but can anyone confirm you were at the game?"

"Señorita, I know what you are suggesting. That is fantasy, but yes there are people who could confirm I was there. We were entertaining clients of Banks, Brown. We had a suite."

"I see. Do you remember any of their names?"

"No, but Maria Garcia, who I think you spoke to before, could give you names."

An hour later, Maria returned her call and confirmed that Hernandez was there, but, not surprisingly, wouldn't give any client names.

"Damn! Looks like we're quickly running out of suspects."

*   *   *   *

Hank found the rental car counter five minutes after hanging up with Alyson. A shuttle bus took him to his car and he was soon behind the wheel of a Jeep Cherokee heading west on Interstate 10. He wanted to visit the ranch and talk to the local police before coming back to San Antonio to talk to the medical examiner. If his calculations were right, he should be able to make it there and back in time to catch his flight home the next afternoon.

On the passenger seat was a sheet of paper with directions to Sandy Creek. It would be a three-hour drive. Heading west, the road seemed to stretch out in front of him as far as he could see. It was going to be a pretty boring drive, he concluded, and switched on the radio. He flipped through the dial and finally found an oldies rock and roll station among all the country and western music. He was soon singing along with the Beatles, the Stones, and the Who. The countryside passed by quickly, changing little from mile to mile.

He pulled into Sandy Creek around three in the afternoon, asked directions to the local police station, and a minute later parked outside a two-story yellow brick building dating back to the thirties. The police department was on the left of the central entrance hall, the town library was on the right, and the sign on the wall told him that the rest of the local government took up the second floor.

"What can I do for you?" a policeman sitting at a desk asked as Hank entered.

"I'd like to talk to someone about the Saunders's murder."

"Y'all a reporter?"

"Yes. Hank Jenkins. I'm with the *New York Times*," Hank said, offering his business card.

"Ooooeee. A Yankee all the way out here. Hey, Sarge," the man bellowed over his shoulder to the man sitting at the bigger desk in the corner. The sergeant was leaning back in his chair, feet propped up on the desk, reading the newspaper's account of the local high school football team's win over their arch rival, Sonora.

"Yeah, what do you want?"

"Hey, I've got me a Yankee reporter wanting to know about the Saunders murder."

"Tell him we're busy."

"That's enough, Billy," a gruff voice bellowed out of the corner office, followed shortly thereafter by a six-foot-four black man wearing a Chief of Police uniform. The sergeant dropped his feet to the floor and sat up straight. "Tommy," the Chief addressed the officer at the front desk, "why don't you get our visitor a cup of coffee." He stepped forward. "And, while you're at it, I'll take one too."

"Sure, Chief. What do you like in it?" Tommy asked Hank.

"Just black, thanks."

"I'm the Chief of what passes for the police department in this town." He glared at the sergeant for a moment before turning back to Hank. He stuck out a hand and said, "I'm Chief Sawyer."

Marcus Sawyer was the first black chief of police the town of Sandy Creek had ever had. In fact, he was the first black chief in the whole county. Who was going to say no to a townie who, upon his return to Sandy Creek after graduating with a degree in criminal justice and ten years on the police force in Houston, wanted the job of chief when the previous one retired? His most important credential for the job in this part of Texas, however, was that he had been a star running back for the Texas leading them to the Cotton Bowl and a shot at the national championship in his sophomore year. Unfortunately, the title went to Oklahoma when the Longhorns lost on a late field goal.

"Hank Jenkins," Hank repeated, holding out his hand.

"Come on back to my office." Marcus led the way and, once inside, motioned for Hank to have a seat in one of the wooden chairs in front of the desk. The sheriff waited for Tommy to put the two cups of coffee on the desk and leave before closing the door and marching around the desk. The leather swivel chair let out a small, sharp squeal of pain as the entire weight of the ex-football player rested on it.

"What brings a New York boy all the way out here? Y'all know we have phones and e-mail now?"

"I've always thought that a good reporter does his best work face to face, especially when the person you're talking to has probably already been asked a million questions by phone and e-mail." Hank pulled out a small notepad and pen. He still liked to do this the old-fashioned way. Some of the younger guys would be writing notes on their personal digital assistants, but he had never found much use for one.

"Now, that's pretty good," the chief said, sizing Hank up. "Just what is it you want to know about the untimely death of Mr. Saunders?"

"I'm interested in your case against the man you've arrested for the murder."

"David Oppenheimer?"

"Yeah, that's him."

The sheriff proceeded to outline their case, although most of what he said had already been reported in newspapers, including the local one. Oppenheimer had been stopped in El Paso trying to cross into Mexico a week after the murder. They had found his prints and DNA on letters sent to Saunders. He was positively identified as being in front of the Hyatt Hotel in Dallas the day Saunders went there for the annual meeting. An hour after the meeting, he had bragged to a bartender at the Remember the Alamo Saloon that he was going to "get" Saunders. He wore a size nine and a half boot, the same size as the boot prints outside the bedroom at the ranch with the broken window.

"Has he confessed?"

"Nope. Not yet. He claims he didn't do it."

"Did he take a lie detector test?"

"His lawyer advised him not to."

"Is there any specific physical evidence placing him at the ranch, prints or DNA?" Hank asked.

"Not really. Most of it was probably lost in the fire."

"Do you have any witnesses that put him at the ranch?"

"Not yet. But Buck Otis saw his truck in town."

"Really?" He hadn't seen that piece of information in the papers."

"It's a red Ford Explorer or Expedition, with out-of-state plates. That Oppenheimer fellow is from Louisiana. He never bothered to change the plates. He was driving it when they picked him up trying to cross into Mexico."

"Did he have an explanation for going to Mexico?"

"He said his girlfriend lives in Juarez."

"Does she?"

"She's from there originally, but she lives in Dallas now. We haven't located her yet."

"Do you have any other suspects?"

"Not at this time. We're pretty sure we got the killer. You got someone else in mind?"

"What about one of Saunders's business associates?" Hank offered.

"Like who?"

"Well, Whittaker Harden for one."

"His lawyer. Nah, we questioned him and don't consider him a suspect."

"What about Charlie Wong?"

"Who's he?"

"A business partner of Saunders," Hank said. "My understanding is that they had a heated argument about a deal just before the murder. We think he might have been at the ranch that night."

"Why do you think that? The ranch hands didn't see anyone that night."

"He was in Atlanta and we think he might have flown over for a secret meeting with Saunders. That's why the ranch hands didn't see him."

"You got any proof of that?" The Chief shifted forward in his chair and wrote down the name on a pad on the desk.

"Not yet."

"So you can't really place him at the ranch that night."

"Not yet, but we're checking on that now."

Chief Sawyer put a big question mark by the name. "Is there anyone else?"

"We're checking out a few others, seeing where they were that night. Did you check out where all the ranch hands were that night?"

"All but Jeb were at Bert's. That's the local watering hole."

"Where was Jeb?"

"He was home with the flu."

"You sure?"

"Yeah. His wife was with him. He had a fever of a hundred and four."

"Was there any evidence of someone being in the house?" Hank's pen stopped over the pad.

"Other than the broken window, you mean? No. We got one print off a mug, but we haven't been able to identify it. Doesn't match any of the employees we talked to or any of the ranch hands."

"Did you run it against the FBI database?"

Chief Sawyer gave him a look that answered his question.

"If we come across anyone who could be a suspect, should we give you the name so you could check it against the print you found?"

"I'd appreciate that. I'll try to run this Charlie Wong fellow's prints and see what we get."

"If you get a match, please let me know. Here's my card," Hank said, extracting a business card from his wallet.

"I'll let you know as soon as I can. I can't always give information to the press as soon as you reporters would always like."

"Well then…thanks for your time." Hank stood up. "Could you give me directions out to Saunders's ranch? I'd like to see it and talk to the ranch hands if you don't have a problem with that."

"I don't have a problem with that." He gave him directions and Hank was soon driving out of town. He pulled through the gate at the ranch a short while later and drove up the two-mile long driveway toward the main house.

As he neared the ranch compound, he saw a long line of assorted trucks and cars parked along the drive. He pulled up behind the last one, parked, and got out. He walked toward the house.

The driveway ended in a circle in front of the house. In the center of the circle stood a monstrous red and black modern steel sculpture, rising directly out of the grass. Hank remembered a reference to it on the list of artwork that Saunders had bought over the years. It was one of the few big pieces that Saunders had bought that was actually worth more today than when he bought it. Hank looked at it for a few moments, trying to figure out what it was, thinking it looked upside down. He gave up and walked over to a small group of men who were standing on the grass smoking and talking among themselves.

Rebuilding had begun on the center and west end of the building where the fire had done the most damage. The rough framing of the first two floors had been completed. Workers were milling about and Hank couldn't tell who was a construction worker and who was a ranch hand. He walked up to the nearest man and asked for Pete Tucker and was directed toward a tall solidly built man emerging from the barn.

"Pete Tucker?" Hank yelled over the noise.

"Yeah. Who wants to know?" He said over his shoulder without looking in Hank's direction. "Hey, Greg!" he yelled at a man apparently still hidden somewhere inside the barn. "We need to get her ready now. The new owner will be here any minute." He spun around to face Hank.

Hank gave him a quizzical look.

"We're selling Love Child, Mr. Saunders's prize stud horse to Ricky Ganter at the next ranch over. He always loved that horse. He was always pestering Mr. Saunders to sell her."

"Could I ask you a few questions?"

"Are you a cop or a reporter?" Hank introduced himself. "Okay. What do you want to know?"

"More about the night that your boss died, but could we go someplace quieter?"

"There ain't no place quieter, not with all the construction going on." He looked around. "Okay. Let's go into the bunkhouse over there." He pointed to a large single-story building. The high pitched roof, which had a row of dormers sticking out of it, also sheltered a raised porch that ran the entire length of the front of the building. They climbed the three stairs, crossed the porch, and entered a large common room with a dining table and chairs down the middle and a half-dozen overstuffed armchairs at one end forming a semicircle around a large-screen TV.

"Okay, shoot," Pete said as soon as the door closed. Despite his earlier comment, the noise level was markedly lower.

"I was just wondering whether Mr. Saunders had any guests the day he died."

"Nope. Not that I was aware of. None of the boys saw anyone either. It's just like we told the police."

"Could someone have come up here after you left?"

"Could be, but then I wouldn't know, now, would I?"

"I suppose that's true. Did Mr. Saunders ever have meetings here where he asked you all to leave so you wouldn't meet his guests?"

"Once or twice that I can remember."

"Who?"

"Lady friends, but that was when he didn't want the missus to find out, if you get my drift." Pete winked.

"Was there anybody else?"

"Nah."

"Was that night one of those times?"

"You kidding? Mr. Saunders's been divorced for years. He didn't need to hide that anymore. Mind you, I doubt that Mrs. Saunders was fooled for a moment."

Hank nodded. "When was the last time his wife was here?"

"Oh, she came out here every once in a while. That was part of their divorce agreement. She could use the place a few times a year. It was supposed to be only when Mr. Saunders wasn't using it."

"Were they ever here together?"

"Yeah. She was here a month or so before he died. She showed up unannounced with her new boyfriend and some friends. Whoooeeee. You should have seen it!"

"What happened?"

"They were like two polecats going at it," Pete said, hands raised shoulder height, fingers outstretched like claws, "if you know what I mean. He tells her to stay away, says he's going to ask the judge to change the decree granting her rights to the place. She yells that she'll see him dead before she gives up the place." Pete stopped suddenly and wiped his chin with his sleeve. "She loved this place. Mr. Saunders bought it for her. I never understood why he held onto it."

Hank nodded. He knew why Saunders had kept it. Under Texas law, creditors couldn't take your house or your horse away from you in bankruptcy. "When did you all leave for town?"

"Like we told the police, it was around seven, maybe seven-fifteen."

"When did Mr. Saunders get here?"

"It was sometime in the late afternoon. I'd say four-thirty or so. We drove over from Dallas in the Hummer."

"We?"

"Yeah. I drove over and picked him up in Dallas. We drove back together right after I got him at the Hyatt."

"Then what?"

"What do you mean, then what?"

"I don't know. What did he do when he got here?"

"Went into the house and had an early dinner. Jackie, she's the cook, made him his favorite, mesquite steak and barbecue chicken with mashed potatoes."

"Anything unusual happen that night?"

He rubbed his chin for a moment or two. "Not that I can remember. Oh, yeah, I was a bit surprised Mr. Saunders had gone somewhere that night."

"How did you know that?"

"His Hummer wasn't in the garage any more. He parked it there when we got back to the ranch that afternoon"

"Do you know where he went?"

"No. Hey, I've got to get back to work." Pete thumbed, hitchhiker style, toward the courtyard. "Is there anything more?"

"Just a few more questions, if I may. Why did Mr. Saunders send you all into town?"

"I don't know, but we weren't going to complain, now were we? Not when it was on his tab."

"Did he do that often when he was here?"

"Not usually. He usually liked to have at least a few of us around. We'd play pool and drink beer. I think he preferred the company of real cowboys to the city folk he usually had to deal with."

"If I show you a few pictures, can you tell me if you've ever seen any of these people?"

Pete took the offered pile of pictures, looked at each one in turn, and then took out three and handed back the rest of them. "I've seen these guys. This here is Mr. Harden, Mr. Saunders's lawyer. Right? He's been up here a bunch of times. Don't remember this guy's name. He was Mexican, I think." He pointed to the picture of César Hernandez. "He was here last summer. I'm not sure exactly when." He flipped to the third picture, which was of Charlie Wong. "I don't know the name of this one either, but he was here a month or so before the fire."

"Are you sure?"

The foreman nodded.

"And none of them were here on the night of the fire?"

Pete shook his head. "Not that I saw."

"I've got just one last question. Do you think any of the other hands would recognize any of these others?" He held up the stack of pictures.

"I doubt it. Besides, there're not many of them here any more with Mr. Saunders's death and all. There ain't enough work to go around any more."

"Could I leave them with you just in case?"

"Sure, but I'm not promising anything."

"Here's my card in case you think of anything else."

The drive back down the driveway was much harder to navigate now that the sun had gone down. There were no lines or markers to show where the drive ended, and there were no lights anywhere to be seen. It was as dark as anything Hank had ever encountered. More than once, he felt the tires leave the gravel as he missed a turn. A long ten minutes later, he reached the road and took a left to get back to the highway to San Antonio.

Three hours later, he pulled into the Holiday Inn on the outskirts of San Antonio where his secretary had booked him a room. After dumping his suitcase in his room, he walked across the street to a Chinese restaurant for a quick late supper. He finished the meal and opened his fortune cookie. It read, "Reflection will reveal your inner desire." What the hell did that mean?

CHAPTER 19

▼

TUESDAY, DECEMBER 5

Hank left his room and went down to the lobby. An overly friendly manager showed him where to find the University of Texas on a map he pulled out from under the counter. Hank pocketed the map, thanked the manager, and scooted out of the hotel.

The university was nearly all the way across town. He parked in front of the Forensics Center. The receptionist directed him to the small cafeteria at the rear of the building where Dr. Pendergast usually had breakfast at that time in the morning.

"Dr. Pendergast?" Hank said to a man sitting by himself at the table nearest the entrance. The man looked up, confused.

"Over here," a man at a table near the back said.

The woman sitting next to him stood up. "Brian, I'll see you later," she said and walked over to the window to return her tray. She nodded politely as she passed Hank.

Hank walked to the table, introduced himself, and sat down.

"I'm sorry to interrupt your breakfast, but they told me you'd be leaving soon for a conference in New Orleans. Could I ask you a few questions about the Saunders autopsy?"

"Okay," the doctor shrugged. He took a gulp of orange juice and a bite of an English muffin smothered in strawberry jam. "As long as you don't mind if I eat while we talk. I've got to get back and finish a report before I leave."

"Not at all. I just want to find out more about your identification of the body, particularly the DNA testing you did."

"There's not much to say about it," the doctor said, before describing the procedure of recovering the DNA from the burned body in gory detail. "Fortunately, we got lucky on the reference sample. As you probably know by now, Saunders had given a DNA sample some years back. So we didn't have to worry about a reference sample. I was pretty confident without it, but I'm not sure that we would have been able to make a positive identification without the DNA tests."

"Any chance there was an error."

The doctor bristled at the suggestion. "No! No chance."

"Sorry. I didn't mean to imply anything. It's just that I read this article."

"Oh, not that Indiana woman and the toes thing again? The old bat was just plain wrong."

"I take it that you think that there's no way she could be right?" Hank wished he had had a chance to interview Edna Grouse.

"You take it right!"

"What about the mix-up with the X-rays? Were they…"

"What about it?" Pendergast cut him off. "The tags were just laid down on the film wrong. I didn't really need them for the autopsy."

"Really, why not?"

"No entrance or exit wounds anywhere. He had a little emphysema, but that wasn't what killed him, was it?" The doctor laughed. "So, the pictures weren't used for the cause of death or the ID."

"So, you're one hundred percent sure the victim was Ted Saunders?"

"No, nothing in this business is one hundred percent, but this is as close as it gets. I'm sorry, but I've got to get back to work." He abruptly pushed his chair back, stood up, grabbed his coffee, and walked away, leaving the tray on the table. Hank watched him go, deciding that he wasn't likely to get anything else from him.

Hank drove out to the airport, returned the Jeep, and checked in at the e-ticket kiosk in the terminal. Security went without incident and he found his gate with more than two hours until his flight. He found a seat by the window and called Alyson. He told her about his visits and that he hadn't made any real progress, except for the tidbit about how Saunders would send everyone away from the ranch if he wanted a tryst. Hank speculated that maybe he did it for other guests.

"So, how'd your search go?" Hank asked.

"About as good as yours," Alyson said.

"Did you get anything on Charlie Wong? The manager out at the ranch said he had been out there about a month ago."

"Wait. The manager said he'd been out there?"

"Yes. Why?"

"Charlie told me he had never been out to the ranch."

"Why would he lie about that? Unless he was out there the night of the murder."

"I don't think so. He says he was in Atlanta that day and left for Bermuda at noon the next day. He said he had a meeting and then had dinner alone in Atlanta that night. We haven't found any record of him charging a dinner that night anywhere in Atlanta."

"Maybe that's because he wasn't in Atlanta that night."

"He could've paid cash for dinner," Alyson offered.

"Unlikely. Who pays cash these days?"

"People do sometimes. We're still checking on it."

"Okay, we know he left the States from Atlanta. Could he get out to Texas and back overnight?"

"Hold on. Let me check." Alyson pulled up an online travel reservation site and put in a search for a round-trip from Atlanta to San Antonio, the closest big city to the ranch, using that day's date. She would have liked to use the day of the murder, but the system didn't allow post-dating of flights. No flights to and from San Antonio would work.

She tried Dallas next, since both Dallas and Atlanta were hub cities for a number of airlines airline. There were a number of flights that might work, but not when you tacked on the long drive needed to get out to the ranch before the ranch hands got back from town. None of the flights to El Paso worked. She then tried Austin. Even though it was the state capital, there were not a lot of flights to choose from. Finally, she tried Abilene. After the last search, she said, "He couldn't make the trip. There's no flight he could take to get out there and back to Atlanta in time for the flight to Bermuda."

"Damn," Hank said. "It looks like we can cross Charlie off the list."

CHAPTER 20

▼

WEDNESDAY, DECEMBER 6

"So, what have you got?" Alyson asked Fred as he walked into her office.

"Do you know how many airports there are in Costa Rica?"

"I don't know. Two?"

"One hundred and forty-five!" He waited a moment to enjoy her incredulous look. "Fortunately, there's no more than five, depending on takeoff weight, that have a runway long enough for a G-IV."

"Really?"

"I talked to the firm that operates the company plane. They weren't aware of any flight to Panama. As far as they know, the plane sat on the ground the whole time. The tower log confirmed it."

"So, we can rule out the company plane. Did you look at commercial flights?"

"Yes, but no Ted Saunders."

"What a surprise. Were you able to get the passenger lists?"

"Yeah, but I had to pull a few strings. I probably broke a number of laws too, but here are lists." He handed her a short stack of paper. "There're seven people making the round trip. Only two were men."

"Hmmm," she murmured scanning the lists. "There was an Edward G. Sanders on the COPA flight from San José to Panama City on the sixth who flew back to San José on the eighth."

"So?"

"I'm not sure, but I've got a hunch we've just found Ted Saunders."

"Why?"

"If it's what I think it is, Ed Sanders is our man."

"I wondered about Sanders, but I thought it would be a bit too obvious."

"Only if someone knew to look for him on those flights."

"But why not take a common name like *John Smith* or something a lot different from Ted Saunders?"

"Why? If you're going to change your name, you've got to change it in a way so you don't screw it up, but make it different enough to miss any sweeps looking for a match on your name. Whatever you change it to, you need to be responsive when someone calls you by it. If your new signature is enough of a scrawl, a similar name could even cover a mistake in signing your name."

"Cool."

"Check out Sanders's nationality for me while you're at it."

"Why?"

"Just humor me."

Fred left with a puzzled look on his face.

Twenty minutes later, Fred waltzed into her office and plopped down in the chair. "You'll never guess what Sanders's nationality is." Fred sat still, waiting with a smug look on his face.

"Belizean. Or whatever you call someone from Belize."

Fred's face fell. "How the hell did you know that?"

"A guess," Alyson said. "But an educated guess. I'm pretty sure Saunders took a trip to Belize."

"That's right. He flew down there for a week of scuba diving after his last trip to Mexico."

"That's it! Now I remember."

"He went there to close some natural gas deal or something. There was a big ceremony, lots of government muck-a-mucks. After it was all over, he hopped over to Belize. The diving's supposed to be about the best in the world."

"I've heard that too. Do you know what else Belize is known for?"

"No." He sat forward in the chair.

"Did you know that Belize offers citizenship to anyone with enough money to make a sizeable investment there?"

"Really! Why would they do that?"

"They're looking for capital investment. It makes sense for them to offer an incentive. It's not illegal to have dual citizenship."

"I know, but," he left the statement hanging in the air. "I still don't understand. How would having a second citizenship help Saunders hide his money?"

"Well, we talked about the possibility that he'd want a new identity to go with the money. Right?"

"Yeah. So?"

"All along I had been thinking he'd take a new U.S. identity, but taking a non-U.S. identity makes more sense. It fits with hiding the money offshore."

"That's true, I guess," Fred said.

"If I'm right and he wanted to have something other than U.S. citizenship, Belize would be an easy one to get. There's no residency requirement like in some other countries, and, with enough cash, he could buy a new identity too."

"You think he was planning to go into hiding overseas?"

"I don't know." Alyson stopped to think that through. "That's certainly one possibility. Maybe he simply planned to keep the cash under a separate name so he didn't have to explain it to anyone."

"But why would he need new citizenship? Why not just set up accounts in the new name?"

"Banks, even in places like Panama or the Cayman Islands, want identification to set up new accounts. And, they'd certainly want some form of identification before they hand over any money. If you're going to go through all the bother of setting up new accounts, you might as well do it as a citizen of another country. A passport is accepted just about everywhere as proof of identity, even one from Belize."

"So, Ed Sanders is Ted Saunders."

"Maybe."

"What do you mean *maybe*?"

"It's just that we shouldn't jump to any quick conclusions. We'd better keep checking. What about charter flights?"

"He could've taken off from any one of about twenty airports near the Nicoya Peninsula," Fred said, much of the enthusiasm vanished from his voice. "There's pretty heavy control over that airspace because of the recent efforts to stop drugs so there'd probably be some record of a flight to Panama from there. Those planes would probably not be the safest things in the world and I'm not sure that he'd want to take the risk of crashing into the mountains down there."

"It might've been safer than a trip to Texas," Alyson said.

Fred grinned. "I'll check into it. I'm not sure if I'll find anything, but I'll see what I can get."

"Great. Don't get too excited about Ed Sanders, at least not yet," Alyson warned him. "See if you can find any Edward G. Sanders in any of the Belize phone books."

"Gotcha." Fred stood up and headed for the door.

"Hey," Alyson said. Fred turned around. "Check into the scuba diving. See if he was certified. See if he actually went diving."

Fred stood up.

"Did you get anything on those calls?"

"Not yet. I'm having a hard time with their system."

"Well, keep working on it."

Fred nodded and strode off down the hall.

Alyson was left alone in her office. If Saunders had planned to create a new identity, he'd want to change his appearance as much as he could. It's hard to disappear without changing your looks, otherwise you're too likely to be recognized by someone, sometime. She picked up the phone.

"Mr. Harden, this is Alyson Murphy."

"Yes. How can I help you?" the lawyer said stiffly.

"Did you notice anything different about the way Mr. Saunders looked when he came back from his trip to Belize?"

"What do you mean? He was tan, if that's what you mean. I was extremely jealous. I usually burn."

"Me too. No, I mean something other than a tan. Was there any change in his hair? Did he grow a beard? Anything like that?"

"Hmmm." Whit Harden thought for a moment. "His hair was a lot lighter. I guess the sun bleached it some."

"Was there anything else?"

"Not that I can think of."

"Do you know if anyone was with him on the trip?"

"I'm not sure why you're asking about this. What does a scuba trip have to do with finding the money?"

"We think he did more than just go on a scuba trip."

"Like what?"

"We're just exploring the possibility that he went to Belize to get a new identity."

"Oh, come on. I think you're taking this a bit too far, don't you?"

"Maybe, but I don't think so. We're checking out all possible paths."

"It sounds as if you're going after the impossible ones now," the lawyer said.

"We don't think that this one is impossible. Actually, we think it's very probable. That's why I'm asking about his appearance when he came back. If he were going to get a new identity, he'd want to change how he looked for his new passport."

"I think this is ridiculous."

"Is it? If we're right about his hiding his assets, it's not much of leap to think that he'd want to be able to spend it without anyone asking questions about it. Right? What do you think the authorities would do if they noticed that he was spending millions without any appreciable income to support that spending?"

"They'd ask a lot of questions and, depending on the answers, look for the source of the money."

"Exactly. So, he'd need a way to spend it without attracting attention, otherwise why bother? The easiest way would be to spend it under a different name."

"So, you think he'd need a new passport to do that?"

"He could probably make do without one, but it would make things a whole lot easier. They're relatively easy to come by. It would allow him to set up new accounts and transfer money."

"It sounds far-fetched, but...Going back to your earlier question, I didn't notice any changes other than his hair. You might want to talk to Betty Goodman. She went with him for the first few days in Mexico to help him get all the paperwork ready and to make the arrangements for the gas deal closing. Ted never trusted the lawyers and accountants to get all that stuff right. He always took her along to make sure everything was all arranged. It was a big PR event too. She flew back to New York after he left for Belize."

"Thanks. I'll give Betty a call."

She replaced the phone and pulled up her address book on her PC to look up Betty Goodman's number. As she reached for the phone, it rang.

"Alyson. This is Miguel."

"Miguel. I didn't expect to hear from you so soon." It was hard to hear him. There was the sound of traffic on his end of the call. She looked at her watch. It was now lunchtime in Panama.

"I know. I'm not done with my search, but there's one investment I wanted to *talk* to you about right away."

"Which one?"

"Argent Trading."

"Go on," Alyson said eagerly.

"It seems that Argent Trading was set up about a month before Saunders bought the mine in Peru. I checked with a friend of mine in the Ministerio de Economia y Finanzas in Peru. It appears that Argent Trading owned the Rio Colca Mine through a company called Colca Compañía de Minas S.A., which was in turn owned by another holding company called Grupo de Plata. Grupo de

Plata was owned by a rich family in Peru. That family had owned the mine for nearly one hundred years. Argent Trading sold the mine to Saunders."

"That's great. Do you know who owns Argent Trading?"

"Yes. Another company by the name of Panamanian Exporters. I'm having some difficulty tracking down the ultimate owner, but I should know that in a couple of days."

"Miguel. This is great. Let me know what you find out as soon as you can. Did you find anything about the other companies on the list?"

"Sure. I'll send that along soon."

"Gracias, Miguel."

"Alyson," his voice suddenly went somber. "You must be careful. I told you that Grupo de Plata had been family-owned."

"Yes."

"The family also exports a lot to the States."

"I see."

"No, I do not think you see. Its biggest export is cocaine."

"Oh. Um. Oh. I see. Thank you for the warning."

"Please be careful."

"I will. You too."

Alyson hung up and sat at her desk, not moving, trying to get her emotions under control. Why was Saunders doing business with a Peruvian drug family? That didn't make sense, not if you wanted to hide your money and live to enjoy it. There must be some explanation. A simple search for missing money was quickly turning into something else. She had had some doubts that Saunders was killed for the money, but now that was suddenly looking much more likely.

The screen on her PC flickered and the image changed to a picture of the Grand Canyon, which she had taken on her last vacation with girlfriends and now used as a screensaver. She hit alt-control-delete and typed in her password. She quickly found the number she needed and dialed.

"Betty Goodman speaking."

"Hi Betty, this is Alyson Murphy." She was struggling to get focused again.

"What can I do for you? Did you get the boxes of documents I sent over?"

"Yes, thank you. I understand you went down to Mexico with your boss last February."

"Yes."

"While you were in Mexico, did you notice any changes in your boss?"

"What do you mean by changes?"

"Oh, I don't know. Did he grow a beard or let his hair grow longer?"

"It's odd that you'd ask that."

"Why's that?"

"I had an argument with Ted about that exact thing. We had arranged for pictures to be taken at the closing ceremony. You know, a big photo op thing."

"What happened?"

"Well, he showed up in Mexico looking pretty grubby. He hadn't shaved for a couple of days. I told him our hosts would be offended, but he didn't seem to care. I had hoped that he would at least clean himself up for the big ceremony, but he didn't. I yelled at him that he looked a mess."

"What happened?"

"We took the pictures anyway, but we never used them. I gave them to Ted, but he decided not to use them in our annual report. We put in some pictures of the refinery and El Presidente of Mexico instead."

"Did he ever tell you why he did that?"

"He said something about a rash or something. I didn't see any sign of it, but I wasn't going to argue with my boss, was I? I had a devil of a time explaining it to everyone, but I think they accepted the rash story in the end."

"Were there any changes about his hair?"

"Not that I remember. It might've been a bit longer than usual, but he had been out at the ranch the week or so before. He always came back a little rough around the edges after being out there."

"Thanks."

"Why are you asking about his appearance?"

"We're trying to identify someone in a picture we found in the files. Someone thought it looked like Mr. Saunders, but he had long hair and a beard." She lied, not wanting to explain.

"Is there anything else you want to know?"

"No. Thank you." She hung up the phone. Okay, so there was a chance that Saunders had altered his appearance just before his trip to Belize. She had seen enough makeovers in magazines and on TV to know that it didn't take big changes to make someone look like a different person. A feeling of foreboding swept over her. If Saunders had been planning this as long as it now seemed, he would have had plenty of time to cover his tracks. Would they be able to find the money? She was no longer sure.

CHAPTER 21

▼

THURSDAY, DECEMBER 7

"Mr. Harden, it's good to see you again," Alyson said as she led the lawyer into her office.

"I hope my stopping by unannounced is not an inconvenience."

"Of course not."

"I know you're busy, but I was in the city on other business and thought I'd stop in for an update. How's the search going?"

"Well. If you'll wait a second, I can print out my notes and a spreadsheet with the numbers." A short while later she pushed the papers across the table to the lawyer.

"I'd like you to walk me through this. I'm a good lawyer, but I'm not so good at all the financial mumbo jumbo."

Alyson described the progress they had made in tracking down the assets. She explained how Saunders had used a series of back-to-back sales to inflate the value of an asset. In most cases, he used multiple layers of companies to hide the true ultimate ownership.

"For most of the investments where there is still value in the underlying asset, he had borrowed heavily to make the purchase. Sometimes using his GenergTex stock as collateral, but usually the loans were collateralized by the asset only or by his personal pledge. For example, the ranch in Texas had a conventional mortgage. The yacht in St. Pete's also had a mortgage."

"What about these?" Harden asked impatiently, pointing to a separate list of assets.

"These investments were typically paid for with cash. Usually from the sale of GenergTex stock that he dumped."

"He didn't *dump* any stock," the lawyer stated emphatically.

"Of course. In any event, he bought these with the proceeds of his sales of GenergTex stock."

"So?"

"It appears that he sold stock before making an investment in each of these and used the cash to make the actual investment. He had to write off the investment in each case shortly after making the actual investment. This pattern fits our theory. Not a single investment made with borrowed money turned out to be worthless like these did."

"That doesn't mean he meant to lose money on them. Maybe the banks would only put money into better investments."

"That might be true, but we don't think so."

"What else have you found?"

"We believe he chose Panama because it's so easy to set up new companies and the country's confidentiality laws are among the strictest in the world, making it almost impossible to find out who really owns the company or trust."

"So, do you know who owns all these companies?" Harden waved his hand over the lists on the table.

"We're close, but it will take a while to determine the true ownership of the parent company."

"I see. So, you really don't have any proof that my client was involved."

"We believe he was, but, no, we don't have *proof* yet."

"And his name wasn't listed anywhere."

"No, but this all fits with our theory and the dates match."

"What dates?"

"We checked your client's credit card and phone records. Did you know Mr. Saunders went to Costa Rica?"

"Of course. GenergTex made a sizeable donation to the Parque Nacional d'Ecologia to protect the ecological preserves in Costa Rica. He was there to present the check to the director of the park."

"True, but did you know that he made a side trip to Panama while he was there?"

"No. When?"

"He went there for a couple of days at the end of the trip when he was supposedly on vacation in Playa Carrillo on the Nicoya Peninsula. The date of that trip matched up with the date of incorporation of some companies we're looking at and the Panamanian trust used in the Argent deal. We believe we'll find that the rest of the deals had companies formed at the same time."

"I don't remember Ted mentioning a trip to Panama," Whit Harden said.

"I'm not surprised. If he were really planning what we're talking about, he wouldn't want anyone to know about that trip. That would especially apply to his lawyer."

"So how do you know he was there?"

"He received a call on his cell phone."

"You place him there on the basis of a phone call?"

"Yes. His secretary says he never goes anywhere without it and he'd never give it to anyone else."

"That's true, I suppose. Were there any other traces of him being there? He would've had to use his credit card there too."

"Not necessarily. Our review of his bank records showed that he took out almost fifty thousand dollars in cash during the week before that trip. That'd be enough for a couple of days and leave plenty left over to set things up down there."

Harden picked up the papers Alyson had given him and read through them again.

Alyson waited until he put them down. "We saw an e-mail from Mr. Saunders to you asking about setting up a company in Panama about eighteen months ago. Do you remember that?"

"Yes. GenergTex was setting up a company there to own a Colombian hydro-electric plant on the Rio Rosada River. GenergTex only had gas-powered turbines down there and it wanted to build a couple of hydro plants as a hedge for its gas-fired plants."

"So, none of that was personal?"

"No, not at all."

"Well, we think that deal may have given Mr. Saunders either the idea to set up this scheme in Panama or the necessary legal knowledge to set it in motion."

"That's a leap, don't you think?" the lawyer protested.

"Not really. Is that where you learned of Banks, Brown and Martinez?"

"No. I've used them many times in the past. Why do you ask?"

"Did you recommend that firm to Mr. Saunders?"

"Of course. Why?"

"They were involved in most of the personal investments that went sour."

"Is all of this in here?" The lawyer asked, pointing to the stack of printouts. Alyson nodded. He picked up the papers and reached down for his briefcase. "Hmmpf." He shook his head and shuffled through the pages again. "I think I've heard enough for today. I've got another appointment in midtown and have to get going."

"Before you go, there's one other thing I'd like to bring up with you."

"What is that?"

"I'd like your permission to fly down to Panama," she said, biting her lip.

"What? Why?"

Alyson took a deep breath and said, "I need to go there in person to find the money."

"Do you know it's there?"

"No, but I'm pretty sure it's there."

"Can't you find it from here?"

"No!" Alyson said, losing her temper slightly.

"Isn't this something you can do over the Internet or by phone?"

"We can do a lot of it that way. In fact, we've done a lot that way so far. It's why I'm recommending I go now rather than a week ago. We now have enough to make the trip worthwhile."

"In what way?"

"First off, as I told you, we know that a number of the assets your client bought were owned by companies in Panama. As I said, we believe that the money is still there."

"I still don't buy this. You keep saying you believe it's there, but you haven't convinced me."

"Well, sir, we believe he used Panama because it has good communications, including online banking so he could get his hands on the money when he needed it. They use the U.S. dollar as a local currency and they have, as I've said, some of the strictest privacy laws in the world. Something Mr. Saunders would want if he wanted to keep the cash hidden. We know that he went to Panama. Secretively. We think that he went there to set up his accounts. We're not aware of any other trips out of the U.S. to any other money-laundering havens. Are you?"

"No, but then I didn't know about Panama either."

"Fair enough, but there weren't any other unexplained absences. We checked with Betty Goodman and she wasn't aware of any."

"Okay, so it's an attractive place to leave money and some or all of the money could still be there, but that doesn't explain why you have to go down there."

"As I told you before, we think that Mr. Saunders hid the money under an alias. We need to show his pictures around and see if we're right. We simply can't do that long distance. The people we need to show it to won't even talk to us long distance, let alone identify someone."

"Why not?"

"The whole reason Panama has grown into a financial center is its reputation for confidentiality. The only way to break that down is in person and with an open wallet."

"I don't think I want to hear this."

"You might not, but it's the way business in my profession is sometimes done."

"That may be, but it's still illegal."

"Don't tell me that you don't sometimes have to pay for expert witnesses or help in support of your cases."

"But, that's not the same."

"Perhaps not, but there's one resource that we desperately need and he's both expensive and wants only cash. He works in the government. I've asked him to track down all the ownership of any of the companies that Saunders bought assets from."

Harden sat back in the chair, fixing his gaze on her.

"We also still think that Mr. Saunders went to Belize for a new identity."

"Not that again!"

"We've determined that a man named Ed Sanders went from Costa Rica to Panama on the right days, and he held a Belize passport."

"That proves nothing!"

"Did you know your client took nearly one hundred thousand dollars in cash out of the bank in the weeks leading up to his scuba trip?"

"So?"

"We think he used that money as part of getting a new identity."

"You don't know that's what he used the money for."

"Can you think of any other explanation? Maybe it was a payoff for the Mexican deal? That's the only other thing we could think of."

"I don't believe he would do either."

"Maybe, maybe not. But we think that the two trips point to his using Panama as part of his scheme."

"What scheme? I don't think you've proven that a scheme existed. You certainly haven't made a case for a trip to Panama."

"Mr. Harden. I know you don't want to spend money needlessly, but my professional opinion is that I need to go there."

"It's not just the money. I still think that this whole thing is a damn wild goose chase."

"I'm more convinced than ever that this *isn't* a wild goose chase."

"Well, I think you need a lot more to convince me to authorize you to go down there."

"But…" Alyson stopped, realizing that it was pointless to argue further. It wouldn't help her case if Harden got angry. She had made her case and didn't have any more arguments at this point.

"If you find out more and show me that such a trip is necessary, then maybe I'll authorize it. Until then? No!" He gathered the pages, put them in his briefcase, and stood up. "So, unless there's more, I think we're finished. Thank you, Ms. Murphy." He shook her hand and marched out of the office, but then turned back at the door and said, "Thank you again. Keep me updated."

Alyson plopped down in her chair and sat staring out the window. She thought back over the conversation with Saunders's lawyer and felt that she had made a strong case for going to Panama. Hank and she had gone over it and thought it was clear why she had to go. But, Harden hadn't bought it. Why, she wondered. Was their case not strong enough or was there some other reason? Harden certainly couldn't believe that much in his client's innocence, could he? She doubted it.

After running through it again, she was more convinced than ever that Saunders had been planning to disappear under a new name so that he could spend the money he had hidden, and Panama had everything going for it. The last place he'd want to go was somewhere where he might be seen by people he knew. Of course, there were a lot of places that he could go where he was unlikely to meet people who knew him as Ted Saunders, but most of them would be unattractive in many ways, like having civil wars, disease, and poverty. Panama had all the advantages she had mentioned to Harden. It had the added advantage that, other than cruising through the Canal, few Americas went there. And, most of those who did were either trying to hide their money, or themselves, or both. It would be highly unlikely that he would run into anyone down there who knew him. That was where he was going and that was where the money was.

She was sure of it. But, to prove that Ed Sanders and Ted Saunders were the same person and that Saunders was planning to make a new life for himself in

Panama, she would have go to Panama. And Harden had just told her she couldn't go. Could she go against her client's wishes?

She knew the answer to that.

CHAPTER 22

▼

FRIDAY, DECEMBER 8

"Are you interested in anything from Starbucks?" Fred asked from the open doorway of Alyson's office.

Alyson jumped.

"Sorry. I didn't mean to scare you. Do you want anything from Starbucks?"

"No thanks."

"I saw Harden in here yesterday. What did he want?"

"Oh, he was in town and stopped by for an update."

"Did you ask him about Panama?" Alyson frowned. "He turned you down, huh?"

"Yup."

"Not a surprise. I don't trust the guy."

"You still think he had a hand in Saunders's murder." It was more of a question than a statement.

"As much as ever. Why don't you?"

"I just can't believe he'd do that."

"But…" Alyson raised her hand to cut him off. They had argued about this more than she needed.

"Now what?" Fred asked.

"Well, I've got reservations for a Sunday afternoon flight. At this point, I see no reason not to be on it."

"You're going anyway?"

"I need to go. I wasn't kidding him when I told Harden that." She looked out the window again and said, "You know, I don't really need his permission."

"That may be, but if Harden finds out he'll be pissed."

"Then we'll work real hard to make sure he doesn't find out, at least not until I find the money."

"Trust me, if you bring home one hundred million dollars, he'll forget all about it."

"That's what I think. And I won't bring it home if we don't act. I'm afraid the money might go missing if it sits there too long. Someone might put two and two together and try to take it. And, if the killer figures out we're looking for the money and he has access to it, it'll be gone for sure."

"Won't that make the trip dangerous?"

"Maybe, but I'm counting on the fact no one knows we're looking for it yet."

"But Harden knows. You just told him for god's sake!" Fred said.

"But he won't know I'm down there now, will he?"

"Sure he will."

"He just told me not to go and, as far as he knows, I would never disobey a direct order from a client, now would I?" She grinned.

"Maybe I should go with you."

"No. I need you here to cover for me. Besides, Mark would kill me if I pulled you off the Cee Group project any more than I already have. He's already pressing me to give you back."

"What are you going to tell Mark?"

"I don't plan to tell him anything. I had a few days of vacation scheduled for next week anyway. I'm just changing my destination, that's all. Mark will never know unless someone screws up!" She glared at him.

"Not me. Never."

"Make sure you don't."

"You know, you shouldn't go alone. It's too dangerous."

"I'm not going alone. Hank's coming down on Tuesday. He's stopping in Belize first. The two of us will be safe enough."

"Hank's going, huh?" Fred said, with a smirk.

"It's not like that. He's just a reporter working on a story." Alyson blushed.

"*Right.*" He said, grinning from ear to ear.

Alyson blushed.

"What else did Harden say? Did he know about Saunders's trip to Panama and the company down there?"

"I don't think so. He said that Ted never mentioned it and I believed him."

"There were certainly e-mails about that company."

"He claimed they were about some GenergTex deal in Colombia."

"Right. I bet he's lying."

"Why do you say that!" Alyson said, getting annoyed at his insistence about the lawyer's involvement.

"He had to know about it. He was Saunders's lawyer."

"Not everyone tells their lawyer everything."

"Someone had to help Saunders put this all together." Fred said.

"But it didn't have to be Harden."

"Have it your way." Fred got up. "You sure you don't want anything from Starbucks?"

"No, thanks."

"You know," Fred blurted out. "I just had a thought. Maybe you shouldn't go to Panama?" Alyson frowned. "No, this is different. Really!"

"How?" She crossed her arms and waited for his explanation.

"Maybe he wants you to find the money."

"What's that supposed to mean? Of course he wants us to find the money."

"But why? Or, more accurately, for whom? No one else knows it's there."

"But we'll know."

"Yeah, but if we're not around, no one else will."

"Great," Alyson sighed. "Now, you've moved from him being a murderer to him being a mass murderer. Please stop. You've read too many murder mysteries."

"I'm serious."

"So am I! Go get your espresso. I've got to finish this up before I leave."

"Sure. Just watch your back down there." Fred marched out the door without looking back.

Alyson shook her head and returned her attention to the report she had been typing before Fred had stopped by.

An hour and a half later, Alyson spun in her chair away from the computer. The report on the screen was still a long way from being finished. Her thoughts kept wandering from the report to her conversation with Fred.

Why didn't she suspect Harden? Fred was right that Harden would likely have had access to Saunders's plan, but the surprise in Harden's voice when she first told him about the missing money and about Belize had seemed genuine. She was sure of it. Again, today, when he learned about Saunders's trip to Panama, there was real surprise, but something else as well. He certainly didn't seem surprised when she asked to go there.

What if she were wrong? If she were, going to Panama might just be the biggest mistake of her life. Alyson shuddered.

Alyson decided it was no use trying to finish the report. And, if she didn't leave soon, she'd be late. Hank had called earlier and wanted to get together tonight, but she already had dinner plans with Gavin. She had agreed to meet Hank for a quick drink before heading uptown for dinner with Gavin. She wasn't looking forward to the dinner. He wasn't going to be happy that she wasn't going out to California with him. But, drinks with Hank would make it easier.

She pushed back her chair and walked toward the elevator. Her step was light as she walked down the hall, Harden momentarily forgotten.

Ten minutes later, she walked into County Clare Restaurant and made her way through the crowd to the bar. "Sorry I'm late," she said to Hank, raising her voice to be heard over the din.

"That's okay. I just got here myself." He ordered her a Chardonnay.

"I've already called and set up a meeting with the Deputy Minister of the Immigration Service in Belize," Hank told her. "Hopefully, I'll be able to find out if Ed Sanders is who we think he is. He might even have a place there instead of Panama and we need to either eliminate or confirm that possibility. There're some leads I've dug up off the net."

"Good. Fred checked on his diving. It seems that Saunders is, um, was a diver. He got PADI certified about fifteen years ago. He did some serious diving for a while, but not in the last few years."

"Did he actually go diving while he was in Belize?"

"Yes, he went nearly every day."

"So, maybe it was just a coincidence. Maybe he just got an urge to dive again," Hank said with a shrug.

"I don't believe in coincidences like that."

"I don't either, but they do happen. I'll try to check that out when I'm down there too." Hank looked at her for a moment. "I think you should come with me. I'm not sure it's safe for you to go to Panama by yourself."

"We went through that on the phone earlier. I've got to meet Miguel on Monday. He's out of pocket the rest of the week. It's the only way."

"I know. I know. Okay. You go to Panama and I go to Belize. Just be careful," he said.

She looked at him with eyes that said "I'll be fine," then checked her watch. "I've got to run. I'm meeting someone for dinner," she said, gathering up her purse and briefcase and starting to force her way back out through the crowd. "I'll see you in Panama," she yelled back over her shoulder.

*   *   *   *

Dan Morris replayed the recording, then took off the headphones and sat still for a moment. So, Hank and Alyson were going to Panama anyway. He'd have to pass that news along. He picked up his cell phone, but stopped.

What had that other voice said? That Harden might want the money for himself. He mulled that over a number of times. What an interesting thought. Whoever had suggested it was right, only a few people even knew the money existed so only a few would know it was gone.

He sat still for a couple of minutes, lost in thought. He pursed his lips and shook his head. "Nah," he said.

Morris flipped open his cell phone and dialed.

*   *   *   *

"Mrs. Radcliffe called and will be fifteen minutes late. I know you want enough time with her so I bumped…"

The private line on his phone rang. "Excuse me, Kate." He hit the speaker-phone. Kate Morgan knew that if her boss had wanted her to leave, he would have waved his hand, so she stood still.

"Mr. Harden. This is Morris."

"What is it?" He glanced up at his secretary and sat back to listen.

"I just wanted to let you know that Miss Murphy seems determined to go to Panama."

"I know."

"She's booked on a flight on Sunday."

"Interesting! Even after I told her not to go. Oh, well. No matter."

"Do you want me to stop her?"

"No. This is perfect. Since I told her not to go, if anything happens down there, I can't be held responsible. Good."

"Okay. Just thought you'd like to know. Also, Hank Jenkins is planning to go with her. He's stopping in Belize first."

Hmmm. Hank Jenkins was certainly a wild card he hadn't counted on when he decided to hire Murphy, but this could be helpful. "Anything else?"

"Not at the moment."

"Thank you." He hung up.

Harden rubbed his chin a few times. This was good, he thought. Given the reporter's reputation, having him involved wouldn't hurt their chances of finding the money. That was what it was all about at this point.

"Ahem."

He looked up at Kate. "Now, where were we?"

She looked down at her pad. "I've bumped Jack Sturgis to five. He wasn't thrilled, but I told him it was an emergency." She had lied. He was a stickler for schedules and she didn't want him to make a scene.

"Thank you."

"Is it all right that I leave a little early tonight? I have an early dinner date."

"Is this with your gentleman friend that I just heard about? What's his name?"

"John Whitman." Out of nervous habit, she reached up and pulled back her shoulder-length dark brown hair and looped it behind her ear. Her other hand tightened its grip on the notebook she was holding.

"How come you've never told me about him before? I had to hear about him from Jenny, over a cup of coffee."

"It wasn't that serious."

"Is it serious now?"

"I think so," she blushed. "I've only been seeing him for a couple of weeks." Her whole face turned crimson.

"I'm sorry. I shouldn't pry. Have a nice dinner."

"Thank you." She left the office.

Harden's next appointment flew by quickly. Fortunately, it was an easy divorce case. The man and woman had signed a pretty airtight prenuptial agreement, which he had drawn up. The wife's attorney had been making noises about contesting it, but then decided to back down yesterday after Harden had pointed out to the wife, much to the annoyance of her attorney, that the offer his client had made would expire in twenty-four hours and what little she would get from her husband without taking the offer would be chewed up in legal fees.

Kate knocked at the door and announced Jack Sturgis, who stepped into the office behind her. She walked over to the desk, took the papers from the out tray, and waltzed out of the office. She quickly sorted the mail, placing about half in the outgoing mail bin, put the rest next to her notepad on her desk, grabbed her coat, and headed out the door.

Harden had never seen his secretary like that before. This John must be special. He hoped he'd get to meet him one day. His thoughts were interrupted by a sudden movement by Jack Sturgis, who was still standing by the door. Harden nodded to the accountant.

"I need to run over your billing hours on the Macarthur case," Sturgis said as he walked over to the desk. "Old man Macarthur thinks we overbilled him."

"Have a seat, Jack."

*   *   *   *

Hank reviewed the information on the screen, hit the confirm selection button, then typed in his credit card information and hit enter. Damn, this trip wasn't going to be cheap. He hoped that when he came back with a story, Adam would let him put all of the costs through on his expense report. In the meantime, he would have to do this on the cheap, including the rental car in Belize that was on his screen. He had wanted a full-size car, but that cost a couple hundred dollars more than a Suzuki Samurai. At least it was a sporty, two-door model rather than one of those small, dumpy compact cars you got from Avis or Hertz. Thank God for frequent flyer miles. He could get down there and back without spending anything, but a ski trip out west this year wasn't going to happen this year.

*   *   *   *

Alyson took a cab uptown to meet Gavin, who had called the day before and told her he was coming back to New York for an unexpected meeting. They had arranged dinner for tonight.

She stepped into the restaurant. Gavin was waiting by the maitre d' stand. He smiled as she came in. He looked every inch the investment banker he was. He was tall and athletically built, without being overtly muscular, and his hair looked like he had just stepped out of the salon. With his tailored dark blue, perfectly pressed pinstripe suit, white shirt starched just right, and power Armani tie, he looked liked he had just stepped out of the pages of *GQ*.

The maitre d' seated them at one of the best tables in the restaurant. The waiter strode over as soon as the maitre d' left the table.

"Bon soir, Mademoiselle. It is a pleasure to see you again, Monsieur Matthews."

"Good evening, Olivier."

"It has been a while, Monsieur."

"Yes. I've been away on business."

Olivier took their order and left.

Most of dinner was spent with Gavin complaining about how long the deal was taking, all in a tone that suggested he was happy to be part of it even as he complained. Each time she tried to change the subject, he found a way to return to his work.

Alyson had decided to wait until the end of dinner to break the bad news. Now that the dishes were being cleared, the time had come. Her mouth was suddenly parched. She drank the last sip of wine from her glass, gripped her napkin tightly, and blurted out, "I can't come with you to California on Saturday. I've got to go to Panama."

"What? You're going to Panama? Why?"

"Business!"

"You're not coming to California with me? It was all set."

"It was, but plans change." Yes, they do, she thought. In fact, next week's vacation was originally supposed to be in Lake Louise in the Canadian Rockies for some early skiing, but he had to be in California for his big deal. All of his deals were big, she had realized soon after they had met.

"Can't you go some other time?" Gavin frowned.

"No. I'm sorry, but it can't wait." That was so like him, she thought. It was okay for him to change their plans at the last minute because of work, but not her. "I'm working on a case that's got a really tight deadline. I'm afraid it can't wait."

"How long will you be gone?" he whined.

"The whole week," she said firmly.

"The whole week," he whined. "I don't want you to go."

"Why, Gavin, so I can be with you next week?"

"Yes."

"But would I? Will you take time off or will I be sitting around by myself while you work?"

He looked at her, not saying a word.

"I thought so." Her tone turned icy.

Olivier came back and asked if they wanted dessert, but could see from their faces that they did not. He quickly retreated.

Later, as he walked her to the door of her apartment, Gavin pulled Alyson close and to give her a good-night kiss, but she pulled away.

"I think we should say good night," she said. "You have an early long flight tomorrow."

"Are you sure?"

She nodded. She allowed him to kiss her cheek. He turned and walked slowly to the elevator.

She almost called him back. Not to stay, but to tell him about Hank. She bit her lip and said nothing. She didn't have the energy to explain about Hank. She stepped into her apartment. What would she have said about Hank had she brought it up? She didn't know.

CHAPTER 23

▼

SATURDAY, DECEMBER 9

The clock read 5:30 AM.

Her body felt warm and soft against his. John Blanchard could hear her breathing. So slow, so rhythmic, so soft. Her face looked almost young again, nowhere near its thirty-seven years. Sleep erased all evidence of cares and worries. Although she never believed him, he really did think she looked good without all the makeup she wore every day. There was a natural beauty in her skin, and her face was radiant, especially when she smiled. He lifted his arm from around her, scratched his neck, then curled his arm around her again. She stirred briefly and then went still again.

His thoughts returned to their lovemaking the night before. It had started tentatively at first, slowly caressing each other, exploring their bodies, becoming more and more frenetic as the night wore on. During their first time together, she had confessed that she had not been with many men before. Maybe because of that, each night they were together thereafter, she gave into their lovemaking with gusto, eager to learn how to be pleased and how to please. He had acted as her teacher at first, but now he was both teacher and pupil. Last night they had climaxed together after a long night of lovemaking. Exhausted, they had lain in each other's arms until they had both fallen asleep.

Lying there in the dark, he had to admit that he had begun to enjoy their nights together. What had started as a job had turned into much more, but he knew that he would have to end it soon, before it was too late. She had served her purpose, had told him what he and his employer needed to know. It wouldn't make sense to see her again. He wanted to, but that was, he knew, a sure way to get himself into trouble. It would be too easy to let something slip. He had to disappear, and she could not be part of that life. No one could. That was the price he had to pay for the career he had chosen.

Buzzzzz. She reached out and turned off the alarm. The blanket fell off as she rolled over to face him and she didn't bother to cover up. He caught sight of her breasts and he could feel himself getting aroused again. Sensing this, she reached down under the blanket and began to fondle him. He needed to get going, had lots to do that day, but his passion was rising again. He moved forward and kissed her again and pulled her tight to him.

The clock read 8:01 AM when they walked out the door of her apartment. She looked at him and smiled, totally unaware that this would be the last time she would see him. They walked to the Bethesda Metro station. They kissed at the top of the escalator and she ran down to hop on the subway that took her to her job at Garrison, Harden and Tilden. It was a shame, he thought, that she had had to go into the office on a Saturday. They could've spent a little more time together, but then again it was probably for the best. It would have been harder to break away.

When she disappeared from view, he walked back to where the blue Toyota Corolla he had rented was parked. He drove the five miles into Silver Springs, Maryland, where he had rented a furnished room for the last couple of weeks. Of course, *furnished* was in the eye of the beholder. The room had a bed, and a night table on which stood a ghastly art deco lamp. A small TV perched on a dresser. At one end of the room was a small, round Formica-topped table with two metal folding chairs that served as an eating area. Against the far wall stood a small cabinet where the plates and a couple of pots were kept. The hotplate on top allowed him to heat up food if he needed to. There was a small bath with a shower. He had to clean the dishes in the bathroom sink. There was a small closet tucked into the corner.

The best part of the room was the landlord took cash without asking any questions. It wasn't much, but at least the price was right. And, he could rent the room by the week.

On the round table was an IBM Thinkpad laptop hooked to the phone jack in the wall next to the bed. He turned on the computer, threw his clothes on the bed, walked into the bathroom, shaved, and took a shower. Putting on fresh clothes, he sat down at the computer and started composing an e-mail to his employer.

He had never met his employer, but in his line of work, it would have been highly unusual if he had done so. He usually communicated by phone, but that had changed a couple of weeks ago when his employer had switched to e-mail only. That wasn't as effective, but he was sure his employer had his reasons. It was certainly harder to trace e-mails than phone numbers, although that was changing rapidly. During their last phone call, he had been given an e-mail address to use, although he was sure that any message was probably forwarded a couple of times before it reached its final destination. He didn't care as long as he was paid, which, for all of his jobs, meant the cash was paid up front, including an advance on expenses.

Satisfied with the message, he logged onto his Internet service provider using a local access number. Once his homepage came up, he hit the send key. Within seconds, a confirmation message came up on the screen. He would now wait for a reply for thirty minutes. If he didn't get one in that timeframe, he knew he wouldn't get one until twenty-four hours later. He hopped up on the bed, grabbed a mystery novel and opened to the dog-eared page about halfway through, and waited.

*   *   *   *

Blanchard walked out of the room forty-five minutes later, there being no need to hang around any longer. He handed the key to the landlord, thanked him, loaded his two suitcases in the Corolla's trunk, and threw his briefcase containing his computer onto the backseat. He crawled in behind the wheel and drove off toward BWI Airport. He pulled into the return lot and parked, waited in the car until he saw the shuttle bus pull up to the front door of the small office building, got out, grabbed his bags, and climbed on board the bus. He got off at the stop for the airline he had mentioned to the driver, walked down the island, and waited for a shuttle bus to long-term parking. The next bus came a few minutes later. The long-term parking lot was the third stop. He walked to his own car, a late-model silver Mercedes CLK350 convertible, which he had parked there a couple of weeks earlier. He left the parking lot and hopped on I-95 North toward New England and his home in Vermont. He missed the cold, the snow, and the skiing. He was sure that Washington had its nice times of the year, but November wasn't one of them.

He sat in the long line waiting to pay the toll to get across the George Washington Bridge and thought about whether to get the new electronic pass that would allow him to avoid waiting in line for a tollbooth. It might save some time, but that would leave a record of his travel, something he preferred not to do. Sitting in traffic, inching forward every once in a while, he thought back to the response he had gotten to his e-mail. It had been short and told him that his services were no longer needed in Washington.

He was glad that the job was over. It had been long and tedious, with the only bright spot being Kate. The thought of her body lying next to his stirred him again. He closed his eyes tight to drive the image of her away. The car behind him honked. He opened his eyes and saw that the cars ahead of him had moved a couple of car lengths forward.

Blanchard pressed down gently on the gas and pulled forward, the thought of Kate not entirely lost. He hoped the note he had sent to her explaining that he was returning to a fictional wife and kids would stop her from looking for him, but even if she tried, she would never be able to locate a man who never existed. He knew she would be devastated, but that couldn't be helped.

Many hours later, Blanchard stepped into the front hall and dropped his two duffel bags on the floor. It was good to be home. It had been a long drive from Washington, made longer by an early snowfall around Hartford. He was sure that most of the other drivers were cursing the snow, but he loved it, even when it made driving a nightmare. The more the better as far as he was concerned.

He was looking forward to staying put for a while. He turned on the television, tuned to the sports channel to watch the end of the Bruins-Rangers game, and then walked into the kitchen, grabbed a beer out of the nearly empty refrigerator, and plopped down into an overstuffed chair. After the game, he reached down, pulled his PC out of briefcase, and walked over to the oval wrought iron glass-topped dining table at the far end of the large combined living and dining room. He pulled out one of the six matching chairs and sat down so he could look out at the mountains through the oversized windows that made up most of the wall at this end of the room.

As soon as he plugged in the power and slipped the Ethernet cable into the port on the rear of his computer, his PC beeped, indicating that he had new e-mails. He was surprised at the address of one of the e-mails. He clicked on it. The message appeared on the screen.

I want you to get down to Belize immediately. I have arranged a reservation on American Flight 455 out of Boston tomorrow, connecting in New York. Stay at the Queen Street Guesthouse. I'll send more later. Check for e-mail when you get there.
There might be additional work in Panama when you're done, but will let you know later.

The message ended with the agreed-on code that authenticated the message.

He was about to hit the reply key, but hesitated and stared out the window at the Green Mountains, now covered with a blanket of new snow. Even though it was dark and he couldn't see them clearly, they still held his imagination in their grip. He had grown up in the mountains, skiing all winter and hiking during the warmer months. He hadn't even left them when he went to college. The only time he had been away for any length of time was time he had spent in the Navy. After his tour was over, he had come back and tried to earn a living, but hadn't found anything he liked to do. The choice of staying or moving out of New England stared him in the face until one night ten years ago when someone he had met in the service needed him to take care of a little problem and was willing to pay handsomely for it to go away discretely. That job led to another and another, until taking care of problems became his full-time job. When problem-solving jobs were not available, he made a modest living as a security consultant.

Did he want to leave again so soon, having been away so much lately? He knew leaving the mountains he loved was just part of the job, but the more immediate and troubling question was whether he should do any more work for this employer. He had made it a policy to limit the amount of work he did for any one individual and rarely ever did repeat work. Although that cut into his potential client base, he made enough to live the way he wanted and still put away enough to provide a reasonably comfortable retirement someday. He knew that violating this rule was the easiest way to get into trouble; too much work for any one employer created connections that even he wasn't smart enough to foresee, let alone prevent. Someone smarter or just plain lucky might make those connections, and then his career, and possibly his life, would be finished. It just wasn't worth the risk.

He felt he had done enough for this one employer, more, actually, than he usually did. Should he risk doing more? Should he tell him he was unavailable? Did it matter the job was in Belize or Panama? He doubted that anyone would be able to connect a job in Belize with his other recent work. The thought of going back to Panama was intriguing.

It would be the first time he'd been back to Central America since he was in Panama helping to oust Manuel Noriega in 1989 as part of *Operation Just Cause*. He and his Seals team had gone in ahead of the main U.S. force to soften up Noriega's Defense Force and to scout out the country. That fight had ended quickly and turned into a farce when Noriega took refuge in the compound of the Vatican embassy. He'd enjoy going back, but this would be it. He resolved that there would be no other jobs for this employer.

He sent a quick reply indicating that he accepted the job, but suggesting a higher fee than his usual scale, knowing it would be accepted, and then deleted the original e-mail. He got up and quickly threw a bag together with enough clothes for three or four days. He would drive down to Boston in the morning. At least he'd have one night at home.

CHAPTER 24

▼

SUNDAY, DECEMBER 10

The jet rolled up to the jetway at Philip Goldson International Airport outside Belize City. John Blanchard, traveling under the name of John Olsen, waited for the plane to be nearly empty before grabbing his bag out of the overhead bin.

The lines still snaked through the immigration hall when he got there. Most people would be unhappy at the thought of waiting, but he preferred being near the end of the line. That way, he reached the immigration officials when they were tired and just wanted to get the line over with. He handed over his U.S. passport and immigration form. The officer behind the counter took the passport, stamped it and the form without much more than a glance, handed them back, and waved him along.

Blanchard quickly found his way to the rental car counter, presented his John Olsen license and credit card to the woman and was soon driving south on the Northern Highway into Belize City.

He pulled up in front of the Queen Street Guesthouse, handed the keys to bellman standing outside, and strode inside.

The Queen Street Guesthouse was a large old Caribbean-style mansion that had clearly been quite elegant in its day, but had seen better times. That suited him just fine. He never stayed at ritzy hotels, as that could draw too much attention to himself, but, on the other hand, he never stayed at flea traps either. He quickly learned that his employers weren't too concerned about expenses, as long as the problem he had been asked to solve was indeed solved.

He was pleased to see, despite the somewhat rundown feel of the hotel, that his room had an Internet connection. He pulled out his computer, connected to the Net, and called up his e-mail. There were a number of messages. He read one with more interest than the others:

> *The man in the picture (download the attachment) is Hank Jenkins. He's in Belize now, staying at the Hotel Victoria on Marine Parade. He is looking into things that he shouldn't and I would like him stopped. My greatest desire is that he stay in Belize. Permanently.*

That shouldn't be much of a problem.

> *He will only be in Belize until Tuesday.*

No wonder his employer made him come down here so soon. He wouldn't have much time. He would have to look for an opening quickly. Hopefully, his target didn't suspect that someone would be here looking for him and he'd have the advantage of surprise.

> *Send me an e-mail when you're finished.*

He hit the download button and opened the JPEG file. The image of Hank Jenkins appeared on the screen. He blew the picture up to full-screen size and sat there for many minutes scanning every feature, burning the image into his memory so there would be no need to carry the picture with him, but, at the same time, making sure that there would be no mistake. He couldn't afford to make any in his business. Once he was sure the picture was in his mind, he closed the file without saving it. He then sent an acknowledgement and shut down his computer.

Blanchard rose from the bed, leaving the laptop lying there, and crossed the room to the windows. He turned the antique latch and pushed. The windows resisted being opened, but finally yielded, the hinges howling in protest. He ignored the sudden change in temperature as the warm, humid outside air replaced the cool air-conditioned air in the room.

He took in the city before him, trying to get his bearings. He knew from the country guide he had studied on the flight that Haulover Creek, directly below his window, ran through the city and effectively cut it in two. Across the river was the business district. On his side of the river was the more historical area of Fort

George and the Newtown Barracks. It was there that Hank Jenkins's hotel was located.

He wrestled the windows shut and relatched them. He changed clothes and left his room.

To accomplish his mission in the timeframe given, he would have to act fast and he'd have to improvise. Although trained to improvise, he preferred jobs that allowed him time to plan out the mission in detail and to choose where and when to carry it out. The where and when of this mission would present themselves and he would have to be ready. He'd have to begin immediately.

Blanchard left the hotel and wandered the streets looking for the seedier parts of town. He would have to ask around carefully for what he needed, but he was sure it would not take too long to find it.

*   *   *   *

Blanchard parked his car behind a shoulder-high overgrown hedge. The hot humid air weighed on him as he stepped from the car and advanced down the street to the agreed rendezvous point, keeping to the shadows as much as possible. He checked his watch. Good, he thought, he was there ten minutes early. He stepped behind a tree and surveyed the street.

There was sudden movement in the shadows. Blanchard became instantly on guard, ready to strike. A man stepped out of the shadows across the road. The light of a nearby street lamp illuminated the man's face and Blanchard could see it was the man he had met an hour earlier at Bluebeard's Bar. He called himself Henry, but Blanchard doubted that was his real name.

Blanchard waited a couple of minutes, watching the man. He stepped out into the light.

"Ah, you are right on time," the man said. "That is good."

"And you."

"Do you have the money?"

"Yes." Good, Blanchard thought, this man was going to be professional and dispense with the small talk. They both wanted to keep this meeting as brief as possible. He slowly reached into the pocket of his dark blue linen blazer and pulled out an envelope. It contained twelve one-hundred-dollar bills, the agreed-upon price. It was a lot to pay for what he needed. It would have probably cost somewhere between seven and eight hundred dollars in the States, but beggars couldn't be choosers, especially when time was an issue. His employer wanted this to happen here, not in the States. He handed his employer the envelope.

The man called Henry put it into the back pocket of his pants without counting it and pulled a Beretta model 92F 9mm semiautomatic pistol from the waist of his pants behind his back and pointed it menacingly in Blanchard's direction. He could see that the safety was off, but didn't know whether a round was chambered or not. He stood there without any visible reaction, although his mind was racing, readying his body to move in case he saw the man's finger so much as twitch.

"Ha, ha, ha," the salesman suddenly burst out laughing, flipped the safety on with his thumb, and released his grip on the gun, letting it spin so it dangled on his finger by the trigger guard. All the time the gun was pointed at him, Blanchard had appeared to remain motionless, but his muscles had tensed and he had nearly lashed out when he heard the laugh.

"Here you go. It's the best on the market, genuine U.S. government issue." The man handed over the pistol and reached into his coat pocket and pulled out two fully loaded extra clips and handed them over too.

Blanchard pulled back the slide, chambering a round, clicked off the safety again, pointed it directly at the man's head, and held it there for a few seconds. The man's eyes went wide, riveted on the black hole at the tip of the muzzle. Seconds ticked by. Although the man didn't move, small beads of sweat ran down his forehead.

Click. The safety was pushed back on and Blanchard lowered the gun. "Thank you. This is just what I ordered."

The man visibly sagged as soon as the gun was no longer aimed at his head. Drops of sweat ran down his cheeks, but he did not reach up to wipe them away.

Blanchard hadn't used a Beretta since he left the Navy. It was an exceptional weapon, with excellent stopping power due to its high muzzle velocity. The gun felt good in his hand. The ten-round clip would be more than he needed, but he never liked to leave anything to chance. The two extra clips were insurance. He rarely ever bothered with firearms, relying instead on his hands or commando knife, which was usually all he needed if he did his job correctly.

Reaching into his pocket slowly, careful now not to alarm his client, the salesman pulled out a small plastic bag filled with smaller bags of white powder. "You asked for these also."

Blanchard looked at the bag for a second or two before reaching for it. He had asked for some drugs, not that he ever touched the stuff, but this was different. He needed to give the police a plausible reason for the murder that would take place tomorrow. Drugs were part of the dark underside of this tropical paradise, as it was for many countries in Central America and the Caribbean, and he was going to take advantage of that in solving this part of his employer's problem.

"Thank you," Blanchard said, slipping the bag into the side pocket of his sports coat. He reached up and yanked a second envelope out of the breast pocket of his coat. The envelope contained the payment for the drugs, and was quickly snatched out of Blanchard's hand.

Their business over, Blanchard turned suddenly on his heel and walked down the street.

The seller pulled out a handkerchief and mopped his face. He waited until the buyer had taken a dozen or so steps, took a deep breath, turned, and walked back into the shadows. In less than a minute, he had covered the distance to his parked car and sped away.

Meanwhile, Blanchard walked the half mile to his car, all the while listening for any sound that might indicate that someone was following him. He knew that the little weasel of a man who had just provided him with the weapon now safely tucked inside his pants would not dare to follow, but that didn't mean that one of his friends or the local police wouldn't, though he considered that to be highly unlikely. He watched carefully anyway; he survived only by carefully ensuring that even the highly unlikely traps could not be successful.

He reached his rental car, slid in behind the wheel, and drove off toward the Hotel Victoria.

John Blanchard parked in a nearly full parking lot a half block away from a bar that, judging from the noise and the crowds, would be open for quite some time, which was perfect for he had in mind. He meandered three blocks, taking his time, making sure it looked as if he was wandering aimlessly, just one more drunken tourist finding his way back to his hotel.

Across from the Hotel Victoria, he turned down a side street, doubled back, keeping to the darker side of the street, stepping into a recessed front door of a men's clothes store. An awning blocked the light from the nearest street light.

There was a good view of the hotel from his vantage point. Blanchard took out a pair of Steiner 5x50 Commander V binoculars. Although it had built-in night vision capability, he needn't have bothered. The Hotel was bathed in plenty of light and the whole street in front clearly visible. Blanchard stood still in the shadows, making mental notes of the traffic patterns, the number of people coming and going, how many rooms still had lights on. Even at this time of night, the hotel was a busy place, which made it a less than ideal location for his needs.

Blanchard had seen enough. He checked up and down the street and seeing no one, stepped from the shadows and strode briskly away from the Hotel.

As he walked back to his car, Blanchard considered his alternatives. The hotel would be his last choice at this point. He would have to find somewhere else to take out his target. But where? His target wouldn't be here long enough to get into a routine that would allow him to plan an attack. Even if his target had a routine, he didn't have the luxury of time to discover what it was. For most targets, the most vulnerable time was when they were getting in or out of their car, particularly if they weren't expecting an attack. Blanchard didn't think there was any reason why his target would expect anything down here, so the element of surprise would be on his side. Still, he would have to be careful.

The real question was when, not whether his target would give him the opening he needed.

*　　*　　*　　*

The Continental Airline plane touched down at Tocumen International Airport outside Panama City and taxied to a stop. Alyson Murphy grabbed her carryon luggage and followed the rest of the passengers toward customs.

"Buenos días, señorita. What brings you to my country?" the officer at the immigration booth asked in a heavy accent.

"Buenos días. I'm on vacation." Alyson replied.

"How many days will you be here?" He flipped open her passport and looked her over a couple of times before turning to the immigration form she had given him.

"Until Sunday."

"Thank you. Enjoy your stay here." The man stamped her passport and form, and placed them back on the counter. "Next," he said, waving a white-haired couple forward.

Alyson grabbed her passport and went in search of her luggage. She was waved through the nothing-to-declare line and walked out of the terminal. During the short wait for a cab, Alyson's hair went limp in the humid air. She tugged at her clothes where they stuck to her skin. The guidebook had said that December was the end of the wet season, but she wouldn't have guessed it.

The taxi took her into the city by way of the Corredor Sur highway, which crossed a long bridge that swung out into the Bahía de Panama, from where she could see Panama City lit up in the distance. From afar, with its tall modern buildings aglow in the night, she could be riding in from the airport to any major city in the United States.

The taxi pulled up in front of the Hotel de la Independencia on Avenida 1a Norte. The hotel had been built shortly after the first world war to cater to the American and European travelers who would arrive by boat and stay in Panama City before continuing through the Canal or heading elsewhere in Central or South America. The hotel was reminiscent of the grand hotels of Europe, but was considerably more rundown than those it tried to emulate. As Alyson entered the hotel, it was obvious that the lobby had gotten much more attention in recent years than the exterior of the building. The wall-to-wall carpet, a deep maroon with gold ribbons running across it forming diamond patterns, looked expensive and fairly new. The walls were freshly painted and the ubiquitous marble shone as if it had all been recently polished.

Alyson walked across the spacious lobby to the reception desk, going past the bar and its four small round marble-topped tables, each filled with people enjoying a nightcap. Her luggage sat on a trolley being escorted by a bellhop. She had purposefully traveled light and could have carried the luggage herself, but had let the taxi driver pass it all to the old man in a uniform on the steps outside.

"Buenos días, señorita. May I help you?" the man behind the desk said.

"Sí. Gracias. Reservation for Murphy."

"Here we are." After Alyson produced a credit card and showed her passport, the manager handed her the key.

"Gracias." Alyson took it and followed the trolley toward the elevator.

"Señorita, wait! You have a message!"

Alyson turned and walked back to the front desk. "Gracias," she said, glancing at the handwritten note saying that Gavin had called. A faint frown crossed her face.

As she walked back across the lobby to the elevator, a sandy-blond-haired man with small close-set eyes followed her progress in the mirror behind the bar. He nursed a Cristal, a local beer. He turned toward the lobby as Alyson passed, keeping his face partially hidden from her view, and watched her enter the elevator. He waited for ten minutes, stood up, paid for the beer, and walked leisurely out of the hotel.

He walked half a block down the street, got into a rented black Ford Focus, and sat inside with the engine off. Even with the windows down, his shirt quickly became soaked in sweat, turning it a dark blue. The man wished he could have stayed inside the air-conditioned lobby, but he knew he had already stayed there too long.

Dan Morris looked around anxiously, but seeing no one on the street, settled further down into the front seat and waited. After an hour-long vigil, he decided that the woman had gone to bed. He started the engine and pulled out quickly into the light traffic, slowly cruised past the hotel for one last peek into the lobby, and then drove off down the street, knowing he would be back first thing in the morning.

∗   ∗   ∗   ∗

Alyson put her bags and briefcase on the luggage rack in the corner, not bothering to unpack for the moment, but instead just lay down on the king-size bed, enjoying the light breeze from the overhead fan. The room hadn't been renovated as recently as the lobby, but more recently than the outside of the hotel. An Empire-style dresser stood beneath an ornate gilded mirror on one wall. A matching pair of night tables stood guard on either side of the bed. The only truly new things in the room were the television and phone, and, less obvious, the Internet connection.

Lying on the bed, she reached over, picked up the phone and dialed an international number, and was soon connected to the operator of the Hotel Victoria.

"Hello," Hank answered, after the second ring.

"Hi. It's Alyson." She was glad to hear his voice, to know that he had made it safely to Belize.

"Alyson. Did you get in okay?"

"Yes, no problem."

They chatted for about thirty minutes, mostly about their hotels and their first impressions of the cities they were in.

Alyson hung up the phone, went into the bathroom to change for bed, crawled under the covers, and turned out the light. Lying there, waiting for sleep to overtake her, she hoped that this wouldn't turn out to be a wild goose chase, as Harden had suggested. Despite what she had told him, there was no real reason, given the ability to move money around, that the cash still had to be in Panama, but she had to start somewhere and her instinct told her that this was the place to look. She just hoped that she was right.

CHAPTER 25

▼

MONDAY, DECEMBER 11

The early morning sunlight streamed through the gap between the heavy chintz drapes, inching up the covers toward her shoulders. Alyson stretched, kicked off the blankets, and rolled out of bed. After throwing cold water on her face, she pulled a pair of lightweight sweat pants over her shorts and threw on a T-shirt and her running shoes. She wanted to take advantage of the fact that her appointment with Miguel wasn't until lunchtime to get her run in before the day got too hot and muggy.

She hailed a taxi to take her out to the Causeway, where the manager recommended she run that morning. As the taxi pulled away from the curb in front of the hotel, a black Ford slid into traffic behind it. Five cars behind the Ford, a nondescript blue sedan inched out of its parking place and took its place in the morning rush-hour traffic.

The Causeway was a strip of land that jutted out into the Pacific, connecting four islands at the mouth of southern end of the Panama Canal. It had been built from the dirt and rock excavated during the construction of the Canal and was now a popular place for both locals and tourists to walk, skate, or run. Even though it was early, the Causeway was fairly crowded and Alyson had to pay attention to avoid collisions. She planned to run two circuits out to the end and back, figuring that would be about five miles, a good run for her lately although she was used to running longer distances.

Running along the Causeway, she made the resolution right there and then to get back into running, even if it meant working later. It was a shame, she thought as she ran, that her usual run along the East River or Central Park was nowhere near as pretty as it was here.

On the second return leg, she turned off the main path on Isla Perico, the closest to shore of the four islands, and stopped at El Pirata, a restaurant near the beach. Most of the restaurant was outside and was defined by a low cinderblock wall that had once been painted white and was covered in spots by vines with purple and white flowers, which Alyson thought looked familiar, but she couldn't come up with the name. Standing outside, she could smell the kitchen inside the small, partially enclosed building, made of the same cinderblocks as the walls. On a patio, underneath a tin roof supported by a lattice of weathered beams, was a small bar with a few tables in front of it. A couple of old men, surrounded by a cloud of cigarette smoke, were drinking beer at the bar.

She decided to stay outside and chose a table under two palm trees next to where the wall separated the restaurant from the beach. From this spot, she could survey the entire length of the beach. She ordered a diet Coke with plenty of ice and watched a number of families that had camped out on the beach. She smiled at the kids running in and out of the water, splashing and frolicking, imaging what it would be like to have kids of own her someday.

The mild breeze off the ocean had made the run enjoyable. Out here by the water, the humidity was less troublesome than in the city the night before. The sky was a deep blue, with only a few white threads of clouds floating across it. This is the life, she thought to herself. The climate, the scenery, the ocean, the people were all beautiful. Who could ask for more? She could understand why Saunders might have chosen this place to retire to.

She put down the glass, thought about ordering another, but decided that she had better get back to the hotel and change if she were to make her lunch meeting with Miguel. If she missed him, she'd have to do it all by phone or e-mail, thus defeating the reason why she flew down here on her own in the first place.

"Ah, Señorita Murphy," the hotel manager said as he handed her the key, "there is a message for you. Señor Alvarez called and said that he could not meet you for lunch. He will meet you at five this afternoon on the seawall in Casco Viejo."

"Gracias." She turned and took the elevator to her room. What was she going to do with the afternoon? She decided there wasn't much else to do until Hank got down here so she might as well go sightseeing or shopping. She smiled as she crossed the lobby.

As she got onto the elevator, the black Ford slid into a parking spot on a side street near the hotel. The driver switched off the engine. After a couple of minutes, he got out and ducked into a cantina across the street from the hotel and walked back to the car carrying a cold Cristal.

Up on her hotel floor, Alyson emerged from her room after a quick shower and a change into a white linen shirt and mid-length beige skirt. As she was closing the door to leave, she stopped, looked over at the phone on the table next to the bed, walked over, and sat down.

"Alyson, where were you last night?" Gavin blurted out upon hearing her voice. "I was worried when you didn't call."

Alyson gritted her teeth and took a deep breath. "I got in late and thought you'd be asleep. I didn't want to wake you." She squirmed as she said each word.

"That would've been okay. The important thing is you're safe." He paused. "I also called to say I'm sorry."

"Sorry? About what?"

"About not understanding about your work. You were right. I wasn't being fair."

"No, you weren't," she said, a bit more blunt than she had wanted.

He was silent for a few seconds. "How can I make it up to you?"

"I don't know. We'll have to talk when we're both back in New York. I've got to go."

Ten minutes later, she was in a taxi riding through the city on the Avenida Justo Arosemena. When she had asked for somewhere to eat and shop, the manager had suggested that she might enjoy the Avenida Central, a shopping mall with authentic Panamanian shops and restaurants. The good news, he told her, was that it was within walking distance of where she was to meet her gentleman friend later that afternoon. She had smiled at the thought of Miguel as her *gentleman friend*.

The streets were full of cars. The traffic was worse than anything she had seen in New York, making her glad she had decided not to rent a car. The city surprised her. Next to fairly modern steel-and-glass skyscrapers were three-and four-story buildings that looked like something right out of an early James Bond movie set somewhere in the Caribbean. They were covered in white or pastel-colored stucco, and many had balconies along each floor overlooking the street. These were clearly residential, although there were shops and restaurants on the ground floor in many of them.

Forty minutes later, she got out at the northeast corner of the Plaza Cinco de Mayo, which formed the northern end of a pedestrian mall that ran along

Avenida Central. Alyson wandered in and out of the stores, dodging the children as they ran around, stopping here and there to look at the arts and crafts sold in the various stalls and carts along the street.

She stopped suddenly to look at a cart covered by *molas*, a traditional handicraft of Panama. A Kuna Indian woman, obviously proud of her work, showed her a number of blouses with the bright, intricate appliqué panels on the back, but Alyson indicated that she was looking for something to hang on a wall. The woman dug into the pile on the cart and quickly pulled out a number for her to choose from. As Alyson leaned down to pick one up, she caught sight of a man in a white shirt stepping inside a shop doorway thirty feet away. Something about him was familiar. She stared at the door of the shop, hoping to see him again. Seeing no one, she shrugged and returned to examining the *mola* in her hand. She pulled a small wallet out of her purse and paid the full price, knowing that if she had haggled, it would have cost her less, but it already seemed like such a good deal that she didn't have the heart to fight over the price.

Shortly after three in the afternoon, Alyson finally succumbed to the aromas of the restaurants that lined the street and decided she needed to eat. She found a seat at an outdoor café and asked for a piña colada. For lunch, she ordered a traditional lunch of fish soup followed by ropa vieja, a dish of spicy shredded beef with green peppers, plantains, and rice. She passed on the salad and ordered a cup of coffee. She looked at her watch and waved at the waiter to bring the bill.

She walked briskly down the pedestrian mall, which ended at the Parque Santa Ana at the edge of the Casco Viejo. Wandering through the Parque, she continued down Avenida Central. A second glance at her watch made her quicken her step.

Seven minutes later, she stood atop the massive stone seawall that jutted out in the Bay of Panama at the southern end of the peninsula on which Casco Viejo was built. Casco Viejo, meaning Old Compound, was the area where the Spanish had rebuilt the city after it was attacked and burned to the ground by the English pirate Harry Morgan back in the late 1600s. It was now home to Palacio de las Garzas, the home of the President of Panama, and numerous museums and restaurants, as well as many government buildings. At the time the Canal was built, Casco Viejo contained most of what was then Panama City. Now it was just one district out of many.

She stood at one corner of the parapet, looking out over the bay, yet keeping an eye out for Miguel, who had suggested meeting on the seawall rather than at his office at the Ministerio de Gobierno y Justicia, which was only a few blocks away. She checked her watch again. It was 5:07 PM. There was still no sign of

Miguel. She glanced around. Where was he? It was unlike him to be late. She jumped at the flapping of wings behind her. She turned. A pelican had landed on the wall behind her.

She decided to walk to the end of the seawall while she waited. In the distance were a number of ships, including two cruise ships, lining up to enter the Canal, which was only a mile or so away to the west on the other side of the Causeway, where she had run that morning.

She hoped that Miguel would get there soon. The sun was nearly gone and it would get dark soon. There were no lights atop the seawall and she might not see him. She also didn't want to be walking out here alone. Her guidebook had said it was unsafe to wander around Casco Viejo at night.

"Alyson," the voice came from somewhere behind her and she turned to see Miguel hurrying toward her, slightly out of breath. "Cómo estás?" He said as he approached. "Sorry for being late."

"Don't be," she said. They gave each other a kiss on both cheeks.

"Thanks for meeting with me," Alyson said.

"It's my pleasure." He smiled in a way that made it clear that it was.

"I hope everything's all right."

"Yes." The smile on his face vanished instantly. "I am sorry about lunch. Too much business."

Alyson could tell there was more to the story, but thought it better not to ask any more questions.

"Did you find anything else?" she asked.

"Let us walk," he said, taking her arm and guiding her along. "I have a list in my pocket of everything I could find. It seems that Señor Saunders did business with a number of companies here in Panama. Most of them were ultimately owned by the same person."

"Edward G. Sanders," Alyson said.

"How did you know?"

"It was an educated guess. We found his name in some files in New York." She didn't think that Miguel needed to know they suspected the two were the same man.

"¡Magnífico! I guess you do not need my help after all," he said, a small, tentative grin emerging on his face.

"You know that's not true. We still need to know how all the companies are connected so we can track down the money. We couldn't do it without you."

"Gracias. I also have a list of the local law firms that manage the companies. Perhaps you would like to pay them a visit."

"I'm hoping to do just that," Alyson said.

"I doubt that I have all of the companies Sanders was involved in, but it's an up-to-date list. There's even one company incorporated only a couple of weeks ago."

"What? What did you say?"

"Solo Financial. It was incorporated just a few weeks ago."

"That's not possible!" She blurted out.

"Why is it not possible?" She did not answer. "Alyson?"

"Because…"

"What is it you are not telling me?" Miguel stared at her.

"Miguel, I'm sorry, but I think it's best that you don't know any more than you do already."

"Is it because you don't trust me?" He looked hurt.

"No. It's not that. I think it would be safer, that's all, safer for you." Despite the warmth, she shivered.

"What is this all about? There's more than just missing money, isn't there?"

"Yes. A man was murdered because of this money."

"Edward Sanders?"

"Yes," she said hesitantly.

"Then he couldn't have opened the account, could he?" It was a question that needed no answer.

They were now standing in the Plaza de Francia below the wall where they had first met. "This is where I leave you. Please take this," he said, pulling a large manila envelope out of his briefcase and handing it to her. She quickly slid the envelope into her purse. She pulled out a smaller envelope and handed it to Miguel, who pushed it into the breast pocket of his suit coat in one smooth motion, not bothering to examine the contents. There would be time for that later, she knew, when there was no one around.

Miguel grabbed her arm and looked into her eyes. "Alyson, be careful."

"I will," she said with as much conviction as she could muster.

He held her for a moment longer, then leaned over and kissed her on the cheek. "If you need anything else, please let me know."

"I will."

"Buenas tardes. Good luck," Miguel said and turned to walk back to his office. He walked a few steps, looked over his shoulder at Alyson, then strode down the street. As she watched walked away, he seemed to shrink before her eyes. His shoulders became more stooped than she remembered and his step was more faltering, like that of a man twice his age.

Her thoughts returned to the envelope in her bag. Was it really possible that someone was using Saunders's new identity? If there was someone, it had to be the killer or an accomplice. Did he know that she and Hank were looking for the money? Whoever it was wouldn't want anyone nosing around.

She looked nervously around the Plaza, suddenly feeling very much alone. She jumped as a rat scurried behind a trash can in search of food. The Plaza, which had been so beautiful in the daylight, was now almost devoid of beauty. Instead, it was full of menacing shadows that shifted on the breeze. She grabbed her bag tightly and started walking, faster with each passing second. She tried in vain to stop her trembling.

Something crashed in the alley to her right. She instinctively stopped to look. A man, dressed in ragged clothes, shuffled out of the darkness toward her. He had something in his hand.

Alyson fought the urge to run, positioning herself to repel an attack. Confidence returned as she remembered her boot camp training. She would not give up without a fight.

The man stepped out into the faint light cast off by the closest street lamp fifty feet away. "Perdón, señorita. Could you spare some money?" He said in a heavy accent. "Por favor." He held out his hand. In his other hand was a nearly empty beer bottle.

"No. Please leave me alone." Alyson retreated a step, but kept herself ready.

"Por favor. ¡Tengo hambre!" he begged, grabbing his stomach with his empty hand.

He was hungry. Alyson relaxed a little. Without taking her eyes off the man, she reached into her bag and retrieved a ten-dollar bill. The man's eyes lit up at the sight. She shrugged and held out the money. He snatched it, turned, and staggered away.

She stood there for a few moments, her heart pounding. The man entered a bar a block away. The light from inside lit up a portion of the street and roused her from her trance. She spun and ran toward the Parque, where she could hear people talking and music. She found a taxi, gave the name of her hotel, and jumped in the backseat.

As soon as the cab pulled up to the front of the hotel, she handed the fare to the driver and bolted into the lobby. She arranged with the manager for room service before going up to her room.

She shut the door behind her, threw the latch and attached the chain, strode across the room, tossed her bag on the bed, and sat down. She looked down at her hands. They were still shaking. Her legs felt like rubber. She fell back onto the bed and lay there for a few minutes, then walked into the bathroom and took a long hot calming shower. Her phone, buried deep in her bag, rang. Alyson never heard it over the sound of the running water.

Alyson walked out of the bathroom, wearing one of the hotel's terrycloth bathrobes and her hair wrapped in a towel. There was a knock at the door and the man identified himself as being from room service. She peeked through the eyehole just to make sure then unlocked the door and let him in. She directed him to put the tray on the bed, signed the bill, and relocked the door after he left.

She picked at her food at first, but then her hunger returned and she ate thankfully. When she was finished, she put the tray on the hall floor and called down for someone to take it away. As she turned from the door, she saw the corner of Miguel's envelope sticking out of her bag. She walked over and pulled it out, ripped open the seal, and dumped its contents onto the bed.

*   *   *   *

Shortly after 8:00 AM, Hank Jenkins stepped out of the shower, having needed the cool water now running down his back to wake him up. He had tossed and turned most of the night and was exhausted. Images of being chased by a faceless man kept invading his dreams. He woke up each time just as the man's face was coming into view. He thought that the man looked familiar, but he just couldn't make it out, no matter how hard he tried.

As he dressed, he thought about Alyson, glad that she had arrived safely in Panama, but still worried about her. He thought back on his dream and couldn't get the idea out of his head that she was in danger. If someone did know about the money, that would provide an extremely compelling motive for murder. And, if that someone had killed once, he wouldn't shy away from killing again.

Fifteen minutes later, Hank walked out of the hotel and got into his car, which the valet had brought around front for him. He drove down Cork Street, took a right onto North Front Street and a left onto Queen Street, passing in front of the Queen Street Guesthouse, and came to a sudden halt. There was a line of cars stopped at the Swing Bridge that crossed over Haulover Creek. The bridge had been built back in the twenties to connect the two halves of the city. To allow boats to pass through on their way to the sea, the bridge would pivot in the center. He hadn't counted on this delay. He drummed the steering wheel with his thumbs in time to a reggae song on the radio.

The bridge finally slipped back into place and the traffic moved forward again. Hank drove across the bridge, took a right on Orange Street, continued over the

Collett Canal, and then headed west on Cemetery Road, going past the stadium on the way out of the city. Seventeen minutes later, he was driving west on the Western Highway, a bit of a misnomer as the road was only two lanes wide. Still, traffic certainly moved along much faster than in the city. He was headed in the direction of Belmopan, the capital of Belize. He figured that the trip should take about an hour.

The countryside was relatively flat, rising gently as the highway left the city. The vegetation on each side of the highway, which started out lush and overgrown in places, slowly began to thin out and become scragglier as the moist tropical air gave way to the drier climate of the inland highlands.

*   *   *   *

Five cars behind Hank, Blanchard checked his speed then pulled out a pair of sunglasses to cut the glare off the cars in front of him. Despite the air conditioning, which was still on maximum, the air inside the car was getting warmer. "Screw this," he said under his breath. He wiggled out of his blazer and tossed it over his shoulder into the backseat.

Where the hell was his target going, Blanchard wondered. He scooped up the road map that he bought in the States and held it up against the steering wheel. The only thing in this direction was the capital city. The good news was that they were heading away from the more crowded coast and up toward the mountains and the rainforest.

Blanchard smiled. The time and place to carry out his mission may be just ahead.

*   *   *   *

Forty-eight minutes after he left the outskirts of Belize City, Hank could see Belmopan in the distance, sitting on top of a low hill. The city had been created from scratch in 1971 in response to the devastation that Hurricane Hattie had inflicted on Belize City in 1961. The capital was now home to only seven thousand people, making it the smallest capital city of any country in the world. It would swell each day to nearly fifteen thousand people as government workers, many of whom still lived in Belize City, arrived at work. Government buildings, including the National Assembly, dominated the city skyline. Although Belmopan was the capital, most countries, including the United States, still had their embassies in Belize City.

Hank took the exit off the Western Highway and drove the short distance along Constitution Drive into the capital. He stopped and got directions to the Old Plaza Building housing the Immigration and Nationalization Service and found it without any problem. He pulled into a parking space on Market Square and walked the two blocks back to his destination. The building was a mix of modern and ancient Maya design and, although relatively new, had aged considerably in the harsh tropical climate.

Based on the research done by Fred Hamilton before Hank left New York, Hank had set up an appointment with Archibald Gordon, the Deputy Minister of the Service. The receptionist directed him to the appropriate office, where Archibald's secretary informed him that the Deputy Minister had been held up in a meeting and asked Hank to wait, offering him a seat in the Deputy Minister's office. The coolness of the chair's leather seeped up through his pants, making his legs feel clammy after the warmth outside.

Hank sat there rehearsing the story he was about to tell the Deputy Minister. He hadn't told Archibald's secretary anything about the purpose of his visit except that he was a *Times* reporter. On the flight down the night before, Hank had decided on using a child pornography ring as the story he was investigating. Hopefully, it would be seamy enough to elicit help from the man he was waiting to see.

A short time later, Archibald Gordon, or Archie as he was known at the local clubs, walked into the room. Archie was the embodiment of the old British Empire. He was tall and lanky, his skin deeply tanned and his hair nearly all white, with just a few patches of darker hair spread here and there, although not enough to determine what the original color had been.

"How may I help you, Mr. Jenkins?" Archie asked in a distinctly Caribbean version of a British accent as Hank stood up to shake hands.

"I need some information. I'm a reporter from the *New York Times* and I'm investigating an Internet child pornography ring that operates out of Belize." Hank pulled a photograph of Saunders out of his pocket and handed it to immigration official. "We believe this man is the ringleader. His name is Ed Sanders. I was hoping you'd be able to help me get some information on him."

"I'm sorry, but I cannot give you any information."

"Is there any way that I could make you change your mind?"

"No. I think not."

"Well, then, I guess I'll just have to mention you in my article when I write about how governmental officials here in Belize condone this kind of behavior. I may have to speculate whether this is because some officials are actually involved in the operations."

"You cannot do that."

"Um, yes I can."

"I don't know much about your American legal system, but I believe that would be slander."

"Libel, actually, since it would be in print. But, no, you won't get very far that way. Besides, any retraction we'd have to make would be years from now after all the litigation and would be buried way back on page twenty-seven. By then, it would be too late. Now, if you could just provide me with a little information, I wouldn't have to mention any names. Reporters never have to reveal their sources."

As they were talking, Archie had typed in "Sanders" and hit the search button. The search returned two entries, Edward and Rose. He knew Rose. She was a member at his club. Her husband had died in the war and had been a widow ever since. Lovely lady, he thought.

He clicked on Edward. He looked at the screen and noticed that the current passport was the first one issued. Hmm. Highly unusual; most people get passports when they're young and this Sanders fellow was over fifty when he got his. That probably meant only one thing. He pulled up another database and searched it for Sanders. Edward Sanders's record showed up on the screen within seconds. Just as he thought, Sanders had bought his citizenship. He hated that his government sold its citizenship like this. It seemed to him to be a Faustian arrangement. Yes, it brought in much-needed investment money, but he believed that they were selling the country's soul at the same time, giving Belize a reputation of corruption that would eventually cost it more than it ever got from those to whom it had sold citizenship.

He returned to the prior screen.

Archie hesitated. If he cooperated, the Minister would be upset, if he ever found out. But how would he ever know? If he didn't cooperate, he ran the risk that this bloody arrogant American might actually go through with his threat. He doubted that he would, and even if he did, what was the downside? His name might appear in a paper in the States. Few people down here would read it. Even if they did, what would be the harm? He doubted that anyone would believe it. He certainly wouldn't be thrown out of the club. His wife would never believe it. There was no reason to assist this man. He should send the bugger on his way.

Another thought suddenly crossed his mind. If he gave this reporter what he wanted and the fact that Sanders had bought his Belize citizenship, that might help swing the tide against this practice. There was already a growing resentment against it. Having one of these people involved in child pornography might just change enough minds to make the government mend its ways. There might also be a need for change at the top of the Service and he'd finally get the position and recognition he deserved.

"Ahhh. Here we are. Yes. Mr. Sanders was issued a passport last April. First issue. Hmm. Highly unusual." He couldn't bring himself to come right out and tell this reporter that this man had purchased his citizenship, but a hint or two might nudge an obviously inquisitive reporter in the right direction.

"How so?"

"Given our size and where we're located, most people get passports when they're young so they can travel abroad or go to school overseas. That sort of thing. Mr. Sanders was over fifty when he got his first passport."

Hank made notes on his pad. Looking up, he asked, "Is there anything else you can tell me."

"Not very much, my dear boy." Archie leaned toward the computer screen and looked over his glasses to get a better look. He held the picture of Sanders up next to the screen. The image on the screen had longer and much lighter hair, although it was unclear from the photograph whether it was blond or gray. In addition, he had a tightly trimmed beard. It looked like the same person, but Archie wouldn't swear to it. "I am not sure that this is the same man, but it could be." Archie waved the picture at Hank. "Are you sure your man is from Belize?"

"What do you mean?"

"I don't know," Archie said. "I'm not sure this is the same man."

"May I see?"

Archie purposefully hesitated for a few moments before swinging the computer screen around so that Hank could compare the pictures. "Is this the same person?" Archie asked.

"Um, I think so," Hank said, with uncertainty. "Could I get a printout of that?"

"I suppose so," Archie said and hit the print button. Soon a copy of the file, including a color picture, was coming out of the printer on the credenza behind him. He looked it over quickly and handed it to Hank.

"Would this be his current address?"

"I wouldn't know. People are not required to update their address when they move until they apply for a new passport."

"Well, thank you for your help. I can assure you that this meeting never took place."

Archie rose and smiled, glad that it did and equally glad that this reporter would not mention it to anyone. "I wish you good hunting for your story. Good day."

Hank turned and left the office. Archibald Gordon sat back down in his chair and smiled at how clever he had been.

Outside, Hank walked over to a small café in Market Square near where he had parked his car and ordered a coffee. He pulled a notebook and a local map out of his briefcase to see if he could find the address that Ed Sanders had listed on his passport application. He flipped through a number of pages until he found the address that Fred had gotten from the Internet search he had done. They did not match.

Hank looked up as the waiter brought a small carafe of coffee and a cup, along with some biscuits. He thanked the man and returned his attention to the map.

Plop, plop. Hank looked up at the noise. Plop, plop, plop. The raindrops came faster. Seconds later, a torrential rainfall started. He could barely see the building on the other side of the square. Thank goodness he wasn't out in the rain. He would have been soaked to the skin almost instantly.

He poured a cup of coffee and took a sip. It was strong, stronger than he usually liked it, but the flavor of the liquid was so deep and rich that he enjoyed it nonetheless. It took him a few minutes to find the addresses on the map. One of them was outside of Belize City and he could stop there on the way back. He looked at his watch. There was no point in trying to get back to his car now. He'd wait out the rain.

He refolded the map and took out the computer printout. He compared the faces again. After a few minutes, he concluded that, despite the poor quality of the pictures, the two men were, indeed, the same person. But could they prove it?

The pot of coffee nearly gone, Hank was wondering how long the rain would last. Then, almost as suddenly as it had started, the rain stopped. He waited for a few more minutes to make sure, then got up and walked over to his car.

He got in and fastened his seatbelt. Although he always wore it back home, he felt he needed it here even more after his drive out of Belize City. The roads were narrow and the local drivers were not shy about passing, even if it meant giving a driver coming from the other direction a heart attack. He switched on the ignition and was about to put the car into gear when the passenger door opened and a man dressed in tan slacks and a white shirt slipped into the seat.

Hank turned and looked straight into the barrel of an automatic pistol pointing at him. "Drive!" John Blanchard said. Hank put the car into gear and drove through the square.

"What do you want?"

"Just drive." The gun remained pointed at his chest, lower now so that no one outside the car would see it.

"I want to know where you're taking me." Hank said firmly, shooting a glance at his abductor.

"Shut up and drive." The man glared menacingly back at Hank.

The man directed Hank to turn south on the highway, away from Belmopan and Belize City, out toward the jungle.

Hank realized that this was, for him, likely to be a one-way trip. This man was taking him somewhere to dispose of him, he was sure of that. Who knew he was here and why? Had Archibald Gordon called this man? Had he accidentally hit some kind of nerve with his story? No, that didn't seem likely. It had been less than an hour from when he had left the deputy minister to when he had gotten into his car. This must have something to do with Saunders. They knew he was in Belize, which meant they probably knew about Alyson too. His heart began to pound in his chest, faster and harder with each passing minute. He took a few deep breaths to regain his composure.

Shit! What was he going to do? Well, he certainly wasn't going to die without a fight. He wracked his brain as he drove along trying to think of how he would get out of this. He looked over at the man next to him once again and noticed that he wasn't wearing his seatbelt. He looked at the steering wheel and the dashboard. No airbags. Of course not! A country like Belize wouldn't mandate airbags. He made up his mind. Now all he had to do was to wait for the right moment. Hopefully that would come before they reached their, or rather his, final destination. He cringed at the thought.

Up ahead, in the distance, Hank saw a large tree standing near the road, big enough to absorb the impact of the car. He let off the accelerator slightly, letting the distance between him and the cars ahead slowly grow. He stole a quick glance over at the man next to him, who did not seem concerned, although Hank wasn't too sure that he'd be able to read the man's emotions anyway. When he judged they were close enough to the tree, he pushed down hard on the accelerator and watched their speed increase to ninety, then one hundred kilometers per hour. He couldn't remember what that was in miles per hour, but he hoped that it would be fast enough for what he needed.

Hank could see out of the corner of his eye that the gun was still pointed at his chest. He would have to take the chance that the gunman wouldn't accidentally pull the trigger in the next few seconds or worse, figure out what Hank was planning to do and shoot him before he could pull it off.

The distance between the car and the tree was shrinking fast. The man next to him still didn't seem to be aware that anything was amiss. When the car was twenty feet from tree, Hank yanked the steering wheel hard to the left, sending the car off the road. He aimed at the tree with the left front end of the car, the passenger side in Belize.

Ten feet from the tree, the gunman finally realized what was happening. He glanced at Hank, dropped the gun in his lap, and braced himself by sticking out his arms against the dashboard.

With a deafening thud, followed by a grinding of metal, the car stuck the tree. The force of the impact lifted Blanchard out of his seat, his momentum carrying him forward, sending his head into the windshield, which instantly looked like the handiwork of a large spider.

Hank was thrown forward at the same time, but his forward progress was sharply checked by his seatbelt. He felt the pressure on his stomach and shoulder and then his head snapped forward. An instant later, he was thrown backward, the back of his head hitting the headrest.

Seconds later, it became eerily silent, as the car settled down next to the base of the tree. Hank looked around. The man next to him was not moving, his body in an awkward position in the seat. Blood was splattered on the windshield and the dashboard. Hank reached over, grabbed the gun, and threw it behind the front seat. He felt the man's throat for a pulse. Good, he was still alive, Hank thought. He hadn't wanted to kill the man.

Cars were stopping now. Three men came running over to the car, trying to pry the doors open. The passenger door was too mangled to open, its window broken in the crash. Hands reached in and pulled out the unconscious man. Hank's door was finally yanked opened and he released his seatbelt. A pair of hands reached in to help him out and he struggled to his feet.

Hank walked unsteadily around to the other side of the car. The man was stretched out on the ground, blood oozing from a gash on his forehead where it had hit the windshield. Two men were talking excitedly into their cell phones. He hoped they were calling the police or an ambulance. He sat back and leaned against the side of the car, his heart still racing, thumping so hard that it felt like it would burst out of his chest at any moment.

A whiff of radiator fluid made him gag. He coughed and turned around to look at the front of the car. The front left was crumpled and pointed upward slightly. Steam was still rising from under the hood. The car looked like a total loss. Fortunately, he had taken out the optional insurance. He wasn't sure if it would cover this. He smiled weakly at the thought of explaining this to Adam McMahon when he put it through on his expense account.

Before long, blue lights could be seen coming down the road; seconds later, the familiar "wah, wah" sound of a police siren reached his ears. A minute later, a police car, followed shortly thereafter by a second, pulled over behind what was left of the rental car. Four policemen got out and walked toward him.

Before they could ask any questions, they turned around at the sound of an approaching ambulance. They waited until it too had stopped by the car and two men in white uniforms jumped out, grabbed their medical kits out of the rear of the ambulance, and ran over to the man lying on the ground. They knelt down next to him and started to administer medical treatment.

"Oy, what 'appened 'ere?" one of the policemen yelled, in a thick British accent, hoping to be heard over all the noise around him. "'ose car is this?"

"Mine," Hank yelled back, holding up his hand to identify himself.

The policeman who had yelled, along with his partner, came walking toward him. "What the bloody 'ell 'appened 'ere?"

The other two policemen went to check on the man getting medical attention.

"It's a complicated story."

"Please tell me." The policeman took out a pad of paper, ready to take notes.

"I drove into that tree on purpose," Hank began. "That man," pointing to the body on the ground, "was going to kill me and this was the only way I could think of to get away."

"You're joking," the second policeman said, giving Hank a look of total disbelief.

"I wish I were. Look in the back of the car. You'll find the gun he held on me." The policeman with the pad motioned to his partner to look inside the car. The partner saw the gun and nodded.

"Oh, shit," Hank shouted suddenly. "I need a phone, I need to call someone."

"Who?"

"A colleague. She's in danger."

"Slow down. Where is she?"

"She's in Panama," Hank shouted, as he struggled to get to his feet.

"'ow do you know she's in danger?"

"Whoever hired this man to kill me will try to kill her too."

The two policemen listening to Hank looked at each other, clearly thinking that this man was either drunk, crazy, or had hit his head against the windshield and didn't show it.

"Please come over 'ere," the first policeman said.

"No, you don't understand. I need to call her. Warn her!" He frantically patted his pants pockets and realized that he had left his cell phone in his hotel room. He looked around, saw one of the men who had been on the phone right after the crash, and walked over to him. "May I borrow your phone? Please. It's a matter of life and death." The man hesitated, then handed him his phone.

"Thank you," Hank said.

"Please, give 'im back 'is phone. We want to talk to you first," one of the policemen said.

Hank ignored him and punched in the number for Alyson's cell phone, praying that it worked in Panama. The phone at the other end rang. He was relieved for a second when he heard her voice, but then realized that it was just her voice mail message.

Hank's mind went blank when the voice asked him to leave a message. He didn't want to leave a crazy message that would only scare her. "Alyson, um, this is Hank." He tried to keep his voice as steady and calm as he could. "Just checking in. Please be careful until I get there. Give me a call as soon as you get this." Where was she? Was he too late?

"We would like you to step over 'ere, please," the policeman said, his voice hard and determined, yanking Hank's mind back to what was going around him. He looked at the policeman, saw the look in his eyes and the hand resting on the gun at his side, and gently flipped the phone closed and handed it to its owner. "Thank you again," Hank said to the man. The man nodded and retreated to stand among the crowd that had gathered.

"Tell us again what 'appened," the policeman continued.

"I told you." Hank told them about the man's getting in the car with the gun, telling him to drive. How he had become convinced that he had to act. Yes, he told them, the gun belonged to the man on the ground.

One of the policemen, who had knelt down beside the injured man to look for identification, held up a passport and small plastic bag, which contained about a half dozen small packets of white powder. Hank told them that he had no idea what that was, although secretly he had a good idea. "Shit," he said under his breath. He was in deep trouble now. He wondered how far his press credentials might get him in this situation.

The ambulance left the scene a half hour later. Two of the police were directing traffic, hoping to get it moving again. A tow truck had arrived to haul the crushed remnants of the rental car off to the scrap yard. Hank got in the back of a police car and rode with them back to Belmopan. At the central police headquarters, they asked him to wait in an interrogation room. While he waited, they checked the hotels in Belize City for a guest named John Olsen and soon found him at the Queen Street Guesthouse. They contacted the police barracks nearest the Guesthouse and asked to have someone sent over to check out the hotel.

The manager of the hotel let the policeman into the room and watched as he rummaged through the single suitcase in the room. As he was about to close it back up, he noticed a slight bulge in the side, felt around and found a small pocket that was sealed with Velcro. Inside were two passports, one Canadian and another U.S., neither in the name of John Olsen.

The policeman looked at the pictures in the passports. They were both of the same man. The policeman showed one of the passports to the manager, who confirmed that it was the man who had checked into that room under the name John Olsen. He slipped the passports into his jacket pocket and marched out of the room.

Back at the barracks, the policeman called and told the inspector in Belmopan what he had found.

"It appears that there may be some truth in your story," the inspector announced as he marched into the interrogation room and sat down in the chair kitty-corner to Hank.

"I told you. I'm a reporter from the *New York Times*," Hank handed him one of his business cards. "You can check with my boss at the paper. His name's Adam McMahon. He'll tell you I'm not likely to make something like this up."

"Yes, that is all very good. It seems that this man has multiple passports and arrived just yesterday. He may have even been on the same flight you arrived on."

"Can I go now? I've got to get in touch with my colleague. She's in danger."

"Yes, you may go...for now"

"I'm supposed to meet her in Panama tomorrow. I assume that I will be allowed to leave the country."

"I don't think that will be possible."

"I can come back if you need me, but I have to get to Panama," Hank pleaded.

The inspector watched Hank for a few moments. "Wait here. I'll be right back." As he shoved his chair back, it screeched against the linoleum floor. He stepped out of the room.

"Great," Hank sighed, sinking back in his chair in despair.

The inspector marched into the room next door and walked over to the desktop monitor that showed Hank sitting at the table in the interrogation room, with his elbows on the table, his head in his hands. The inspector looked for any signs of insincerity, but found none. He turned and left the room and strode down the hall into his office and closed the door.

He sat in his office for a couple of minutes, silently evaluating the man in this interrogation room, whose story sounded fanciful, yet had a ring of truth to it. He picked up his phone and dialed the main number of the *New York Times* in New York and asked for Adam McMahon.

"Hello," Adam McMahon said.

"Hello. This is Inspector Clarke from the Belize police."

"Yes."

The inspector briefly explained what had happened and what Hank was claiming. "So, can you vouch for this man?"

"Absolutely. If he told you that the man was threatening him, you can believe it."

"But how will I know that he will come back here."

"I will do everything I can to make sure that he does. You have my word and that of the *New York Times*."

Inspector Clarke considered that for a moment. "Thank you, Mr. McMahon. I will be in touch." He hung up the phone and dialed the hospital. He asked to speak with the doctor in charge of the alleged assailant.

Half a minute later, Dr. Nigel Hathaway came on the phone. "He suffered a severe head injury, which is not, in my opinion, life-threatening. I didn't see any signs of permanent spinal cord or neck injury. His wrist is broken, probably from bracing himself before the impact, but that will mend. My main worry is the severity of the cranial contusion caused when his head hit the windshield. At this stage, however, the prognosis is good."

"Thank you, doctor." The inspector hung up. Good, he thought, at least he wasn't dealing with a fatality, just an auto accident. There was the matter of the cocaine and he had to consider whether this was simply a drug buy gone badly, but he believed the man in the next room when he claimed to know nothing about the drugs or the man in the hospital. Then there was the issue of his colleague in Panama. He walked back to the interrogation room and stood in front of Hank. He did not seem to be delusional in any way, and gave the inspector no reason to doubt his story. He decided to take a chance and let him leave. "I would want you to come back if we need you," he said.

"Yes, I will," Hank said, relieved that he wouldn't be stuck in Belize. "May I go now?"

"Yes. You are free to go."

"Um, do you know if there are any flights to Panama this evening?"

"You may use my telephone."

Hank grabbed his coat and walked briskly out of the room. Hank had been relieved to learn that there were seats available on an 8:00 PM Panama flight that evening. He reserved one and gave the woman on the phone his credit card number. The inspector ordered him a cab, and Hank was soon on his way back toward Belize City. He walked into his hotel at 6:25 PM, ran up to his room, threw all his things into his suitcase, and hurried back down to the lobby. By 6:50 PM, he had checked out and found another cab to take him to the airport.

He squirmed in the backseat of the taxi, willing it to go faster, not wanting to miss the flight. There had been no messages for him at the desk and none on his cell phone. The cab pulled up to the curb outside the departure area. He paid the man and ran into the terminal. There were six people in front of him to check in and it took nearly a half hour before he walked through the security check point, showed his passport again, and hurried to his gate. He hadn't bothered to stop by the rental car counter. He'd have to figure out what to tell the rental company, but that could wait. The car wasn't due back until the next day anyway and he would deal with it later.

As he sat at the gate for the ten minutes before his flight boarded, he tried to reach Alyson again. He was relieved to see she had called him back earlier. He called her cell phone again and again her voice mail answered. He left another message to be extra careful, but still couldn't bring himself to tell her about his close encounter with the gunman. He didn't want to get her overly worried. His stomach twisted into knots as he imagined her in trouble. What would he do if he were too late?

They announced his flight and Hank got in line between two couples from Florida who were on some kind of eco-tour and a family of five heading home. They walked out onto the tarmac and Hank's face dropped. The plane was a twenty-passenger turboprop. He stopped at the bottom of the short set of stairs and let all of the other passengers go ahead of him. After the last of the other passengers was seated, the flight attendant stuck her head out the door and said, "Sir, you have to come on board now so we can take off."

Hank hesitated.

"Is there a problem, sir?"

He looked at her for a couple of seconds more. The thought of Alyson in trouble welled up in his chest. He gritted his teeth and climbed on board. Seconds after he sat down, the door closed and the engines came to life, their vibrations reverberating through the fuselage and into his seat. He pulled his seatbelt tight across his lap and closed his eyes. The knuckles of both hands, which clenched the armrests, were white by the time they were airborne.

The plane landed at a little after 9:00 PM outside Panama City, just before a flight from New York, so the line at immigration was fairly short and Hank was soon on his way into the city. Just before ten, he walked into the lobby of the Hotel de la Independencia, asked for Alyson Murphy, and was relieved to hear that she had returned. If he wanted, the manager would call up and tell Señorita Murphy that he was in the lobby.

"Hank, what are you doing here?" Alyson asked as she got off the elevator and flew across the lobby toward him. She was clearly worried. "You weren't supposed to be here until tomorrow."

"I know, but…" He averted his eyes.

"Something's happened, hasn't it?"

Hank glanced around. "Not here."

They walked two blocks and stepped into a restaurant that looked inviting. As they waited for their drinks, Hank kept his gaze down, but could feel Alyson's eyes watching him.

"Um, Alyson, I don't know where to start," he finally blurted out after the waitress had delivered their drinks and taken their order. He quickly told her about his visit with Archibald Gordon and getting the information about Ed Sanders. She thought that that was great news, but then he told her about the man in the car and the "accident."

"Are you sure this was related to Saunders?" she asked, keeping her voice low, when he had finished.

"Yes. Well, no, not one hundred percent sure. But I can't imagine it's anything else unless my cockamamie story about a child porn ring was on the mark and I didn't know it."

"That's unlikely! What should we do now?"

"I'm not sure we're safe here. Maybe we should go back to the States."

She thought about that for a moment. "No. That's no good. If it's true that man tried to kill you because of Saunders, the only way we'll be safe is to find the money and figure out who's behind all this."

Hank knew she was right, but it worried him to have her in the line of fire. He wished he'd never started this. Well, that wasn't exactly true. If he hadn't, he wouldn't have made the first move to contact her again and that, in the long run, would have been bad.

"Well, if we're going to do this, we'd better figure out how." They spent the rest of the dinner making a plan for the rest of the week.

*　　　*　　　*　　　*

Alyson walked straight out of the bathroom to the door to the hall and inserted the chain into the catch, then turned to get into bed. The message light blinked on the phone next to the bed. Alyson groaned. She couldn't believe that she hadn't noticed that before. She trod over to the phone and wearily picked it up and hit the message button.

Thankfully there was only one message. Gavin had called to check on her and to say goodnight. She looked at her watch. It was nearly 11:30 PM, but it felt like much later. She hit the key to delete the message and stood holding the receiver for a few seconds, shrugged and dialed California.

"Is everything all right?" Gavin asked.

"Yes, everything's fine," Alyson said, trying to sound as reassuring as possible.

"You don't sound like everything's all right."

"I am, really. I went for a nice run today and met with my friend in the government down here, but now I'm really bushed."

"Are you still going to be there all week?"

"Yes," she said coolly, switching the phone from one ear to the other.

There was a knock at the door. "Alyson," Hank called out.

Alyson put her hand over the receiver and yelled back, "Just a sec. I'm on the phone."

"Who was that?" Gavin asked.

"The manager," she lied. "I asked him for extra towels."

"I see," he said in a tone that told her he didn't believe her.

"I've got to go," she said, with an edge to her voice. "I've got a pretty full schedule of stuff to do tomorrow."

"Okay. I'll call again tomorrow night. Good luck. Luv ya."

"Luv ya too." She said automatically and hung up the phone, glad to be off the line. She rubbed her sweaty palm on her pant leg and got up and walked to the door and opened it.

"What do you want?" she said sharply.

"I, um, just wanted to read Miguel's file before tomorrow," Hank replied. "I'm sorry I interrupted."

"That's okay," her tone softened. She spun on her heel, walked over to her bag, pulled out the file, and handed it to him.

A few minutes later, she climbed into bed and turned off the light. She stared up at the ceiling without being able to see it. What was she going to do about

Gavin? Maybe she should fly out to California when they were done down here and tell him it was over. Or, should she wait until he came back to New York? It wasn't fair to have him think they were still in a relationship when they weren't. Sleep finally overcame her, but her dreams were not restful.

*   *   *   *

In his hotel room a mile away, Dan Morris tossed a shopping bag on the bed, walked into the bathroom and took a quick, cold shower, and donned a T-shirt and a pair of blue striped boxer shorts. He pulled a box of 9mm ammunition and a gun cleaning kit out of the bag. He pulled his suitcase across the bed and retrieved a brand new Glock 9mm pistol and held it in his hand, turning it from side to side. He smiled at the feel of it. He liked the model 17 with the ten-shot magazine. It had stopping power and was extremely accurate and versatile.

He also smiled because his plan had worked. He had bought the gun in New York and purposefully never put any ammunition in it to reduce the chances of it being found during airport screening. He didn't want to take a chance that the spectrometers would pick up faint traces of the gunpowder. If he had been caught, he would have simply claimed he was licensed to carry a firearm and he needed to be armed to act as bodyguard. He wasn't sure how the police down here would have reacted, but he thought it would be a lot easier than trying to buy a gun down here.

He disassembled the pistol, cleaned it, and reassembled it in a manner that showed his intimate familiarity with the Glock model. He picked up the two empty magazines and quickly loaded them with ten rounds each and slipped one magazine into the butt. He rechecked that the safety was on before laying the Glock on the night table next to the extra clip.

He walked to the mini-bar, grabbed a beer, and popped the top off. He picked up a picture of Alyson Murphy off the bed next to the shopping bag, raised the bottle, and tilted it slightly. "Here's to you, that your search is successful."

CHAPTER 26

▼

TUESDAY, DECEMBER 12

"Come on in," Alyson said as she opened the door. She wore one of the hotel's terrycloth bathrobes, open enough to show the lacy light blue teddy underneath. "Sorry, I overslept. Do I still have time for a quick shower?"

"Um...sure," Hank said. "I'll meet you downstairs."

"No. That's all right. I won't be long." She waltzed over to the dresser, pulled out clothes for the day, and went into the bathroom.

Hank sat on the edge of the bed to wait. Before long, he heard the water turn on in the shower and a few seconds later, heard the shower curtain being pulled across the metal bar. The bathroom door, which had not been fully latched, slowly inched inward until it stood about halfway open. Hank could see the shower reflected in the full-length mirror on the door. The shower curtain was nearly transparent and he could see the outline of Alyson's body as she washed her hair, could see the white bubbles run down her breasts, stomach, and legs. He was mesmerized, knowing he shouldn't be looking, but unable to help himself.

Suddenly, Alyson pulled back the curtain a little to reach for the soap from the sink, looked out, turned her head, and saw Hank on the bed. She paused for a moment and, without saying a word, grabbed the soap, and pulled the curtain shut. Behind the curtain, she laughed and yelled, "You can shut your jaw now."

"I think I'll go down and get us a table for breakfast after all," he announced.

She heard him leave and a wry smirk crossed her face

He walked down to the lobby, totally embarrassed, yet wondering about what had just happened. She didn't seem to be upset when she caught him watching her. In fact, she had playfully teased him about it. Maybe she didn't realize how transparent the curtain was. He pictured her body in the shower and he could feel himself getting aroused. Put those thoughts away, he said to himself, she has a boyfriend. In fact, she had been talking to him the night before and had gotten angry when he interrupted the call. She's just playing with you, you idiot, he said to himself.

They had a quick breakfast in the lobby and, afterward, took a cab down Avenida Frederico Boyd to Avenida Balboa, which ran along the water nearly the whole length of the city, passing La Marina, the local yacht club, and the U.S. embassy. The cab dropped them off across the street from the monument to Vasco Núñez de Balboa, a large copper green statue of the famous explorer, standing atop a white globe, dressed as a conquistador and holding his sword by the blade making it look like a cross in one hand and a Panama flag in the other. They walked two blocks up Avenida Ecuador and entered a small whitewashed three-story building that housed the office of Henriquez y de Santos, a law firm that specialized in managing the local affairs of international companies incorporated in Panama.

Although most of the companies it managed were nothing more than mailboxes, the amount of paperwork and other corporate activity needed to maintain corporate registration kept their staff of thirty-three busy. According to Miguel's papers, Henriquez y de Santos was one of two firms that Edward Sanders used to manage his companies. Hank and Alyson climbed the stairs to the second floor. There was a single door on the landing with a sign announcing the law offices of Henriquez y de Santos. They tried the door and it was unlocked. They entered the office and walked up to a young woman sitting behind the desk nearest the door and asked for Isabel Menes, who was the specific manager listed in some of the documentation that Miguel had given them.

"May I say who is calling?" the woman asked. They gave their names and told her that they were interesting in forming a new company and that a friend had recommended the firm to them.

"Buenos días. I am Isabel Menes," a woman said as she made her way through the maze of desks that occupied the center of the office. She was of medium height and a tad overweight, though she carried it well, and looked to be around forty to forty-five years old, but dressed younger than that.

"Thank you for seeing us without an appointment. I'm about to come into a large inheritance from my uncle, who made much of his fortune in South Africa and Zimbabwe. My wife and I decided that the IRS didn't need to know anything about it," Hank said, immediately going into the story they had agreed on over dinner the night before.

"I see. Maria said that you heard about us through a friend. Yes?"

"Yes. Ed Sanders suggested we contact you. He spoke highly of you in particular."

"You know Señor Sanders?" she asked skeptically.

"Yes. My dad and Mr. Sanders were college buddies a long time ago." They hoped this woman wouldn't ask any more questions, but they had prepared a short story just in case. Besides, they doubted this woman would have any way to check on it.

"I see. And exactly what do you need?" There was still suspicion in her voice.

"Well, we're not exactly sure. Ed said that he had set up a personal trust account," Hank said, using some of the information that Miguel had given them, "and an IBC, whatever that is. He didn't go into a lot of details."

"An IBC is an international business company. It is just another name for a company here in Panama, but one that is not allowed to do any business in Panama."

"What does it do then?" Alyson asked, playing the role of uninformed spouse.

"It conducts only your business, whatever that may be."

"Oh, I see," Alyson said. "That's okay. We don't plan to do any business down here."

"Few of our clients do." She gave them a knowing smile.

They spent the next forty-five minutes going through how to set up a company and the needed accounts. Every once in a while, but not so often as to raise the woman's suspicions, Hank tried to compare what they were discussing to what Ed Sanders had done, but Isabel Menes wasn't too accommodating in that regard. As they finished, Hank said, "I haven't seen Ed for a while. He seems to have dropped out of sight, if you get my drift. I hope he's enjoying his retirement. Could you say hello for me the next time you see him?"

"I will."

As they reached the front door, he turned and asked casually, "When was the last time you saw Ed?"

"Um, a couple of weeks ago," the woman said. A look of dismay immediately crossed her face.

"Don't worry. We won't tell him you said anything." The woman looked relieved. They thanked her again. Hank promised to get back in touch in a couple of days, after they thought more about what she had told them and they had figured out exactly what they needed.

They walked back to Avenida Balboa to catch a cab.

"What do you think?" Alyson asked.

"I was surprised to hear that Ms. Menes had seen Sanders recently. Either she's off in her timing or someone's been successful in taking over Saunders's alter ego. Or…" He laughed as he shrugged off a stray thought.

"Or what?"

"Oh, nothing," he shrugged.

"That seems to support what Miguel told us. We need to find out who's doing it or the money will disappear before we can track it down."

"I just hope she doesn't tell anyone that we were there."

"I don't know. She might not want to. She probably wouldn't want to admit she even acknowledged his name to us."

It was twenty minutes before a cab stopped to pick them up. They asked the driver to take them to the airport, where they quickly found the office for COPA Airline.

The manager rose as his assistant ushered Hank and Alyson into his office.

"How can I help you," he asked, sticking out a big, stubby hand.

"We're here to locate someone," Alyson said.

The manager looked confused. "I'm not sure how I can help."

Alyson looked around the room, pleased to see pictures of the manager surrounded by numerous children. "We're looking for a man who abandoned his wife and three children without any money." She hesitated. The manager leaned forward slightly. "We've tracked his movements outside of the U.S. over the last year and we think he took a number of your flights earlier this year. We were hoping you might be able to confirm this."

"We don't usually release the names of our passengers."

"We understand. Here's his picture." Hank slid the photo across the desk. Underneath was a crisp, new one-hundred-dollar bill.

The man picked up the picture and deftly pocketed the bill. "I may be able to help. What is his name?"

"That's just it," Hank said. "We think he was traveling under an alias, but we don't know what that is." The manager shrugged his shoulders as if to say that he wouldn't be able to help. "We are hoping you'd let us show that picture to some of your ground crew to see if they recognize him."

"How long ago was this flight?"

"About six months ago."

"I doubt that anyone would be able to remember a passenger from that long ago."

The manager checked the employee records for the dates in question. Both of the people who would have checked in passengers the day that Ed Sanders left Panama were on duty. He stood up and led them out to the main terminal. As they walked, he said, "It will be unlikely that either one would remember a single passenger from six months earlier. It will be a big help that he was traveling under a Belize passport. We don't get that many from that country."

The two women looked at the pictures. Neither one was sure whether they had seen him or not, but one thought that she may have seen him check in that day. She thought she remembered questioning whether the picture in the passport and the man checking in were the same person. The passport picture showed a man with a beard and light hair and the passenger had much darker hair and no beard. She recalled that they had had a good laugh about how bad passport pictures were, although she wasn't sure that she was remembering the same person.

Hank and Alyson thanked the women, left the airport, and headed back into town, disappointed and excited at the same time. The case that Ed Sanders was Ted Saunders was getting stronger and stronger. That meant Panama had certainly been the right place to start looking for the money.

An hour later, they were standing in front of a twenty-seven-story, steel-and-glass building in Punta Paitilla, at the western end of Panama City. They marched into the lobby, found the name they were looking for, and got off on the seventeenth floor. They were soon standing in the lobby of Tottingham, Wentworth and Sayer, one of the local law firms that Maria Garcia used in her deals for Saunders. To Hank, the name sounded more appropriate for a New York firm than one in Panama. They asked for John Sayer, the partner that had been directly involved in the deals handled by this firm.

They were told to take a seat and that Señor Sayer would be out in a few minutes.

The few minutes had stretched to nearly forty when a fiftyish man dressed in a dark gray suit walked out to greet them. He extended his hand, and a Rolex watch poked out from under the cuff of his sleeve.

"I'm John Sayer. How can I help you?" He said in impeccable American English, sounding like a high-priced lawyer on Park Avenue or Wall Street. His smile was clearly the result of very expensive dental work.

They introduced themselves. "Perhaps we could move this someplace more private," Hank suggested quietly.

"Of course." He led them to his office, offered them two of the chairs surrounding a small conference table, and ordered them coffee. "Now, how can I help you?"

"We're here to ask some questions about a couple of deals you were involved in with Ted Saunders."

"Ah, yes, but I'm afraid that we can't divulge that kind of information."

Alyson picked up her purse, reached inside, and withdrew an envelope, which she handed to the lawyer. "This is authorization from Mr. Whittaker Harden, Mr. Saunders's executor. We are acting on his behalf. There's also a notarized copy of Mr. Harden's appointment as Mr. Saunders's executor." The letter was a copy of the one she had sent to Maria Garcia at Brown, Banks and Martinez.

The lawyer opened the envelope, read the enclosed documents, folded them neatly, and put them back inside, then handed it back to Alyson. "What do you want to know?"

"Could you explain your involvement in Mr. Saunders's deals?"

"We got involved through Banks, Brown and Martinez, Mr. Saunders's attorneys in the States. We often act as local counsel on deals. Don't let our name fool you. We have tremendous local experience and a lot of contacts here and throughout the area. I, myself, was raised in the Canal Zone, but left to go to Harvard and then to Harvard Law School. I spent a number of years in the States at a small law firm in New York, but my wife—who's from here too—and I missed Panama too much. So, we moved back here. At first, I practiced in the Canal Zone, but then expanded out from there. It's a similar story for Ben Wentworth, but Donald Tottingham's a Brit. We were all raised here, but can offer good connections elsewhere."

"We understand you hired the firm that did the appraisal on the cattle ranch in Argentina. We'd like to see a copy of the report."

"We're under a confidentiality agreement."

"What about the silver mine in Peru?"

"I'm sorry, but we're under one for that one too."

"We understand that, but since we're Mr. Saunders's agents, we fall under that agreement and are entitled to see the report. If you want, we can sign a separate confidentiality agreement."

"I still don't think that I can give you a copy."

"What if we read them here?"

The lawyer considered that for a moment, stood up, and walked out of the office. Three minutes later, he walked back in with a sheaf of papers and sat down.

"This is all I have down here on the appraisals. Banks, Brown must have the rest of it." He slid the pages across the table to Alyson. The appraisal for the cattle ranch was on top. It was a mere seven pages long. Most of that document was filled with caveats, with just four short paragraphs at the end that said anything about the value of the ranch. The report offered little that could be used to establish the true value of the ranch. She handed it to Hank, who read it quickly and handed it back to the lawyer.

She picked up the report on the mine. It appeared to be more substantive at ninety-eight pages. Despite its additional length, which was mostly appendices with lists of equipment and a ten-page description of the process of extracting the silver from the ore, the key information needed for setting the mine's value was contained in another document and only referenced in this one.

"Is this all there is?"

"As I said, that's all I have."

"No wonder they don't want anyone to see it."

"I understand how this would look to anyone used to the American legal system, by you have to understand this is how business is done down here."

"Do you know if Mr. Saunders saw these reports?"

"I assume he did, but, no, I don't know for sure."

"Was he willing to buy the mine on the basis of this?" Hank asked, tapping the mining appraisal on the table in front of him.

"He bought it, didn't he?" the lawyer replied.

"Don't you think it odd," Alyson jumped in, "that a Panamanian company would own a cattle ranch in Argentina for an American?"

"Are you kidding?" The lawyer laughed. "Do you know how many companies are incorporated here? You wouldn't believe all the things that companies are set up to own. Real estate from all over the world is common. I had one company a couple of years ago that owned a dog."

Alyson and Hank looked at each other and shrugged.

"Can we see the rest of the files on these deals?" Alyson asked.

"No," the lawyer said bluntly, gathering in the documents and resting his hand on them. "I really don't think that is possible."

"You don't think it's possible," Hank asked. "When will you know for sure?"

Alyson touched his arm to get him to check his temper, then turned to the lawyer and said, "I don't think you understand. We're authorized agents of Mr. Saunders's estate."

"In the States you might be, but not down here. I probably went too far even talking to you, but I hoped that showing you these reports would satisfy you. Apparently, they did not. I think we're finished here."

"We were told that Panama recognized this kind of agency authority."

"It might, but not until it's certified by a court down here. Otherwise, anyone could waltz in here and ask for information."

Alyson looked at Hank. She hadn't thought of that.

"Well, then," Hank said, "we've probably taken up enough of your time."

"We'll be back after we get a court to certify our agency status," Alyson said.

"Then I will see you sometime next June." He smirked. "The court that would deal with your petition has a six-month backlog."

"We'll see about that," Alyson said with a bravado she didn't feel.

"Ms. Murphy. If you're trying to piece together Mr. Saunders's investments down here, please be careful. Panama can be a dangerous place."

"Are you trying to scare us?" He was succeeding, Alyson decided.

"Not at all. Just trying to make you aware of what you may have gotten yourself into. Just watch your step while you're down here. You might just ruffle some feathers the wrong way, that's all."

They left the office and started walking down the street in the direction of their hotel.

"Can you believe how bad those appraisals were?" Alyson said. "What a joke."

"You think they were the whole reports?" Hank asked.

"I don't know. They could be. That may be how they do it down here. Besides, if we're right about Saunders, he didn't really need much of an appraisal."

"I suppose not," he said softly.

Alyson stumbled.

"Are you all right?"

"Yes. I just remembered the not-so-veiled threat." She quickened her pace and began looking over her shoulder as they walked. "I'd like to get back to the hotel."

A black Ford eased out of its parking place, inched along slowly for a minute, and sped past them, pulling down a side street a few blocks ahead. It turned around and parked facing the main street. Morris pulled out a cigarette, lit it, sat back, and waited for them to pass. He pulled out his spiral notebook and started scribbling notes. He had followed them to the building, watched them get on the elevator, and waited to see which floor they had stopped on. A quick check of the large directory on the wall across from the elevators told him which firm they had visited.

Hank and Alyson strode across the entrance to the street he was parked on. He got out, walked to the corner, stubbed out his cigarette against the side of the building and dropped the butt on the ground, turned the corner, and followed them at a distance.

They arrived back at the hotel a little before 5:00 PM and went straight up to Alyson's room. Alyson opened her e-mail and clicked on a message from Fred Hamilton.

"Fred got the name of the person that Saunders called. He had a friend hack into the phone database of Cable & Wireless Panamá. It took a while to match up the record. It didn't help that everything was in Spanish. Hmm. Wait a minute." She read the message again. "Oh, my gosh," she cried out.

"What is it?"

"The number that Saunders called when he was here was Alberto Ramirez."

"Who?"

"Miguel's boss."

"So? If Saunders needed to get everything done in twenty-four hours, he would call the top guy."

"At home?"

"What?"

"Saunders called Ramirez at home."

"Oh, that's not good."

She reached for her bag and frenetically looked for her cell phone. Finding it, she flipped it open and hit one of the preprogrammed numbers on her list.

"'Allo," a woman answered.

"Buenos días. ¿Habla usted Inglés?" Alyson asked.

"Sí. Some," the woman answered hesitantly.

"Is Señor Alvarez there?"

"Señor Alvarez is not available," the woman answered in heavily accented English.

"When will he be back?"

"Lo siento. I am sorry. He is in hospital."

"What happened?"

Alyson listened as the woman explained in a mixture of Spanish and English. Alyson's eyes widened and began to moisten as she listened, trying hard to make sense of what she was hearing.

"Gracias," Alyson said at last. She closed the phone and sat frozen in place.

Hank reached out and touched her knee with his fingertips. "What's wrong?"

"Miguel! He's in the hospital. He's been shot."

"What! When?"

"He was robbed on the way home from work yesterday."

"Is he going to be okay?"

"They don't know yet. He's still in intensive care." She dropped her head into her hands, sobbing. "It's…all…my…fault."

"No, it's not." Hank took her into his arms, feeling each sob rolling through her like a crashing wave. "You had nothing to do with it. It was a robbery, that's all." She didn't say anything, couldn't say anything. He held her tight for a few minutes, until the sobs began to lessen and become less frequent.

Alyson pulled away slightly and looked at him, her eyes red and swollen. "If only I hadn't called him…"

"You don't know that. Can we go see him?"

"No. His secretary said the hospital won't let anyone see him except family."

▼

CHAPTER 27

WEDNESDAY, DECEMBER 13

"Hank! Wake up." Alyson was knocking on the door. "We've got to get going or we'll miss our flight."

"I'll be out in a minute."

They hurried through the lobby, which was deserted. The cab they had requested the night before was waiting at the curb. Minutes later, they were heading east toward the airport.

"Explain to me again why we're up at this godforsaken hour." He looked at his watch, which read 6:12 AM.

"The only way to get out to Contadora without spending the whole day there, or an overnight, is to catch the 8:00 AM flight." They had discovered that Ed Sanders owned a house on a small island called Isla Contadora, about forty miles off the coast, out in the Bay of Panama.

"But why do we need to see Sanders's house?"

"I'd like to see it and I thought that maybe we'd be able to talk our way inside. Maybe he left some documents there that we could use."

"I doubt it. He died before he got to move in."

"You never know. He might have shipped stuff there."

"But we'll only have an hour."

"That's if we don't find anything. If we do, we can catch the 5:15 flight back."

The de Haviland Twin Otter plane taxied to the runway and took off for its fifteen-minute flight. There were thirteen other passengers aboard. Hank gripped the armrests. Alyson looked out the small window watching the city below.

The plane flew low out over the Bahía de Panamá. The water was a mixture of turquoise in the shallower water and dark blue in the deeper water. The bay was full of sailboats and yachts, as well as a number of larger ships coming from or going to the Canal.

The de Haviland touched down on the single narrow runway that ran the width of the island and taxied to a stop outside a hut that served as the terminal. They looked around for a taxi. Seeing none, they walked inside and asked about a cab. They were told that the island was so small there weren't any taxis on the island. They could, if they wanted, rent a couple of Honda ATVs, which were essentially four-wheeled dirt bikes. They agreed to rent two ATVs for an hour and were soon driving away from the airport along Paseo de los Guaymies, one of two main roads that traversed the length of the island.

They drove down the middle of the road, staying away form the deep concrete gullies that lined both sides of the road, which were designed to carry away the floodwaters caused by torrential downpours during the rainy season. They prayed they wouldn't meet any oncoming traffic. The trees and the low undergrowth grew right down to the sides of the gullies, sometimes obscuring the view when the road turned sharply.

Seven minutes after leaving the airport, they pulled up in front of a set of gates. Alyson stepped off her four-wheeler and pushed the call button on the gatepost.

"¡Hola!" A woman's voice said.

"Buenos días. ¿Habla usted Inglés?"

"Sí. Yes," the voice answered, a bit tentatively.

"We are looking for Señor Sanders. Is he home?"

"Señor Sanders?"

"Yes. I understand that this is his house."

After some hesitation, "Señor Sanders does not live here."

"Oh, we were sure that this was his house."

"Lo siento. You are mistaken."

"Are you sure this is the right house?" Hank said from behind her.

She turned and glared at him. "Yes."

"Okay, now what?"

Alyson hit the call button again.

"Sí," the woman answered.

"Could you tell us whose house this is?"

"No."

"Could you tell us if Señor Sanders lives around here?"

"No. Lo siento."

"Gracias."

Alyson climbed back onto her ATV and they turned around in the driveway. As they approached the airport, Alyson pulled over to the side of the road in front of the police station. Hank, who was ahead of her, pulled over fifty feet down the road, turned around, and parked next to her. She got off her bike and walked inside. Four minutes later, she walked back out and got on.

"The police think that's his house."

"How did you get them to tell you that?"

"I just said that we were visiting and couldn't find it. They were very friendly and gave me directions to the house."

"So she lied," Hank said.

"It seems so."

"Did the police give any hint as to whether they've ever seen Ed Sanders?"

"That's the funny thing. They seem to think that he's living there now."

They drove back to the airport, dropped off their ATVs, leaving them only ten minutes to wait for the return flight. They climbed into the plane and found their seats. They had to sit apart as it was a work day and the flight was full with no assigned seating.

They were back to the hotel by half past eleven and stopped in the hotel restaurant for a cup of coffee and a late breakfast of rolls and jam.

The woman from behind the reception desk ambled across the lobby and stopped next to their table. "¡Perdón! You are Señorita Murphy, yes?" she asked.

"Sí." The woman handed Alyson a piece of paper. "Joyce Howard called," Alyson read it aloud. She reached into her bag and pulled out her cell phone. "Hi, Joyce. What's up?"

"I thought I'd give you an update. We finally cracked the last password last night. The one for that big accounting file on that CD Betty gave us."

"That's great. How?"

"I interviewed Betty again since we weren't getting anywhere with the stuff we had. I thought that maybe she could give us other info we might be able to use."

"Like what?"

"A whole bunch of stuff about work and his personal life we didn't get before. The clincher was telling me about Alicia Dubin."

"Who's that?"

"Believe it or not, it's Saunders's mother."

"I thought her name was Mary or Martha or something like that."

"That was his adoptive mother. Alicia Dubin was his biological mother. Betty remembered her name from something she saw a few years ago when Saunders's biological mother died. I fed that name and the year of her death into the Social Security database and got two hits. I then found her birth date and Passbreaker morphed all that into the password."

"That's great! I assume you found something or you wouldn't have called."

"I'm not sure what we've got yet. I've e-mailed a copy of the file to you with the password. It has a list of assets that Fred's still trying to reconcile to the hard copies of his account statements you got out of his office that day. He says there's a bunch of assets that aren't on any of the account balances."

"What kind of assets?"

"They're mostly bank and brokerage accounts. There's a list of these accounts with some codes assigned to them, probably numbered accounts. Some of them list the banks and some just have initials. We're trying to track those down."

"Can you fax them to me?"

"I can fax the summary. The reconciliation isn't done yet."

Alyson gave her the hotel's fax number. "Send me what you've got. And when the reconciliation is ready, give me a call so I can be down there to get it right off the machine. Don't send it otherwise." She didn't want that kind of information lying around anywhere or possibly copied, not after the warning they had gotten the day before.

"I'm setting it up right now." Alyson could hear Joyce typing at her keyboard. She would fax the summary directly from her PC. "Oh, before I forget. Did you get the e-mail from Fred? He got the number that Saunders called in Panama."

"Yes, I did," she said sadly. Tears began to fill her eyes. She reached up and wiped them with her paper napkin.

"Are you okay?" Joyce asked.

"Yes. No. That number belonged to Miguel's boss. I called Miguel to ask him about it and to warn him..." Alyson choked.

"What happened?" Joyce cried.

Hank reached over and took the phone. "Joyce, it's Hank."

"What happened?"

"Miguel's in the hospital. He was shot during a robbery."

"Oh, my god. You guys have to get out of there. It's gotten too dangerous."

"We've got to stay. It's the only way. We won't be safe until we find the money."

"But you could be killed."

"We'll be extra careful. We'll be on the lookout for anyone after us."

"I don't like it."

"I don't either, but we don't have a choice. We're in it now and the only way out is to see it through to the end."

"I hope you know what you're doing."

"Me too. Why don't you send the fax? We'll walk over and get it. Just give us a minute of two to collect our things."

Hank hung up the phone. "Are you okay?"

"Yes." Alyson wiped her eyes again, then blew her nose. "I'll be okay. Let's go and get the fax."

They were soon standing by the hotel's fax machine. The first page was already printing. The manager didn't object to their being there once they explained they were expecting a highly confidential fax. The manager didn't seem a bit surprised at the request.

Thirteen pages later, the machine signaled the end of the incoming fax. They rode up the elevator and were soon in Alyson's room.

"Where do we start?" Hank asked as soon as the door closed behind him.

"I thought we'd try to match it up with Miguel's list." She picked up her purse, pulled out the manila envelope containing Miguel's list, threw it on the bed, and sat down. They spent the next forty-five minutes comparing the two lists. There were only a few accounts that seemed to be connected, either because the dates of deposits were the same or because the amounts were a close match.

"This isn't much help. The two aren't similar at all," Hank said, frustrated.

"That's not surprising, I guess. Saunders would have moved the cash out of those companies as soon as possible. There're a number of contact names here. Let's start with them."

"I know, let's use the accounts and the codes and see if we could take some of the cash out. He won't miss it." Hank suggested with a smile.

"That would be a very bad idea." She glared at him.

"I was just kidding." He laughed and held up his hands as if surrendering.

"I know, but besides being illegal and unethical, that would tip off anyone using the accounts that we've got the codes and the account numbers. We know there's someone out there who knows we're looking for him. The last thing we need to do is tell him we're getting close to the money."

"What's preventing him from moving it already?"

"He won't until he gets nervous enough. It takes time to set up all the accounts and transfer the assets."

"Can't he just wire transfer it to new accounts overnight?"

"Yes, but not if he doesn't want to leave a trail we could follow."

"But if we move it all, do we care? It would be safe then."

"Yes, we care. We want to catch the guy who's using the accounts. He's likely the killer or could lead us to him."

"But…we could go online and look around."

Alyson pulled her laptop out of her briefcase. She connected it to the Internet port and was soon online. "Let's see, where should we go first?"

"I'm not sure which of these accounts are at which banks."

"There's a few with bank info, let's try those first."

The first account they tried had already been closed, as was the second. "We're too late! The money's been moved."

"Let's not give up," Hank said encouragingly. "You said he probably moved it. There's more than a couple dozen other numbers here. Maybe only the ones with a bank listed are closed. Maybe the others are still open."

"Maybe," Alyson said forlornly.

"Let's just check them all. We've got plenty of time before we've got to leave to get to the bank before it closes."

They had a list of Panamanian banks that Fred had put together before they left New York. They tried each of the account numbers in the first name on the list. With each succeeding bank, their spirits dripped away like the water in a pail with a slow leak. By the fifth bank, Alyson was ready to concede defeat. Hank looked at his watch. They had time for one more try. He typed the online address for the next bank on the list and brought up the login screen for Banco de Colón, then keyed in the first account number. No luck. He tried the second account, with the same result. He tried the third account number. The screen fluttered for a moment after hitting the log-in button, then came up with a new screen showing the balance in Ed Sanders's account. He stared at it for a moment, not believing what he saw. He spun the laptop around so Alyson could see it. "Bingo," he said, with a smile as broad as his face.

Alyson didn't understand for a second or two. She smiled as she realized what it meant.

"Are you sure we can't just siphon off a little?" Hank asked mischievously.

"No, I told you…"

"I'm just kidding."

Even though they should have left ten minutes earlier, they couldn't bring themselves to leave right then, now that they had gotten into one of the accounts. They spent the next fifteen minutes looking around. There was nearly twenty-five million dollars of securities in the account, most of them U.S. stocks and bonds, with a smattering of stocks of some of the largest European companies.

"We've got to get going," Hank announced, looking at his watch again. "If we don't, the bank will be closed."

"Okay! Let's go." She pulled herself away from the PC.

"Maybe we don't need to go to the banks. Maybe we can just do it over the Net."

"No. We've still got to go. If our calculations are right, this is maybe, at most, about a quarter of the total. We can't count on finding it all this way."

"But the rest might be in one of these other accounts."

"But it might not be. Besides, it'll be here when we get back," Alyson said, hoping that would be true.

They quickly gathered up the papers, shoving them and the laptop into Alyson's bag. They were soon on their way toward the Marabella section of the city, which formed the eastern edge of the financial center of Panama City.

"Do you think that he'll talk to us?" Hank asked.

"I don't know, but it's worth a try." Alyson replied and then turned to watch the city pass by. "It sure is pretty, isn't it?"

"Yes, it is," he said, looking at her, not at the city.

They were dropped off outside a large white stucco building. Four ornate marble columns held up the part of the roof that extended out over the entrance. On the exterior wall to the left of the main entrance was a shiny brass plaque that announced the name of the bank, Banco Internacional de Panama. Under the name was 1897, the year the bank was founded.

Upon entering, they felt as if they had stepped into a Victorian-era men's club rather than a bank. The ceiling was twelve feet above their heads and the walls were richly paneled in dark mahogany for the first eight feet, then plastered and painted white the rest of the way up to the thick crown molding. That space was filled with large oil portraits in ornate gilded frames of former presidents and directors of the bank. There was a row of offices along the back wall. One half of the open floor was covered with rows of desks, each in a style that matched the paneling. Behind each one sat a clerk, probably doing much the same work that his or her counterpart had done a hundred years earlier, only now using computers. The other half of the floor looked more like a comfortable seating area where gentlemen could enjoy their after-dinner cigars or cognacs than the lobby of a bank. Overstuffed leather chairs and couches invited customers, and tables were covered with magazines and current issues of the *Wall Street Journal* and the *New York Times*, as well as several London papers. Perhaps one of the most telling indications of who the bank's clientele were was the complete absence of any local newspapers.

"Buenos días," Alyson said, holding out her hand to the man sitting in the office the receptionist had directed them to. The man they were meeting was responsible for setting up most of the new accounts and had been doing so for the past four years. They hoped that the bank had few enough customers that he would remember Ed Sanders.

"Buenos días. My name is Fidel Morales. How may I help you?" he said comfortably in English. He was conservatively dressed, as a typical banker would be anywhere in the world, in a gray pinstriped suit that he had bought in London, a white shirt, and a colorful striped school tie. Neither Hank nor Alyson could determine how old the banker was. The creases in his face made him look like he was ready for retirement, but his dark hair and taut body were those of a much younger man.

"We're thinking about opening an account here," Hank said.

"Very good. Please be seated."

They sat in the deep maroon leather seats in front of the desk.

"Before we start, you do realize we require a minimum deposit of ten million dollars…U.S." He put emphasis on the *U.S.*

"We realize that," Hank said nonchalantly.

The banker's face brightened at the prospect of a new account. He sat forward and smiled.

"What kind of documentation would we need to open up an account here?" Alyson asked.

"Our bank is committed to complying with the international standards that require us to obtain positive identification from all of our clients," he said, spouting the official bank policy. "In order to do that, we usually require a valid passport and at least one letter of reference. We usually require one from your current bank and others from a current client in good standing or from some other well-respected person."

"We have all those," Alyson said.

"Are there any exceptions to these requirements?" Hank asked.

"Sometimes, if the person can produce other forms of identification, we might accept them."

"But you generally know who your customer is before you'll open an account."

"Of course," Fidel said with an emphasis that told them it wasn't always true.

"I see. That's good."

"Now, you said you had references?"

"Of course. We have a letter from Edward Sanders, who we think is a customer of yours." Hank waited for a second. "You do know Ed, don't you?" Hank waited again until the banker finally nodded. The letter was a forgery she had created before they left New York. She hoped that the banker wouldn't compare the signatures right away, or if he did, the modified version of Saunders's signature would pass for that of Ed Sanders. "Here are our passports."

The banker looked over the documents. "They seem to be in order. I'll need to take a copy of these for our files. Is that acceptable?" They nodded. "Now about setting up the account, what kind of account would you like?"

"We're not sure. Could you please explain the different accounts you offer." Hank asked.

The banker pulled out a file from his desk and opened it in front of them. He then described each of the various accounts the bank offered and the services and fees each one commanded. There were seven in all. "Now what do you need."

"Hmmmm." Hank rubbed his chin as if thinking about the choices.

"Darling," Alyson said, "I don't think that I'm ready to put our money into this bank."

"Why not honey?"

"It's just…I don't know."

"But Ed thinks that this is one of the best banks in Panama."

"I know, but there are so many others to choose from."

Hank turned to the banker and said, "Mr. Morales, what kind of account does Ed have? Maybe we should start there."

The banker looked from one then to the other, clearly not knowing what to do. He pressed the tips of his fingers together, as his rested his hands on the desk, and tapped his thumbs together.

Alyson started to stand up. "I think that we should go. I liked the man from Pacific Asset Managers. We should put our money there. He was cute."

"But Ed told us that PAM wasn't as good as this bank," Hank pleaded.

Alyson reached down for her bag and took a step away from the desk, as if to leave.

"Just a moment," the banker said, then typed in a name and hit enter. "Mr. Sanders has the Premier Private Banking Account with us. That's this one here." He pointed to the description in the brochure. Alyson returned to her chair. The banker smiled. He spent the next ten minutes explaining the features of the account, including the fact that the minimum balance was twenty-five million dollars.

Hank and Alyson were debating the pros and cons of the account in front of the banker, when Alyson suddenly held her hand to head. "I can't do this. I've got such a migraine."

"Are you sure? We're so close to making a decision."

"This won't take much longer," the banker insisted.

Alyson continued to hold her head, shaking it slowly.

"Are you okay, honey?"

Alyson shook her head.

"Well, er…okay," Hank said to Alyson. Turning to the banker, he said, "I'm sorry, but we're going to have to leave. Do you have a card? Can I take these?" He gathered up the business card, their documents, and the brochures.

Alyson said, "I'm sorry." She started to stand up, letting some of the papers from her bag spill onto the floor. Fidel Morales reached down to help her pick them up.

Hank leaned forward and scanned the screen. It still showed Ed Sanders' account information. He tried to memorize the account number. The balance was more than thirty million dollars.

The banker sat up, saw Hank standing in front of the desk, and noticed that he had left the account information on his screen. He reached over and punched a button. The screen went dark for a second before a picture of the bank popped up.

They set an appointment for the next morning, although it was not an appointment they meant to keep.

Letting Alyson get a few steps ahead of him, Hank turned back to the banker. "Thank you." Hank extended his hand. "Please forgive my wife," he said, in a low, conspiratorial voice. "She gets like this whenever she's close to making a decision. You should have seen her when she was picking out the drapes for our living room."

*   *   *   *

Alyson took a shower before getting ready to go to dinner and was about to leave the room when the phone rang. She threw a towel around her and walked into the bedroom.

"Hi Alyson, it's Gavin."

"Oh, hi," she said, her voice flat.

"How's it going? I miss you."

"I miss you too," she answered without thinking. "Things are going well."

"I was worried about you. You sounded like you were in trouble last night."

"No. Everything's fine."

"I worry about you being down there all by yourself. Maybe I should fly down."

"No!" she blurted out, a little stronger than she meant to.

"Why not? I could rearrange things, I'm sure that Alex could take over for me for a couple of days."

"No, that's not necessary. Besides by the time you'd get down here, I'd be ready to come home."

"Are you sure?" He sounded disappointed.

"Yes." They chatted awkwardly for a few more minutes and then said good night. She stared at the phone in her hand for a while before putting it down. She hurriedly dressed and met Hank in the lobby.

Hank and Alyson had a late dinner and returned to the hotel around eleven.

"Un momento, señor," the night manager said as Hank and Alyson were walking toward the elevator after returning from dinner. "You have a message."

"It's from Bobbie Roth," Hank read the message softly aloud as they walked toward the elevator. "She wants me to call her any time between nine and ten tomorrow."

"Who's she?"

"She's a medical examiner with the NYPD. I asked her about DNA profiling after I talked to Edna Grouse. You know, the one who claimed the toes were on the wrong foot."

"Oh, right. How do you know her?"

"Um, we used to date." After a short pause, "That was many moons ago."

"I was just wondering how a financial reporter would know a medical examiner."

"I wonder what she wants," Hank said, ignoring her question.

Chapter 28

▼

Thursday, December 14

"Why are you dressed in a running outfit?" he asked as she walked into the restaurant where they had agreed to meet for breakfast.

"I need to go for a run. Our first appointment isn't until after lunch."

"That's not a good idea."

"Yes it is. It will help me deal with all this. I ran out on the Causeway the other day and it's safe. There're huge crowds. I figured I could run while you call Robbie, or Roberta, or whatever her name is."

"Bobbie. I still think running is a bad idea."

"No. It's a good one. You talk and I run. Nothing's going to happen." Although she was still worried, the risk seemed to be so much less with the new day, its bright sunshine driving away the gloom of the night before. She was sure that she'd be safe on the Causeway with all the people around.

Alyson had orange juice and a piece of toast. Hank ordered two eggs, over easy, sausage, toast, and coffee.

"Is that all you're having?" he asked.

"I always eat light before I run."

They finished their breakfast quickly. Alyson bought a bottle of water at the small store off the lobby. They hopped into the back of a taxi on the way across town. A black sedan pulled out from a parking space half a block away and followed them.

The cab hurtled down Via Espana, one of the main boulevards that ran through the main part of the city. The driver zigzagged from lane to lane, nearly hitting one car after another. The black car kept pace without drawing the attention of the cab driver.

A terrifying twenty-five minutes later, they stepped out of the cab amazed that they had made it in one piece. They walked partway out onto the Causeway and stopped at the restaurant where Alyson had stopped on her prior run.

"Okay. I'll be back in about forty minutes. You'll be safe here. Just don't pick up any strange women." She smiled playfully.

"How about non-strange women?" he shot back with a grin.

She gave him a dirty look, turned, and jogged off. Hank watched her until she was lost in the crowd. He couldn't believe that he was letting her go alone. They had argued about it all the way over in the cab. He had even volunteered to run with her, but they both knew that he wouldn't be able to keep up with her. He finally gave in when he realized that he wasn't going to change her mind. He also saw that she needed the release that the physical activity would give her. A lot had happened, and she needed to get away from it all. This was the only way. He shook his head.

Hank pulled out his cell phone and dialed Bobbie's number in New York.

Meanwhile, the black Ford had pulled into a parking space and the driver had gotten out and walked past Hank and Alyson. He wore a light blue loose-fitting short-sleeve shirt and khaki pants, similar in style to dozens of local men on the Causeway. He sat down on a park bench, replaced his wire-rimmed glasses with sunglasses, and pulled out a copy of *La Pensa*, a local Spanish-language newspaper. He watched Alyson run off and then switched his attention to the man she had just left. The man watched Hank for a few minutes, folded his newspaper and tucked it under his arm, and walked back to his car. The black sedan pulled out of the parking lot and headed east on Via España.

"Hey, Bobbie, it's Hank."

"Hi. How's Panama?"

"It's pretty nice. I'm actually sitting in a restaurant on the beach. It's a beautiful, bright sunny day."

"Okay. Stop rubbing it in or I won't tell you why I called."

"Sorry. But it is beautiful down here."

"I've always wanted to cruise the Canal."

"I'm hoping we can get out there before we leave."

"I hope you do. Take some pictures for me, okay?"

"I will. Now, what's up?"

"I gave our conversation some more thought and I think I have something that might interest you."

"What is it?"

"Your comment about that old woman who claimed the toes were on the wrong foot got me thinking. Something about it stuck in my head, so yesterday I did some research. I called Texas and got a copy of the autopsy report. Did you read it?"

"I skimmed it." He felt a little guilty admitting that. Autopsy reports made him queasy, something he would never admit to a medical examiner.

"Do you remember anything unusual in it?"

"Not really."

"Do you remember reading about the mix-up with the chest X-rays? They noted that the tags were wrong."

"Yes. I do remember that. In fact, I asked the doctor who did the autopsy about it. He said it was just a mistake and it didn't mean anything since they didn't need the X-rays for the ID."

"That may be true, but it may not be a mistake."

"But that would mean Saunders's heart was on the wrong side."

"Maybe it wasn't Saunders."

"Wait a minute. I thought you said that given the DNA results, the body had to be Saunders."

"That's what I thought too. But have you ever heard of mirror twins?"

"Sounds like something out of *Alice in Wonderland*. Just kidding. No."

"Actually, you're right. Tweedledee and Tweedledum were mirror twins."

"No kidding! I didn't know that. What's a mirror twin and how does that apply to Saunders?"

"Well, mirror twins are a type of identical twins. Identical twins happen when a single fertilized egg splits at some point after the cells begin to divide. If the split happens late enough, you end up with mirror twins. The most extreme case is when even internal organs end up on the opposite sides of the body, like the heart being on the right side instead of the left. About one in four identical twins are to some degree mirror twins. Do you know what's special about all identical twins?"

"No, what?"

"They've got identical DNA."

Hank thought about that for a moment. "Makes sense, I guess. So?"

"Well, maybe the body in that fire wasn't Saunders after all. Maybe it was his identical, but mirror, twin."

"But he didn't have any brothers."

"Maybe he did. You said he was adopted."

"Yeah, so?"

"Maybe his twin brother was adopted by someone else."

"Could be, I guess."

"That would explain the toes and the heart. Well, anyway, think about it. You asked me how it could be someone else. This is the only way I can think of."

"If you're right…"

"Then Ted Saunders didn't die in the fire."

Hank sat silently. Could Saunders really still be alive? It seemed like a stretch. How was he going to find out if Saunders had a biological brother? And how likely was it that such a brother would be a mirror identical twin?

"Hank, are you still there?"

"Huh? Yeah. Sorry. I was just thinking."

"I realize this is a longshot, but it was the only thing I could come up with to answer your question."

"Bobbie. This is great. Thanks. I owe you one."

"Sure. Good luck."

"Thanks. I think I'm going to need it."

He hung up and quickly dialed another number. "Carol, it's Hank."

"Oh, hi Hank," Carol Somers cooed. "I thought you were on vacation."

"I am, but I need some help."

"Oh." He hated taking advantage of her feelings, but he was desperate. "You're not in jail, are you? I don't think…"

"No. Nothing like that. It's for a story I'm working on."

"Okay. What do you need?" Carol's voice became serious, businesslike.

"I need you to get as much information on Ted Saunders's adoption as you can. I need to know if he had any brothers."

"I didn't think he had any brothers or sisters."

"Well, none that we know of. I want to know whether he has a biological brother, one that got adopted by somebody else."

"Don't they usually keep kids together?"

"Now, yes. Back then, who knows?"

"Okay, but it's going be hard. You know they've tightened up the laws on this kind of stuff. Everyone's worried about privacy these days."

"Yeah, I know," Hank said.

"Okay. When do you need it?"

"ASAP, sooner if you can. I'm using part of my vacation to research a story."
Then an idea hit him. "I know how you can get the information and it's partly
true if my theory for my story is right."

"What is it?"

"Tell them you're working for Whittaker Harden, Ted Saunders's executor,
and that you're looking for heirs to a multimillion dollar fortune. That should
open them up."

"That might work. I'll let you know if I get anything."

Hank sat silently for many minutes. A mirror twin would certainly explain a
lot of things, but the odds of that had to be a million to one when you factored in
the odds of being a mirror twin in the first place and then the odds that Saunders
had an unaccounted-for brother and on top of that the likelihood that the
brother had been found and ended up at Saunders's Texas ranch. Still, it was
worth exploring. They didn't have any other real leads at this point.

A gust of wind ruffled the stack of papers on his lap. He looked down at
Joyce's list and looked for the account number he had seen in on the banker's
screen yesterday. He found it on the seventh page. The bank was listed only by a
code number. He scribbled some notes in the margin.

He looked at his watch. Alyson had been gone for nearly an hour. Maybe she
decided to take an extra lap out to the end of the Causeway and back, he thought.
That would take only fifteen minutes, he calculated, assuming Alyson was still
running seven-minute miles. If she had waited for a few minutes and then gone
for another lap, she'd be back any minute. Fifteen minutes later, Hank was
beginning to get nervous. Where was she? Another wave of guilt swept over him.
Why had he agreed to let her go running on her own?

He started to get up, determined to walk out to the end of the Causeway,
when he saw her walking toward him, talking to another woman who was pushing a baby stroller.

"Sorry I'm late," she called out, as she came up to him. "Were you getting nervous?"

"Not at all."

"Liar!" She laughed.

"Where were you?"

"I finished my first run and, believe it or not, bumped into a girlfriend from
high school. She's down here with her husband and new son, Aaron. Hank, I'd
like you to meet Lynn Gutterman." They shook hands. "And Aaron."

"We haven't seen each other in years," Lynn said, "but it seems like just yesterday."

"Oh, yeah. We got caught up on what we've been doing, swapping stories of old friends," Alyson said.

"Old boyfriends," Lynn said. The two women laughed.

"Really?" Hank said.

"Like Jerry Townsend," Lynn began.

"Don't!" Alyson protested.

"Tell me," Hank pleaded.

"We both had a crush on him. He was the captain of the high school baseball team and selected as most likely to be the first to earn a million dollars. Alyson won and he took her to the senior prom." Lynn paused. "The last thing I heard was he's going through his second divorce and working as the manager of a small shoe store at Park City Mall back home." They both giggled.

"Good men are so hard to find," Lynn said. "I found mine, although it seems I've misplaced him somewhere around here." She laughed. "When are you going to find yours, Alyson?"

Alyson blushed and then said, "How do you know I haven't?" She winked at Lynn.

"Oh, there's Ben. I've got to go. Let's talk when you're back in the States. We leave tomorrow."

They said their farewells and gave each other a kiss. Lynn pushed the stroller over to a compact car, put Aaron in the baby seat, and threw the folding stroller in the backseat next to him. Lynn waved as they drove away.

"Well, she seemed nice," Hank said, not knowing what else to say.

"Yes. We were best friends and still are." Alyson stood quiet for a few moments. "I'm starved. Are you hungry?"

"Yes. Should we go back or stay here for lunch?" Hank asked.

"Let's go back," she said, smiling.

After another torturous ride through the city, the cab pulled to a sudden stop in front of the hotel. They were both thrown forward, Alyson's bag spilling out onto the seat. Hank helped her gather the contents of her bag.

"What's this?" Hank said, holding up the canister of pepper spray and tear gas.

"Oh, that. My friend at the twenty-fourth suggested I buy it. I had forgotten it was in there."

"Did you get on the plane with it?"

"I guess so. So much for airport security." Alyson laughed nervously.

She held the canister in her hand and looked at it for a couple of seconds. She shivered.

"You okay?" Hank asked.

"Yes. I just got a chill."

Hank looked at her for a second, opened the door, and stepped out onto the curb, then reached back inside the cab to take Alyson's hand to help her out. A few minutes later, they got off the elevator on the third floor and he escorted her to her room.

As she turned the key in the lock, they heard a noise from inside. Hank pushed open the door and there, next to her bed, stood a man who was clearly not one of the hotel staff. He was dressed in a blue loose-fitting shirt and khaki pants. The contents of Alyson's briefcase were strewn all over the bed. The man turned to face them. His face was deeply tanned and his dark brown eyes glowered through wire-rimmed glasses.

Hank stepped in front of Alyson. "What are you doing?" he demanded.

The man's only response was to reach behind his back and, in one swift movement, swing a knife from its hiding place and flick his wrist to open it. Menacingly, he took a step toward them, holding the knife out in front of him. Hank took a step to one side, pushing Alyson further behind him. "Just go," Hank demanded.

The man took another tentative step forward. Seeing that Hank was not making a move to stop him, he started to run from the room. As he passed them, Hank stuck out his leg and sent the man sprawling into the hallway, the knife flying against the far wall. Before the man could get up, Hank jumped on top of him, trying to hold him down.

"Hank!" Alyson screamed. "What are you doing?" She fumbled with her bag, looking for the spray canister.

Hank didn't answer, focusing instead on trying to pin the man's arms to the floor. Even though the man was shorter and slighter than Hank, he was stronger than Hank had bargained for. The man locked his foot against the doorjamb, using it for leverage to suddenly push up with his leg, rolling the two of them over so that he was on top. With his newly freed hand, he punched Hank in the face. Then, taking advantage of the momentary break in Hank's grip, the man jumped up, stomped on Hank's stomach, and jumped to retrieve his knife. Hank recovered enough to grab the man's foot, causing him to lose his balance, sending him crashing headfirst into the wall across the hall. Hank rolled over still holding the ankle and scrambled to his knees.

The man reached out, his fingers inching toward the knife. Hank pulled back on his leg, but the man twisted his body and lashed out with his left hand, the back of which caught Hank in the chin. A sharp pain caused Hank to loosen his grip, and the man squirmed away. The man's fingers curled around the knife, which he swung in an arc toward Hank's shoulder. Hank rolled to his right and the blade missed him by an inch, but the movement caused Hank to lose his grip on the man's leg completely. The man scrambled to a standing position and stood there for a moment before bolting down the hall. Hank hopped up and took a step to follow him. Alyson reached out and grabbed his shirt. "Don't!" She yelled. "Let him go. It's not worth it."

The pull on his shirt broke his attention on the intruder and he stopped and turned toward her. "You're right," he said.

"Hank, you're bleeding," she cried out. Hank reached up to feel his chin. It was wet with blood. There was also blood on his shirt. She pulled him into the room and washed the wound. It was jagged but not too deep. It was clear that it wasn't a knife wound. She brought a Band-Aid from the bathroom and covered the wound.

A couple minutes later, she checked his chin and was satisfied that the bleeding had stopped. Her eyes widened, then she stood up suddenly, grabbed her bag, and dumped its contents on the bed.

"What are you doing?" Hank asked.

She ignored him and rummaged through the items until she found the spray canister and held it up.

"Whoa. I don't think I need that." He brought his hand up to his chin. "A Band-Aid is enough." He smiled.

"Ha, ha. This doesn't do any good if I can't find it when I need it." She placed it on the bed, then scooped up the rest of the contents and dropped them back into her back. The spray canister went into a small interior pocket so that she could get to it quickly. "There," she announced and placed the bag on the floor.

An hour later, a policeman knocked on their door. "Señor Henkins."

"Yes. That's me." Without waiting to be invited, the policeman stepped into the room. "This is Alyson Murphy," Hank said, pointing toward Alyson, who sat on the bed. The policeman nodded.

"Tell me what happened, por favor," the policeman asked.

Hank described their coming back to Alyson's room, finding the man going through her things, the fight in the hall, and the man running away. They gave a description of the man. The policeman took notes.

"Nothing seems to be missing." Alyson said when Hank was finished. They had done a quick check around the room as best they could without disturbing things in case the police wanted to look for evidence. It was becoming clear from the policeman's manner that they needn't have bothered to be so careful. He was clearly not interested in investigating what he viewed as a botched robbery attempt.

"It was good that you did not follow him, señor. He may have had friends waiting for him."

"I suppose," Hank said. He hadn't considered that, but was still a little disappointed in himself that he hadn't gone after him.

"How is your face?"

"It's just a scratch."

"You are lucky. It could have been worse."

"Do you think you can catch him?" Alyson asked.

"We will try, señorita, but I have to be honest with you. There are a lot of robberies in Panama City. Too many, I am afraid."

"But this wasn't a burglary."

"What do you mean?"

"We're down here trying to recover stolen money."

"Are you policía?"

"No, but that's irrelevant. I was attacked in Belize on Monday."

"¡Perdón! What do you mean attacked?"

"A man tried to kidnap me in my car, but I escaped."

The policeman thought about that for a moment. "Señor, it is unlikely that the two are related. They are, what do you call it, a coincidence. This is a simple burglary. I am sure of it."

"I don't believe in that kind of coincidence," Hank exclaimed.

The policeman shrugged his shoulders. "That may be, but it does not change the fact that it will be difficult to find this man. You say nothing was stolen, no one was hurt," he looked at the bandage on Hank's chin, then correcting himself, "hurt seriously. We do not have the manpower to put men on this kind of crime."

"So, you're not going to do anything!" Alyson said, anger replacing fear.

"We will give this report to all policía with his description. They will be on the lookout for him. I am sorry. That is the best I can do."

"That's the same as doing nothing," Hank groused.

"That may be, señor, but that is all I can do at the moment."

Hank and Alyson sat there in silence.

"I will go now. When are you leaving Panama?"

"Sunday."

"If you find anything missing, call this number, por favor," the policeman said, handing them a small card. "I am sorry that this happened. I hope that you enjoy the rest of your stay." They policeman left the room a few minutes later.

They sat unmoving for a few moments. "I can't believe it! They're not going to do anything," Alyson said, breaking the silence.

"I know. But, to be fair, I doubt that it would be any different in New York."

"I guess that's true," Alyson had to admit. "But it wasn't just a simple burglary."

"You and I know that, but he doesn't. You heard him! He didn't believe this had anything to do with what happened to me in Belize."

"I agree, but…" There was a knock on the door. Hank opened it to find a squat, balding man standing there who introduced himself as the general manager of the hotel. He stepped into the room and started to apologize profusely, alternating between Spanish and English. Hank and Alyson assured him that they were all right. After a few more minutes of apologies, they finally figured out that he was offering Alyson a new room, the best in the hotel, at no additional cost, assuring her that she'd be safer there.

"No one would know she switched rooms, yes?" Hank asked the manager.

"¡Sí! ¡Sí!" He replied, obviously relieved that they had decided to take him up on his offer.

They quickly packed up her things, again confirming in the process that nothing had been taken. They rode up in the elevator to the fifth and top floor of the hotel. The room was at one end of the corridor. The manager escorted them in and showed them around the presidential suite. There were two bedrooms, each with its own bathroom, and a large living room with a small dining area at one end. It also had a small balcony with two chaise lounges and a tiny table, surrounded by an ornate wrought iron railing. In the distance, they could see cloud-enshrouded mountains, which ran down the center of the country like a spine.

"You will like it here?" the manager asked.

She nodded. "Please do not tell anyone we moved to this suite. If anyone asks, we checked out today and you don't know where we went."

"I understand, señorita." The manager bowed and left.

"I'll go get my stuff." They had quickly agreed that Hank would also move to the suite and take the second bedroom.

They ordered room service and ate lunch on the balcony. "Are we still trying to see someone at Banco Nacional Popular this afternoon?"

"I don't think I'm up to it. Do you mind if we hang out here for the rest of the day?"

"Sure. We could try the rest of the account numbers. We've only got about eight or ten left, don't we?"

She nodded, reached into her purse, and pulled out the fax sheets she'd gotten from Joyce Howard. They hooked up her laptop and spent the rest of the afternoon trying the account numbers at all the banks they could find. Between the phone book and a Google search for banks in Panama, they had over fifty banks to try. By six o'clock, they had located three more accounts. That left six numbers on the list unaccounted for with about half the banks still to be checked. Not all of the banks had online banking.

At the last bank they tried before stopping to get ready for dinner, they discovered nearly ten million dollars in the account. "Do you realize that we've already found almost eighty-five million dollars?" Alyson's face brightened and, in the excitement, she jumped across the space separating them on the couch and gave Hank a hug and, without thinking, kissed him hard on the lips. Surprised, he retreated slightly.

"Don't you want to kiss me?"

"Of course. I just wasn't expecting…"

"Well, what are you waiting for now?" Her hand came up and pulled him closer. He didn't resist at all this time. Her hand moved down from his neck, reaching down to the small of his back and then under his shirt. Soon, her hand was exploring all of his back, her fingers occasionally inching under the waist of his pants.

He followed her lead and began caressing her back. He reached under her blouse and ran his hands over her skin. He reached up to unfasten her bra. She groaned in anticipation. He continued to massage her back for a minute or two and then moved to her stomach. She pulled away from him slightly to give him more room. He inscribed circles on her stomach alternating with the back and palm of his hand. On one circle he allowed his hand to brush lightly over her nipples. Another groan. He moved his hand and cupped it over her breast, fondling it gently. She responded by kissing him harder and moving her hand to massage the insides of his thighs.

He pulled his hand out from under her blouse and began to unbutton it. He took his time, ready to stop at the slightest hint that he had gone too far. He was down to the last button when the phone rang. She grabbed up the front of her shirt and reached for the phone.

"Oh, hi, Gavin." Alyson's face bloomed scarlet and she motioned to Hank to leave her alone.

Hank looked at her, confused. After some hesitation, he stood up in response to her second attempt at motioning him to leave. He walked into his bedroom, closed the door, and lay down on the bed. He strained to hear what she was saying, but gave up. A couple of minutes later, Hank popped up, walked into his bathroom, shaved, and stepped resignedly into the shower. After rinsing off all the soap, he slowly turned the hot water lower. "Brrr." He scrambled to turn off the water.

Later, they walked to the restaurant in silence.

"What did Gavin want?" he asked over an appetizer of ceviche, a local specialty of sea bass, chopped onions, and chili peppers, marinated in lemon juice.

"Oh, he just wanted to make sure I was okay." She blushed, looking down and picking at her fish.

"I see," he said. He waited for her to say something. After a short, uncomfortable silence, he said, "How much more money do you think we'll find?"

"I don't know," she replied, looking at him with a faint smile. "How much did we think was missing? It was more than a hundred million."

"Yeah. Something like that."

"So, we might find another twenty or thirty, but I'd be happy if we could get what we've found back to the States. That would be an excellent outcome."

He grunted in agreement as he reached out suddenly for his glass of water and a piece of bread. He had just bitten into one of the peppers, an ají chombo, and discovered that it lived up to its reputation as one of the hottest peppers in the world. He poured most of the water in his glass straight down his throat and took two mammoth bites of bread. He heaved a sigh of relief.

"Are you okay?" she asked. Seeing that he was, she laughed. Hank stared at her, his nostrils flaring. Then, suddenly, he laughed too, as he realized how funny he must have looked.

The conversation during the rest of dinner stayed away from any mention of what had happened that afternoon. They returned to the hotel relatively early for Panama City, where the nightlife usually doesn't get started until ten or later.

Entering their suite, Alyson gave Hank a quick kiss on the cheek goodnight and walked into her bedroom and closed the door.

Hank stood in the living room for a moment after Alyson closed her door, hoping that it would open again. The door stayed closed. He turned and wandered into his room. As he lay in bed, he stared up at the ceiling in the dark. After a few minutes, he turned his head to look at the clock. *It's going to be a long* night, he thought. He stared at the ceiling again, his arm resting across his forehead. "Damn," he whispered, and rolled over on his side, facing away from the door.

Alyson walked into her bedroom and shut the door, leaned back against the doorframe, closed her eyes, and waited for a few moments. The attempt on Hank's life had unnerved her, but it hadn't seemed real—she had convinced herself that it wasn't part of this, that he had been in the wrong place at the wrong time. The man in her room changed all that. There could be no mistake about what he wanted. As much as she wanted to believe that it had been a simple burglary, she knew different. She had seen the look of recognition in the man's eyes.

She walked over to the bathroom, washed up, put on a nightie, and climbed into bed. Every time she closed her eyes, the man from her room smiled at her, hissing at her that he would be back. Each time, her body shook. She tossed off the sheet—it was soaked through with sweat despite the air conditioning. She tried to drive him from her mind by thinking of fun times from her past, but nothing worked. She then tried to think about Gavin and imagining their trip to Bali, lying on the sand. Try as she might, she couldn't clearly see his face.

She then thought of Hank and smiled at the memories of their college days together. She slipped out of bed and tip-toed through the living room, stopping in front of Hank's bedroom door. Hesitantly, she turned the doorknob, pushed the door slowly open and stepped into the room. The door closed with an audible click. She waited to see if Hank reacted to the noise, but he remained still. She padded silently across the room, lifted the covers, and slid underneath, then sidled over next to Hank, who rolled over onto his back at the touch of her hand.

"What are you doing here?" he asked sleepily.

"I don't want to be alone. Is it okay if I sleep here?"

"Sure."

"Thanks." She gave him a quick kiss on the lips and nestled next to him, her head on his shoulder, her fingertips lightly caressing his chest for a few moments. Within minutes, her hand fell still and her breathing became shallow.

Hank lay next to her, not saying a word, just enjoying the feel of her lying next to him. He could smell her hair and feel her breathing on his chest. He sighed contentedly, then shook his head gently in thought.

He wanted to caress her and hold her tight, but it was clear that Alyson just needed him to be there; the events of the afternoon had been too much for her. That was enough for him, for now. Maybe there would be more later. But what about Gavin? He still hovered in the background. Alyson seemed to be wavering in her feelings for Gavin. Sometimes she appeared to be trying to make it work and at other times, she seemed to be trying way too much. That was understand-able given all that they've been through. Besides, what could he honestly expect? He hadn't shown any interest in years.

Alyson stirred. "Hmmmm." She rolled over and pulled a pillow under her head. Hank curled up next to her, draping his arm over her waist. She reached out and took his hand.

CHAPTER 29

▼

FRIDAY, DECEMBER 15

Hank awoke alone. He had expected Alyson to be lying next to him. Had last night been a dream? No, he was sure that it hadn't been. He flipped off the covers and spun to an upright, sitting position on the bed with his feet on the floor. He sat there for a few moments, listening, waiting in case Alyson came back. When she didn't, he got up, walked into his bathroom, and took a shower. By the time he finished dressing, he could hear the shower running in the other bathroom.

He dressed and sat down in the living room to read the copy of the local English language newspaper that had been left at the door that morning. He flipped from page to page without really reading anything.

Alyson emerged from her room a half hour later. "Good morning."

"Good morning. Um…"

She held up a hand. "Thank you for last night. You don't know how much I needed not to be alone. I hope I didn't keep you awake."

"I understand. You're welcome and, no, you didn't keep me awake." That was only partly true.

"We'd better get going. It's already nine-thirty." She grabbed her purse and headed for the door. He dropped the paper on the coffee table, jumped up, and followed her.

After stopping for a quick bite of breakfast, Hank and Alyson walked into the lobby of the main office of Banco Nacional Popular and were soon directed to the commercial banking group's office. They weren't sure that there was much they would learn there, but the bank held a large account that they had identified from Joyce's list as well as handling most of the international wire transfers for a couple of Saunders's deals and the original trust account for Argent Trading. That trust account had nominee directors and, although his name was not among them, they were convinced that the real owner was Ted Saunders.

"Can I help you?" Emanuel Bonilla asked.

"We'd like to get some information," Hank said. "We would make it worthwhile."

"What kind of information?" The man asked, clearly interested.

"Our client has asked us to track someone down. We know that he has an account here. He is missing and our client is concerned about him."

"I cannot tell you anything about our clients or their accounts."

"We understand that. We're not interested in information about anyone's account at this point. We just want to know whether you might have seen him about six months ago."

"I do not know." A demure glance: the international symbol for *bribe me*.

"Just look at these pictures and see if you recognize anyone." They slid a small pile of pictures across the desk to him. All of them were of Ted Saunders, but they had been digitally altered to add stubble, lengthen his hair, and made the hair darker and lighter. Emanuel picked up the pile somewhat reluctantly.

After looking at all of them, he said, "I am not sure that I recognize any of these persons. They are mostly of the same person, no?"

"Yes. We're not sure how he would have looked when he came in here to open an account."

"I might be able to remember better later, somewhere else," the man said, looking around nervously. "Perhaps we could meet during my lunch break. That will be," he looked up at the clock on the wall, "in an hour. I also might need a little something to prompt my memory."

"I understand. Where should we meet you?"

"There's a small cantina around the corner. I am not sure the señorita will feel comfortable in there. It can be pretty rough." The bank officer slid the pile of pictures discreetly back across the desk.

"We'll see you then," Alyson said defiantly.

"I am sorry that I was not able to help you open your account," Bonilla said, in a voice louder than he had used during the rest of their conversation.

"Well, thank you anyway," Hank said, going along. They stood up, shook hands, and walked out of the bank.

An hour later, Hank and Alyson walked into the cantina. While Alyson found an empty table near the back, Hank walked up to the bar, ordered drinks, carried them back to the their table, and waited. The men at the bar, glancing furtively at Alyson, made comments to one another, only loud enough for themselves to hear, and broke out into raucous laughter. Hank and Alyson were both sure that Alyson was likely to be the source of their amusement, but chose to ignore them.

Five minutes later, the banker walked in, looking around furtively. After a few seconds, he spied Alyson and Hank and walked between the men to their table and sat down in the empty seat. Hank pushed a bottle of Cristal toward him.

"I am sorry for my countrymen over there," he said, jerking his thumb over his shoulder. He took a long drink from the bottle.

"That's okay. I'm sure that there are many places in the U.S. where I'd get the same treatment. I was once in the Navy and trust me, none of them could say anything I haven't heard before."

"May I see the pictures again," he asked, holding out his hand. Alyson dug the pictures from her bag and handed them to him. Under the pile was a single one-hundred-dollar bill. He deftly pocketed the money, with expertise that showed he had performed the move many times before. He looked at the pictures again. "This is the man."

"So you're sure it was Edward Sanders who came into the bank to set up the accounts?" Alyson said, purposefully using Sanders's name, hoping the banker would inadvertently confirm the name.

"Sí. His hair was lighter. Hmm, how would you say it? More gray…and a little longer."

"Are you sure?"

"Sí." Bonilla handed the pictures back to Alyson with the one he had identified on top.

"Did he also set up the accounts for Argent Trading?"

"Sí." The banker grimaced at the mention of the company and looked around to make sure that no one was paying attention to them.

"Do you remember when this was?"

"He came last spring."

"In May? Mayo?" Alyson asked in Spanish.

"Sí. Mayo."

"Have you seen him since?

"No. Nunca." Never.

"Is there anything more you can tell us about Mr. Sanders?" Hank asked.

"No."

"Was there anything unusual about his visit?" Alyson asked.

"I remember it because it was, how do you say it, a crazy house. I had to work very late that night. He says he needed all of the paperwork finished the next morning." Bonilla glanced around the bar again and then at his watch. "I must return now."

"Gracias."

"¡Salud!" the banker said quietly, raised his bottle, and drained it. He stood up, looked around the room nervously, and quickly fled the cantina.

Hank and Alyson waited a few seconds before walking toward the door. The group of men let Hank through easily, but formed a gauntlet for Alyson, each making sure to bump her or touch some part of her body. One large, unkempt man put his arm out to block Alyson's path.

"Let me through, por favor," Alyson said.

The man grinned.

"Por favor."

The man smiled broadly, showing teeth that were yellow from too much coffee and nicotine, but remained quiet.

Without warning, Alyson brought her knee swiftly up into the man's groin. The man exhaled sharply and grabbed his crotch with both hands. Alyson's hand shot out and stabbed the man's throat. One of his hands cradled his neck, then he slumped to his knees. Alyson looked around. The men around her stepped back and a path to the door emerged. Alyson stepped defiantly through the opening and out to the street.

"What happened?" Hank said.

"Nothing I couldn't take care of." Alyson's hands were trembling. "Let's get out of here."

They marched down the street, wanting to put some distance between them and the cantina. They walked on in silence for the first few minutes and looked around for some place to have lunch.

After lunch, Hank and Alyson went back to their hotel room. They pulled out their notes and Alyson's computer to continue their online search.

"Just a minute, I want to make a call," Alyson said, taking her phone out onto the balcony. "You get started. I'll be right back in."

She stood out on the balcony, talking softly for a few minutes. She was smiling as she sat down next to Hank.

"Well?"

"I just called Miguel's secretary. He's been moved out of ICU. He's not out of the woods, yet, but they think he's going to make it."

"That's great!" Hank said with sincerity, but he was already thinking of the work ahead of them.

By mid-afternoon, the air in their room had gotten heavy and warm, despite the air conditioning.

"Let's take a break," Alyson said suddenly.

"Good idea. I want to make a quick call. You order some coffee or tea. I think I need some." Hank pulled out his cell phone and dialed Carol Somers.

"Hi, Hank."

"Any news?"

"Yes, but I'm not sure if it's good or bad."

"What is it?"

"Ted Saunders didn't have a brother. At least not according to the records at the Sisters of Charity Orphanage where he grew up."

"Damn. Are you sure?"

"Yep. I talked to the director. She was very cooperative once I told her I was looking for Saunders's heirs and could offer a sizeable reward to anyone who helped me find them."

"Nice touch."

"I thought you'd like it. I just embellished your idea."

"Well, thanks anyway. I knew it was a long shot." Hank snapped his phone shut and walked out onto the balcony where Alyson was sitting.

"Who were you talking to?" she asked.

"Carol Somers. She works at the *Times* with me." Hank related the conversation.

"That would have been an interesting twist."

"Twist was right, but it didn't work out."

*   *   *   *

The phone on Isabel Menes desk rang. "Buenos días," she answered.

"I understand you had visitors yesterday." She had called a number and left a message the night before as she had been instructed to do if anyone asked about Ed Sanders.

"Sí, señor."

"A friend of my father's. How interesting."

"Do you know Señor Jenkins?"

"Oh, yes, we go way back."

Isabel Menes relaxed at the news.

"I need you to make a call for me."

"Sí, señor. Who do you want me to call?" the lawyer asked.

"I would like you to call Señor Jenkins and ask him to meet you tomorrow. Say you want to give them more information, but it has to be someplace outside of town where a lot of tourists go so no one will notice you meeting with them. I'm sure they'll understand."

"There are many such places."

"I know. I would like you to tell them to meet you out at the pier in Balboa where the boats leave for the Canal tours. Tell them that they could go on a cruise afterwards."

"Sí, señor. What am I to tell them when I meet with them?"

"Nothing. I don't want you to be anywhere close to the pier. I will meet with them, but I want it to be a surprise."

She hung up the phone, relieved that she wouldn't get any more involved in the affairs of Señor Sanders than was necessary. She knew that there would be clients like this one when she came back from working in the United States at Banks, Brown and Martinez, but the less she knew about what they did, the better. And, what was going to happen to the Americanos? Did she want to know? No, she decided with finality, and attacked the pile of paperwork on her desk, driving any further thoughts about their fate out of her head for the time being.

A little after five in the afternoon, Isabel Menes called the cell phone number that Hank had given her. After the third ring, Hank retrieved the phone out of his pants pocket.

"Hello," he said.

Isabel told him exactly what she had been instructed to, set the time for their meeting at ten minutes before the morning tour boat left, and hung up before Hank could ask any questions.

*   *   *   *

"What was that all about?" Alyson asked, seeing the look on Hank's face.

"Isabel wants to meet us tomorrow."

"Where?"

Hank told her.

"You think she's too nervous to talk in the office?" Alyson asked.

"Probably, or maybe she lives out near there. It will be Saturday, you know."

"It probably couldn't hurt to go out there. Nothing's going to be open on Saturday anyway and we're pretty much finished down here. We can take the day off and take a tour of the Canal."

"Hmmm. That's what she suggested too."

As they were getting ready for dinner, Alyson's cell phone rang again.

"Ms. Murphy?"

"Mr. Harden. What a nice surprise." She looked over at Hank and shrugged her shoulders as if to say, 'What does he want?'

"I was calling to get an update. I hope I'm not interrupting anything."

"Not at all." She wondered what he meant by that. "I was going to call you soon."

"Oh, good. I'm glad to hear that. My first question is how's the weather down in Panama? I hear it's muggy and warm this time of the year."

Alyson's face froze. She held the phone away from her mouth and put her thumb over the mouthpiece and whispered, "He knows we're here."

"How?" Hank asked in an equally low voice.

She shrugged. "Mr. Harden, I can explain…"

"Ms. Murphy, I'm sure you have a plausible reason for disobeying me, but that's just water under the bridge at this point, isn't it? Just tell me you've found the money."

"We did. Not all of it, but a big chunk." Alyson proceeded to tell him that they had confirmed that Ed Sanders was actually Ted Saunders and that they had tracked down many of the accounts using the account numbers and access codes they had salvaged from the CD retrieved from the trash from Saunders's apartment. She also told him of her concern that someone knew they were in Panama and suggested that he act fast if he wanted to make sure the money didn't disappear.

"I'll start proceedings to freeze the money immediately," Harden said. "But it'll take time."

"Good. But, as I said, we haven't found it all, but we think we will, given more time. We were thinking about staying a few days next week."

"You've done a great job." He cleared his throat. "That makes what I'm about to say difficult. Have you told your boss about what you've found?"

"Not yet," she said tentatively.

"What about your friend Mr. Jenkins? I assume that he's there with you as we speak."

"He knows you're here too," she whispered.

"How?" he mouthed without a sound. Alyson shook her head.

"Oh, come on, Ms Murphy. Your silence tells me the answer."

"Um, yes. He's right here"

"Please put him on," the lawyer demanded.

She handed the phone to Hank.

"Mr. Jenkins. It's so nice to talk to you at last. I've read all your articles about my late client. That was quite a hatchet job you did on him."

"Um…"

"That's okay. He's dead and beyond your reach now. My question to you is this: have you told your editor anything, yet, about what you've found down here?"

"Not yet. I discussed the story with him before I came down here, but I haven't spoken to him since we found the money. He'll be excited. It'll be a great story once I get back."

"I don't think so."

"I'm sorry?" Hank said, perplexed.

"Let me make this perfectly clear, neither of you are to tell anyone about this until I give you permission to do so."

"What?"

"You're both under a confidentiality agreement and you're not allowed to release any of this information without my permission."

"I'm not under any confidentiality agreement," Hank announced confidently.

"I believe you were aware of Ms. Murphy's agreement, were you not?"

"Um, yes."

"Then, by working on this with her, you implicitly accepted the terms of that agreement. I am sure the lawyers at your paper will agree with that."

"That doesn't apply to the press."

"Yes it does. This isn't a freedom of the press issue. This is contract law 101. You print, I sue. This will cause immeasurable damage to my client's estate. Once you publish, there's a risk that the money will disappear."

"But…But…" Hank stammered. He hadn't thought of that. "I can see your point. I'll agree to an embargo for now, but once you get the money back, the story's all mine."

"Agreed. At that point, I won't care. Now, Ms. Murphy…"

"Just a second," Hank said, handing the phone to Alyson. "He wants to speak to you."

"Ms. Murphy?"

"Yes?"

"I expect you to turn over all of your notes to me as soon as you get back. Also, all of your computer records, and return all the copies of material you were given, including anything your colleagues have."

"I don't think that's a good idea," she said. She frowned at the idea.

"This isn't open to discussion. You contractually agreed to give it all back to me immediately upon my requesting you to do so. I am doing that now."

"I know what the agreement says. All I'm saying is that I don't think that we're finished with the investigation."

"I'm the one to determine that."

There were a few moments of silence.

"All right," she said finally, frowning as she said it.

"We'll talk again when you get back to the States. In the meantime, do some sightseeing. Go out and see the Canal that Mr. Jenkins's grandfather built." Alyson looked at Hank with a quizzical look.

"Good afternoon and," almost as an afterthought, "thank you." The line went dead.

"Damn," Alyson said.

"That was odd," Hank said.

They filled each other in on their sides of the call.

"That's odd that he'd mention my grandfather, though it was my great-grand-father."

"I must have mentioned it at some point, although I don't remember when."

"You can give him your notes, but I'm not returning mine. Otherwise, I've got no story."

"That was the strangest request of all. He must know that we can't find the rest of the money without this stuff." She said, waving her hand over the pile of papers in front of her.

Neither one spoke again, each caught up in his or her thoughts.

"Shall we go to dinner?" Hank said dejectedly. "I'm not in the mood, but we should probably get something to eat."

"I'm not sure I'm all that hungry either."

"There's nothing we can do now anyway. We might as well go get something to eat."

After finding the restaurant recommended by the hotel manager, they were seated at a table overlooking the city. The waiter brought a bottle of Pinot Grigio and filled their glasses.

Hank lifted his glass and said, "What should we drink to?"

"I'm not sure there is anything to drink to. Not yet, at least."

"Oh, come on. We cracked the case. We found the money."

"But it feels so unfinished somehow after that call from Harden."

"Well, maybe, but admit it, we accomplished a lot more than you thought we would," he smiled at her.

"Okay, I admit it. I originally thought you were crazy. Although the jury is still out on you being crazy," she grinned, some of the tension falling away, "You were right about the money. I feel bad that you won't get your story."

"That's okay. I'll get it eventually. In the meantime, there'll be other stories. I'll talk to McMahon when we get back and find out about this confidentiality thing."

They walked out of the restaurant. There were people everywhere enjoying a night out on the town. The temperature had dropped ten degrees as a breeze blew in off the ocean. They decided to walk back to the hotel. Halfway there, Alyson stopped under a streetlamp, turned to Hank, and said, "Do you ever wonder why Harden agreed to have us track down the money?"

"He's the executor of the estate. He had to."

"Maybe." She took a few more steps and stopped again, looking left and right, and said in not much more than a whisper, "Did you ever think that he might have wanted us to find the money so he could keep it for himself?"

"What? He wouldn't…" He left the sentence. "Wow. That would certainly explain that phone call."

"Exactly."

"So, would do we do now?"

"I don't know."

"I do. I write the story. Then I send it and copies of my files and notes to my boss so the story's safe. Then we need to be careful until we get home."

CHAPTER 30

▼

SATURDAY, DECEMBER 16

The cab pulled into the parking lot at the marina, just downriver from the first set of locks of the Canal. A crowd of tourists had already gathered. Hank and Alyson scrambled out of the cab. The cab turned as soon as the door closed and sped out of the parking lot, kicking up a thick cloud of dust as it drove away. They walked around the pier looking for Isabel Menes.

"I wonder where she is," Alyson said. "You sure we're in the right place?"

"I think so," Hank said with conviction. "This is the tour company she mentioned."

They continued to look for her. "Let's get on line. Maybe she wants to meet us on board." They walked toward the ticket booth, bought two tickets, then joined the line of people waiting to get aboard the tour boat.

The boat moored at the dock had a fresh coat of blue and white paint, but it couldn't fully hide its age. Much of the exposed metal was pitted with rust. The upper deck was lined with benches. The wheelhouse sat forward, leaving very little foredeck. It reminded Hank of the boats he had seen in the pictures that his great-grandfather had shown him when he was a child.

As they chatted in line, a man got out of the passenger side of a car that sat in the corner of the parking lot and walk directly over to the back of the line, not bothering to go to the ticket booth. He slowly made his way past the four or five people in front of him. When the people at the front of the line began to move forward to hand in their tickets, Hank looked at his watch. The boat would be leaving in two minutes, he calculated, looking around and still not seeing Isabel. He wished he'd taken her cell phone number. As Hank turned back to talk to Alyson, the man moved to a space directly behind Hank.

A second later, Hank felt a hard object in the small of his back. The man leaned closer and whispered in Hank's ear, "Por favor, do not do anything stupid. I have a gun in your back. Ask the señorita to follow us."

"Alyson, let's go over there for a moment," Hank said quickly.

"What? Did you see Isabel?"

"No."

"Then why get out of line? They're loading."

"I know. Please," Hank pleaded.

At that moment, Alyson saw the man behind Hank and then looked at Hank. Seeing the look on his face, she gasped. "What do you want?" she said to the man behind Hank, finally getting the breath to speak.

"Señorita, por favor. Do as I say and no one will get hurt."

Alyson wavered.

"Let's do as he says," Hank said in response to a nudge of the barrel in his back. He indicated with a tilt of his head for her to obey.

Alyson noticed the man's arm and said, "Oh." She brought her hand up to her lips.

"Walk over to the silver BMW. Yes, that one over there. Get in, por favor." The man got in the front passenger seat after Hank and Alyson had climbed in the back then turned around holding the pistol between the seats and pointed directly at Hank's chest.

"Where are you taking us?" Alyson demanded. Neither the man nor the driver gave an answer. The BMW left the parking lot and turned north, away from Panama City.

She looked over at Hank and saw a look of dread in his eyes. She swallowed hard and returned her gaze to the man in the front passenger seat. She looked at the driver. Something about him was familiar. Shifting to her left, she glanced in the rearview mirror. Dark brown eyes returned her gaze. Even without the glasses, she recognized them. "It's you," she blurted out.

"Who?"

"The man from my room."

The man turned. A thin sinister grin appeared on his face. He shot a glance at Hank, saw the bandage and smiled, then returned his attention to the road ahead.

"So you know my friend, sí?" The man with the gun asked.

"Yes. We've had the dubious honor of meeting him."

"And you lived to tell about it?" His head shifted slightly toward the driver, without taking the gun or his eyes off his guests in the back seat. "You are getting sloppy, Raul." He laughed.

Alyson could see by the look in the eyes in the rearview mirror that Raul did not find the taunt the least bit funny. The car suddenly began to close in around her. She reached over and grabbed Hank's hand. They stole a glance at each other, then locked their eyes on the men sitting in front of them, neither one knowing what to do or say.

They traveled about two miles and pulled into a driveway, past two large stone pillars. A large plaque on one of the pillars welcomed them to the Balboa y Panama Yacht Club. They drove past the clubhouse, a two-story-high white stucco throwback to the heyday of Canal travel, with green shutters on the windows, and continued toward the docks. The car pulled to a stop under a large ceiba tree, its lowest, outermost spindly branches and leaves scraping along the top of the car. The driver winced at the sound. The man in the front passenger seat jumped out of the car as soon as it stopped, yanked open the rear door, and, without saying a word, motioned with the pistol for Hank and Alyson to get out.

They climbed out of the car. A light breeze rustled the leaves of the ceiba above them. Sunlight flickered off the water. A pelican flew by and landed on a piling near the dock. The peacefulness deepened their sense of foreboding. They walked in front of him, out onto a main dock, past the sailboats and the motorboats bobbing up and down in their slips.

"Come aboard, por favor," he said, pointing at a white Sea Scorpion, a fifty-foot-long motorboat near the end of the pier, with the name *Alicia* painted in black on the stern. Under the name was painted *Balboa, Panama*. They were ushered down into the cabin. Once the cabin door was closed behind them and with the curtains pulled across the small portholes, the cabin was nearly pitch black. Their eyes struggled to adjust after the brightness outside.

Their escort flicked on a small reading light and pointed to the bench on the starboard side of the cabin, indicating that he wanted them to sit. He pulled a roll of duct tape down off a shelf by the stairs and tossed it to Alyson, all the while keeping the gun trained on them. "Tape his ankles and his wrists," he instructed her. "Please turn around," he said to Hank, who spun on the bench. "Tape his hands behind his back."

The man with the gun waited until that was completed and said, "Now your ankles, señorita, por favor." She did as she was told. He reached out and took the roll of tape back and asked her to turn around and put her arms behind her back.

Now that they were bound, he put the pistol into the waist of his pants. Cutting a short piece of tape, he reached out to put it over Hank's mouth. "Please don't. It's too…hhhmmp." His words were muffled as the tape was put in place. The man then cut a second piece of tape.

"Please. We won't be able to breathe in here," she begged. The man ignored her plea. She move her head back and forth so he couldn't put the tape on her mouth, causing him to reach up with one of his hands and clamp it down on the top of her head, holding it still for the time it took to put the tape in place. The man watched them for a few seconds to make sure that they could breathe and then stood up.

"Please stay here," the man warned—the sudden politeness in his voice ominous to Hank and Alyson. The man turned, switched off the light, climbed the stairs, and closed the cabin door. The lock clicked. The room was plunged into darkness again. The cabin was stifling.

Hank looked at Alyson. His eyes began to adjust to the darkness and he could make out her face. Her eyes were wide with fear, her nostrils splayed wide as she tried to get enough air in through her nose. He nodded his head, trying to tell her everything was going to be all right. He wasn't sure that he believed that himself, but he knew they both had to stay calm if they were going to survive.

Seconds later, they heard a number of men scramble aboard the boat, speaking excitedly to each other in Spanish. A minute later, they felt the vibration of the engines start and grow stronger as they were put into reverse. Hank and Alyson could feel the boat backing out of the slip. There was a slight shudder as the engines were shifted into forward and the boat left the marina.

Where were they? What was happening? Hank struggled to stand up, leaned against the cupboards behind the bench, and tried to move a curtain aside with his head to see out a porthole. He lost his balance as the engines were put into gear again and the boat lunged forward, causing him to fall on top of Alyson. With some effort, he regained his seat, breathing hard from the exertion, the heat, and the lack of air.

A short while later, the engine noise died and the boat began slowing. The voices outside became animated again and there seemed to be much running up and down the sides of the boat. The sound of something hitting the water alongside the boat was accompanied by a rash of Spanish obscenities. This was followed a minute later by a loud metallic thud on the deck above that reverberated inside the cabin.

Hank looked at Alyson. Her breathing was fast and irregular, and sweat was pouring down her face. At least the look of panic was dissipating, he decided. He focused on his own breathing, trying to get it under control. It was difficult getting enough air with the tape covering his mouth.

He struggled to his feet again, propping himself against the cabin wall, then turned around and jerked his head backward and down. He grunted and wiggled his index finger in a motion for Alyson to come nearer. Turning his head, he saw her staring at him in confusion. He grunted again and repeated the wiggling. Alyson still looked at him without understanding.

Fighting the rocking of the bock, he climbed up onto the bench to kneel in front of her. It was amazing how difficult it was to maintain his balance without his hands and ability to spread his legs apart. The boat rolled to one side and Hank's head and shoulder slammed against the wall, momentarily dazing him. He shook his head to clear it, then shimmied back toward Alyson until he was right next to her. He straightened as far as he could so that his hands were nearly at Alyson's shoulder height, then turned his head again and nodded it downward, wiggling his finger again.

Sweat was running his face. His clothes were nearly soaked through. He was winded. If Alyson didn't understand soon, he would have to give up.

He wiggled his finger one last time and looked behind him. Alyson nodded and bent down so that her mouth was next to his hands. Thank God, he said to himself.

He stretched out his fingers and found the edge of the tape covering her mouth. His fingernails pried a corner loose. Slowly, he peeled a bigger piece loose. It was now large enough for him to grab hold of it. His fingers held it tight. Just as he was about to pull, he felt her head snap back violently. The idea that the man with the gun had come in without them knowing it somehow flashed through his mind. He swung his head around.

Alyson sat there, moving her jaw back and forth. She saw the look of concern on his face and responded with a faint smile.

"That hurt," she said softly. "Thank God I can breathe again. Would you like me to do you too?

He gave her a look that said, *What do you think?* He scrambled back into a sitting position and turned toward her.

Alyson stood up unsteadily, tottering back and forth on the floor in front of him. Hank leaned forward so that his face met her hands. A second later, he felt her nails picking at the tape.

"Umph," he involuntarily let out.

"Sorry," she said. Her probing at the tape became a little less frantic. A few moments later, she had enough to hold onto. Hank jerked his head back, but the tape remained in place.

"Sorry..." The force of his pulling his head away upset her precarious stance and she fell backward onto his lap, then toppling into wall. "Ouch," she cried.

They both froze, listening for any sound that indicated that someone had heard her. Seconds passed like minutes. No one came.

Alyson struggled to her feet again and positioned herself in from of Hank. "Wait until I get a better grip this time," she whispered. Her fingers found the loose end of the tape and squeezed it tight. "Okay, I'm ready."

Hank pulled his head back and the tape leapt off his face. It felt as if the outer couple of layers of skin had been ripped away. He stifled a cry.

"Thanks. You okay?" He asked.

"I can breathe if that's what you mean."

"Listen, I'm not sure how they'll react if they see we've taken off the tape, so if anyone comes, turn away from the door."

"Okay," she said, a bit unnerved by the thought. "What do you think they're going to do to us?"

"I don't know." Hank ducked his head to hide his sense of prevarication. Certainly they couldn't be planning anything good. "They obviously want information or they wouldn't have kidnapped us." Hank's stomach tightened at the sight of Alyson's reaction to the word *kidnapped*. "The good news is that they need us. Otherwise, we wouldn't be here." Being here was both good and bad. The fact that they were still alive was good. Most other signs pointed to *bad*. The fact that no one knew where they were and that they had no clue who had kidnapped them was definitively bad.

Hank looked at Alyson, who was staring at him, waiting for him to come up with something, some way out of this. He smiled weakly.

"They're going to kill us, aren't they?" Her voice nearly broke. The tension of the last few days was washing over her, threatening to overwhelm her.

"We don't know that. Maybe they just want to scare us." He cringed, knowing that she would see through an obvious lie. "We've got to convince whoever is behind all this that we're not a threat, that he has nothing to fear from us."

"Do you really believe that?" she asked skeptically.

No, he didn't really believe it, but it was all they had to work with and sometimes you have to play the cards you're dealt. "I don't know. I think it's our only chance. We've got to make them think that we came up empty and were about to go back to the States."

"They'll never buy that." Her voice was rising.

"Shh. They'll hear us."

"I don't care." She lowered her voice anyway. "Is it really going to matter?"

"I figure as long as they don't know we have the tape off, they won't come back and retape us."

Alyson looked at him. She clearly hadn't thought of that.

It was hard to tell the passage of time in the dark cabin. The boat began rocking back and forth erratically, twisting left and right. The boat groaned and they could hear the straining of ropes, which were obviously being stretched to their maximum. A cabinet on the portside popped opened and a couple of cans toppled out. Hank looked at Alyson. She looked around nervously.

"What the hell's going on?" Alyson said nervously.

"I don't know."

The motion of the boat started to ease. Hank and Alyson spent the time rehearsing their story. Hank had to admit that, even with the practice, the story didn't sound convincing.

The voices started yelling again and men were running on the port side. A bump shuddered through the boat and they heard a loud thud again, followed by the same turbulence. This was followed by the sound of the engines revving up and they could feel the motion of the boat moving across open water.

The door of the cabin suddenly opened, flooding the room with light. Hank and Alyson blinked and turned away, unable to stand the sudden brightness. The man from the car peered down at them, checking to make sure his captives hadn't moved. The door closed and they were plunged back into darkness again. The engines began to slow and finally idled gently. The same routine was heard from above, followed by an equally rough movement of the boat. The engine once again came to life, but for not more than ten minutes or so, then idled briefly as the boat came up against a dock or something hard and a number of people could be heard getting off the boat. The engine revved up and the boat was moving freely now.

The door of the cabin was pushed open again. A man came down the stairs, closing the door behind him. Hank could tell it was not the man from before. The man stood silently for a few seconds, then pulled out a knife and held it in front of their faces. Even in the dark, they could see glints of light bounce off the six-inch blade. Their eyes opened wide, fixed on the blade. Their breathing became irregular.

Without saying a word, he indicated to Alyson to turn around. She hesitated at first, then slowly turned. The man reached down and cut through the tape holding her hands together. He waited for her to pull the tape off her wrists. Next, he unexpectedly handed the knife, hilt first, to Alyson and said without any local accent, "Please cut yourselves loose. I see that you've already taken some of it off already." He took a step backward and pulled out a pistol that had been stuffed into his pants. He watched them free themselves. Pulling the tape off his wrists caused Hank to utter an involuntary yelp. "Sorry about that," the man said. "Please put the knife on the floor and kick it over here."

Alyson did as she was told.

"What do you want?" Hank demanded.

"All in due course. First, let me apologize for the accommodations," he said, holding up his arms shoulder high, palms outward. "I wanted to make sure that you didn't try anything stupid before we had a chance to get to know each other. Besides, if you were walking about the boat, you might have gotten in the way of the line handlers. They've all gone ashore for the moment so that won't be a problem."

"Line handlers?" Alyson asked.

"They're a necessary part of going through the locks. We won't need them again until we go back down."

"We're on the Canal. Of course!" Hank said. Now the intermittent noise and turbulence made sense.

"We just passed through the Miraflores and Pedro Miguel locks. That was the turbulence you felt. There's quite a rush of water as it pours into the chamber of the lock. Something like a million and a half gallons flood into each one in less than fifteen minutes."

"Who are you?" Hank asked. It was too dark to make out his features clearly.

The man sat there silent and unmoving.

"If I'm not mistaken," Alyson answered, "we're talking to Ted Saunders, a.k.a. Ed Sanders."

"Give the lady a cigar," the man with the pistol said. "How'd you know?"

"Well, you're about the right build. The accent is clearly Midwestern, although you tried to hide it. The ring was the clincher. University of Michigan, I believe."

"Yes. I knew I should have gotten rid of it, but couldn't bring myself to throw it away."

He reached up and turned on the light. The man who sat there was outwardly much changed from the man everyone knew as Ted Saunders, much thinner and his hair was now gray instead of dark brown and nearly collar-length in the back rather than closely cropped as he had worn it as CEO of GenergTex. Wire-rimmed glasses completed the transformation.

"The glasses are a nice touch."

"Bifocals, believe it or not," he took them off and held them out for a moment and then put them back on. "The upper is plain glass, but I need them to read. In my case, it's a welcome advantage of getting older."

"Now what's going to happen?" Alyson asked.

"I think that it's time to go."

"Go where?"

"You wanted to see the Canal, Mr. Jenkins, I believe. Let's go up and enjoy the cruise. I'm sorry you missed the locks." Saunders stood up, walked over to the cabin door, and pushed it open. Sunlight flooded in and Hank and Alyson had to cover their eyes until they adjusted to the brightness. Neither one moved immediately, afraid that this was some kind of trick.

"There's nothing to be afraid of. At least, not for the moment," Saunders said.

Hank and Alyson climbed up onto the main deck and Saunders followed them, not taking the gun off them the entire time. They stepped into the cockpit and Saunders pointed to a bench. "Please take a seat so we can talk."

Hank looked around. Other than the man behind the wheel, he didn't see anyone else on board. He didn't know where the man who had taped them was, but figured he must have gotten off with the line handlers. He felt some hope returning. At least the numbers were even, although Saunders held the upper hand with the pistol.

"This is Herve," Saunders said, noticing Hank's interest. "He's the captain on the boat. Fortunately, among his other accomplishments, he's a qualified Canal pilot so we needn't be bothered with guests on our cruise. I thought that it would be better if we weren't disturbed. But don't let his size fool you. He was a lieutenant colonel in the Fuergas de Defensa de Panama, Noriega's defense force. Given his reputation, I'm surprised that he's not in prison somewhere. Isn't that right, Herve?" The man at the wheel nodded and flashed a toothy smile that, although it instantly vanished, was enough to make Alyson shudder from the pure malevolence it showed.

Hank gave the man a second look. His skin was weathered and pockmarked, his eyes cold and distant, as if he wanted to be somewhere else, yet was taking in everything around him. His head was covered by dark brown stubble. He stood about five foot nine and his white linen shirt and pants hung loosely on his unimposing frame. Yet, despite his stature, he looked in total command of the vessel and surprisingly lethal.

Astern, they could see the Pedro Miguel locks receding. They were now cruising at about ten knots through the Gaillard Cut. The Cut, a nine-mile excavation through the continental divide, rose more than three hundred feet in steps on either side of them, making the sides of the Canal look like Inca pyramids.

Saunders put the hand holding the pistol under a pile of towels that sat on the table next to him in a way that told Hank the barrel was still pointed at them. The reason for the move became clear as the shadow of a large cruise ship, on its southward transit through the Canal, swept over them.

"There is one thing I'd like to know," Alyson said, not waiting for Saunders to ask any questions.

"Just one?"

"To start. Why did you kill your brother? Not only your brother, but your identical twin." As soon as she had met Saunders below, Alyson had realized that Hank's theory about the identical twin had to be right after all, even though Hank's friend Carol had said that Saunders didn't have one. It was the only thing that made sense.

Hank turned and glanced at her with surprise, then returned his eyes to Saunders.

"Hmmm." Saunders gave her a look of mild amusement. "How did you know about him?"

"You didn't count on him being a mirror twin."

"A what?"

"A mirror twin. You and…what was your brother's name anyway?"

"Kevin. Armstrong was his adopted name."

"Wait a minute. Carol said you didn't have a brother. He checked with the orphanage."

"Well, he wouldn't know that they changed the documents years ago."

"Why would they do that?"

"They were afraid that Kevin's adoptive parents might try to return him."

"Why would they?"

"Enough," Saunders shouted.

"That doesn't change the fact that you and Kevin were mirror twins. You both have webbed toes. Yours were on the right. Unfortunately for you, his were on the left."

"How do you know that?"

"Edna Grouse," Hank said. "You remember her? She remembered you. Is that why you killed her?"

"I have no idea what you're talking about. I didn't even know she was still alive." His tone and manner convinced them both he was telling the truth.

"But you did kill your brother," Alyson said accusingly. "How could you do that?"

"He wasn't my brother!" Saunders said adamantly.

"Yes, he was! You were blood brothers. No! You were more than that. You were twins!"

"Hah! What does that matter? Blood is meaningless!" Saunders was beginning to get worked up. They had clearly hit a nerve.

"How can you say that?" Hank asked.

"How would you know anything? Your mother didn't give you up for adoption. You weren't picked over like a head of lettuce by all those *nice* people." The word "nice" came out as a hiss.

"That's true, but I'm sure that your new parents loved you very much." Alyson observed.

"Are you trying to psychoanalyze me, now, Miss Murphy, hoping that I'll suddenly come to my senses?"

"No, I...er..."

"Save your breath. Kevin Armstrong meant absolutely nothing to me. All that crap about twins is just that. Crap."

"Okay. So he didn't mean anything to you. You still killed him. Why?" Alyson asked.

"Isn't it obvious? I was going to jail. My life was over. Kevin Armstrong had never amounted to anything. He was a drunk, couldn't hold down a job. No one was going to miss him."

"I still don't understand?" Alyson said.

"I couldn't just disappear, now could I? There had to be a body to convince everyone I was dead."

"I get it," Hank jumped in. "You had to kill your brother. Your DNA was on record and you couldn't afford to have someone check and find out the body wasn't really you."

"You get the gold star, Mr. Jenkins. I may have been able to fake my death some other way. But I couldn't risk someone going back and checking my old profile, now could I? So, you see, I didn't have a choice."

"But..." Hank started to respond.

"Enough!" Saunders yelled again, waving the gun in his left hand back and forth. "Discussion closed."

"Why did they split up you and your brother up in the first place?" Alyson ventured warily, so as to avoid another outburst.

"I said the discussion was closed."

"But I was just curious. No psychoanalysis."

"My adoptive parents didn't know about him at first. No one wanted the two of us, said we were too much to handle. Two girls, maybe, but no one wanted two boys. Plus Kevin was already a problem. He'd probably be labeled ADHD today. Instead, they gave us away one at a time."

"Didn't you tell your parents about your brother?" Alyson said with a touch of sorrow.

"Yes, but only later. That *evil woman* at the adoption agency told me not to say anything, otherwise my new parents wouldn't want to keep me and they'd send me back. By the time I realized, years later, that she had lied to me, it was too late. I was nearly twelve. My parents tried to find my brother, but they couldn't. He had been taken out of state. It wasn't like it is now. No Internet or computers. Hell, we barely had phone service. My parents tried, but they couldn't find him."

"So how did you find him?"

"I tracked him down a couple of years ago when I heard my real mother died."

"Did you try to contact him then?" Hank asked.

"No. I didn't. I didn't want the memory. I thought I did, but I didn't, especially after I saw what he had become."

"Did you know you were identical twins?"

"Yes."

"When was it you decided to kill him?"

"If you must know," Saunders said very softly at first, his voice growing only slightly louder as he continued, "it was when I realized I was going to jail and was going to lose everything. I was watching the Discovery Channel, of all things, some show about DNA, and they mentioned that identical twins had identical DNA. That's when the idea hit me." He sat silently again, looking down at the deck. "I didn't know about mirror twins or I would have done something about the toes." He sat there deep in thought.

Herve turned and pointed out that they were now about seven miles into the Cut. Saunders told him to come about and head back. Hank and Alyson both turned. They had forgotten Herve was on board.

"I think you've seen enough," Saunders said. "We got to get back or we'll miss our reservation to get back through the locks. We wouldn't want to get a late fee." Saunders laughed.

"I have question," Hank said. "How'd you get your brother up to the ranch and then get away."

"He was drugged and left in a local motel by someone I hired to help me. I drove out and picked him up after all the ranch hands went into town."

"That explains how the Hummer ended up in the garage." Hank mused softly, not realizing he had said it out loud.

"What did you say?"

"Oh, nothing. How you'd get away from the house? Your Hummer was still there."

"I love to ride. I took Solo out, threw an old saddle that I knew no one would miss on him, and rode out to south range. There's a small barn out there where I usually kept some farm equipment. I had parked an old car out there on my last visit to the ranch. I threw the saddle in the back of the car and then let Solo find his way back to the barn. I figured everyone would think he got out somehow during the fire. After that, I simply hopped in and drove away. The highway's close by out there."

"Clever," Hank said. This was a thoroughly dangerous man sitting across from him, Hank thought. It was clear that killing someone to get what he wanted was not a problem for him.

Saunders grinned thinly.

"Seriously, Ted, can I call you Ted?" Alyson asked. Saunders nodded. "What are you going to do now?"

"Well, once we've finished our little talk, I was thinking that we'd take a ride back to my house out on Isla Contadora. I understand you visited me the other day."

"We were told you didn't live there." Alyson said.

"Rosetta has instructions to tell that to everyone who stops by unless I tell her otherwise."

"How'd you know we were there? We didn't give her our names."

"Closed-circuit TV," Saunders said. Alyson nodded in understanding.

"Now, depending on what you both do next, you can either be my guests on Contadora or you can go for a swim on the way out there. I'm sure that the sharks would be happy to get a meal. Don't you think, Herve?" Saunders laughed, looking toward the man behind the wheel.

"Sí," Herve said with a broad, thin sneer. He then turned his attention back to steering the boat. At that moment, they were approaching a mooring area where a number of boats were waiting to go through the lock. They were heading toward a distant dock where they would pick up the line handlers.

"Now back to business!" Saunders said, turning his attention back to his passengers. "Who have you told about me?" He leaned back in his seat, elbow on the armrest, chin resting lightly on his left hand, index finger running up his cheek alongside his ear, the gun hand resting nonchalantly in his lap.

"Why should we tell you anything?"

"Beyond the obvious?" he said, grinning and brandishing his gun.

"You're not going to risk firing that gun in the middle of the Canal just to make us talk. Let's be serious." Hank said, hoping it was true.

"Listen to me." Saunders's voice lost all humor as he leaned forward, bringing both hands together and his elbows down on top of his knees, the pistol pointing straight at them. "I am deadly serious. As you pointed out, Miss Murphy, I've killed my own brother. I will have zero, I repeat zero, compunction about killing the both of you unless you tell me what I want to know."

Hank and Alyson were left with no doubt that he meant it. "You're going to do that anyway." Hank said.

"That may be," Saunders's voice softened slightly as he leaned back into the seat once more, "but the sharks don't care whether they eat live or dead meat. That is a choice I can still give you."

Hank looked at Alyson and could see in her eyes the same fear he struggled to control. The best they could hope for was to play for time and hope they got a chance to get away.

"We've told a number of people about you," Alyson said, who must have been thinking the same thing.

"Really? For some reason, I doubt that's true." Saunders stared at Alyson. "Like who?"

"Your lawyer for one," Alyson said.

"I know everything you've told my former lawyer. Without her knowing it, his secretary Kate has been indirectly telling me everything you've been telling him. That's one of the downsides of having a loyal secretary to whom you tell everything. I warned him about that years ago. It serves him right for not listening to me, the punctilious bastard."

"I see, but this was only in the last couple of days since we've been down here. When did you last talk to his secretary? We figured out it was you only in the last few days."

"That's unlikely. You were surprised when you saw me down below. I could tell," Saunders said, although there was a slight twinge of doubt in his eyes. "I'm betting you weren't sure enough to tell anyone about me. At least, not yet. So, who else?"

"Well, all the bankers we've talked to," Hank said.

Saunders laughed. "Bankers. Do you really think they'll say anything?"

"Once they hear that something happened to us, they will," Hank said as confidently as possible.

"I doubt that very much."

"I also told my editor. In fact, I sent him my story and a copy of all my notes and files."

Saunders reached down into a black canvas briefcase next to his chair and pulled out a FedEx package. "You mean this?"

Hank blanched. "How'd you get that?"

"This is Panama. A few dollars goes a long way down here."

"That's okay," Alyson said bravely. Hank also sent his story by e-mail. So, you see, his editor still knows."

"I don't doubt you sent it by e-mail, but without all the notes in here, it will be difficult to prove anything. Besides, your story wasn't all that detailed."

"It's enough," Hank declared.

"Perhaps, but by the time your editor acts on this, I'll have moved all the money out of reach. He'll also find that the two of you left here to go to Argentina to visit my ranch down there. That's where you'll disappear. Without you two, the story will soon peter out."

"No way!" Alyson interjected. "Face it, Ted, we've told a lot of people about you. Having us disappear isn't going to help you. You might as well give it up and let us go."

"I don't think so. I'll take my chances," Saunders said with a malignant sneer. "No one's going to care about you. You're simply going to disappear. No one even knows where you are."

Hank stole a quick glance at Alyson. What Saunders had said was true, and he could tell that Alyson realized that too.

"I notice you didn't mention your friend in the Ministry of the Economy," Saunders said directly to Alyson.

Alyson suddenly turned pale. "You know about Miguel?"

"Of course. I've had you followed since the moment you stepped off the plane. It seems that Raul wasn't as lethal as I had hoped. Of course, that oversight will be corrected." Saunders's malevolent sneer peeled back the last veneer of humanity.

"You bastard!" Alyson screamed.

"Now, now, Ms. Murphy. Remember, if you hadn't gotten him involved…"

"You'll regret this," Hank said.

"I doubt that very much. But, not that it hasn't been fun, I think it's time to end our little chat. I think I'll get even more pleasure out of seeing you go for a swim." He laughed devilishly, keeping the gun pointed at them. "We'll soon be out of the Canal. Take a last look." His comment was cut short by a woman's cry from a sixty-foot ketch that motored up close to them.

"Ahoy! Aboard the *Alicia*," a gray-haired, middle-aged woman in a bright floral sundress on the sailboat shouted. Saunders lowered the pistol, but kept it pointed straight at Alyson.

"Don't say a word or try anything heroic," Saunders hissed under his breath, then turned his head partially toward the woman. "Yes," he yelled.

"Who's Alicia? That's my daughter's name," the woman yelled back.

"My mother," Saunders replied.

"Where are you from? We're from Miami."

Saunders was clearly irritated by the intrusion. The last thing he needed was a busybody hanging around who could later recognize him and his passengers.

"New York," Hank yelled out before Saunders could stop him.

"That's nice. Are you on vacation?"

Saunders looked at Hank with a look that told him to keep his mouth shut.

"Yes," Saunders said, turning to the woman, "but, not to be rude, we're having a private conversation here if you don't mind." The woman was taken aback and started to sit down.

Before Saunders could turn his head back around, Hank jumped forward, grabbed the gun hand and pushed it away from pointing at Alyson. There was a loud crack as the gun went off, the bullet embedding in the side of the portable bar on the port side of the boat. The woman in the ketch screamed. Her husband quickly spun the wheel hard to port, trying to put distance between the two boats, which caused the ketch to swing dangerously into the northbound lane of traffic. A blast from the horn of a tanker made the skipper of the ketch swing his wheel back to starboard, sending the ketch back in front of the Sea Scorpion. Herve spun the wheel, forcing the Sea Scorpion to veer suddenly to starboard.

Hank and Saunders were wrestling for the control of the gun when the shift of the Sea Scorpion to starboard gave Hank a momentary advantage, which he used to slam the hand holding the pistol against the port railing, sending the pistol overboard. With his free hand, Saunders landed a solid jab into Hank's ribs, causing Hank to lose his balance. Hank toppled over without letting go of Saunders's arm and the two of them crashed to the deck.

"Get Herve," Hank yelled.

Alyson jumped up and tried to grab Herve from behind. Herve pushed her away, trying to maintain control of the boat amidst the chaos that had erupted around him. As Herve struggled to get away from Alyson, he accidentally pushed the throttle forward. The boat jumped as its twin MerCruiser inboard V-drive engines responded to the extra gasoline pumping into them. Within seconds, the Sea Scorpion was hurtling along at more than twenty knots, well in excess of the speed limit anywhere within the Canal. The sudden acceleration threw Herve momentarily backward, and he focused on steering the out-of-control boat. As the gasoline kept racing through the MerCruisers, the Sea Scorpion was soon approaching thirty-three knots, its top speed.

Hank and Saunders had gotten to their feet again, but were thrown to the deck again when the boat shot forward, Saunders landing on top of Hank. Saunders tried to land a couple of punches, but the heaving of the boat made it all but impossible to put any weight behind his fists.

Alyson started to fall backward. At the last moment, she stretched out and grabbed onto the only thing within her reach—Herve's shirt. Herve had taken his right hand off the wheel to reach for the throttle and didn't have a strong enough grip on the wheel with his other hand to prevent him from being pulled backward. Alyson and Herve landed hard on top of Saunders and Hank. The four of them formed a tangle of arms and legs as they all struggled to gain their footing. Herve was desperately trying to get back to the controls and slow the boat down.

Without anyone at the helm, the Sea Scorpion drove forward heedless of anything in its path. It bumped the side of a tour boat returning from a day trip on the Canal, generating a slew of screams from the passengers and obscenities from the crew. The collision threw Herve to the deck again. Saunders pushed Herve away and tried to punch Hank again. As Hank and Saunders struggled to regain their balance, the boat swerved from side to side. The boat was headed toward the southbound entrance to the Pedro Miguel locks. At thirty knots, the remaining distance to the lock ahead of them was shrinking rapidly.

A boat horn sounded. Saunders looked out over the rail and could see they were hurtling straight toward the lock. He scrambled to a near-standing position and began scrambling forward to the helm. Not fully aware of the danger ahead, Hank grabbed at his leg, pulling him back. Saunders kicked frantically at the arms clawing at him.

A frightened look spread across Herve's face. He too knew what was happening. He lumbered to his feet, leaned out over the starboard rail and saw the two massive gates of the lock closing. He could tell that they were headed straight toward the quickly narrowing gap between the closing huge arms of the lock. He fought to move toward the captain's chair and the controls.

The gates were nearly closed and the boat was now only seconds away. In desperation, Herve lunged forward, pulled back hard on the throttle, throwing the engine into reverse, and spun the wheel hard to starboard. The boat shuddered as the props began to grab at the water, but there wasn't enough time or distance for them to have much effect on the vessel's speed. The Sea Scorpion slammed into the leading edge of one of the gates, which bored deep into the side of the fiberglass hull, and carried it forward as the gate continued to close.

Inside the boat, everything not nailed down was sent flying. Hank was thrown against the side of the boat and Alyson slammed into him, momentarily knocking the wind out of both of them. Herve had grabbed the armrest of the captain's chair to stop himself from being thrown to one side. Saunders was not as lucky. Standing on deck with nothing to hold onto, he went flying out of the boat. His momentum carried him over the port railing, across most of the gate's seven-foot width, landing him hard on its top. He rolled to the far edge, where he tottered for a second before tumbling into the water inside the lock's chamber.

The sharp turn had caused the starboard side of the boat to dip deep into the water so that the edge of the gate cut low into the hull, preventing the boat from regaining a level trim. Hank and Alyson groaned and then struggled to their feet. Hank coughed, pain shooting through his ribs. Hank winced and grabbed his side.

"Are you okay?" she asked.

Hank nodded. "Let's get out of here!"

They scrambled up and over the side of the boat and out onto the gate, where Herve was standing looking at his wounded boat. They watched in horror as the two gates crushed the Sea Scorpion's hull as if it were made of balsa wood.

"Saunders," Alyson screamed and suddenly jumped into the water inside the lock, swam over to Saunders, who was floating face-down in the water, and dragged him to the side of the gate. She held him with one arm and reached for the top of the gate with the other. Herve reached down and grabbed his boss and effortlessly hauled him up onto the top of the gate.

By this time, the man in the control tower had seen the accident and had stopped the gates from closing farther. Seconds later, the gates shuddered and began to slowly open again. The sudden shift of the gates shook the boat free and it began to sink almost instantly.

Two men, wearing bright orange life jackets, made their way slowly out on the gate to them. One of them called for medical help on his walkie-talkie. After some protestations, the other life-jacketed man escorted Hank, Alyson, and Herve off the gate, leaving Saunders there to be attended to by the medical team now hurrying toward the gate.

The emergency squad of the Authoridad del Canal de Panamá turned the three over to the police and then returned to the lock to join a growing number of workers busily assessing whether there was any damage to the gate and debating how they were going to remove the sunken boat.

The police ushered Hank, Alyson, and Herve into an interrogation room, where it quickly became apparent that there were two different stories about what had caused the accident. Hank and Alyson were moved to a separate room, where they told two policemen their side of the story. Neither policeman gave any indication of whether they believed it.

Two hours after the accident, there was a knock on the door and another ACP policeman stuck his head in and asked the two policemen in the room to come out. They excused themselves and left Hank and Alyson in the room alone. Hank looked over at Alyson. The fear in her eyes had been replaced by a look of fatigue and numbness, which he was sure mirrored the look in his own eyes. He reached out and took her hand and squeezed it gently. She closed her eyes and tears ran down her face. They sat in silence, lost in their own thoughts.

A few minutes later, the same two policemen came back in. "It seems that we have found someone to back up your story."

"Who?" Hank and Alyson asked at the same time. Alyson was trying to think of who even knew they were there.

"A Señor and Señorita Ashford."

"Who?"

"An Americanos couple from Miami. They say they saw what happened."

"Oh, yeah. The couple in the sailboat. Are they all right?" Hank asked.

"Sí. They say you jumped on the man and a gun went off."

"Yes. Like I told you, he was going to kill us."

After another hour of questioning, the policeman in charge said, "You are free to go for the time being."

CHAPTER 31

SUNDAY, DECEMBER 17

The morning light found its way through the heavy curtains, illuminating the room in a soft, yellow glow. Hank blinked several times then rubbed his eyes. He threw off the lightweight blanket, not remembering having a blanket on when he went to bed the night before.

He gingerly rolled to one side and sat up, grabbed his ribs, and stifled a cry. He sat motionless and took a couple of shallow breaths, then reached over and picked up the bottle of Advil from the nightstand. Dropping three tablets into his hand, he rose slowly to his feet, gently put on a bathrobe, and walked out into the living room. Alyson was lying on a chaise lounge on the balcony, looking out at the mountains. Hank checked his watch and was surprised to see it was nearly 10:00 AM.

"Good morning," Hank said as he stepped out onto the balcony. The air was fresh from a light breeze that blew down out of the mountains. The morning sun already felt warm, much warmer than the bedroom he had just left. In the distance, he heard church bells announcing the start of Sunday mass.

"Morning," Alyson said, looking up at him. Her eyes were red and puffy.

"How long have you been up?" he asked.

"I came out here around three, I guess. Maybe a little later. I couldn't sleep." That meant that she had gotten at most an hour or so of sleep. They had stayed up late talking about the events of the day. Despite her brave front out at the

Canal, Alyson had clearly been shaken by being nearly killed and at the death of Ted Saunders. "How do you feel?" she asked.

"Fine." He sat down deliberately, poured a glass of orange from the pitcher on the table, popped the pills into his mouth, and washed them down, draining the glass.

"You don't look fine."

"I'll be okay. At least nothing's broken." They had wasted three hours in a local hospital the previous night, waiting to get his ribs X-rayed, then another hour for a doctor to come out and tell them nothing was broken.

"The airline called earlier and told us that we got on the Tuesday flight. They didn't have any seats tomorrow." They had already canceled their flight back today figuring Hank wouldn't be up to flying for a couple of days.

He shifted his position on the chaise lounge to look at her, winced again, and said, "That's great."

"I figure Harden can pick up the tab for the extra couple of days." She laughed.

Hank grinned. "Did you call him yet?"

"I tried, but his message said he was away for the weekend. I left a detailed message and asked him to call."

He pointed at the coffee pot on the table and said, "Is there any left?" She nodded. He poured himself a cup and took a long swallow.

"Do you want, um," he stopped, not sure if he should go on, "to talk about yesterday some more."

"No. I'm okay."

"Are you sure?"

"Yes." She turned toward him and gave him a smile, a genuine one that told him that perhaps she was going to be all right. She leaned over, reached down, and picked up a tumbled pile of newspaper. "I picked up the *Times* when I went down to the lobby to get the coffee," she said as she handed it to him. "It's yesterday's. That's all they had."

"Thanks." He gently reached out, took the paper, and put it on his lap. He pulled out the unread sports section and began to read. His eyes strayed from the paper to Alyson from time to time. She closed her eyes. A peaceful look slowly spread across her face. Soon her breathing told him that she was asleep. He sipped his coffee and turned his attention to the article detailing how the Celtics had lost another game at the buzzer to the Knicks.

Alyson's phone rang. Hank turned. He rose slowly and walked into the living room. Her cell phone was in her bag on the table next to the sofa. He flipped it open on the fifth ring. "Hello."

"Mr. Jenkins?" A female voice asked, in a very slight accent.

"Speaking." Hank didn't recognize the voice at all.

"I'm Kathy Morton," the woman said. "Mr. Harden's secretary."

"Yes."

"I'm calling you to tell you that Mr. Harden would like you to meet him for dinner, tonight around eight."

"Where? In Washington?"

"No. In Panama. Mr. Harden will arrive on the late afternoon flight and wants to meet you…and Miss Murphy." She gave him the name of a restaurant and he repeated it back to her.

"We just spoke to Mr. Harden yesterday. He didn't mention this."

"He decided to fly there late last night. That is all I know."

"We'll be there."

"You will tell Miss Murphy? Yes?"

"I will tell her."

"I will let Mr. Harden know everything is all arranged. Thank you." The line went dead.

Hank walked back out to the balcony. Alyson was yawning and stretching. Damn, Hank said to himself. He had hoped the phone wouldn't wake her. She obviously needed the sleep.

"Who was that?" Alyson said, sleepily.

"Whit Harden's secretary. We're having dinner with him tonight."

"What?' She sat up and looked at him, her legs dropping so she straddled the chaise lounge. "We won't be in Washington until Tuesday."

"No, he's coming here."

"He's flying down here?"

"It looks that way."

"Really?" Alyson said.

"It makes no sense at all."

"No, it doesn't. Not after our call with him yesterday."

They sat there in silence for a few moments until Alyson said, almost under her breath, "I don't like this."

"What was that?"

Alyson turned her head toward Hank. "I don't like this."

"Why?"

"Think about it. Why would Harden fly all the way down here? We'll be back in the States in a couple of days."

"I don't know. Maybe he's scared after what happened yesterday or maybe he needs to deal with Saunders's body."

"No, that doesn't make sense."

"Could be he just wants to get his hands on the money right away?"

"That's what I'm afraid of."

"Oh, come on. Now that everyone knows about Saunders, we're safe. Besides, you said there's a lot of legal work to do to recover the money. If we had to come down here, wouldn't he need to come here, too?"

"That could be," Alyson said, sounding unconvinced. She leaned back and closed her eyes.

"Well, we'll find out tonight."

"Yes, we will." She became silent and distracted.

Seeing she didn't want to talk about it anymore, Hank returned to reading the sports section. After finishing with that section, he glanced over and saw that Alyson was lying motionless and staring at the mountains.

"Let's get some lunch," he said, hoping that getting out of the room would help.

"What? Ah, sure." She stood up. "Let me take a shower first." Without waiting for an answer, she ambled into her bedroom. Seconds later, Hank heard the shower running in her bathroom.

Hank walked into his own bathroom, turned on the hot water, threw some on his face, lathered, and began to shave. Fifteen minutes later, he was sitting out on the balcony again, reading the paper as he waited for Alyson to finish dressing.

Alyson came out of her bedroom a few minutes later, walked to the sofa, and grabbed her bag. "Let's go," she yelled out to Hank, as if she had been the one waiting.

The two of them rode down the elevator in silence and left the hotel quickly. It being Sunday, there were few cars on the street. The sun beating down on the pavement made it much warmer than on their balcony. Hank stood at the foot of the stairs leading up to the hotel entrance, enjoying the sun and the warmth.

Alyson had taken five steps, turned around, and waited. Hank hobbled up to her, trying not to twist his ribs as he walked. She looked at him as if to say, *are you sure you want to go out?* "I'm okay," he said, answering the unspoken question.

They wandered slowly down Avenida Federico Boyd toward the harbor, passing a number of small curbside cafes with tables and chairs outside filled mainly with tourists. Hank's stomach started to growl as the smell of the food reached him. At Avenida Balboa, they turned west to walk along the water and passed the marina again. Two blocks later, they found a restaurant with a balcony overlooking the street and the Bahía of Panama.

They were soon seated on the balcony, watching the few cars pass by below. Beyond the street, the bay was filled with sails of all colors gliding across the deep blue of the sea. A north wind raised a light chop; a white cap could be seen here or there.

Hank looked at her, uncertain as to what to say, so they sat there in silence until their meals came.

"How's your chicken?" he asked.

"Great. How's yours?" Alyson had ordered *sancocho*, a dish of spicy chicken and vegetable stew. Hank had ordered a hamburger, wanting something "American."

"I still can't believe that Harden's coming down here. What did Kate Morgan say again?"

"Not a lot." Hank frowned. Was that the name of the woman who had called? It must have been, he decided with a shrug.

"But it doesn't make sense."

"I know. I guess we'll find out what this is all about when we see him later tonight."

"That's true." A forkful of chicken hovered in midair. "Did she mention which hotel he was staying at?"

"No. She didn't. Does it matter?"

"I suppose not, but I would have liked to have met Harden on our terms rather than on his."

Hank looked at her, not knowing exactly what she meant.

"At least he picked a good restaurant," Hank said.

"Yes, it is." She sat lost in thought, only picking at her food. The plate was half full when the waiter came to clear the table.

"At you okay?" Hank asked.

"Yes. I'm fine." Hank didn't believe her, but could tell by the look in her eye that she didn't want to discuss it.

They spent the afternoon leisurely touring around the city, most of which was closed on Sunday. They arrived back at their hotel at 5:30 PM. As they crossed the lobby, the people at one of the tables in front of the lobby bar stood up and walked toward the elevator. Hank reached out and took Alyson's hand and guided her toward the open table. "I think we have time for a quick drink. We're on vacation, now." He said in a vain effort to lighten her mood.

They sat down and ordered drinks. Forty-five minutes later, they went up to their suite to get ready for dinner.

At exactly 8:00 PM, Hank and Alyson walked into the restaurant and went straight to the maitre d' and asked for Whittaker Harden. They were seated and each ordered a glass of wine.

Thirty minutes passed.

"Where do you think he is?" Alyson asked Hank, instinctively lowering her voice.

"I don't know. I'm sure this is the right restaurant," he said, answering her next question before she could ask it. "His secretary was very specific about the location. She made sure that I had it right. What should we do?"

The waitress returned and asked if they wanted another round of drinks. Hank looked at his watch again. He shook his head and asked for the bill.

"I guess he's not coming," Hank said as he put money on the table to cover the drinks and the tip. "Let's go back to the hotel. Maybe he left a message for us there. If not, we can go get something to eat near the hotel."

Twenty minutes later, they walked into the lobby of their hotel and asked the woman behind the front desk if there were any messages. There were none. Hank took the key from the woman and played with it nervously as they rode up the elevator to their room. Neither spoke, each lost in thought.

Hank stood before the door of their suite, inserted his key, and pushed the door open. He reached inside to flip the switch on the wall that turned on a lamp that sat on the desk in the living room and stepped aside to let Alyson go in first. She took one step inside and gasped.

"What's wrong?" Hank said as he stepped into the room.

Some of the furniture had been overturned and the cushions from the sofas and chairs were strewn around the floor. The contents of Hank's briefcase were spread out on the desk. Hank took a step toward the phone to call the front desk, but Alyson grabbed his arm. "Don't," she said. "Someone might still be here."

"You're absolutely right, Miss Murphy," a voice from Hank's bedroom said. A second later, a man stepped into the living room. The light from the lamp revealed a pistol in his hand. "Please come in." The man stepped farther into the room and the light fell on his face for the first time.

"You!" Alyson yelled. "What are you doing here?"

"Who is he?" Hank asked, looking first to Alyson and then toward the man.

"He's my stalker from New York."

"What?" Hank looked from Alyson to the stranger, totally confused.

"Ah. I knew you caught me following you," Dan Morris said. "That was sloppy of me."

"What do you want?" Alyson demanded.

"You guys have been pretty busy, going all over town, visiting banks, shopping."

"That was you the other day," Alyson said after the sudden realization of where she had last seen him.

"Yup. Did you ever end up buying anything from that old Indian woman?"

Alyson didn't say a word. Her gaze alternated between the gun and the man's face.

"What are you doing in our room?" Hank said.

"Well, I realized after your experience out on the Canal yesterday, you'd be returning to the States soon. I couldn't let that happen."

"What do you mean?"

"You didn't think that I'd come all the way down here to let you go back and tell everyone where the money was, did you?"

Hank and Alyson exchanged worried glances.

"I assume that you have your computer and files in your bag," Morris said, pointing at the strap slung over her shoulder, "since I didn't find them here."

Instinctively, Alyson grabbed the strap with both of her hands.

"Come now. Don't be foolish." He waved the barrel of the gun at them. "Why don't we sit down? Please close the door, Mr. Jenkins." The man pointed at the door with the pistol. Hank turned and slowly closed the door, then stepped forward to get in front of Alyson.

"Oh, how noble, but do you really think you'll be able to protect her if I really want to hurt her?"

"Perhaps."

"Hank! What are you doing?" She pulled on his arm. He turned to look at her.

"That's the right idea, Ms. Murphy. Please." He gestured again with the pistol then stepped aside to let them pass. "Excuse the mess. I had to make sure you didn't hide anything around the room. Plus I had to make it look good."

Alyson shot Hank a look. That didn't sound good.

Hank and Alyson stepped forward into the room. On the way to the sofa, Hank bent over to pick up the cushions.

"Leave them," the man with the gun said.

Hank let the pillow drop from his hand.

Morris followed them at a safe distance, ready in case either Hank or Alyson tried anything heroic. Once Hank and Alyson were seated, he pulled over the desk chair and positioned it on the other side of the coffee table. "Now that we're comfortable, perhaps you'd empty out your bag for me," Morris said to Alyson.

"I hope your computer is still okay after you dropped it in the cab the other day," Hank said.

Alyson looked at him with a confused look. Hank winked, hoping the man sitting across the table wouldn't see it. A second later Alyson's look changed to one of understanding.

"I do too," Alyson said, reaching into her bag. She pulled out her computer and placed it on the table, then pulled out her Saunders file and purposefully placed it on the edge of the table, where it teetered for a moment before falling to the floor. "Oops," she said as her hand returned to her bag.

Morris's eyes followed the file to the floor. Alyson noticed his gaze drop from her as she had hoped and quickly reached into the inner pocket of her bag, pulled out the canister of spray, aimed, and pulled the trigger.

White liquid squirted from the nozzle, hitting the gunman in the face. He dropped the gun and reached up to cover his face.

"Ayyyyeeeee," Morris screamed. He coughed violently, bending over trying to clear his lungs. His left hand rubbed his eyes to wipe the spray off.

Hank started to jump up.

"Wait," Alyson yelled as she grabbed his arm. "Or you'll get it too."

They waited impatiently as the mist began to dissipate. He watched the man clutch at his stomach as his body was wracked with coughing. He was thankful that Alyson had stopped him. Ten seconds later, Hank jumped off the sofa and stepped toward Morris. As Morris sat up straight, trying to catch his breath, Hank hit him in the face, sending him crashing to the floor. Hank stepped over him to get the gun.

Morris lashed out with his fist and caught Hank in the ribcage. Hank screamed, doubled over, and fell on top of him. Morris grabbed Hank around the neck.

Alyson saw what was happening and jumped around the table and picked up the gun.

"Stop," she demanded.

Morris squinted a few times, trying to rid his eyes of the spray. "Give me that gun, little lady, before someone gets hurt."

"The only one getting hurt will be you."

He tightened his hold around Hank's neck. "Drop it or your boyfriend here will have more than some sore ribs."

"Let him go," she said coldly, now so sick of the whole mess that she wouldn't let anything else hurt her.

Morris tightened his grip further. Hank coughed. He was having trouble breathing.

Alyson dropped the barrel of the gun. Morris relaxed a little. She aimed at his thigh and fired.

Morris screamed, letting go of Hank to grab his leg.

Hank crawled out of the reach of the man on the floor, ignoring the pain in his side.

"Get something to tie him up with," Alyson said to Hank, holding the gun pointed at the writhing figure on the floor.

"You bitch. You shot me." He reached an arm out at her.

Alyson took a step back. "I warned you that you might get hurt."

Hank reappeared seconds later with a towel and the belt from the hotel bathrobe. "Turn around and put your hands behind you," he demanded. Morris hissed and slowly put his arms behind him. Hank made a loop in the belt, grabbed one wrist and slipped the loop over it and pulled the belt tight. He looped the belt around the man's other wrist and pulled sharply on the other end, binding Morris's wrists together.

Hank rolled him over and pressed the towel on the wound. Morris screamed in pain. "Sorry, but I've got to stop the bleeding," he said. "You'd better call the police." He looked down at the leg and then back at Alyson, "Did you learn that in the Navy?"

"I guess it was good for something after all." She grinned.

Alyson picked up the phone, but a knock came at the door before she could dial. She ran to the door. "Who is it?" she asked, looking through the eyehole. It was the manager.

"We heard a gunshot," the manager said nervously, through the closed door.

She opened the door. "Call the police."

"I have called them already." He looked past her into the room. "¡Ay! ¡Dios mío! What happened?"

"He broke in and tried to kill us," Alyson said.

Thirty minutes later, there was a knock and two policemen walked through the still-open door into the suite. "Señorita Murphy, we meet again," the taller of two said.

"It seems so."

"Is this the same man who attacked you before?" the policeman asked, standing over the prone man. His partner reached down and replaced the bathrobe belt with handcuffs.

"No. But we saw *that man* the other day at the tour boat dock."

"Yes, I heard about that. You closed the Canal for more than five hours."

"That was the least of our worries at the time."

"I understand. I am sorry I did not take the first robbery more seriously. What happened here?"

Alyson and Hank told the police what had happened.

As they were finishing their story, two medics wheeled a stretcher into the room and walked straight over to the man on the floor and began to treat the leg wound. Within minutes, they had stopped the bleeding and determined that the wound was not life-threatening. The bullet had passed cleanly through the fleshy part of the thigh, missing the main arteries and veins. They lifted him onto the stretcher, pulled it up to waist height, and began to wheel it out of the room.

"Wait," Alyson said, reaching out a hand to stop them. "I need to ask him a few questions."

"Of course, señorita." The policeman nodded to the medics.

Alyson leaned over the stretcher. "Who are you?"

Hack. The man coughed, but didn't say a word.

"Where's Harden? What did you do to him?"

Again, silence. Morris looked up at the policeman, then over at Alyson.

"Where is he? Have you hurt him?" She paused for an answer, but getting none, said, "Is he involved in this?"

At the last question, Morris coughed again and then laughed. The resulting smile and red, rash-mottled face gave Morris the look of someone straight out of a horror movie. "Harden involved in this?" he hissed. "You've got to be kidding. You think he'd go along with any of this? Not likely! Besides, why would I want to share any of the money with him?"

"Then where is he?"

"Probably shacking up with some bimbo somewhere for all I know."

"In Panama?"

"Not as far as I know."

"What about dinner?"

Morris looked at Alyson and smirked.

"Oh. I get it. There was no dinner."

The man's eyes narrowed and the smile left his face. "Of course not. I wanted to get you out of your room for a while. When I didn't find the computer and your files, I had to wait for you to get back."

Alyson shuddered at the memory of seeing him step from the dark bedroom with the gun in his hand.

"Señorita. Are you finished now? We need to take him to hospital."

Alyson nodded.

The medics left. The tall policeman asked Alyson and Hank to join him in Alyson's bedroom, so they could be away from the blood. He questioned Hank and Alyson for an hour and then left. Hank showed the police to the door and came back into the bedroom.

"Are you going to be okay?" Hank asked.

"I don't know anymore," she responded and then burst into tears. Hank sat back down on the bed and pulled her into his arms. They sat there in silence for ten minutes, each thinking through the events of the past days. There was another knock on the door.

"Now what?" Alyson blurted out and started to rise.

"I'll get it," Hank said. He walked out of the bedroom. Alyson followed him a few seconds later when she heard the manager's voice.

The manager walked meekly into the living room. "Señorita, señor. I am so very sorry."

"That's okay. It wasn't your fault." Alyson nodded in agreement.

The manager looked down, wringing his hand. "Gracias," he said softly.

"Is there anything I can do for you?" the manager pleaded.

"Maybe you could find someone to sit outside our door tonight," Alyson said softly. "I'd sleep much better." They had decided to stay in the room that night instead of changing rooms again.

"Sí. Of course! I will see to it." The manager bowed, shook hands profusely with both of them and left. Twenty minutes later, Hank and Alyson heard a chair scrape along the floor outside their door. They locked the door and placed a chair under the doorknob.

Alyson walked into her bathroom, changed, and walked back into Hank's bedroom and climbed under the covers. Hank walked out of his bathroom and climbed into bed. Alyson rolled over and cuddled with him. Ten minutes later she was asleep.

Hank lay awake for an hour, enjoying being near her and wondering what would happen when they got back to New York. How did Gavin fit in? Was any of what they had down here real, or was it just her way of dealing with the stress and the fear? He didn't know. He finally fell into a fitful sleep.

▼

CHAPTER 32

WEDNESDAY, DECEMBER

20

John Blanchard rolled gingerly out of bed, his head pounding whenever he made any sudden movements, and walked over to the small stainless steel sink in the corner of his cell. He let the water run for a few seconds before he caught some in his cupped hands and splashed his face.

"Ah, you're awake," a voice from behind him said.

Blanchard slowly lifted his head and turned. On the other side of the bars stood a uniformed guard and a man dressed in a suit.

"I'm Inspector Duncan," the man in the suit said. "I came down here to see how you were doing. The doctors told me you were over the worst of it and up and around, but I wanted to see for myself."

Blanchard stood silently. He had nothing to gain by talking to the police.

"Since you appear to be in reasonable good health, I can talk to the magistrate about setting a trial date. We don't let things linger for months or years like they do in the States."

"I want to talk to a lawyer."

"Yes, you're going to need one. Given the charges, kidnapping, attempted murder, drug possession, you'll be our *guest* for a very long time."

"When can I set bail?"

"I've already talked to the magistrate about that. Given the charges and your background...Oh, yes, we checked with FBI and the U.S. Navy and know all about your background, both the official and, shall I say, unofficial, I've convinced the magistrate that you're a flight risk. There will be no bail." The Inspector smiled wryly.

Blanchard glared at the policeman.

"We arrange for a lawyer to meet with you." The Inspector turned and strode away, the uniformed guard following behind him. Blanchard heard the footsteps recede down the corridor. Ten seconds later, there was the clang of a metal door closing.

Blanchard sat down on the bed, the metal springs creaking under his weight. Shit! How was he going to get out of this mess? That Inspector was right. If they get him on all of those charges, he was going to be an old man by the time he got out of jail. But it wasn't the jail time that worried him—he knew he could handle that, just like he had boot camp and the Seals training, which were worse than anything they could do to him here.

He closed his eyes and saw his beloved Green Mountains and realized that he may never see them again. His head drooped.

CHAPTER 33

▼

FRIDAY, DECEMBER 22

"Thanks again for all your hard work," Harden said, standing in Alyson's office and shaking hands with them both. "I still can't believe all that happened. Imagine Ted having a twin brother all these years and…that he could be such a cold-blooded murderer. I thought I knew him."

"It's amazing how money can change people," Hank said.

"I'm not sure that it changed him all that much. He must have always had it in him somewhere," Alyson concluded.

"You might be right," the lawyer said.

"What about Dan Morris?"

"He'll go to jail for a long time. I don't understand why he'd try something like that. I've used him so many times before."

"I bet you've never used him to look for that much money before."

"That's true. I guess that much money could tempt anyone."

"That thought had crossed our minds about you on more than one occasion."

"Really. Hmm. I guess that's not surprising. The real reason I stopped by, besides to say thank you, was to tell you that I was able to put a freeze on the money. Looks like it'll be returned as soon as I can get all paperwork down there. Most of it based on your work." He gave them an appreciative look.

"Mr. Harden. Were you ever able to find out anything about Saunders's brother?" Hank asked.

"Yes. Kevin Armstrong was reported missing a couple of days before Ted's death—his first death—and presumed drowned. The local cops have been told about this. Thankfully, he didn't leave any family behind."

"That's sad," Alyson said, meaning it despite all that had happened.

"Yes, it is, but…" Harden said, stopping in mid-sentence.

"Did you ever find out about the man who attacked Hank?" she asked.

"Yes. His name is John Blanchard. He's an ex—Navy Seal and now a security consultant in Vermont, but the FBI suspects he might have been much more than that. They think he was probably the person Ted hired to help him kidnap his brother, but they can't prove it. They showed his picture around Larned, Kansas, where Ted's brother lived and several people think they saw him around town, but couldn't be sure."

"It's too bad they can't get him for that."

"True, but don't worry. He'll spend a long time in prison down in Belize. They don't like paid killers any more than we do, but they don't have the hassle of proving anything so complex. The drug charges alone are enough to get him life there."

"I hope that's true," Hank trembled at the thought of how close his escape had been.

"Sorry to cut this short, but I've got to go. I want to beat the holiday traffic and I still have to find something to put under the tree for my wife. Your Christmas present should come shortly after New Year's. There will be a check for your expenses…and yours too, Mr. Jenkins, with my thanks. The rest will come when we actually get the money back." He paused, momentarily lost in thought. "Based on my calculations, that should be around four million dollars." Alyson's and Hank's eyes popped wide open. "And you can have your story now too."

"Thank you," they both said, enthusiastically. They turned and smiled at each other.

The lawyer stood up. "Thank you both again. Happy holidays!"

"Happy holidays to you too," Alyson and Hank replied.

The lawyer left the office.

"Speaking of the holidays, what are you doing for Christmas?" Hank asked, as nonchalantly as he could.

"I'm going home to see my folks in Pennsylvania."

"What about Gavin?" Hank asked, figuring he might as well know where he stood.

"Oh, he's back in New York. He asked me to go skiing." Hank's shoulders drooped slightly. "But I told him no." Hank's face brightened. "Too much work."

"Oh."

"I think I need some time by myself." She looked at him for a moment or two, then leaned forward and kissed him on the cheek. "Call me after New Year's. Don't wait six months this time."

Hank left the building and hailed a cab. The taxi pulled up to the curb and Hank opened the door and paused.

"Hey, get in or get lost," the cabbie yelled.

"On second thought," hank replied, "I think I'll walk for a while." He stood planted in the spot and watched the cab stop twenty feet farther up the street. He smiled, turned up the collar on his coat against the cold and marched up Broadway, not knowing where he was headed, but looking forward to the trip.

978-0-595-37210-2
0-595-37210-4

Printed in the United States
47349LVS00003B/70-78